The creature screamed, enraged, and charged

The companions broke before the rush, folding away on both sides, then stepping in. The creature was trapped in a killing box, with every blaster firing.

It slashed out a clawed wing, which drooped as the cartilage was smashed. Pain overwhelming sense, it continued to rush the humans, but the blasters never ceased, a person reloading while the one alongside kept firing, until finally the broken, bloody thing collapsed, yellow blood pooling around the riddled ⟨...⟩se. Then Ryan stepped close and cut off ⟨...⟩ panga.

"Good thing De⟨...⟩ "If that thing had cau⟨...⟩euver, we'd be in its ⟨...⟩

"Where's Dean ⟨...⟩

"Dean!" Ryan sh⟨...⟩ are you?"

Only the wind w⟨...⟩ ⟨...⟩d in reply.

JAMES AXLER

DEATH LANDS®

Zero City

A GOLD EAGLE BOOK FROM
WORLDWIDE®

TORONTO • NEW YORK • LONDON
AMSTERDAM • PARIS • SYDNEY • HAMBURG
STOCKHOLM • ATHENS • TOKYO • MILAN
MADRID • WARSAW • BUDAPEST • AUCKLAND

For Melissa, who understands

First edition December 2000

ISBN 0-373-62562-6

ZERO CITY

Printed in U.S.A.

...no sane man who has ever fought in a war ever wishes to do so again. It is madness and chaos and nightmare combined. Yet most will do so again and again for the most ordinary of reasons: honor, duty, a solemn promise, and of course, to protect or avenge their kith and kin. Black powder may charge our guns, sir, but it is red blood that charges the common soldier...

—General John Gibbon, 1862
Army of the Potomac

THE DEATHLANDS SAGA

This world is their legacy, a world born in the violent nuclear spasm of 2001 that was the bitter outcome of a struggle for global dominance.

There is no real escape from this shockscape where life always hangs in the balance, vulnerable to newly demonic nature, barbarism, lawlessness.

But they are the warrior survivalists, and they endure—in the way of the lion, the hawk and the tiger, true to nature's heart despite its ruination.

Ryan Cawdor: The privileged son of an East Coast baron. Acquainted with betrayal from a tender age, he is a master of the hard realities.

Krysty Wroth: Harmony ville's own Titian-haired beauty, a woman with the strength of tempered steel. Her premonitions and Gaia powers have been fostered by her Mother Sonja.

J. B. Dix, the Armorer: Weapons master and Ryan's close ally, he, too, honed his skills traversing the Deathlands with the legendary Trader.

Doctor Theophilus Tanner: Torn from his family and a gentler life in 1896, Doc has been thrown into a future he couldn't have imagined.

Dr. Mildred Wyeth: Her father was killed by the Ku Klux Klan, but her fate is not much lighter. Restored from predark cryogenic suspension, she brings twentieth-century healing skills to a nightmare.

Jak Lauren: A true child of the wastelands, reared on adversity, loss and danger, the albino teenager is a fierce fighter and loyal friend.

Dean Cawdor: Ryan's young son by Sharona accepts the only world he knows, and yet he is the seedling bearing the promise of tomorrow.

In a world where all was lost, they are humanity's last hope....

Chapter One

As the swirling mists of the trans-mat chamber faded away, the seven people inside the unit tumbled to the cold floor, gasping for breath.

In silent agony, the companions lay where they fell, waiting for their tortured bodies to finally overcome the horrid sickness that always accompanied a jump. Almost an hour passed before the first of them was able to stir.

"N-no m-more," J. B. Dix whispered, a string of drool hanging from his mouth. His wire-rimmed glasses slid from his shirt pocket and fell to the floor as a tremor shook the man. "D-dark night, I can't take...another bastard jump."

Panting for breath, Ryan Cawdor swallowed before being able to answer. Fireblast! He had known they were pushing the envelope with three jumps in a single day, and now they were paying the price. It felt as if fire ants were eating his guts.

"A-agreed," the man croaked. "Don't...give a motherless damn if we find any food in this redoubt or not. No more jumps for a while. Win, lose or draw, this is it."

Mumbled agreements from the others answered his decision.

"About time," drawled Jak Lauren. The albino teenager was lying on his side, fighting to control his rebellious stomach. His pale skin looked even whiter than usual, almost the same color as his long snowy hair. The armpits of his shirt were stained dark with sweat. "N-not done six before."

"Won't ever again, either," gasped Krysty Wroth, unbuttoning the front of her khaki overalls to expose a wealth of creamy cleavage. Rivulets of sweat streamed off her lovely face, the woman's fiery red hair flexing and moving as if stirred by secret winds.

"Don't exaggerate. It was six in a week," corrected Dr. Mildred Wyeth, leaning against the chamber wall. She rubbed the back of a hand across her mouth as if trying to remove an unpleasant taste. "Only did three in the same day."

"More than enough."

"Agreed."

Resembling a Civil War college professor with his silvery hair and old-fashioned clothing, Dr. Theophilus Tanner lay on the cold floor, savoring the coolness against his cheek, his hands white-knuckled about his ebony walking stick. Patiently, he waited for the world around him to stop spinning and settle down. For some reason, the jumps hit him harder than the others. Perhaps it was a legacy from the time-travel experiments done to him by the whitecoats of Operation Chronos. Doc didn't know, and for the moment, he didn't care. Every peaceful second brought him away from the debilitating jump sickness and put strength into his body.

Grimacing in determination, Dean Cawdor forced himself to stand upright, then crashed back down on his ass. The eleven-year-old blinked away the hurt pride, and began the struggle to rise again.

"Stay still, son," Ryan ordered brusquely. "Rushing only makes the aftereffects last longer."

"Okay," the boy agreed, relaxing into a heap.

Disregarding his own advice, Ryan struggled to his hands and knees, concentrating on every move as he struggled upright. His vision was clearing, and he was feeling stronger by the second. Briefly, he wondered if he was acclimatizing to the shock of disintegration. Doc had once theorized that the sickness was actually a person's soul searching for the body so rudely taken away. Foolishness, of course. But the time traveler often talked utter nonsense.

Adjusting the patch over his left eye and squinting to focus the right, Ryan glanced about the chamber. The walls and floor were made of a smooth blue material speckled with flecks of gold. He didn't recognize the color combination, so they had never been in this redoubt before. For the millionth time, he wondered why the predark scientists had decided to color code the redoubts instead of just putting up signs listing the locations. Just another of the endless ancient mysteries they would probably never solve.

Drawing in a lungful of air, Cawdor noted the atmosphere tasted flat and smelled antiseptically clean, as if every possible sign of life were missing. On the rare occasions they found an inhabited redoubt, there were faint odors of sweat, sex, blasters and food, hot oil in machines, the sharp stink of ozone from the nuclear reactor. Both life and death carried a perfume easily recognizable. This one smelled deserted.

"Terra incognita," Doc said, sitting upright. "Albeit, an aesthetically pleasing locale."

"Talk English, you old coot," Mildred muttered, brushing the long beaded hair off her face. Automatically, the healer started to reach for the canteen at her belt, then stopped. Damn, she had forgotten that they ran out of juice two jumps ago. Although, to be honest, none of her herbal concoctions ever seemed to ease their jump sickness much. But the physician was grimly determined to keep searching until she found a combination that worked.

"We've never been here before," Doc explained.

"I know that."

"Company," Jak barked, pointing at the floor.

That jarred everybody awake. Stumbling closer to the teenager, Ryan saw a series of boots scuffs marring the floor, which had gone unnoticed in the aftermath of the multiple jump.

"Those are Army boots," Ryan snapped, drawing the 9 mm SIG-Sauer pistol from his belt. "Triple red, people!" Metallic clicks and clacks filled the room as the companions drew their assorted weapons.

"Are they going in or coming out?" Krysty asked, easing back the hammer on her S&W .38 revolver. Her bearskin coat billowed about the redhead's legs as she walked closer to the door, carefully keeping to one side. Only a fool approached an unknown door straight on.

"Seem to be both," J.B. said, retrieving his spectacles and setting them onto his bony nose. Unfolding the wire stock of his 9 mm Uzi submachine gun, he eased off the safety and slid the selector switch to burst. Now every time he pulled the trigger, the blaster would fire three times in less than a second. More than enough firepower for any conceivable danger.

"New or old?" Doc asked, laying his swordstick against the wall to free his hands. With oft practiced ease, Doc emptied a few pockets and began the laborious process of loading his huge .44 LeMat. The Civil War handgun was a percussion piece and each chamber in the rotating cylinder had to be purged and hand charged with black powder, cloth wad and lead ball, and then a copper nipple of fulminating mercury slid into the notch at the base of each individual chamber before it was ready to fire. Although old and slow, under the control of the gentleman from Vermont, the LeMat was a weapon of mass destruction fully capable of blowing a man in half. It was cumbersome to reload, but the 9-shot capacity more than made up for that small flaw.

Blaster in hand, Jak dropped to a knee and rubbed a finger across the scuff marks. "Not tell," he announced. The bright fluorescent lights overhead glinted off the six-inch blue-steel barrel of his .357 Colt Python. The handcannon was almost the rival of Doc's monstrous LeMat.

"Maybe old and new on top each other," Dean offered. Drawing his Browning Hi-Power pistol, the boy dropped the clip to check the load, then slammed it back and jacked the slide.

"Only one way to find out," Mildred stated, holding the strap of her med kit with one hand, the other full of a Czech-made .38-caliber ZKR target pistol. The precision revolver was amazingly accurate over long distances, as many enemies and muties had found out the hard way.

"I'll take point," Ryan said, holstering his handblaster and sliding a Steyr SSG-70 rifle off his shoulder. He worked the bolt to check the magazine inside. Satisfied, he slammed it back, chambering a long 7.62 mm round for immediate use. "J.B., cover the rear, Dean and Jak with Mildred and Krysty."

Listening for a while, Ryan eased open the door and stepped quickly into the next area, automatically moving to the side to clear the field of fire for the people behind him. The precautions proved unnecessary, as this was merely the standard antechamber to the mat-trans room, little more than a ready room for the personnel using the mat-trans chamber to check their equipment before a jump. Across the antechamber was a plain door that led to the main corridor of the redoubt, and another to the side made of burnished steel. That caught their attention.

Krysty covered the men as Ryan checked for booby traps and J.B. picked the lock. Going through first, Ryan glanced around the office and gave a sharp whistle, announcing that the room was clear. The others followed close behind. It was a standard military office with an American flag covering one wall. A large steel desk stood beneath it, the top covered with an elaborate communications console. There were a few chairs scattered about for visitors, and a sofa in the corner. This was probably the base commander's office.

Taking a position near the sofa, Ryan motioned Krysty forward with his rifle, and she opened the door leading to the corridor outside. When nothing happened, she knelt low and took a quick look outside in both directions.

"Clear," the redhead announced, standing. "No sign of anybody."

"Leave it open," Ryan decided with caution. "Doc, go stand guard." The old man saluted with his sword-stick and moved into the corridor, his LeMat resting comfortably in the crook of an arm. Longblaster in hand, Ryan stood guard while Mildred glanced under the furniture and J.B. peeked into a corner. Checking behind the door leading into the trans-mat chamber, Dean saw the usual sign posted there: Entry Absolutely

Forbidden To All But B12-Cleared Personnel. It was the same in every redoubt they had ever visited.

Suddenly, Ryan glanced about. Had he just heard music? The man held his breath and listened hard, but heard nothing.

"Anything in the desk?" Mildred asked, rifling through a file cabinet. Officers often hid things inside the locked cabinets they didn't want to share, but not this time. Nothing but status reports, correspondence and shipping-receiving manifests, the endless effluvia of the predark military. In triplicate.

"Just papers and comp disks so far," J.B. reported, checking drawer after drawer. Paperclips, rubberbands. He slammed the last one shut. "Nothing useful."

Walking over to the small wet bar, Jak checked over the array of bottles. Liquor was a good item for trade, and vodka could also be used for cleaning wounds and degreasing weapons. "Son bitch," the Cajun said in surprise. "Look that!"

The others gathered close as he turned, holding a squashed cardboard box in the palm of his hand. The lid was ripped off, exposing the neat rows of red and brass shotgun shells nestled inside.

"Army issue," Ryan said, scowling. "The owners of those boots must have left in a hurry."

"And left ammo behind?" J.B. scoffed, lifting a round. Sixteen gauge, too small for his 12-bore shotgun, but he pocketed the shell anyway. "Damn good condition. Almost perfect."

Jak agreed as he put the rest of the box into a pocket of his vest. "Air dry," he offered as a possible explanation.

"Or the armory has been recently emptied," Krysty

countered dourly. Just what they needed, another empty redoubt.

"No signs of battle, so they weren't attacked," Ryan said thoughtfully. "Not directly anyway. Could have been chased out."

Hoisting the Uzi onto his shoulder, J.B. checked the radiation counter on his shirt collar. "No rads," he announced. "Place is clean."

"It's clean now," Ryan said, the barrel of the Steyr steady as a rock. "Mebbe it wasn't when they departed."

Feeling ill to his stomach, Dean stood firm and addressed his father. "I'm ready for another jump, Dad."

The elder Cawdor almost smiled, then reached out to ruffle his son's hair. "First we recce the redoubt," he said. "Jumping is what you do when a plan fails. It's never the plan."

The boy nodded in understanding.

"Check the barracks first?" Krysty asked.

"Armory," Ryan replied, wrapping the strap of his longblaster around his forearm for a better grip. "We're almost as low on ammo as food. With any luck, we'll find something there."

"Sure as hell hope so," Mildred stated, shifting her backpack into a more comfortable position. "I'm about six shots away from throwing rocks."

"And me," Dean added.

Jak snorted. "Why got so many knives."

"Agreed, my friend. The one great benefit of blades," Doc espoused, leaning on his ebony stick, the silver lion's head peeking out from between his laced fingers, "is their complete lack of ever needing to be reloaded."

Heading for the stairs, the companions swept through

the corridor in a standard two-on-two coverage pattern. At an intersection, Ryan and Krysty stopped, allowing Doc and Dean to move past and secure the other side.

At the stairs, Doc and Dean stood as anchor while Jak and J.B. moved up the steps. Mildred followed grumpily along with the others. The landing was covered with trash, MRE food pack wrappings and empty cig packs. The bright yellow of an official military notice peeked out from among the refuse, and Ryan speared it with his rifle.

"'A summary notice of execution for two soldiers who tried to leave the redoubt without proper authorization,'" he read aloud. "'The charge is treason.'"

"Probably trying to get back to their families," J.B. said. Then he saw the pained expression on Doc's face and stopped talking. The man had been yanked away from his family in 1896 by Overproject Whisper.

"Could have been plain old thieves," Mildred said, quickly changing the topic. "Maybe black market runners."

"Don't care," Jak said, his stomach rumbling audibly. "Need find food."

Continuing up to the next level, Ryan paused before opening the door and tilted his head against a cloth-covered grille in the wall.

"Music," he said, sounding amazed. "Weak and off tune."

"Mebbe this place isn't deserted," J.B. said grimly.

With a rusty creak, the door swung open on a long chemical laboratory. The tables were stacked with retorts and beakers in a wild state of disarray, and the wall shelves were stacked with countless bottles of unknown chemicals. A pile of animal cages was filled with tiny bones.

"Germ warfare?" Dean asked nervously.

"Wrong equipment," Mildred stated. "Don't know what it's for."

Walking through the cold, sterile laboratory, Ryan curled a lip in disgust. "Science rules," he muttered softly. But that had been months ago, at the redoubt filled with Kaa's army. This one was stripped clean as a fresh corpse.

Leaving the lab, they went past a communications room and at the end of the corridor found the heavy door to the Armory. Behind the veined portal of burnished titanium, the U.S. government had stashed away food and blasters for the troops to utilize after skydark. Unfortunately for the companions, the redoubts were usually picked clean during evacuation.

"Mebbe we'll find some reloading equipment," J.B. said hopefully, tilting back his fedora. "Not many folks thought to take those, and I can make enough ammo to hold us for a good while if the tins of cordite are still good. Even make something for Doc."

"Smokeless gunpowder will not function in my black powder gun," the tall man rumbled.

"Will if I cut it enough."

"And the primers?"

A shrug. "There you're out of luck. I can't make those."

Doc touched the cardboard box in the pocket of his frock coat that held the precious copper nipples for his handgun. He was down to eighteen. Maybe it was time for him to switch to a modern breechloader. He savagely shook those thoughts from his mind. No, that would never happen.

Shouldering his rifle, Ryan grabbed the release lever of the vault door and released it instantly. "Cold," he said, sounding amazed. "The bastard door is freezing cold!"

"Heavy armored and arctic cold," Krysty whispered. "Gaia, you…you don't think this might be a deep-storage locker?"

"Naw," Jak drawled contemptuously. "Impossible."

"More than likely, you are right, my young friend," Doc rumbled thoughtfully, reaching out to touch the icy metal. "We never found one before."

"But if it was…" Mildred started. "My God, we could find anything in there. Enough food to feed an army for a year, clothes, medicine, anything, everything!"

"What's a deep storage?" Dean asked. The term puzzled the boy until suddenly he remembered his father telling him about them over a campfire one night. Or rather, his father had relayed the tales told by the Trader. Deep-storage lockers were very special vaults designed to protect food and ammo for centuries, not just for a few years like a regular armory. It was to be the predark government's emergency reserves in case food couldn't be grown outside, or the fighting was worse than ever imagined.

"A DS locker," J.B. whispered, trying to keep the excitement from his voice. "All the equipment needed to rebuild a high-tech civilization from scratch behind one door."

"Mebbe, mebbe not," Ryan said, grabbing the lever and easing it downward. "Let's find out." The handle resisted his efforts, and it took all of the man's prodigious strength to shift its position until the main lock disengaged.

Silently, the massive door swung ponderously open

a hairline crack, pale gases loudly streaming out from the thin opening.

"Back," Mildred snapped, and the companions retreated to a safe distance while the vault disgorged its contents of nonbreathable inert gases into the air system of the redoubt.

Involuntarily, the physician shivered at the temperature drop. God, she hated the cold! Two hundred years ago she had gone into a hospital for a simple operation. There had been complications, and the doctors had been forced to put her in an experimental cryogenic freezer to try to save her life. Decades later, Ryan thawed her from the living death, her illness mysteriously cured.

Eventually, the hissing stopped, and the companions eagerly advanced. Doc and J.B. grabbed hold of the door and started to pull, while Jak and Ryan waited until it was far enough away from the jamb for them to start pushing. Dean and Krysty kept guard, watching the laboratory for any suspicious movements. Even when there was no discernible danger, it was wise to stay alert. The Deathlands were carpeted with the bones of people who let down their guard at the wrong moment.

"How the hell did they get this open in the past?" J.B. grunted, his face distended from the effort. "Damn thing must weigh a ton!"

"Two tons, by my calculations," Mildred corrected, her hands splayed. She wanted to help, but only four people could reach the door at a time. "Perhaps there's a system we haven't found to mechanically open the locker. Or some machine we're supposed to attach that does the work for us."

"Like those jimmy things on submarines," Dean added, bobbing his head to try and see between the mass of bodies and sneak a peek inside the locker. A deep-storage locker could have food in there, maybe those terrific U.S. Army MRE packs with condensed soup, and bread and salt and coffee and nut cake, and cigarettes and toilet paper. The companions had found a few items in the past; the cigs they traded for food to the sec men at different villes, but everything else they kept for themselves. Once there had even been chocolate bars.

"That's enough," Ryan said, and the group broke away from the metal slab. The portal was a good foot away from the jamb, more than sufficient room for them to wiggle through. It was pitch-black inside.

Reaching around the jamb, Ryan slid his hand along until he found the wall switch. He flicked it on. Nothing happened. Then a soft high-pitched humming could be heard, and the ceiling began to strobe with flashes of light that came faster and brighter until most of the florescent tubes in the drop ceiling burst into blinding illumination. Eagerly, the companions shoved their way into the locker. Krysty stayed outside to guard the only exit, while Dean shoved a chair between the door and the jamb to make sure it stayed open.

Faintly in the background, the ghostly music was heard again, then was gone.

The air was still chilly inside the vault, the temperature deliberately reduced to help retard the damage to food and weapons from the passage of time. Their breath fogged before them, the tiny clouds instantly disappearing as the redoubt finally began to pump power into the locker. The vents blossomed into life, a steady stream of delicious warm air wafting over them battling the centuries-old chill.

Then faces fell. Empty plastic shelving stretched for yards in every direction. Only a few scraps of plastic wrapping lay here and there to show where once thousands of ration packs had been stored.

Craning his neck, Doc scrutinized the top shelves. Reaching out, he retrieved two clear plastic bottles. "Mineral water," he announced.

Mildred inspected the containers for leaks or mold, then added them to her med kit. "Better than nothing."

J.B. opened a metal bin. Damnation, even the bedrolls and spare blankets were gone.

Following the maze of empty shelves, the companions turned a corner into the main area of the locker. Bare shelves stretched to the far wall, dozens of empty wooden pallets lying on the floor in mute testimony of the vanished cornucopia.

"Nothing," Ryan said bitterly. "Not a bastard thing left."

"On the contrary sir. Over here is a collection of office supplies," Doc offered, sounding perturbed. "Yes, indeed. Fax paper and staplers are extremely useful nowadays. Shall we each take an armload or ferry them out one at a time?"

Nobody even bothered to comment on the snide remarks. All of their hopes had been pinned on finding something in storage. The last few redoubts had been emptied like this one.

"Hey, what's this?" J.B. asked, peering behind a cabinet slightly angled away from the frosty wall. "Never found a second door before."

Snapping his fingers, Ryan pointed about the room. The companions moved into defensive positions as the Deathlands warrior holstered his pistol and unslung his longblaster. They had once found sentinels hidden in the redoubts, armed robots designed to protect the mil-

itary bases from exactly what the companions were doing.

"If its a tin can," J.B. muttered, using their slang
name for the machines while extending the wire stock
of his Uzi and nestling it into his shoulder for greater
stability, "aim for the mouth. Once it's down, we can
chill the machine easy."

Holding the LeMat pistol firmly in one hand, Doc
grabbed the hammer and pulled back until it clicked
solidly in place. The big-bore blaster was deadly at
close quarters. The soft lead miniball hit like a sledgehammer.

Ryan glanced at the others and held up three fingers.
They nodded. He took a breath, counted to three and
threw open the door, diving to the side.

Chapter Two

Everybody paused, braced for an attack as the door hit the wall with a crash. Only darkness was beyond. The light streaming in from their side illuminated only a small section of the concrete floor and several dark lumps of what could be anything.

Rummaging in her med kit, Mildred unearthed her old battered flashlight and squeezed the handle a few times to charge the battery inside the handle. The survivalist tool was a recent acquisition for her, a precious find, but was unfortunately already starting to show signs it was dying. It took more and more squeezing to get the light to work, and the weak beam was taking on a more pronounced yellowish tinge, marking the end of its service. The physician had a single spare bulb as a replacement, and then it was back to oil lanterns and candles.

She played the feeble beam about in the darkness, illuminating nothing. Then suddenly there was an audible crackle of electricity, and the room beyond exploded with light as banks of halogen bulbs in the ceiling came to brilliant life.

"Holy shit," Jak said, lowering his .357 Python.

"Eureka," Doc shouted happily. "The eagle has landed!"

The tiny room was full of gun cases and ammo boxes.

Piles and piles of them. Rows of lockers lined the back wall.

"Excellent. There has got to be food here," Mildred said in delight, and she started forward, but then abruptly stopped.

Ryan nodded in approval as J.B. moved among the boxes and crates looking for booby traps, his expert hands touching nothing but caressing the air itself as if deciding where to lay the traps himself.

"Clear," the Armorer announced after a while. "Come and get it."

Shouldering his weapon, Cawdor whistled for Krysty and Dean to join them as the others converged on the supplies, ripping open boxes and cases in grim concentration.

"What was this?" Krysty asked, appearing in the open doorway behind them. "Somebody's private stash?"

"Not know," Jak stated, placing aside a box full of Claymore mines. "Dean, look for grens."

The boy rushed forward. "On it!"

Sliding his Uzi out of the way, J.B. went straight to a wall locker and began to rearrange the boxes inside. He figured this had to have been the stash of a Navy SEAL or Green Beret team. There were military-style disposable garrotes, the kind that locked once you pulled them closed and couldn't be opened or removed without a knife. Excellent stuff. He hadn't seen its like in decades.

Under a pile of flak jackets was a flat box lined with screw-on acoustical silencers for U.S. Army Colt .45 pistols, but no pistols. However, there was an unlocked steel box the size of a shoebox packed with oily cloths and a good dozen Ruger .44 derringers. Very illegal blasters in predark days, and he wondered how the base commander got his hands on them. A squat red plastic box bearing the emblem of the Air Force contained a Veri-Pistol and some flares. Useless.

On the next shelf down, he found a collection of what resembled wax-covered bricks. But under closer inspection, they proved to be ammo boxes, the cellophane wrapping under the layer of wax still intact. Triple sealed, he marveled, the ammo would be in perfect condition! There was a good assortment of the standard calibers, but no .44 rounds for the derringers. Damn.

"Jak, .357 ammo!" J.B. called, and tossed the teenager a box.

The albino teen made the catch, shoved the box into the hip pocket of his fatigue pants and went straight back to his search for explosives.

"Any 9 mil?" Ryan asked, looking up from a stack of crates covered with shrink wrap. The military markings on the crates identified the contents as light antitank weapons, a 75 mm, single-shot, disposable bazooka called a LAW. The deadliest handheld weapon in existence during its day, and even more so in the present.

"Nine millimeters?" J.B. rummaged among the boxes. "Yep, regular and Parabellum."

"I'll take those," Ryan said, and he filled his pockets with spare ammo. "Any clips?"

"Lots, but just for Colt autos," J.B. replied, tossing another box to Dean. "Nothing for a nine."

"Any .38s?" Krysty asked, walking around a .50-caliber machine gun on a tripod."

"Not yet, but I'm still digging." Lifting an empty grenade tray off a stack, he found only more empties underneath. "Crap, they took all of the implosion grenades!"

"Wouldn't you?" Ryan asked, dusting off his hands.

The Armorer gave a half smile. "Yeah, still annoying, though."

"What about food packs?" Mildred asked, shoving away a big box stuffed full of a coiled ammo belt for a .50-caliber machine gun. If they still had the Leviathan, this would have been a major find, but now it was deadweight.

"No MRE packs, not even a box of K-rations," J.B. answered sourly. "Just ammo. Hey, .38 bullets!" He threw a box to Krysty.

"I have located a stack of MRE crates over here," Doc announced in jubilation, ripping off the tops barehanded. The man stared for a moment, then sighed. "Empty, as expected."

"Damnation!"

"Agreed, madam. Agreed. We cannot eat blasters."

"Or a Hafla," Jak announced, tossing aside the canvas tarp from a stack of canvas backpacks. Each pack was stuffed with six elongated tubes strongly resembling a LAW, except for a fluted nose and different markings on the pipe.

"What's that?" Dean asked, coming closer.

"A sort of LAW rocket," Ryan said. "Only loaded with napalm instead of high explosives."

Jak dropped the tarp. "Trade a month eating for one these."

Shifting through the empty boxes hoping to find a few packs missed, Doc paused to smile at the outpouring. For the Cajun, that was a long speech.

"Leave them till later," Ryan directed. "We don't

know if there is a ville within walking distance outside.''

''Be just the thing to convince a stubborn baron we mean business,'' the Armorer suggested.

''True, but for the moment, we have no need of them.''

As the others ripped through the military stash, Doc gave up his search among the MRE crates and started to check the back areas of the room. According to the Trader, the U.S. government had stocked the redoubts with the idea in mind that there was no telling how low civilization might fall after the nuke war. When the troops emerged, they might find savage cannibals wearing wolf-skin breechclouts and armed with wood clubs roaming the streets of New York and Chicago. So aside from clothes, medicine, wags, fuel, weapons and the like, the Trader claimed there were also very basic supplies, plows and seed, swords, crossbows and blackpowder weapons, to help rebuild America from the ashes.

In a corner, Doc found a large unmarked trunk and smashed off the padlock with the butt of his pistol, then was forced to rip away a plastic tape running along the edges of the trunk doubly insuring it was airtight. Lifting the lid, Doc dodged the exhalation of inert gas and then gazed inside with unabashed glee. The top tray was full of luxury items for trading—packs of chewing gum, cigars, butane lighters, hairbrushes and boxes of condoms. Lifting that aside, he found strings of cheap beads, fake jewelry and plastic mirrors. Pure tosh, a nice antiquarian word from his grandfather's time meaning utter and complete crap. So the predark government had also included trinkets to bribe the simple natives, eh? It was embarrassing to think that whole nations had been stolen with such trash.

Underneath the junk tray was a third filled with bundles of Bowie knives, graphic crossbows and quivers of arrows. Better, but not quite what he needed. However, the bottom area contained tiny kegs of black powder, cotton wadding in plastic jars, lead bars and balls for ammo and a collection of muzzle-loading pistols, huge .75-caliber horse pistols with flint firing mechanisms. Doc knew from experience that he could utilize the black powder, wadding and lead in his own LeMat.

Then with a cry of delight, he unearthed a tiny cardboard box of copper primer nipples and a brace of Remington muzzle-loading revolvers. They were the standard .44-caliber, exactly the same as his hog-leg LeMat, but heavily gilded with swirls and filigree. Choosing carefully, Doc filled the leather pouches on his ammo belt with more powder and shot than he'd seen in years.

"Hey, Doc!" J.B. called out.

Standing slightly off balance with the unaccustomed weight of a full pack, Doc turned to grin widely with his oddly perfect teeth. "Speak, Horatio, I am rapt attention."

"Found a brand-new Webley .44," the Armorer said, displaying the top-break wheelgun. "She's a beauty. Want to upgrade from that Civil War museum piece of yours?"

"What? Never. It is impossible. Unthinkable!" Doc said resolutely. Then he eased his tone to add, "However, I sincerely do appreciate the consideration, old friend."

Watching the exchange, Ryan draped a bandolier of 5-shot clips for the Steyr across his chest. "Reminds you of home, doesn't it?"

Fondly, Doc stroked the carved wooden handle of the massive weapon. "Indeed, it does, and more." He spoke softly as if lost in remembrance. "In its own curious way, this is my home."

Ryan understood. Both weapon and man were from the 1800s. To Doc, it was a direct physical link to his family, as dead as ashes now, but still living in another time. The old-style blaster helped keep them alive in his mind.

Pragmatic as always, J.B. shrugged in response and went back to his hunting.

"Hey, what's this?" Dean called out, holstering his Browning and lifting an oddly shaped blaster into view. It was an angular rectangle, with a thick holding grip on top, and a pistollike grip on the bottom. A safety switch was on the left, and a fire selector on the right. Aside from the muzzle, there didn't seem to be any other openings in the weapon.

"'Heckler & Koch G-12 4.7 mm caseless,'" Dean read from the lettering on the breech. "You used to have one of these didn't you, Dad?"

Ryan looked up from unpacking the Hafla rockets. "Yeah, I did, although a slightly different model, and it's a damn fine blaster. Holds a hundred rounds and weighs next to nothing. Put a hole through a flak jacket at five hundred yards."

Curiously, Dean turned the weapon over and upside down.

"There's no ejector port."

"That's because no brass comes out. The ammo is caseless. There's only propellant and lead in the stock. No brass. That's why it is so lightweight."

The boy loomed at the sleek blaster, impressed. It sort of reminded him of the laser weapons they had faced on Wizard Island, except that it didn't have a dial to adjust the burning power of a beam.

"Why did you stop carrying it if it's so great?" he asked bluntly.

"I have the Steyr, which has a longer range, and ammo is easier to find. And I can save the brass and do reloads if necessary. The HK can only be reloaded with blocks of caseless ammo. Nothing else. When you're out, that's it. She's deadweight."

Getting the balance of the odd rifle, Dean tried the weapon at port arms, then shoulder arms, like he had seen predark soldiers do in the videos the redoubts sometimes had. "I like it," he stated, slinging the blaster over a shoulder.

The elder Cawdor came over and placed it in his hands. "Okay, then I'll teach you long-range tactics. The Browning is good, but only at short distances. Keep this on the first setting, single shot. One trigger pull fires one round. The next is burst, one trigger pull, three rounds damn near instantly. Sounds like a single round firing."

"Wow."

"Last setting is full-auto, the HK fires so fast—"

"Six thousand rounds a minute," J.B. chimed in.

Impressed, Dean raised both eyebrows. "This would empty in seconds!"

"So stay on single shot, remember that. Reloads fast, but you have got to keep the ammo blocks sealed in plas until just before you slide them in. The block gets wet, it's dead."

He released the catch on the stock and lifted up the top of the magazine. "When you're done, there's nothing inside to dump, and no spent brass to collect or get underfoot. You drop in the new block, close the top and go.''

''Mebbe we should find you another one,'' the boy suggested.

''I'll stick with what I have.''

''Nothing,'' Mildred reported from the doorway, her expression a mixture of disappointment and anger. ''We have enough weapons to stage a war, but there's not a single scrap of food here.''

Ryan looked over the assemblage of his friends, noticing how thin they were becoming, faces haggard and belts tightened. Short rations for a month had turned them into skeletons.

''Okay, everybody load up on ammo,'' Ryan ordered brusquely. ''First, we'll do a recce of the base to make sure we're alone, then we go shopping. There has to be some supplies here.''

In perfect synchronicity, his stomach loudly rumbled.

''Let's go find them,'' the one-eyed man stated, starting for the exit.

Fully armed, the companions started at the bottom level and worked their way upward. Reactor room, maintenance, offices, barracks, were deserted. Not a sign of life, not even a mouse seemed to have breached the integrity of the underground bunker.

On the level above the bio labs, they found a communications room with a CD player still struggling to play ghostly music over the intercom system. There was no jewel case for the worn disk, and so whatever the distorted tune actually was would remain a mystery. But at least they made the eerie noise stop. Oddly, the music had added a touch of life to the redoubt, and now it seemed even more deserted than before.

Unfortunately, the kitchen was devoid of anything

edible, the big freezers deactivated and empty as the pantry. Resting a boot on the seat of a molded plastic chair, Ryan glanced over the rows of long tables lining the cafeteria. The one positive aspect was that life support was starting to react to their presence and the water pumps were coming on-line. The kitchen taps spewed forth trapped air at first, then brownish gunk unfit to wash a corpse in and finally cool clear water. It wasn't much, but they took it as a positive omen.

Moving to the top floor, the companions found the garage equally devoid of useful items. Bits and pieces of vehicles lay scattered about, but none in working condition. Heaps of trash were everywhere, string and paper and excelsior packing material, along with numerous crumpled cardboard boxes. The others moved about the huge room, giving it a quick once-over.

J.B. headed directly for a battered Hummer near a workbench. The tires were flat, its headlights busted and the hood was up, exposing the partially disassembled engine. Tools lay on the block, and tiny boxes holding new spark plugs were stacked on the bumper.

"Old plugs have never been removed," J.B. said thoughtfully. He wiggled a hose and tried yanking an insulated cable free without success. "Engine is still sealed."

"Think we could get it working again?" Dean asked eagerly. Machines were his passion, and he could never ride long enough in any vehicle. The boy was still irked that he had never gotten a chance to drive the Leviathan before they were forced to abandon the giant war wag.

"No prob fixing," Jak said, surveying the other wrecks. "Tires from that, headlights there."

"What about the battery?"

"That's a nuke battery," J.B. stated, pointing out the

shielded box under the hood. "Those babies last forever and have enough juice to fry a griz bear, so be careful."

The boy swallowed hard. "Yes, sir."

J.B. bent over the radiator and started to fiddle with the distributor. "Find me a three-quarter-inch combination wrench, will you?"

"Sure!"

"Hold on there," Ryan ordered, joining them. "It would take hours, if not days, to get that junk pile into shape. Let's recce outside first. Might not be needed. A ville may be only walking distance away."

"Or mebbe on top of mountain," Jak added in wry humor, raking back his snowy white hair with stiff fingers.

Extracting himself from under the hood, J.B. laid aside the distributor cap. "Fair enough. No sense doing work if it isn't necessary."

Leading the way toward the exit tunnel, Ryan passed one of the many busted boxes scattered about and nudged it with his boot to shove it aside. The sagging sides split asunder, and a wealth of tiny cylinders came tumbling out.

"I'll be damned," he said aloud, bending to see what they were. The labels on the cans were badly faded but still readable. "Hash! This is corned-beef hash. Dozens of cans! Enough for months!"

Across the room, Mildred spun about. "Excellent!"

Dropping the power drill he had been inspecting, J.B. hurried over at a lope with Dean and Jak at his heels. Doc and Krysty walked over at a more leisurely pace.

Grabbing a can from the pile to show them, Ryan's own elation faded when he saw the side and tops of the container bulging from massive internal pressure.

"Dammit, they're spoiled," he announced, dropping

the container as if it were unclean on the outside. "Probably why they weren't taken along by whoever cleaned this base out so efficiently. God alone knows how long they've been lying there."

The rush slowed to a walk and the companions gathered around the deadly food, the happy smiles gone as quickly as they came.

"There's so much," Krysty said woodenly. The memory of what pan-fried hash tasted like surfaced in her memory, and she savagely killed the recollection. It was bad enough looking at the stuff without remembering how good corned beef was.

Swallowing twice to clear his mouth, Jak felt his stomach churn at the mere sight of the cans. "All bad?" he asked.

Ryan nudged another box with his boot, and more rounded cans spilled across the floor. "Seems to be," he stated coldly. "One mouthful of this could chill an army."

Kicking apart another box, J.B. sent cans rolling across the cold floor of the garage in every direction. "Shit!" he yelled, then stomped one flat. The thick contents gushed out like speckled mud, the salty meat streaked with vile greens and blues. That killed his anger and his appetite at the same time.

"Mebbe we could boil the cans without opening them first," Dean suggested hopefully. "You know, to kill the germs and stuff inside."

"Still be deadly," Mildred explained sadly. "Toxicity is also a chemical composition, not just a bacteriological infection."

"Oh. Nothing we can do to fix them?"

"No," Ryan and Mildred said together.

His arms full of cloth, J.B. returned and threw an old

tarp over the boxes and cans. "Out of sight, out of mind," he stated.

"Mildred, how much do we have?" Krysty asked, putting some distance between herself and the rotting meat. The stench was ghastly, worse than the breath of a Louisiana vampire.

"Six cans of beans and a pound of rice. Enough food for two, maybe three days," Mildred reported stolidly, the meager weight of her backpack not very reassuring. "After which we start boiling our belts."

"Huh?" Dean said.

His father answered. "Remember that leather is edible, if cleaned sufficiently." He surveyed the redhead in her bearskin coat. "We could stay alive off the soup that fur would make for at least a week."

Registering disdain, Krysty glanced at her coat.

"Not hungry enough to eat boots," Jak remarked.

"Not yet," J.B. said. "Come on, let's check outside. Been a while since I've been hunting."

An entire stanza of a Walt Whitman poem came unbidden to mind, but Doc refrained the impulse. Literary allusions seemed pointless before the specter of starvation, the only enemy ever faced they couldn't stop by force of arms.

Moments later, the companions reached the door to the redoubt. Twice the height of man and wide enough to allow a tank passage, the titanium steel was as perfect as the day it rolled out of the foundry. Nothing encountered could even scratch the resilient material.

Ryan tapped in the access code on the armored keypad. Nothing happened. Ryan tapped in the code more carefully. There was no lever, and, obediently, the portal rumbled aside, exposing a dark tunnel.

"Now that's odd," Ryan murmured. "Don't recall ever finding a redoubt with an exterior tunnel."

"Looks handmade," Krysty said, squinting.

"Let me check this," J.B. suggested, removing the rad counter from his shirt collar and pointing it toward the opening. Everybody remembered when they had nearly gotten fried alive trying to exit a redoubt that was at the bottom of radioactive blast crater.

"Got no readings," J.B. said, lowering the silent device.

"Check them," Mildred told him, digging a tiny wristwatch from her backpack. The mechanism was long broken, but that wasn't why she still kept the time piece. The physician held it out, and both J.B. and Ryan waved their rad counters over the timepiece. Each counter gave off a click when over the tiny radium-lined hands of the watch.

"Okay, let's go," Ryan said, attaching his rad counter to the collar again. "Standard positions, single-yard spread."

As they walked into the tunnel, the huge door rumbled shut behind them, loudly bolting closed with a series of dull mechanical thuds. Lighting a few candles, the companions proceeded along the rocky tunnel. The passageway was clearly artificial, the rough walls supported by concrete columns set at regular intervals. The tunnel curved gently to the left, and suddenly their way was blocked by something huge and leathery, the object barely visible in the flickering candlelight.

"What is that?" Dean asked curiously. "A pile of luggage?"

Instantly, the obstruction turned and snarled loudly, inhuman eyes dominating a misshapen face.

"Mutie!" Ryan yelled, drawing his blaster and firing.

J.B. brought up the Uzi, the muzzle-blasts strobing the passageway in flashes and giving them a brief glimpse of wings and a fang-filled mouth on the end of a serpentine neck.

Screaming and spitting in rage, the beast jerked at the impact of the 9 mm rounds, then advanced toward the humans, seemingly unaffected from the lead and steel coming its way.

Now they all discharged their blasters, the noise almost deafening in the tight confines of the shaft. Then a thunderous boom overwhelmed the irregular barrage as Doc unleashed the LeMat, a foot-long lance of flame extending from the muzzle.

Oddly, the beast wailed in pain, covering its gnarled features with both wings. Then turning tail, it rushed away from the companions and disappeared.

Staying in combat formation, Ryan and the others moved forward slowly until reaching the end of the tunnel. A soft breeze threatened their candles, and the companions cupped hands around the tiny flames. The underground passage fronted at the crest of a low hillock, the ground gently sloping away into the night. Overhead, a full moon was struggling to send grayish light through a heavily clouded sky. Not a star was visible, but they did spot a tinged figure flapping for the horizon as if running for its life.

As they walked farther out, the friends watched where they stepped. In the cracks of the stone flooring, a single small flower was growing, the delicate white petals spread wide to challenge the world.

"Some sort of bat, I think," J.B. commented, tracking the passage of the beast with his Uzi just in case it returned. "Ugly bastard."

Ryan scanned the ground. "Don't see any blood. Our blasters did as much damage as pissing would."

"Did you see those eyes?" Mildred asked, her ZKR pistol still in her hand. "Solid black with no pupils. Definitely nocturnal."

"Night feeder," Jak said, then he sniffed loudly. "Not smell spoor. Not home."

"Just waiting for prey, like a vulture sitting in a tree," Ryan said, resting the stock of the Steyr on his hip. "This is a good vantage spot. Probably can see for miles in the daylight." He paused. "Look over there."

The windswept dunes of the desert below formed gentle ripples in a flat sandy sea that reached out to the horizon. There stood the ruins of a predark city, a ragged array of skyscrapers reaching into the clouds proud and majestic. Very few predark cities had escaped the bombs, or the firestorms that followed.

"Where are we?" Doc asked, staring. The ruins didn't resemble any metropolis he knew from the past.

J.B. shrugged. "Sky is too cloudy to get a reading with the minisextant. Could be anywhere."

Unexpectedly, twin rods of light erupted from the ruins, the beams steadily sweeping across the sky, casting lucent circles on the bottoms of the cloud banks overhead.

"Searchlights," Mildred breathed, amazed. "I'll be damned."

"Mebbe just machines," Ryan said thoughtfully. "Comps still trying to fight a war over for centuries."

J.B. checked his chron. "Too irregular," he said, winding the timepiece and returning it to his pocket. "Those are hand operated."

"People," Jak stated with a smile. "Folks gotta eat."

"And we have goods to trade," Krysty said confidently. "I would guess it's about a three-, four-day walk from here."

"Only be a few hours in the Hummer," Dean offered hopefully.

J.B. rubbed the back of his neck. "It *is* fixable."

"Sounds good," Ryan said, hitching up his belt, a finger feeling the new hole in the strap to make it smaller. "We'll rest up tonight and leave at first light."

"It is odd, though," Krysty remarked thoughtfully. "Why would anybody advertise their presence these days? Likely to get you attacked."

"Could be throwbacks," Mildred suggested. "Savages still doing a job their great-great-great-grandfathers were supposed to. And now it's a religion to them."

"Or slaver trying to lure in fresh merchandise." Doc scowled. "Great Scott, what a disagreeable notion."

"Cannibals," Jak added, a knife appearing in his hands as if from nowhere. The teenager flipped the blade and tucked it away again.

So many questions, with only one way to get any answers. Ryan turned away from the city. "We'll find out in the morning. Come on, we have work to do."

Chapter Three

On the far side of the dead river, the darkness descended upon the large ville, sealing them in for the night like the lid on an iron pot. Bobbing points of light came from the dozens of bright lanterns held by the sec men patrolling the outer wall, the lamps giving off an odd bluish light from the burning alcohol-soaked wicks. A stationary series of crackling pitch torches dotted the repaired main streets and the baron's huge mansion.

Closing the wooden shutters on the glassless windows, the blacksmith shut down her forges, letting them cool for the night. The glassmakers did the same, but banked their kiln to keep it warm until the following day. The prisoners assigned to sewer digging were unwrapping the rags from their hands used in lieu of gloves and washing the stinking grime of their toils off tired bodies.

Behind a barricade of pungi sticks and barbed wire, the shine gang ate its dinner and tossed lumps of black coal into the dull reddish fire underneath the huge distillation vat of the still. From the top, the coils of copper angled downward, leading to rows of painfully clean metal barrels waiting to be filled with alcohol for the next day—juice for the vehicles and fuel for the lanterns. And the dreaded Machine.

Murmuring voices came from the patched houses of the full citizens, joining soft conversation from the patched tents of the immigrants yet to be rewarded by full status. The crack of a whip sounded from a three-story building secreted among the ruins yet to be reclaimed by the workers. Downtown, happy laughter sallied as a family celebrated the birth of a child. A singing drunk fell to the ground in front of some sec men, who stepped over the man and kept walking. A husband and wife were screaming at each other, with the neighbors listening for any good details. And faint tinkling music drifted out from the well-illuminated gaudy house set prestigiously between the market square and the barracks of the sec men.

But from one tiny oasis came an endless barrage of cursing and grunting. A partially built greenhouse towered above the streets, the framework roof draped in folds of protective canvas.

Straining from the load in their grips, the two men shuffled away from a huge rock pile, their bare hands desperately clutching a tremendous granite slab.

"Easy, dammit, Felix," the tall man cursed. "Not so fast. Nearly tripped me!"

"Blow it out your ass, Ben," the other retorted. "This thing weighs a ton!"

"Do we have to finish this now?"

"The sec men says we don't get fed till this wall is up," Felix grunted, the smell of dinner a tantalizing torment in the air. He tried not to think about baked potatoes smothered in fried onions with all the mushroom soup he could eat, and failed miserably. The baron may beat a person at a whim here, but a person was fed! "First thing they taught me when I arrived here, no work means no food."

Rivulets of sweat running down his hairy forearms, Ben struggled with his grip, the slab of stone shifting dangerously in his slick hands. "Watch it!" he cried out.

Releasing his end, Felix jumped backward as the stone hit the ground like an earthquake.

"Is it broke?" Ben asked fearfully, dropping to the ground and running his hands over the granite. "Please, no. I can't take another whipping."

Scampering nimbly through the stacks of wood beams and salvaged nails, Felix returned with the old battered lantern. Standing over the granite, he recklessly turned up the wick, bluish light washing over the deserted construction site.

"It's okay." He sighed, lowering the light to the bare minimum again. This was all the alcohol they would get for today. When it was exhausted, they'd have to work in the dark if that stone wasn't in place. And that was a sure way to lose fingers. Wasn't a man or woman among the crew whose hands weren't covered with scars from the rigors of masonry.

"We'll never get this freaking thing in place," Ben grumbled, flexing his aching shoulder muscles. "Why can't we bust it into pieces?"

"Baron Strichland wants this greenhouse twice the size of his private one," Felix stated, "which means bigger end walls, which means stronger foundations." He glared hostilely. "Unless you want to tell the foreman to go jump a mutie."

"And get fed to the Machine? Fuck that."

In the distance behind them, the great beams of the Alphaville searchlights swept the sky in their endless motions, back and forth, a slight wobble every now and then as a prisoner slowed at his task and a sec man encouraged him to do better with a lash from a knotted bullwhip.

"So what do we do?" Ben asked, eyeing the slab hopelessly.

"Gotta ask for more men on the job." Felix sighed, rubbing his lower back. "We'll take a few lashes, but that's better than busting this thing."

Ben shook his head. Another whipping. He was starting to lose feeling in his back from the accumulation of scars. Felix said the outside world was a lot worse than this place. He was an immigrant and should know. But Ben was born here and couldn't imagine a worse hell then living in Alphaville.

"How about we take another rest, try again in a—" Ben stopped and smiled broadly. "Never mind. Here comes the answer."

Out of the dark, a huge figure was shambling along the street, moving hunched over as if struggling against a fierce wind.

"Hey, Sarge!" Ben called out with a wave. "Over here!"

Shuffling along, Harold paused and stared at the men with his good eye. Many people, when they first met him, instantly thought him to be a mutie, with his bent back, mottled hair and distorted features. But in truth, he had been one of the most handsome men in the ville until he fell through the top of a greenhouse, the shards of glass reducing his good looks into a grotesque mockery in less than seconds. And even worse, a sliver of glass had stabbed into his head, producing little blood and healing quickly, but his mind was gone, terminated like a cut cable. All that remained of the master sergeant of the Alphaville sec men was a powerful body, forged to even greater strength by the endless toil of brutally hard work.

Harold came their way at a leisurely pace, trying to

smile, but only managing to distend his lips and drool slightly. In his powerful arms, he clutched a tiny box covered with flowery wallpaper.

"What's prob?" he said with slurred words, bobbing slightly. "Bad rock?"

Hands resting on his hips, Ben laughed. "Yeah, that's right. It's a bad rock. Toss it on top of the wall for us, would you, pal?"

Harold blinked at the titanic stone as if registering its existence for the first time. A soft wind blew over the work site, carrying the smell of hot dust from the outer desert. Somewhere, a wolf briefly howled and was abruptly silenced.

"Sure." Harold grinned. Putting aside his package, he started to bend to grab the rock, when a song repeated in his addled mind about lifting big things "up from the knees." He had to listen to the voices in his head, he admonished himself. They were friends.

Bending his knees, Harold slid his thick sausage fingers underneath the rock and grunted slightly as he lifted the quarter ton of polished granite to his chest.

"Where?" he asked in an embarrassed tone. "Forgot."

Openmouthed, Felix could only stare as Ben directed Harold to the wall. Gingerly, so as to not hurt the puny wall, Harold placed the slab on top and stepped away quickly. Sometimes when he moved things they fell over, and he didn't want to get hurt. For a split second, there flashed through his mind a kaleidoscope of images—a ladder, a push from below, falling toward the wall...but then they were gone and forgotten.

"Good job, Sarge," Ben said, slapping the giant on the shoulder. "Get along. Dinner is waiting."

"Yar," he said, drooling. Tenderly retrieving his

box, Harold ambled away, so very pleased to have helped a friend in need. Softly, the voices in his head started to whisper that they really weren't his friends, but he covered his cauliflower ears and shouted until they stopped. Everybody in the ville was his friend. Didn't they always ask him for help? He was as important as the baron! And today was a special day. He clutched the canvas bundle in his arm even tighter. Harold was going to get married today!

Watching the broken goliath shuffle away, Felix fanned himself with a battered cloth cap. "Son of a bitch. I ain't never seen nothing like him!"

"Strong as a machine," Ben agreed, finding his shirt and pulling it on over his head. "And just as dumb. We get him to do a lot of our work for us."

"Doesn't the foreman know?" Felix asked suspiciously.

"Naw, he does it, too. We all do."

Unwrapping the rags from his hands, Felix privately smiled at the news. That was important information to file away if he ever decided to rat to the baron on laziness in the construction crews. Might become foreman himself that away. "If that thing ever goes insane, be mighty hard to stop."

"Crap," Ben scoffed, reclaiming his own hat, a battered baseball cap with the letters removed from on the bill. Only a few loose threads showed where the embroidered logo of some predark company had once been. "A bullet in the head will stop anything."

Felix scowled deeply and cast his eyes to the cloudy sky. "No," he said. "There are some things a blaster can't stop."

Fully understanding what the immigrant was referring to, Ben felt a rush of fear and turned up the wick on the lantern as high as it would go. The area was filled with brilliant light for several yards in every direction.

"Come on, let's get inside," Ben suggested. Staying near the lantern, they hurried toward the barracks and a meal long overdue.

THE TINY GRAY HOUSE stood alone on a cracked parking lot, the single plastic window solid white from the sandstorms that occasionally swept over the ville from the desert. The roof was tough plastic and withstood the acid rains in the spring just fine. Although kind of small, it had been comfy for two, tight for three, and now was too damn big for just him alone.

When Philip Arnstein and his wife first found the place, there had been a chart posted on the exterior listing the prices for the privilege of parking in the lot. But he had found a rusty can of paint decades ago and used half to paint the exterior twice, giving it a new look that pleased his wife greatly. She had shown him how much that night, by doing things she had only hinted about earlier. He still remembered that night and always would.

Naturally, the other half of the paint was given to the baron. Sex was nice, but not even the wolves scared him as much as the thought of going to the Machine.

Sitting in a lawn chair by the open door, the old man shook off those thoughts and lit a corncob pipe with a piece of smoldering oakum. In his withered hands was a whole fresh corncob, nicely dried and completely devoid of anything edible. Smoking contentedly, the oldster started to whittle a new pipe. This one was getting a bit oily in taste and was soon for the mash pot of the brewers. The baron didn't let anything go to waste. It was his only good point, the bloody bastard.

Then from out of the darkness, a monstrous shape lunged forward, and the old man screamed in fright, dropping his pipe.

"Hi, Mr. Arnstein," Harold said, grinning sloppily. "I got speak about Laura."

"Harold, don't ever do that again!" Arnstein admonished angrily, searching on the ground for his pipe. He found it under his chair and lit it with trembling hands. "Damn near made me jump out of my skin. Thought you was a mutie."

"Sorry. Laura?" he asked plaintively, trying to sneak a peek inside the tiny house.

"Not here," Arnstein said, surprised he got the name right. Poor dumb thing got lost inside a walled ville. It was pathetic. The new baron should have shot him years ago, but Strichland wasn't exactly famous for his mercy.

"Marry," Harold gushed. "Wanna marry her." He held out a package. "Brought gift. Dowry."

The former sec man stumbled over the big word, and wasn't exactly sure what it meant. But the voices in his head keep screaming it was the correct thing to do. Ask first. Always ask first.

"You want to marry my daughter, Laura." The old man chewed over the pronouncement as if it were unknown meat. Damnedest thing he had ever heard. Why would even this half-wit want to marry a retarded whore?

"You fucking her?" he asked bluntly.

Harold felt his face burn bright red, and his vision clouded, dots of blackness swimming before him with a cloud of flies.

"Yes," he blurted honestly, remembering how they had once kissed. "We in love."

Rad-blast it! The hunchback and the girl were having sex.

"Sorry, son, but you're a day late," Arnstein said kindly. "She was just too much trouble here, knocking over things, setting fires, so I sold her to the gaudy house."

Raw horror seized the goliath, his heart pounding savagely in his barrel chest. "She at bad place?" he squeaked like a child. He grabbed the old man and lifted him effortlessly off the chair. A massive hand closed around Arnstein's neck, cutting off the air. "No! No! I marry her! She mine! You hear me? Mine!"

Feebly, Arnstein clawed at the hand holding him aloft. He tried to kick Harold between the legs, but he was too far away, his skinny foot only flailing helplessly. Finally, Harold realized what he was doing and eased his grip.

"Baron made me," Arnstein wheezed. "Everybody has got to work. You know the rules, same as me. Hell, boy, you wrote them! No work means no food. Or worse, expulsion."

Frightened, Harold glanced at the rusty wall of smashed cars rising above the ville. Outside, the muties would get you. Laura was too little to go there. He could, but he was strong and knew the great secret.

But Laura sold to the gaudy house! Raw fury seized the man, and he felt the adrenaline rush of killing flood his body when the ghostly voices commanded him to release the whitehair. He was Laura's father. Would Laura marry the man who killed her blood kin? Conflicting emotions shook his fragile mind. On impulse, he released the man as if gesturing in surprise.

"Back," Harold rumbled menacingly at the man cowering on the pavement. "You get back!"

"C-can't," Arnstein gasped, massaging his bruised throat. "She belongs to the house now. They own her. Probably already at work doing some sec man or farmer."

The words so simply said hit Harold like punches, driving the madness from his mind and replacing it with a deadly cold fire. He turned and stumbled, going down the streets between the array of finished greenhouses. His pace quickly became a sprint, then a lope, as he dashed across the ville to save the woman he loved from being forced into kissing other men.

The blocks flew beneath his shoes, and the greenhouses passed by in the glittering majesty as if crystal phantoms. Reaching the market square, he plowed into numerous people, his every thought on reaching his goal.

Music, light and laughter came from every window and door of the building. A few men lounged against the wall, smiling and smoking on corncob pipes. The front door was garishly painted with a vulgar cartoon for patrons who couldn't read, and the picture fueled Harold into an insane rage. Charging, he simply plowed through the door, ripping it off the hinges. The crash stunned him for a moment, then he found himself standing inside the gaudy house, with a burly man advancing upon him holding a dented baseball bat.

"What's wrong with you, Sarge?" the bouncer demanded, brandishing the weapon. "You finally gone crazy, or forgot how to knock?"

Harold wasn't sure how to answer the man, so he said nothing. Okay, he was inside, but now what? The giant couldn't think. His thoughts were muddled and confused. Looking about hopefully, he saw a group of men drinking at tables in the next room. The walls were covered with mirrors, and a pretty girl with garish makeup stood behind the makeshift counter, polishing a plastic tumbler, her red satin dress skintight, her bound breasts nearly spilling out for display.

"Mebbe he's been smoking wolfweed!" called out a drunken tailor, who immediately regretted the words as the hunchback stared at him directly with eyes filled with death.

"You're going to have to replace that door!" the bouncer stated.

"No," he rumbled. "Where Laura?"

"She's not here," the girl behind the bar told him. "Pat sent her home."

Was that true? Could it be? Harold felt even more confused when he saw the slut glance nervously at the steps leading to the second floor, and some small part of his brain that could still process information told him she was lying, that Laura had to be up there. Turning, he started for the staircase. The bouncer blocked his way, and Harold shoved him aside. The man flew across the room and hit the wall with a crunch, his limp body sliding to the floor, blood dribbling from a slack mouth.

"Laura!" he bellowed at the top of his lungs. "Laura!"

"She's upstairs with a customer," the tailor shouted callously. "Wait your turn. She'll be down in a second."

Screaming in fury, Harold took the stairs three at a time to the upper level. A long corridor stretched before him, lined with doors on each side. He could hear odd noises from the other side, squeaking and muffled cries. Choosing one at random, he kicked it open, the door coming off the hinges and sagging to the floor. Inside, two people were on a bed wrestling. They froze in surprise. Without comment, Harold went to the next door and tried again. That room was empty, but strange items made of leather hung from the walls and bedposts. He didn't understand and left feeling oddly unclean.

In the room across the hall, Harold found three nude women lying on the bed covers, their limbs entangled to the point where it was impossible to tell where one ended and the next began. He grabbed a random leg and started to separate the moaning women. Each began to scream as he forced their faces upward to see which was Laura. None of them was.

Leaving the room, Harold shouted her name again as a skinny teenager appeared at the end of the corridor brandishing a homemade blaster, a thin metal barrel attached to the wooden grip by baling wire.

"Hold it right there, buddy!" the runt cried out, and slid a .22 cartridge into breech of the zip gun. With the other hand, he pulled back a nail attached to a rubber band. "Ain't no fighting on the fuck floor allowed!"

His beleaguered mind couldn't comprehend the full meaning of what was said, but he recognized a threat, and panic for Laura seized him worse than before. Finding he still held the broken handle from the first door in his hand, he threw it at the teenager, catching him in the stomach. The boy doubled over, vomiting, and dropped the blaster. The weapon fired as it hit the floor, a puff of dust exploding from the wall near Harold.

Not connecting the two events, Harold went unconcerned to the next door and kicked it open to find more people wrestling.

"What the hell is going on here?" shouted the man on top of a woman with raven-black hair. "Scram, gimp! I paid for this slut—she's mine for another hour.''

But as the stranger resumed his actions, Harold saw in horror that it was Laura under him. Her slim arms were tied to the bedposts, her nude body splayed like a cow for slaughter. Her blue eyes were closed, a dirty rag stuffed in her mouth, and his new wife made little whimpering noises as the big man between her legs began pumping again.

Stepping to the bed, Harold punched the man in the face as hard as he could. Blood sprayed from the impact, and the stranger flew off the bed, tumbling to the floor in a tangle of clothes.

Looking down at Laura, he saw she wasn't really naked. Her clothes were undone and in wild disarray, her breasts fully visible and the tangle of ebony hair between her legs exposed.

A moist pink slit ran along the downy triangle, and it fueled a strange new hunger inside the hunchback.

"Don't you move!" a cold voice said from the doorway.

Instincts honed in a hundred battles before his accident, Harold sensed real danger now and spun with his hands clenched for a fight.

Standing in the ruined doorway was a hugely overweight woman dressed in frilly clothes and holding a longblaster. Not a homemade model like the kid in the hall, but a proper shotgun. She worked the pump and pointed the muzzle not at him, but straight toward Laura. Harold moved between them to protect the girl.

"Smart move, Sarge," Patrica stated. "But this is loaded with bent nails and glass, boy. Cut you open like a fish.''

"Mine," he offered in simple explanation, pointing at the bound girl. "Mine!"

The gaudy house madam shook her head, never taking her eyes off the hunchbacked giant. "No, Harold," Patrica said quietly. "Laura is mine. Her father sold her to me. I own her."

Harold lowered his head and took a step forward.

Instantly, the madam triggered the blaster, blowing a hole in the plasterboard wall the size of a sewer grating. He stopped the advance as she worked the pump action again, but didn't relax.

"Mine," Harold repeated, his deadly hands still extended.

"Sergeant O'Malley, listen to me," the madam said slowly. She was armed, but if the shotgun didn't kill him on the spot, he'd rip her head off before dying.

"Harold, by the law of the ville, this was a legal transaction," Patrica said in a motherly tone. Sex appeal wouldn't work on the enraged idiot. She had to be nice. "The baron himself is a client here and encourages whoring. It's a service to the ville. We forge treaties between families. Immigrants don't get raped anymore. It's a good thing. Sluts are special people. The ville needs sluts."

"Gonna marry her!" he screamed, spittle coming from his slack lips. "Father said okay. Called me son!

"She mine!" Harold repeated, glancing at the bound girl supine on the sweat-stained bed. "Mine."

"Interesting." Now the madam felt more in control. His tone was softening, and she was starting to understand. So old man Arnstein had sold his daughter cheap, knowing the ville hunchback was in love with her. That's why nobody else wanted the girl, in spite of her incredible beauty. Well, she'd settled the score with the old cheat later. Right now, she had a brain-dead Hercules who wanted to walk off with her prize slut. No way Pat was going to let that happen. At least not without making a profit. Maybe the sarge could be of use to her in certain matters. Debts to be collected, break a few legs. She might have him under her control for years.

"Well, that's too bad about her father, Sarge. I paid for her fair and square. Canned food and shoes. A good knife and two blankets without holes."

"Me buy," he mumbled, not sure of what to do. Things that had to be moved or broken, invaders or muties to kill—these he could fathom, real things you could touch. This was beyond him, and the voices were beginning to whisper terrible bloody suggestions.

Tucking the shotgun under her arm, Patrica laughed heartily, making her whole body jiggle. "Oh, my poor young fool. You work shoveling boiled crap in the greenhouses. You could never steal enough vegetables to pay for a beauty like this!"

Behind her, the skinny kid reappeared, the tiny blaster in his grip, a savage expression on his face. Harold looked directly at the boy the way he did with the desert wolves, and the teen went pale, backing into the corridor.

The package in his back pocket suddenly felt warm, and Harold removed it. "Got this," he said, tossing the bundle to the woman. It landed on the floor between them.

Wary of a trick, Patrica moved aside and let her assistant get the package. Opening it carefully, the madam almost dropped the shotgun in shock. Inside was a predark handblaster, a Smith & Wesson .357 Magnum in perfect condition, the barrel shining with oil, as smooth as winter ice. Even the cushioned grip was intact, without a single crack or tiny piece missing. Unfamiliar with the blaster, she fumbled a bit before managing to release the cylinder and check the barrel. Perfect. The damn thing might as well be brand-new. She dry fired it a few times to check the spring, the solid sound of the hammer falling music to her ears.

Shutting the cylinder with fingertip pressure, Patrica stared at Harold, standing as if braced for a whipping. He was fully capable of tearing this whole house down to the foundation, and now he stood in fear of her words. Did he know what this actually was, and what it was truly worth?

"And bullets," Harold hastily added, showing a fistful of cartridges, fearing her lack of response was an indication the blaster wasn't good enough. It was the best he could find. He was supposed to give it to her father as dowry, but was it enough to buy his wife free from the bed?

Without fear, Patrica walked closer and took the bullets from his trembling palm. "This is forbidden. None but the baron and his men can own blasters." But the madam took them and tucked them into the fold of her dress. With a blaster like this, a person could risk leaving the ville. Be free of the bastard Machine forever. Anybody could leave the ville, but outside there were many muties and animals who waited for norms to risk crossing the desert. Not many ever came back. A working blaster in this condition could have bought him the whole damn gaudy house for a week. Ten times enough to buy a retarded slut who had to be tied to the bed to keep her from rolling over and offering the wrong end to a customer.

"Enough?" Harold asked, hope burgeoning within. "We go now."

"No. This doesn't buy her, boy," the woman lied with a straight face. "A lovely quiff like Laura can earn more than this each moon for years. The baron himself wants her, and who can risk angering him?"

Choking slightly on her gag, Laura shivered on the bed, and Harold gently reached down to lay a blanket over her partially nude form. She smiled around the rag at him and closed her eyes, drifting off to sleep.

"Buy me a month," he said, staring at his wife. "A month no kissing?"

Kissing. How sweet, the poor dullard. "No, Harold. Everybody works," Patrica said, crossing her arms. "No work, no food." An animal growl started low in the man's throat, and the madam realized she had gone too far.

"But it will buy you a week off her back, if that's what you mean," she hastily corrected, smiling for her life. "She can scrub pots in the kitchen and clean the lavs. Mop the floors."

Ask for more, screamed the voices in his head. "Two weeks!"

"One," Patrica said, surprised he would even try to bargain. Mebbe he wasn't as insane as she had heard. "Plus, I don't tell the baron you found a blaster...in the ville?"

Harold shrugged noncommittally.

Damn, he wasn't talking. "However, if you want to marry her, it will cost a lot more than this one poor blaster." She pressed her thumb against the hammer and pulled the trigger a few times. "See? It's no good. Broken already."

The man frowned, contorting his face into a grimace.

"I know longblasters," he said slowly, testing each word as if they were rotting timbers on a bridge. One wrong move and he would fall to his death. "Bag full."

"A duffel bag?" Patrica asked, trying not to show her excitement.

A glum nod. "That enough?"

In the hallway, her assistant sharply whistled.

"Yes, dear Harold. That's enough. Come back in a week with a bag full of working blasters, and Laura is your wife. Working, mind you," she scolded. "Not junk, like this!"

He nodded again.

"And ammo, of course," the madam added hastily. "Blasters are useless without ammo." She smiled as sweetly as possible. "That sounds fair, doesn't it, Sarge?"

A minute passed, then two. The only sounds were of labored breathing from the customer bleeding on the floor, and the muffled noise of sex from down the corridor. A fight in another room.

"Ammo," he repeated in agreement. "All I can."

"Your word of honor?"

"Yes," he said in a perfectly normal tone.

The momentary transition to sanity frightened the madam worse than his growling. This was a dangerously unstable individual.

"Done," Patrica said, offering her plump hand for a shake. "In one week, you deliver a duffel bag of working rifles and ammo, and she's yours forever."

With a massive effort of will, Harold tried to concentrate enough to recall how many days in a week. "Six days," he said. "Back six day." He brushed past her, ignoring the offered hand and moving down the hallway as indomitable as an express train.

"What a freak!" exhaled the teenager, tucking his zip gun into his belt.

Patrica grabbed the boy by the arm. "You heard nothing," she snapped. "Not a fucking thing, or I'll whip you to death myself."

"And risk the Machine? Bullshit." The boy smiled. "I want a cut."

Impressed, she released him. "One blaster."

"Five."

"Two."

"Done."

They shook on the deal.

With a soft groan, the customer stirred and struggled to sit upright. His nose was mashed flat, and the lower half of his face was clotted with dried blood.

"Gonna kill that mutie," he mumbled, struggling to his feet. "I got an ax. That'll do him!"

Surprisingly quick, Patrica walked over and grabbed the man between the legs. He gasped as she squeezed hard.

"Touch him before the next moon," she whispered, "and I'll remove these with blunt scissors."

Nearly wetting himself, the man nodded emphatically. She released him and smiled seductively.

"Still got one coming," Patrica added, loosening the frilly top of her dress and pulling it down to expose her fat sagging breasts. She pinched the nipples, making the wrinkled bags of flesh harden. "Come on, I'll do you right here."

Yanking up his clothing, the man backed out of the room. "I'll come back later. Got to get a healer to fix my nose. Later."

As he dashed away, Patrica stepped into the hall and hoisted up her skirts, showing that she wasn't wearing anything underneath. "I'll be waiting for you, lover," she called.

Gagging and pale, the man scurried down the stairs.

"He won't be coming back." The teenager laughed. "But I'll do you, boss."

"On Tuesday, as usual," the madam stated, fixing her clothes. "Not before, Jimmy."

"Fair enough. But what about the girl?" he asked, jerking a dirty thumb at the sleeping form.

Her lips pursed in thought, Patrica slowly walked over and slapped the girl. Laura awoke with a start, struggling against the ropes.

"Just throw a bucket of water over her to cut the smell," the madam said, "and tell the boys downstairs the line forms to the left."

Chapter Four

In the kitchen of the redoubt, Mildred, J.B. and Doc were assistants with the preparation of dinner for the group. It was their turn, and having ovens at their command was making the usually odious task easy.

Especially since, while the redoubt may have been out of food, the life-support system still functioned, and everybody had luxuriated in a hot shower. After three jumps in one day, the group needed a good scrubbing to get out the sour stink of sweat. They each took turns while somebody else stood guard in the hallway. It was a basic survival plan that all members of the group were never unarmed at the same time.

Sneaking a glance at J.B. busy working at the table, Mildred remembered being joined in the shower, and they used the rare privacy to make love. Privacy was hard to come by these days. Unfortunately, the sex had really put an edge on her appetite.

Scrubbed and shaved, they happily found that the laundry worked fine, if somewhat noisily, and donned clean clothes afterward. As well, many of the officers' quarters hadn't been completely cleaned out, and they located replacement boots for her, a fresh shirt for Dean and underwear for everybody. Reaching inside her denim shirt, Mildred shifted the strap on her U.S. Army–issue bra. It wasn't a perfect fit, but a hell of lot more comfortable than the old Air Force one, which had been one cup size too small.

Rooting about in the cabinets, Mildred had made a lucky find of a few staples lost amid the petrified breakfast cereals and dust-filled plastic wrappers of granola bars: tea, honey and rice, items that didn't go bad with age if kept away from dampness. Keep rice dry, and it lasted forever. Not a lot of nourishment, but it would bulk up their meager meal of beans. The group needed fresh food supplies quick, or else they really would be reduced to eating their leather goods. After which, she didn't care to think about.

Lowering the heat of an electric grill under a small saucepan, Mildred placed the open jar of honey on a folded cloth lying at the bottom of the softly boiling water.

"Can't believe that stuff is still good after a hundred years," J.B. said from his work table.

The table nearest the stove was covered with full water pitchers, napkins, disposable plates and cups for the evening meal. Spread out before the Armorer at the next table over were several pairs of Army boots, and he was meticulously removing the laces from one to insert in another. His own battered boots were lying on the floor, the souls worn paper thin in spots, the leather badly cracked. His feet were wrapped in brand-new woolen socks taken from the base PX. He wiggled his toes at the sensation, savoring the feeling.

"Honey doesn't ever go bad," she informed him, lifting the lid on the pot full of rice and stirring the contents with a long fork. "Over a few years, honey crystallizes as solid as a rock, but low heat will melt it again. I caught on TV once how honey from Egyptian times had been recovered and found to be edible, and that was a hell of a lot longer than the big blow.''

"Hot tea, with honey for desert,'' Doc observed, sitting patiently before the chugging dishwasher. "What a delightful treat. What kind is it, madam? Orange pekoe?''

"U.S. Army–issue food stuff. Classification—tea, for drinking.''

"Oh.'' His face fell, then rose. "Still, better than naught.''

"Sorry there aren't any scones,'' she joked, adding some water to the stew. The delicious smell was a knife in her belly, and the physician had to restrain herself from tasting it constantly. At least with the rice, they would all be able to eat their fill.

"Scones and jelly.'' Doc sighed. "How I miss that.''

"Bananas,'' Mildred said after a moment. "Hurts to think I might never have another banana.''

"Vids,'' J.B. added, finishing the first boot and starting on the next. "Back in Alaska, we found a redoubt once with a working vid player and a ton of vids.''

"Denzel Washington.'' Mildred sighed, then stole a glance at J.B. and winked. He returned it with emphasis.

"Jeremy Brett,'' Doc said. "A superlative thespian, compounded by the fact that we look so similar.''

"Even if you sound like James Earl Jones.''

"Who?''

The dishwasher musically chimed and stopped working.

"Ah, at last,'' Doc cried. Opening the door, he moved aside to avoid the outpouring of steam. Using his handkerchief with the blue swallow design, he retrieved his LeMat from the drying rack and laid it on the table to cool.

"Never seen anybody clean a blaster that way." J.B. laughed, his hands weaving laces in and out. "That'd wreck my Uzi."

"Dissolve the nylon bushings, yes," Doc said, carefully replacing the wooden handle on the bare metal frame of the handcannon. "But I recall reading how J. E. B. Stuart used to boil his once a week to clean away the oily residue, while General George S. Patton soaked his in whiskey."

"Would have thought that would be Ulysses S. Grant."

"General Grant waste whiskey on a gun?"

J.B. chuckled. "I stand corrected."

"So, it's good for the LeMat?" Mildred asked, wiping her hands on a dish towel.

"Mandatory!" Doc exclaimed, juggling the hot blaster from hand to hand. "Absolutely mandatory. I seal the loading holes with grease to prevent a cross-firing. The old girl needs to be scrubbed every now and then, or else the works clog."

Scowling, J.B. opened his mouth to speak, then shut it. Doc was never going to upgrade to a decent blaster, and that was the end of the matter.

"Well, dinner is done," Mildred announced, turning down the heat and draining the excess water from the rice. A kitchen this big and no measuring cups? She poured it into a huge ceramic bowl, steam rising from the crumbling mound. "Start serving, Professor Tanner."

With a flourish, Doc slid his empty weapon back into its holster. Clean as a whistle, it was still much too warm to load. That would have to wait till later. "My pleasure, madam."

"I'll call the others," J.B. said, tying off the laces

and going to the intercom on the wall. "Dean and Jak are still in the garage patching the Hummer together?"

"Last I heard," Mildred replied, lounging in a chair. Her part of the meal was over. Doc would serve and J.B wash up.

"So Ryan and Krysty are..."

She smiled. "Where else?"

Taking another seat, Doc barked a laugh, and then apologized for the rude behavior.

Smiling himself, J.B. glanced at the digital clock on the wall. "Well, okay, then. We'll give them another couple of minutes."

THE UNDERGROUND REDOUBT was designed to support a hundred soldiers and command staff, so there were plenty of private showers for the officers and spacious group showers for the troops. Ryan and Krysty had investigated the commander's private bathroom, but the stall was too small for a couple, so they moved to one of the main showers in the barracks. Exactly as J.B. and Mildred had done earlier.

Clean warm water cascaded steadily from the sixteen showerheads onto the naked couple as Ryan soaped Krysty's back in long steady motions. The suds trickled down, covering her perfect buttocks like the finest lace.

"Feels wonderful," Krysty purred as his hands moved over her shoulders, more massaging than scrubbing, then swept lightly forward to brush the outside of her breasts.

The redhead glanced backward and smiled. "You better be serious," she said deep in her throat.

"Always," Ryan replied, stepping closer to slide his hands over her slippery form to cup her full breasts. He could feel her nipples instantly harden, and the woman arched her back, thrusting her buttocks firmly against him. He stiffened in response, but didn't move, and for a brief period of time, they stayed that way, allowing the warm water to flow freely over them, easing away the rigors of the past week, savoring the moment of privacy and peace.

"Dinner will be ready soon," Ryan finally said, hating to break the mood.

Krysty turned and kissed him full on the mouth. "Then shut up," she whispered, running her hands down his muscular torso.

Breathing deeply, Ryan crushed Krysty to his chest, her full breasts spreading a warmth across him that quickly spread to his groin. In spite of being damp from the water, her long red hair moved wildly about, forming a fiery corona around them as it responded to her excited emotional state.

They kissed again, deeply, tongues and hands traveling everywhere. As Ryan cupped her buttocks and squeezed, Krysty wrapped one leg around his waist, and then the other. The man shifted position to accommodate her weight, as she hoisted herself upward and he slid deep inside her, the heat of their joining overwhelming the warmth of the shower. She cried out softly in pleasure, digging her nails into his muscles.

Vividly, Ryan remembered how he had wanted the voluptuous redhead the first moment he had seen her, and it seemed like the most logical thing in the world for them to have sex. But both were surprised when the casual fornication changed along the way, and instead they found themselves making love that night.

No words were needed or spoken as they gently rocked back and forth, feeling the excitement build until neither could stand any more.

Holding her tight, Ryan carefully eased to his knees, then laid the woman on the Army blanket covering the tiled floor. He started to climb on top, but Krysty forced him over instead, her velvet thighs straddling his muscular waist, the fiery snatch rubbing deliciously over his hard penis, rough and smooth at the same time.

Her magnificent breasts dangling in his face, Ryan licked a nipple and nipped the other. Raking her nails down his chest, Krysty moaned in passion, and arched her pelvis. They both inhaled sharply as he slid deep into her once more.

She rose and fell in curving motions, the soft flesh engulfing him as her unique internal muscles caressed the man in ways no other living woman could.

His hands gripped her waist hard as the gentle tempo became quicker, more urgent. She met his fervor, and thoughts of foreplay ceased, the sounds of slapping flesh masked by the falling waters of the military shower.

Softly in the background, the intercom chimed and J.B.'s voice announced dinner was ready, but neither noticed or cared. And for a few precious seconds, the two lovers enjoyed their private celebration of life and love, giving no thoughts at all to combat or death.

THE WINGED MUTIE watched the opening of the cave from the air above, waiting impatiently for the food to reemerge. Her belly crawled with hunger as her metabolism raced to heal the holes in her wings caused by the barking sticks of the two-legs. Fury welled within at the remembrance, and she cut loose a scream of rage at the meat escaping so easily.

However, the mutie knew better than to try for them in the terrible light, the most fleeting glance making her blind and helpless as if she were prey. Soon the sky fire would return, forcing her into hiding once more, and the prey would be safe to leave and travel away from the hunting ground. The thought was intolerable. There were young to feed! Then instincts flared and the rage slowly calmed. Eventually, the meat would be forced to come out, and she would gather them in the coming night before they could reach the terrible beams of light. Darkness was her mantle of safety.

Fluttering her great wings, the mutie took flight and circled above the cave one last time before turning her attention to the smaller creatures of the desert. Lizard eggs would do for now, but she could already taste the fresh blood and imagined it running down her fangs and chest. Soon enough, she would return and feast upon their living flesh.

Chapter Five

The black clouds slowly became tinted with hints of orange and gray with the coming of dawn as Harold darted from the shadows and moved to the outer wall of the ville. The hunchback looked both ways for the sec men on patrol, but his timing was good. They were beyond the curve of the circular wall, and the buildings blocked their view of this area. But only for a moment. The second team would be here in a few moments.

Taking a battered brass key from a pocket of his dirty clothes, Harold unlocked the smashed trunk of a big luxury car and stepped inside. Crouching low, he closed the lid tight, pulling until hearing the click that told him the lock was engaged. After waiting a few minutes to become adjusted to the darkness, Harold pushed down the back seat, wiggled into the front, clambered over the dashboard and out the gap where the windshield used to be. Crumpled cars and wags surrounded him on every side, tireless wheels jutting out, sprinklings of greenish glass squares everywhere, and seat belts dangling from above. From outside, the wall appeared to be impenetrable, a solidly compacted mass of smashed metal, but the hunchback knew that was false. The old baron had designed this area himself, and after the workers were finished, Harold had done something to them that made his head hurt to remember. And sometimes he woke from fevered nightmares of screaming men begging for life.

Able to see somewhat better now, Harold wiggled forward between an array of tires and tailpipes, ducking under a transmission and into an explosion hole in the side of a military APC. Climbing up the sloped interior, he left by the escape hatch in the roof, slid across the armor and climbed down the undercarriage of a slanted school bus.

A rat scurried from the wreckage and Harold stomped it flat, then moved on. Nasty things. Folks got sick and sometimes died when they got bitten. The old baron and the new both had a reward on the rats—kill a hundred and get a day off from work. Nowadays, it was getting hard to find a hundred. The rats wouldn't come into the ville anymore, which made Harold sad. The first gift he had ever given Laura was a box of a hundred dead rats. That was the first day she kissed him, and he knew they were in love.

Carefully sliding through the split top of an armored bank truck, Harold maneuvered up the wall shelves and into the front seats. Unlocking the passenger-side door, he swung out and dropped the full yard to the concrete apron outside the ville.

Directly before him was the dead river, the stink of sulfur hurting his nose and eyes. On the other side of the stained concrete banks were the ruins of the predark city that he had been named after. Holding his breath, Harold listened for any movement on the wall above. But the world was still asleep; not even the sting-wings or the lizards were up and moving yet.

However, the clouds seemed more yellowish than normal, and panic seized the man as he wondered if the deadly acid rain was coming early this year. But in spite of his proximity to the polluted river, the smell in the morning air was wrong, not strong enough. He gratefully relaxed his powerful shoulders. No storm was forthcoming, and it would be safe for him to leave the ville and do what had to be done to save his poor wife.

Closely following the rusted wrecks composing the wall, Harold watched the searchlights crisscross the brightening sky. Dawn was when the night crew went home to sleep, and the day crew turned off the colossal lights and did maintenance on the alcohol-driven generators, transformers and jennies.

Shivering slightly from a damp chill in the air, Harold waited until the beams winked out. Moving fast, he dashed forward a dozen yards and dropped to the rough ground. Prying off the grate of a storm drain with his bare hands, Harold scrambled inside and eased the hundred pounds of rusty iron gently back into place.

He was halfway there.

WITH A SMOOTH hydraulic hiss, the black metal door to the redoubt moved aside and the sputtering Hummer rolled though the opening, bluish smoke coughing from the muffler. At the steering wheel, Ryan gave it some gas and worked the choke until the engine smoothed somewhat.

"You sure the timing is right?" he asked gruffly, studying the gauges on the dashboard. Plenty of fuel, and the battery was charged, oil pressure and water temp at acceptable levels.

"Sounds like bad piston rings," J.B. told him, standing in the cargo area, an arm resting on the long M-60 machine rifle attached to an upright gimbal, a linked belt of ammo traveling from its breech to a big box attached to the stand.

There was another sputtering cough, and a small explosion of blue smoke.

"Is this going to make it to the ruins?" Krysty asked from the front passenger seat, the Steyr SSG-70 cradled in her arms. With Ryan doing the driving, she was the point guard for the journey. "Be a long walk back."

"Especially, sir, conveying the rest of us on your back," Doc added from his perch on top of a stack of weapons crates. The Hummer was much larger than a military-style jeep, but not quite of sufficient size to comfortably hold seven people and a load of supplies. Doc had lost the coin toss, and so was resigned to the cargo area with the water barrel and bazookas. A folded towel offered his bony hindquarters some comfort, but not much.

"Be okay, just old," Jak said from the back seat, jammed between Dean and Mildred, with boxes of supplies at their feet.

"The engine is just burning off the excess oil buildup. We flushed it twice, but there's always a bit left over," Dean explained as the engine suddenly smoothed into a powerful hum. "See? Told you."

"Better," Ryan agreed, gunning the gas a few times to check the response. The big Detroit engine obeyed promptly, so the Deathlands warrior put the Hummer into gear and started following the tunnel to the exit.

Krysty bobbed her head about to see where they were going. The damn snorkel for the power plant was next to her window, partially blocking her view, but they hadn't been able to get the thing to retract, so she was stuck. At least it was only the air intake and wasn't blowing exhaust into the wag. The snorkel was designed to automatically cut in if the vehicle went into water deeper than a few feet. Jeeps were faster, and APCs offered serious protection, but for general work, Krysty thought the Hummer was damn near perfect. It did everything well, even if the only armor it had was in the floorboards to protect the crew from land mines. The doors were only stretched canvas and wouldn't stop a newborn sting-wing.

A faint grayish light was emanating from the distant opening to the outside world, giving enough illumination for driving, but Ryan hit the headlights just the same. The brilliant halogen bulbs flashed on, filling the tunnel with blinding white light, almost painful to see.

"That should blind the mutie, if it returned in the night," Mildred said, blocking her face with a raised hand. "Damn near blinds me, as it is."

Jak, an albino, said nothing, and simply slid on a pair of old cracked sunglasses.

"Well, if it did come back, this will chew it to bits," J.B. boasted, jacking the big arming bolt on the M-60. "But watch for the brass. She spits them fast and far."

"Too bad that .50 cal from storage wouldn't fit," Dean said wistfully. "That'd chill any mutie."

J.B. ducked under a roof support beam. "And most war wags."

"And flip over the vehicle," Ryan commented, both hands on the wheel. "Not even a Hummer can support a .50 cal in full fire."

"Thirty fine," Jak stated. "Not need nukes chill ants."

"John, be sure to aim for the center," Mildred said, sitting uncomfortably on top of a field-surgery kit. "The wings are only membrane with no real circulatory system."

"Like shooting fish in a barrel," Dean stated confidently.

"No, son. Only a fool aims for the fish," his father said, concentrating on driving. "You shoot the barrel. It can't dodge."

"Just spend the brass, and save your ass, because I don't want to have to use this," the physician said, affectionately patting the belted canvas lump between her boots. It was the find of her life, and one that she had been searching for since she awoke in the twenty-second century. A field-surgery kit. A real, honest to God, fully equipped, U.S. Army MASH medical kit. Mildred had found the incredible treasure in the first-aid station, which had the only locked room in the redoubt. Probably to keep the troops out of the brandy and drugs in the supply cabinet. And as Mildred wasn't registered with the redoubt's mainframe as the doctor on duty, the palm lock had refused her admittance, but a crowbar convinced the door to open for her anyway. Neatly jammed with surgical instruments specifically designed for soldiers in combat, the pack was as heavy as hell, but the physician couldn't have been more pleased. Dr. Mildred Wyeth was a trained doctor, but without instruments, there wasn't much she could do for serious injuries.

The external light got brighter, and the companions prepped their weapons. Ryan slowed the Hummer to a crawl, but as they rounded a turn they found the outside ledge completely empty, only a few of their spent brass from the previous night on the rocky ground.

Braking to a halt, Ryan killed the engine to save fuel. The companions disembarked, with J.B. staying at the machine gun to give them cover if necessary. Warily stepping outside, the friends found the tunnel ended at the top of a gently sloping hillock that flowed downward into a vast expanse of sandy desert, low dunes rising and falling across the barren vista like waves on a calm sea. In the far distance, completely dominating the horizon, were the sprawling ruins of the huge pre-dark city.

"Spread out and look for the mutie. Five yards, one on one," Ryan directed, blaster in hand. A breeze wafted over them from the desert, carrying the smell of heat and dust. Instinctively, he checked the rad counter on his shirt collar and was relieved to see the background count was normal. This wasn't a hot area.

"Not circling above us," Dean said, squinting at the overcast sky. "But it sure looks like a storm is on the way."

"Those are the wrong type of formations for rain," Mildred commented, studying the overcast sky. "They more resemble dust clouds."

"Nukes," Jak said, frowning, scratching his cheek with the muzzle of his .357 Magnum. The tinted lenses of the sunglasses made the teenager seem even paler than usual.

"Or a chem storm."

"No spoor, or bones from a kill," Ryan said, kneeling on the ground and studying the soil for tracks or prints.

"Quite right. We seem to be alone, captain, O my captain," Doc said, holstering his huge blaster. "Our uninvited guest has sought lodgings elsewhere."

"Unless it has a nest on another ledge," Krysty suggested, moving away from the tunnel to check above them. The tunnel opened near the base of a large outcropping, a mesa actually, the main column of the granite mountain had shattered into splinters and boulders from some terrible geological event.

"But with all this light, I don't think the night feeder

will be out and about to bother us much." Her voice faded away, then came back strong. "Mother Gaia protect us!"

Blasters at the ready, the others quickly joined the redhead and stared in wonderment. Where huge sections of the mesa were gone, smooth sections of a dull black material could be plainly seen in the shadowy light. The material wasn't marred or scratched in any way.

"That's the exterior of the redoubt," Ryan said, rubbing his freshly shaved chin. Then he glanced about. "This whole area must have been underground before the war."

"Then it became desert, and the winds unearthed the redoubt," Mildred agreed.

"Now we know where that odd tunnel came from," Dean said grimly. "Somebody saw the base and was trying to gain access."

The elder Cawdor shook his head. "No, that was old tech that built the tunnel. Those beams were ferroconcrete. That can't be made anymore."

"Yes, sir." The boy nodded, but kept a grip on his blaster.

The sound of a starting engine shattered the early-morning quiet. The companions dropped into combat positions, with Dean crouching to fire his new blaster from a kneeling position for greater stability. A moment later, their Hummer bounced into view with J.B. behind the wheel.

"Everything okay?" he asked suspiciously, one hand strategically out of sight. "You were taking too long… Dark night! The outside of the redoubt!"

"No other ledges or caves along this face of the mesa," Ryan said, then turned to stare into the distance. "Mebbe the mutie came from the ruins."

"Sure seems a lot bigger than it did last night," Dean stated, cradling the longblaster in his arms, but making sure the muzzle wasn't pointed at anybody. He had caught hell for accidentally doing that once, and he'd never repeat the mistake.

"Seems like the buildings reach for miles," Krysty stated.

The darkness had to have masked the true size of the predark city. The outlying structures stretched in every direction, and there were rows of tall buildings downtown, some slashed on a diagonal cut from erosion, or with jagged tops from fires. But one marble edifice towered above the others, a single shining skyscraper untouched by the ravages of time or war.

"Gulliver in Lilliput," Doc observed, resting both hands on his cane, the silver lion's head peeking out between his laced fingers.

"Not Chicago," Jak said, squinting, "Miami, or Big D."

"Not any place I know. Anybody else?" Ryan asked, easing the safety on his blaster before holstering the weapon. There was a negative chorus.

"And no sign of people," Mildred said, craning her neck for a better view. "That I can see."

"We couldn't spot a wag at this range," J.B. said, retrieving a spyglass from a cushioned pouch on his belt. He extended the brass scope to its full length and closed an eye to look through it.

"Well?" Ryan asked.

"Still too far," J.B. reported, collapsing the tube. "We need binocs to see details at this range."

"Might be deserted, then," Dean said, sounding disappointed.

"Or it could have a thousand people," Krysty

warned over her shoulder. "Somebody was operating the searchlights. And much as I hate killing, I sure hope they have a lot of enemies. We'll get a better price with folks who have a fight coming."

"Everybody has enemies," Ryan rationalized coldly. "We'll do fine with this lot of blasters and rockets."

"Blasters always good," Jak stated. "Heard 'bout man bought life by giving baron can opener."

"Really?" Dean asked in disbelief. He touched the Swiss army knife in his pocket. Was it that valuable?

"Believe it," Ryan said, climbing back into the Hummer and starting the engine, which caught on the first try. "You ever try to open a can of stew with just a knife or a rock?"

"Yes," Krysty said, taking her seat.

One boot resting on the back wheel, J.B. laughed and displayed a finger. "And I still have the scar."

As the rest jammed into their seats, straddling boxes and crates, Ryan studied the slope of the hillock. Off to their west was a flat section of desert, a nice long stretch of hard-packed sand. Maybe an ancient highway, or a dried riverbed.

"We'll head for that natural road," Ryan said, starting the engine again. "Should make good time."

"Others might have the same idea," Krysty cautioned, wrapping the strap of the Steyr around her forearm so it couldn't be dropped. "Best be ready for an ambush."

"Gotcha," J.B. said, straightening a kink in the ammo belt of the M-60. "Stay sharp, folks."

"An ambush. From whom?" Doc asked, sounding perturbed. "A tumbleweed, perhaps?"

"No, she's right. Those searchlights can be seen for miles," Ryan said, shifting gears and releasing the hand brake. "Could have every coldheart bastard, junker and nomad from the whole countryside down there."

"Wherever down there is," Mildred added, using a strip of cloth to tie back her long beaded plaits. The city was vaguely familiar to the woman, but that was all, nothing specific. Then again, most big cities resembled each other. Who could tell Toronto from Seattle if their major landmarks were gone?

"We'll find out when the stars appear tonight," J.B. said confidently, straightening his fedora. "That cloud cover is going to break soon. I can smell it."

"We used to sled down a hill like this," Doc said softly. "All covered with snow and twinkling with ice. My wife would have hot chocolate waiting for the children and I when we came home afterward. Cold. It was so cold in Vermont that winter." His voice faded away, and he stared into the distance, reliving another life in another world.

"Hold on tight," Ryan said, dropping into low gear and starting down the slope.

The grade was steep, but the Hummer dug in and he began zigzagging to control their speed. However, they were still going faster than he liked when the Hummer bounced over a hidden gully. The companions cursed, and the supplies jumped about wildly, but none left the wag.

"Warn us next time, will you?" J.B. snapped, clinging to the M-60 with both arms, the ammo box jingling with every jolt. Mildred handed him back his dropped fedora, and he stuffed it on.

Ryan dodged another gully, then a cactus. "You want to drive instead?"

"Sure! Pass me the wheel."

At the bottom of the slope, the Hummer dipped into

a ravine and rolled up gracefully onto flat land. Ryan gunned the engine and started in the direction of the crude road they had spotted from the hill.

Keeping a grip on the M-60, J.B. looked around, studying the horizon for any suspicious movements. "The landscape is bare for miles. At least nobody can sneak up on us until we reach the city."

"And if the locals won't trade, there must be some stores to loot," Mildred noted, altering her grip on the med kit. A shopping list of supplies was already forming in her mind.

"Mebbe some canned goods that haven't gone bad," Dean suggested.

"In this heat?" Jak scoffed, elbowing the lad.

"Not likely," the elder Cawdor added pointedly, watching a tumbleweed roll across the road. "Mebbe some homemade preserves in a glass jar, but nothing in a tin can."

Sweeping the vented barrel of the M-60 from side to side, J.B. shrugged. "Hell, anything is possible. Just look at the place."

"Indeed," Doc said, leaning on his swordstick. "It could be the veritable cornucopia, a bacchanalian trove of treasure!"

Everybody hung on as the Hummer rolled up an incline and came to rest on the path. The dried sand had cracked into a crazy jigsaw pattern. Dunes rose on either side, offering some protection from the warming desert winds. But they all realized that if this was dawn, by noon the city would be an inferno.

The miles went by in steady progression, the three-hour-plus trip to the ruins uneventful. A cooling breeze blew into the military wag from their speed, but also a contrail of dust rose from the Hummer's studded tires on the loose sand. Any hope of sneaking into the ruins was now completely gone.

Spotting a moving shadow on the sand, Jak intently watched a sting-wing cruise through the murky sky. The bird sailed off toward the east as if the ancient city ahead of them held no interest to the little mutie. That was a good indication. Sting-wings feared nothing and ate everything. Perhaps the ruins were deserted.

As the Hummer approached the outskirts of the ruins, the buildings rapidly rose above the horizon. Oddly, there seemed to be no houses or stores to show the gradual expansion of the metropolis. The structures simply jutted from the sunbaked soil like fence posts with windows. Most of the windows were a dull white in color.

"Desert storms sandblasted them white," Mildred stated, wiping the sweat off her face with a moist towelette.

Nobody contradicted her theory. An octagonal sheet of metal on a post heralded their entrance into the nameless city, and Ryan immediately slowed the progress of the Hummer. The streets were completely bare, not a car, a truck or even a piece of a vehicle was in sight.

"Strange," Ryan said, furrowing his brow. "No cars, yet the buildings are intact."

"Another neutron bomb," Krysty suggested, curling a lip in disgust.

"Seems that way. No bodies, property undamaged. Only where are the vehicles?"

"Mebbe the survivors drove away," Dean offered.

"Could be. But if the city was hit by a nuke, the engines would have been deactivated by the EMP blast," Mildred said. "And if it was a chem storm or germ warfare, then all the people would be dead, but the cars okay.''

"So somebody took them afterward,'' the boy stated as if the fact were obvious.

The Hummer rolled past a parking garage. The gates were smashed, and every level they could see into was vacant.

"Mebbe,'' the elder Cawdor agreed hesitantly, not liking where this conversation was going. "But what would you need a thousand, mebbe ten thousand bastard cars for?''

"Wall,'' Jak said.

"Makes sense,'' J.B. stated, his finger resting on the trigger of the M-60. "We've seen it done before. Just not on this scale.''

They rolled past a new-car showroom, the window gone, the sales floor deserted.

"But it's got to be one huge ville to need every car,'' Krysty said.

The ruins seemed to be thinning ahead of them, so Ryan took a left at an intersection heading toward the skyscraper. Soon, bits and pieces of broken asphalt started to show under the sand covering the road, and within a block they were driving on cracked pavement. It was a rare experience.

"Stay sharp,'' Ryan warned as he slowed their speed to get a better view of the ruins.

Large snowy windows fronted the street on each side, the same down every side street. Above stores, empty metal frames swung in the soft breeze, the plastic long ago eroded, and the tattered remains of a movie-theater marquee seemed bullet-riddled from the hundreds of empty lightbulb sockets. Street signs of different shapes stood wordless on shiny metal poles, every trace of paint completely removed.

"No rust," Ryan commented, bringing the Hummer to a halt. "Must get a lot of acid rain here."

"That stops rust from forming?" Dean asked in surprise.

"Washes it off," Mildred answered. "Sandstorms and acid rain. Not a good area to try farming."

"Storm damage is minimal," Doc noted, glancing around carefully. "Mayhap the buildings themselves act as a sort of windbreak."

"I'd of thought they'd funnel the wind and worsen the damage," J.B. said.

"Close," Ryan replied, driving around a huge pothole in the middle of an intersection. "Faster wind means less sand to form piles."

"I'm surprised that mutie was around," J.B. stated, removing his hat to wipe his forehead with a sleeve. Even with the unbroken cloud cover, it was still getting too damn warm. He replaced the fedora with a pat. "Wonder what it eats."

"Lizards," Krysty said, watching a fat lizard with a twitching spider in its mouth dart out from underneath the mailbox and scuttle away into a sewer grating at their approach. The lizard's claws churned the sand and left a little contrail of dust to mark its passage. "Lots of them around."

"And what do they eat?" Dean asked.

"Bug, worms, old shoes, leather couches and mink stoles," Mildred said patiently. "Any old thing. After sharks, reptiles are the only true omnivores."

"The desert is an ocean with its life underground, and a perfect disguise above," Doc said softly to himself.

Past a corner, the squat buildings became neat rows of apartments and strip malls. A yellow sheet of newspaper blew by the wag, the faded headlines touting vital information from a century ago.

"Place gives me the creeps," J.B. said unexpectedly. "Got the damnedest feeling we're being watched."

Studying the white windows on the buildings, Jak nervously clicked back the hammer of the Python and eased it down again with his thumb. "Yeah. Me, too," he said. "Eerie."

Holding the Steyr, Krysty said nothing, but her hair was coiled tightly in response to her disturbed frame of mind.

"Thought it was just me," Ryan added, increasing their speed slightly. One important question kept repeating itself over and over in his mind. Why hadn't a predark city this large and in excellent condition been looted yet? Suddenly, he had the strangest urge to turn the wag and head straight back to the redoubt.

"Hey, look there!" Dean cried, pointing ahead.

Visible over the rooftops of the two-story apartment complexes was a pair of curved metal arches.

"Must be bridges," Ryan said, shifting gears and heading in that direction. There had been no evidence of the searchlights or the owners in this section of town. Perhaps they were across the river. It made sense to stay near running water in a desert. Then a strong whiff of sulfur made the man wonder if they were heading toward an acid rain lake?

As the Hummer took a corner, a dockyard spread before them in crumbling majesty. Rows upon rows of long warehouses lined the concrete apron of the shore. Deep recesses clearly designed for drydocking vessels notched the embankment with tall derricks standing alongside for ferrying cargo.

An opening dropped away from the dockside, some kind of a storm drain or river. But more importantly, across the span was a jumbled wall of smashed cars and trucks towering thirty feet high, and extending in both directions to curve out of sight.

"We found the source of the searchlights," Ryan remarked, parking the Hummer a safe distance from the docks. The concrete looked solid, but the five tons of the Hummer might send them all plummeting into whatever was at the bottom of the smelly trench. Best to take no chances.

"They raided this side to fix the other," Krysty said. "Smart folks."

"Architectural cannibals," Doc stated thoughtfully. "How unique."

Removing his glasses, J.B. extracted his folding telescope and extended it to its full length. Carefully, he traversed the other side.

"Nobody in sight," he reported, collapsing the telescope.

Killing the purring engine, Ryan nodded and climbed out of the wag. "I'll take point. J.B. you're on guard."

J.B. slid his glasses back on. "Check," he replied, patting the breech of the M-60. "Any trouble and I'll sound the alarm."

Spreading out so they didn't offer any snipers a nice clustered target, the companions proceeded closer to the edge of the concrete. The smell was worse here, the reason soon painfully obvious. A hundred feet down was a sluggish yellow river reeking of sulfur and other chems.

"Must be runoff water from the desert," Krysty

guessed. "We already knew they got bad acid rain here."

"Now how the hell do we get across this?" Mildred asked, clutching her med kit.

"We don't," Jak said, jerking a thumb to their left.

Nearby, the great arches of steel were all that remained of the predark bridge crossing the river. A wide road led to paved ramp extensions that ended in melted gobbets of cooled metal only feet from the embankments. An identical section stood on the other side of the river. But the center span of the bridge was completely gone. Worse, two more smashed bridges were visible upriver, hundreds of severed steel cables dangling limply into the brackish flow of the polluted river.

"Well, if we dive in, the fall wouldn't hurt us," Mildred said, sounding half serious. "But nobody could live for long in that water. Plus, there's no way to climb up the other side. Those support pillions are thicker than the Hummer."

"Mebbe after they took the cars, the people smashed the bridges," Dean suggested.

"And permanently cut themselves off from all the material on this side? Doubtful," Ryan said, rubbing his jaw. "I think if we follow the shoreline for long enough, we'll find how they get across."

"Mebbe fly like muties," Jak said.

Resting the longblaster on her shoulder, Krysty merely arched a fiery eyebrow at the unsettling suggestion when a piercing scream of terror sounded from their left, followed closely by the telltale rattle of autofire.

"That was a child," Mildred said, aghast.

Ryan agreed, and friend or foe, combat was always

something that should be investigated. The next minute it might very well be coming their way.

"Silent probe, single-yard spread," Ryan ordered, drawing his pistol and starting forward at an easy run.

Chapter Six

Clutching a headless doll, a small girl was running madly down the sandy street, her long hair flying in the wind. She slowed to glance over her shoulder to see if the monsters were still after them.

"Keep running!" her father screamed, dropping to one knee and discharging a handblaster at the pack of wolves chasing them. The weapon banged in smoke and sparks, and a store window down the street exploded into pieces.

Cursing the inaccuracy of his blaster, the man turned and ran, trying to reload, but paper and lead balls dropped from his fumbling hands. His wife ran without pausing, a small crying bundle held tight in her arms.

Straight ahead, the road angled into the ground and ended at a tiled wall with two huge openings. The left side was crudely bricked solid, ivy growing up the stones to show the age of the work. But the left side was open. Two large wooden doors swung aside, exposing a brick-lined tunnel extending into the darkness. Two gigantic machines of some sort bracketed the tiled wall and formed an impressive barricade. In front was a sandbag wall topped with twisted coils of barbed wire. Behind the sandbags were three men in predark uniforms, two in military fatigues, the third dressed as a policeman. The soldiers were frantically working nimrods to charge their muzzle-loading rifles. The policeman was notching a barbed arrow into a crossbow made from the spring leaves of a car.

"Here!" the policeman screamed, taking aim at the family with his weapon. "This way! Keep coming!"

"Don't look back!" added the short private, locking back the hammer on his museum-piece rifle.

The other private leveled his rifle and fired. The longblaster thundered like a bazooka, volumes of smoke exploding from the barrel almost hiding him. But no yelp of pain came from the snarling animals so very close behind the runners.

Turning, the father fired again, and the lead wolf yipped in pain. Shoving his blaster into a pocket, the elderly man then ran for all he was worth, losing items from pockets at every step of the way.

Almost losing the doll in her arms, the girl reached the wall of sandbags and stopped looking for a way past the obstruction. The tall policeman reached out to grab her arm and brutally hauled the child over. She gasped in pain and landed sprawling on the side, losing her toy. The short private scooped it up and thrust it back into her tiny arms as he shoved her toward the opening in the tiled wall.

"Run to the end of the tunnel!" he barked. "Go! Don't stop!"

Pausing for a moment, the child glanced at her folks, then took to her heels into the darkness beyond.

The mother made it next, the sleeve of her thin shirt ripping off as it brushed the barbed wire coils. She wasn't wearing a bra, but the men pretended not to notice. Two of them boldly leaped out to gently assist her and the crying baby over the sandbags while the policeman fired the crossbow. The arrow appeared to go straight for the father, but it missed him and kept on going. A wolf howled as the man sprinted forward in renewed speed and dived over the barricade.

The clean-shaved soldier escorted her inside, while the private with a beard stood between her and the oncoming wolves. Coolly raising his weapon, he cocked the hammer and fired, thunder and smoke vomiting from the crude rifle.

Diving over the sandbags, the father landed hard, but rolled over and came up with a machete in his hand. The policeman knocked that aside.

"We have blasters!" he snapped. "Inside, they won't get past us! Save your family, man!" Sheathing the blade, the father nodded in thanks and dashed into the darkness.

Instantly, the guards relaxed their tense posture and, smirking in satisfaction, lowered their weapons. Then they shared a grin, ran inside, firing their blasters into the air.

"The wolves are here!" one private cried, firing his rifle straight into the air.

The other started to walk casually toward the wooden doors. "Stand firm, men! Don't let them pass!

"Hurry! Hurry!" the policeman added, lighting a cig and blowing a smoke ring. "Get the axes!"

Reaching the barricade, the wolves stopped and milled about looked expectantly at the men. The lead wolf started to wag his tail in anticipation. Smiling widely, the policeman tossed the pack something from his pockets, which the animals happily devoured and then dashed off into the ruins barking and yipping.

RETREATING A FEW BLOCKS, the companions convened behind a garbage bin before allowing themselves to speak.

"Fireblast!" Ryan breathed. "Did you see that?"

Leaning wearily against a brick wall, Krysty nodded. "A sham. This is all a sham!"

"Longblasters firing not one wolf hurt?" Jak snorted, sitting on his haunches.

"And no dust kicking up from misses, either," Ryan said. "It's a new sham on me, and I thought I had seen them all."

"Bastards," Mildred spit furiously. "Utter contemptible bastards."

"What do you think they do with the people?" Dean asked, staring at the junkyard wall across the river. No sounds could be heard from this distance. Even blasterfire would become lost in the wind, so anything could be happening out of sight behind the imposing barrier.

"I don't know, son," Ryan said. "Slaves, mebbe."

Returning to the Hummer, they informed J.B. about the situation.

"Blanks," the Armorer stated, sitting on the bumper of the Hummer. "Shit-eating sec men were firing blanks! You sure about that?"

"Makes sense," Ryan agreed. "Searchlights draw in folks to investigate. Then somewhere along the way, a pack of pet wolves attack, herding the people into the ville. The sec men pretend to fight off the muties, and the victims rush inside for protection, while actually thanking their captors."

"Deuced clever way to increase your population," Doc admitted in grudging admiration. "Highly contemptible, but I must admit that I am impressed by its sheer audacity."

"Bastards," Mildred repeated.

"Agreed, good Doctor. But still brilliant."

"So what about that winged thing we found in the

cave,'' Dean asked, holding his new rifle, his eyes never pausing as they searched the shadowy ruins for possible enemies. ''Think that's another sheepdog?''

Krysty dismissed the idea. ''Head was too small. No way it was smart as a wolf.''

''I'd guess that was for real,'' Ryan agreed. ''Or possibly, the stick to the carrot. If anybody tries to escape, it'll be at night and the bird, whatever, attacks for real.''

''Why doesn't it attack the ville, then?''

''Weak eyes,'' Mildred reminded. ''Those search-lights would keep the mutie far away.''

''More tricks and games,'' Krysty said grimly.

''However, you all seemed to have missed the most important point,'' J.B. said, adjusting his glasses until he had their full attention, then he smiled broadly.

''We now know where dinner is coming from,'' he continued, chocking the bolt on the Uzi.

Faces brightened in understanding.

''Wolf hard to kill?'' Dean asked, feeling a rush of adrenaline. He wanted to do something for the poor trapped folks, and if he couldn't free them somehow, then chilling the wolves was the next best thing.

''Most pack animals are,'' Ryan said, nodding at J.B. The wiry Armorer saluted in return. ''Just have to catch one off by itself away from the others.''

''And once we ace the wolves,'' Ryan continued, ''tomorrow it'll be much easier to cut a deal with the baron of the ville without getting caught between two enemies. He'll keep expecting the wolves to show. That'll keep him off balance and give us an extra bargaining edge.''

''And if we can't find them?'' Dean asked in concern.

Standing, J.B. went over to pat the long ventilated

barrel of the M-60. "Then we'll just have to reason with them the old-fashioned way," he said grimly.

"WENT NORTH," Jak said, brushing back his snowy hair. "Wind going muddle tracks. Go now."

"Agreed." Ryan climbed into the Hummer and started the engine. "We'll circle around and approach from the west, so the guards at the tunnel won't hear us."

Taking their seats amid the cargo, Ryan kept the Hummer in low gear to be as quiet as possible as they drove along the zigzagging maze of streets until finally reaching the park just west of the great skyscraper.

"Thank Gaia for that building," Krysty said. "Without street signs or maps, it'd be easy to get lost in here. But just check the angle of the sun and you have a location."

"Like a sundial," Dean said, chewing over the notion. "Pretty smart."

She smiled. "Your father taught me that."

"Stop," Jak said, leaning way out of the wag, studying the ground.

Shifting into neutral, Ryan eased to a fast halt, and the Cajun hopped out, walking back a few yards to bend low to the ground and brush his fingertips across the smooth sand. To Dean, there didn't appear to be any marks on the sand, but Jak stood and pointed decisively.

"Eight," he stated, then pointed down an alleyway. "Six."

"Damn alley is too small for the Hummer," J.B. noted, estimating the opening. "Want to circle around again?"

"Too close," Jak said, frowning. "Hear and run."

"And we don't want to go chasing them all over the

ruins," Krysty said. "There are far too many places they can reach that we can't."

"On foot, then," Ryan said, leaving the wag. "Krysty, stay with the Hummer. We'll follow the six."

"If you come back running, I'll be ready," she promised, handing over the Steyr. "The M-60 might reduce dinner to hamburger instead of steaks, but at least it'll be us on the outside digesting them, instead of the other way around."

Snorting a laugh, Ryan bent close to exchange a fast kiss, then checked the longblaster and ammo belt. Satisfied, he started across the street. "Full weapons, everybody, and stay close. Packs fear other packs."

With Jak in the lead, the companions eased into the alleyway, following the trail of faint depressions in the loose sand. The next street down came into sight, but the two companions conferred and took a side alley. Coming out a block to the east, Jak raised a hand, then closed it into a fist. The group froze and got ready for combat.

Just a block away was a smashed store window, the only gap in the endless seam of white store windows that lined the street.

Spreading out, the companions eased toward the gaping hole, Dean and Mildred watching the windows above for any signs of snipers. It could be another trap, and better safe than dead.

Above the smashed window, words were chiseled into the marble lintel of the building, but time and the winds had worn the engraving down to vague unreadable squiggles. But recently somebody had neatly painted the huge single word across the stone lintel.

"'Supirmarkit,'" Doc quietly read in disgust. "Not only thieves and liars, but illiterates, as well."

Mildred scowled in agreement while Ryan studied the crude sign. Another bastard trick for travelers in the city. Solos or explorers looking to loot would find this open food store and naturally go inside to check for canned goods. That's when the wolves charged and the victims would get herded straight to the ville like sheep.

"Hopefully not to the slaughter," J.B. whispered, obviously having the same train of thought.

Jagged daggers of glass jutted like teeth ringing the opening. From their vantage point on the sidewalk, they could see bare floors inside, a bank of linked carts to the left, registers to the right and rows upon rows of shelves stretching out of sight. A fine sprinkling of sand lay over top of everything for yards, and the rear of the store was masked in darkness.

Signaling for silence, Ryan tapped his eye and gestured at the store. Rifle in one hand, he drew his SIG-Sauer and knelt on the sidewalk, listening for any sounds of movement inside. The ghostly moan of the desert wind whispering down the street was discernible, but nothing else. No dripping pipes, no ticking clocks, not a snarl or a cough.

Extracting a small plastic mirror, J.B. eased it past the jamb of the window and tilted it inward to scan the area.

"Behind the registers," he silently mouthed, pocketing the mirror.

Eagerly, Dean started forward, but Ryan stopped him with a single raised finger. The boy retreated, and the elder Cawdor first pointed at Jak, then Doc. Keeping his blind, left side to the wall, Ryan poked the muzzle of his Steyr around the jamb just as J.B. did the same on the other side with the Uzi.

The lead wolf was large and heavily muscled, with

brindle markings showing it was from the forestlands. The rest were smaller and leaner, similar to whippets, but none seemed to be starving and that was a bad sign. Hungry animals would just attack, and any organized group of defenders could easily withstand them. However, a well-fed pack would wait and watch until a mistake was made, then charge when its victims weren't paying attention.

"Wait for it," Ryan said quietly. Then with a roar, the Hummer bounded into view, a barking pack of wolves surrounding the vehicle. Driving with one hand, Krysty was firing at the leaping animals with a blaster gripped in a bloody fist.

"Behind us!" Doc cried, firing the LeMat into the store.

Ryan spun, and there were the other six wolves crawling around the registers moving as silently as ghosts. In a heartbeat, the hunters had been the hunted.

"Hummer!" Dean shouted, announcing his target as he cut loose with the G-12. The blaster hissed a stuttering zip of caseless rounds, and six of the eight animals were torn into pieces under the incredible fusillade of subsonic steel. But then the HK stopped, and the youth realized he was out of ammo. Dropping the spent weapon, he drew his handblaster. Ryan discharged the Steyr, and a wolf in the store flipped over, crashing into an ancient display rack.

Free from the attentions of the beasts for a moment, Krysty scrambled into the back of the Hummer and cut loose with the M-60, the weapon chattering a deadly hellstorm at the beasts. Two danced in the air as their bodies were torn to pieces before the rest spread out, running wildly in every direction, one even darting under the vehicle.

But there was method to the madness, and Ryan cursed as he realized the wolves were combining into a pack again; the running around was merely intended to disorient the humans before a unified charge.

"Move to the wall!" he shouted, dropping the empty Steyr and drawing his panga while firing the SIG-Sauer. "Get the leader!"

The largest wolf snarled at the one-eyed warrior, and the rest of them repeated the challenge.

"Brace!" J.B. cursed, fumbling in his munitions bag. "Going to use a gren!"

But as if they knew what those words meant, the animals stopped running and crouched in fear, their haunches raising in submission. Uncaring, J.B. raised a gren and pulled the pin, pausing to gauge for distance. But then their eyes glazed over and a third eye blossomed wide, the yellowish orb glaring with monstrous hatred.

"They're muties!" Mildred yelled. At her words, the foreheads of the wolf pack split open to display a third eye with a large square pupil, like a goat's. Then they charged, moving across the sandy street with nightmare speed.

Krysty got in one more shot, and J.B. burped the Uzi twice in short controlled bursts, chilling one wolf and wounding another, before the animals swarmed over them from every direction.

Kicking at the slavering muties, the companions fired nonstop, wounding the animals over and over, but not one dropped. Snarling and snapping, the animals took wild bites, but only got layers of cloth. They spit the material out in disgust. Krysty fired the M-60 one final time, then was forced to stop, her hands helpless on the trigger of the deadly machine gun. Without a clear view, she could chill her own people instead.

Slamming in a fresh clip, Ryan shot the leader in the leg and as it closed upon him, he kicked the wolf in the jaw, his steel-toed Army crunching bone. Spitting teeth, the animal backed away, drooling blood.

Sidestepping a charge by two wolves working together, Dean punched one in the face with his empty blaster and buried his knife into the other one's muscular shoulder. Jak quickly fired his booming Magnum pistol twice, nicking a darting wolf, then his blaster clicked on a spent shell. He was out of ammo, and there was no chance in hell of reloading it. Sputtering a virulent curse, the albino teen dropped the blaster, and two knives appeared in his pale hands. With a flip, one was reversed with the flat of the blade resting along the bone of his forearm, and the teenager went into a knife fighter's attack crouch. A wolf flew past him, and he slit the beast's belly open as it went by. Spilling out its writhing guts, the wolf trembled and fell over, its long legs starting to paw the sand as if it were still charging. Incredibly, it started to rise again, so J.B. discharged his shotgun directly into the hole where the third eye had been. Its head blew apart into bones and blood, and the animal dropped.

Darting and dodging, the wolves bit more cloth, the rips now exposing vulnerable flesh. Steady as a rock, Doc stood amid the yipping muties and calmly fired a seventh, eighth and ninth time, his huge .44 LeMat booming hot lead death. The booms shook the walls of the store, and blood sprayed out from the hip of the wolf. But the animal neither slowed nor stopped from the glancing blow.

Her back against the wall, med kit laying protectively

at her feet, Mildred banged away carefully with her ZKR 551 target pistol, finally wounding one animal in the shoulder, blood forming a geyser from the severed femoral artery. The wolf staggered from the wound, and Ryan rammed the stock of his Steyr into its face, bursting apart the third eye. Puss and wiggling filaments gushed from the cranial wound, and the wolf froze, motionless from the pain. Ramming his 9 mm blaster into its ear, Ryan fired and brains sprayed out the other side of its head. The corpse stiffly toppled over to the bloody sand.

Dean charged a wolf, shoving his Browning blaster into its misshapen face. He yanked the trigger as the wolf dodged. The bullet missed, but the muzzle-blast seared the unblinking third eye and the wolf retreated, howling in agony.

A wild honking noise announced the violent arrival of the Hummer as Krysty slammed the military wag against the brick wall alongside the companions, the headlights shattering as she crushed a wolf into pulp. Now safely bracketed in a corner, the companions concentrated their weapons on the animals, blowing away chunks of flesh with every round.

The alpha wolf recoiled as half its head was torn away, and two smaller muties alongside it crumpled from the impact of the hollowpoint rounds. Another pair of muties was slammed to the ground, blood gushing from hideous wounds.

The last mutie dashed madly about between the moving human legs, zigzagging wildly as it sought escape. Blasters fired and knives stabbed, but missed. Desperate, it leaped onto the hood of the Hummer. Krysty burped the M-60, but the .38 hollowpoint rounds only grazed its body, removing wads of mangy fur.

Diving among the humans, it bounced off the side of Dean, ducked between Ryan's legs and broke free from the group, sprinting for freedom. But it suddenly stopped with a full yard of shining steel thrust through its laboring chest. Snarling himself, Doc twisted the blade of his sword, enlarging the wound, and dark blood gushed onto the sidewalk. Whimpering in agony, the mutie struggled to get away, its goat eye rolling backward into its head until only the yellow showed. Bracing a boot on the writhing beast, Doc yanked the blade free and thrust it back in again and again, skewering the chest, the stomach, the throat, searching for the vulnerable heart. Still trying to crawl away, the beast emptied its bowels as its whole body violently shuddered and went abruptly still.

Withdrawing his blade from the corpse, Doc cleaned the Toledo steel on the animal's fur, then again on a bit of cloth from a pocket. Visually inspecting the long shaft for any damage, he returned it to the ebony sheath of his walking cane, where it snapped tightly into place.

"Blasted muties," Jak growled. Watching the interior of the supermarket for any further movement, he cracked open the cylinder of his Colt Python, pocketed the spent .357 shells and thumbed in fresh ammo.

Retrieving a dropped clip for the Uzi, J.B. stood and tucked it away. "Never seen this type before."

The filaments of her hair waving about in agitation, Krysty clicked shut the reloaded cylinder of her S&W .38, tucking the blaster in a holster at her hip. "Thankfully, these wolves are a lot easier to kill than those hellhounds we encountered in Ohio," she remarked without humor.

"Easier ain't easy," Jak said, rubbing a set of parallel scratches on his throat. "Bastards fast."

Mildred walked over and took hold of his jaw, turning the teenager's head to inspect the red marks on his albino skin. "Didn't break the dermis," the physician announced, and released him. "You should be okay. But let me clean it, so you don't go septic." Opening her bag, she anointed him with a splash of alcohol.

"Thanks," he muttered, gingerly touching the scratch.

"Just be glad it didn't chew your ass." She grinned.

Brushing the snowy hair off his face, Jak snorted in response.

The distant rumble of an approaching storm sounded in the cloudy sky as Dean picked up the ejected brass from his blaster and dropped it into a pocket for later reloading. One of them seemed bent, which meant it was useless, but he could check on that later. Carefully, the boy inspected his Browning for any signs of fouling from being dropped in the sand, and when satisfied, he inserted a fresh magazine. Snapping off the safety and working the slide, the boy walked away from the group and stood guard at the corner of the intersection.

"Mildred, check the bodies," Ryan directed, retrieving his rifle from the ground.

Kneeling at a warm corpse, the woman displayed a bloody knife. "Already doing that."

"Good." Brushing the sand off his dropped rifle, Ryan worked the bolt, slid in a fresh clip and slung the weapon over a shoulder. Then checking the area, he noted that Dean was already standing guard without waiting for directions. He felt a rush of pride.

"J.B., Doc, recce the market," Ryan ordered, the longblaster held easily in both hands. "See if there are any more of these bastards around."

"Or supplies," Jak added.

Doc eased back the hammer on the LeMat as the Armorer pulled out a gren. Together, the men stepped through the broken window and into the grocery store, J.B. pausing at the registers to let Doc proceed, then the old man doing the same at the head of the first aisle as J.B. crept past him in a standard two-man defensive rotation pattern.

"Slick move with the Hummer," Ryan told the redhead as he walked over. "You okay?"

"Fine," Krysty replied, pumping gas and trying to start the engine. It took two tries before the big power plant caught. "Just angry that they got so close before I saw them."

As she backed the wag away from the brick wall, the wolf's body stayed where it was as if nailed in place.

"Headlight's broken," Ryan reported. "So no more night driving until we can replace it at the redoubt. Pop the hood."

She did, and he listened to the humming engine.

"No real damage," Ryan stated, closing the hood and latching it in place. "Thankfully, the Army built these things to take damage and keep going."

A whistle heralded the appearance of J.B. and Doc from within the predark store.

"Clear," J.B. reported. "No more wolves, not even cubs. Also, nothing much usable on the shelves. All of the cans are empties, just there to make the store look like it's full of goods. It was expertly cleaned out long ago."

"This was all we appropriated," Doc added, lifting a plastic bag of bottles and glass jugs. "Some grape preserves, Band-Aid bandages and a few odds and ends."

"I expected as much," Ryan said with a sour expression. "But it never hurts to check. Stow it away, and check the side streets, will you?"

Doc deposited the bag of food carefully in the cargo area of the Hummer, while J.B. climbed into the wag and set the safety on the M-60 before easing off the bolt. The military blaster was one hundred years old, and even though it was in perfect operational condition, it wasn't wise to keep tension on the firing spring. Otherwise, next time he used it the weapon would break, becoming a twenty-two-pound paperweight.

A brisk wind formed little dust devils on the street, the miniature tornadoes twirling madly before slowing into nonexistence.

"Storm coming," Jak said. "Soon."

"Yeah, I know. How's it going, Mildred?" Ryan asked, cradling the Steyr in his arms.

"This is the last," the black woman replied, running her hands over the corpse of another wolf. Not all of the beasts had that third eye of a mutant, but this was the last one to check. Carefully, she inspected its forehead, teeth, eyes, then legs, bending the joints to observe the configurations.

Satisfied for the moment, she pulled a knife from a sheath inside her boot and began to make incisions in the chest and abdomen, turning the internal organs around to review everything. Ryan and the others waited impatiently, watching her every move.

A tumbleweed rolled across the intersection, traveling with the wind on a endless journey to nowhere.

After a few minutes, Mildred raised her head, smiling. "Clean!" she declared. "This one isn't a mutie."

Pushing his hat into a more comfortable position, J.B. smiled. "Hot damn. Steak tonight."

Jak and Dean stayed at their posts, while Ryan and

Krysty joined Mildred at the dead animal. They produced knives and began dressing the stiffening carcass. Incisions were circled around the paws and throat, then down the belly to the tail. The skin was peeled off, the fur carefully kept whole and the meat wrapped in the skin with pieces of bloody ligament used to tie the package closed.

"Time to leave," Ryan announced, wiping his sticky hands on a rag from the Hummer's toolbox. "The gunshots and the smell of blood will attract both kinds of animals we don't want to deal with right now."

"One additional problem," Mildred said, shouldering her med kit. "All of these were males. Not one bitch among the pack."

Passing off the rag, Ryan frowned. "Great. So this was just a hunting party, and the rest are out there somewhere."

"Probably a whole lot more than fourteen," Krysty said. "And when their mates don't come back, the females will come hunting."

With a guttural cry, Doc spun, drawing his blaster. The rest of the companions copied the action and separated slightly, an automatic reaction learned the hard way from countless ambushes.

"What is it, Doc?" Ryan snapped, the long barrel of the Steyr resting on the hood of the wag, giving him stability and cover.

"Somebody on the roofs?" Krysty asked, her S&W .38 tracking the sky.

Doc didn't reply for a moment, but just stood there in the street, the Civil War blaster tightly held in both hands while another tiny dust devil danced about his worn shoes. His face was scrunched, head tilted as if concentrating on hearing something.

"Could have sworn I heard a car engine," Doc said slowly, as if unsure of his words. "Mayhap I was mistaken."

Jak and Dean exchanged glances, but kept their weapons in a ready stance. Neither had heard a thing, certainly not a working engine, and the Deathlands winds were famous for playing tricks with sound.

"An engine?" J.B. said thoughtfully. "Could be the sec men coming to check out the blaster noise."

Ryan looked over the group. They were ready to keep going, to negotiate with the sec men right here and now. But he knew they were as tired as he was. Too little food and too many jumps had weakened all of them. And tired people made mistakes, which got them chilled.

"Let's go and find some place to cook dinner," he directed, climbing behind the wheel of the vehicle and starting the engine. "We'll deal with the baron tomorrow after a full stomach and a good night's sleep."

"Sounds good to me," Krysty said, taking the passenger seat with a sigh. The others hesitated, but finally relented, the hunger in their bellies overcoming their impatience to deal with the tricksters from the ville.

LETTING GO of the rotting curtain, Harold stepped away from the second-floor window of the predark hotel. This was where he rested before journeying across the desert to the secret armory of the old baron. But there was no need to make the trip when those people across the street had everything he wanted. Blasters, and a wag that still worked. That alone should buy Laura her freedom.

Watching them drive off, Harold scrambled down the stairs to follow them, a plan already forming in his mind. He wanted to jump onto their wag from above, but the voices told him to follow the strangers and wait until after they had eaten. Food would make them sleepy. That was the time to strike.

Chapter Seven

"Dinner will be ready soon," Ryan announced, turning over the steaks with a pair of tongs. The tantalizing smell was making everyone anxious in anticipation, but the meat wouldn't be served until thoroughly cooked and there wasn't the slightest trace of pink on the inside. He was going to make damn sure there would be no case of poisoning from the wild animal.

The interior of the pawnshop was warm and well lit. There had been some camping lanterns, which still contained a quantity of kerosene, and gave them all the light needed. The windows were covered with layers of thick blankets from the upstairs apartments to keep the lights from giving away their location through the frosty windows.

Ryan remembered the Trader teaching him that while banks made good bolt-holes with their stout walls and bulletproof windows, and high schools were excellent for long-term bases with their machine shops, libraries and such, for a short stay, pawnshops were the best. Stout iron bars covered the windows, and a flexible steel grating completely masked the front window. Even the back door was a solid slab of wood with 54-gauge sheet steel bolted over the whole thing. And they were often undisturbed, as most folks had no idea what the classic three brass balls of the store meant anymore. Almost always there were piles of useful supplies inside.

The shop consisted of one large room with a center island of heavy tables covered with speakers, stereos, air conditioners, television sets and assorted electrical equipment. A brace of sec cameras hung impotently from the ceiling, and a glass-topped counter ran around the walls. The left-side counter was covered with racks of musical instruments, while the right was jammed full of blasters—rifles and shotguns of every type imaginable. Not an inch of wall space was unused. Inside the waist-high glass cases were rows of wallets, watches, cell phones, pagers and a vast array of pistols.

He flipped over the steaks and dodged a fat spit of frying grease. True, the ancient blasters were useless, the barrels and mechanisms clogged with clots of dried oil, but with a good cleaning there were enough blasters here to outfit an army. And a whole display case of handblasters, also deadweight until disassembled and cleaned and oiled. A few were still in their sales boxes; being unused, they were in a lot better condition than the rest. In the back vault—actually an old-fashioned standing safe resembling a cast-iron refrigerator—they had located trays of diamond rings, and other pretty jewelry, deeds to cars and homes that no longer existed and a lot of ammo. Also dead. Cordite lasted a lot longer than black powder or gunpowder, but after two hundred years even the best deteriorated into a goop as explosive as dandruff.

A bowling trophy case in the corner of the pawnshop had been easily converted into a rough kitchen, the trophies removed to hold any of the canned goods from the apartment upstairs that Mildred deemed edible. Incredibly, there had even been a spice rack, and the Deathlands warrior knew from experience that a few centuries only made most spices tastier. Which was just about the only good thing that ever came out of skydark.

"Mmm. Smells ready," Jak said, his stomach rumbling at the idea of cooked meat. It had been hours since their meager breakfast of cold beans, and even the raw wolf was starting to smell good. He remembered being hungrier than this, but not for a while.

"Anytime is good for me," J.B. added, sitting in a cane-back chair, the Uzi in his lap. He was situated right next to the front door, keeping an ear on the street outside. The only sounds were the whispery desert winds and the occasional hoot of an owl.

Repacking the instruments from the med kit in precise order for ease of use in an emergency, Mildred glanced up from her work. "Are you sure the Hummer is going to be okay in that garage next door? Without it, we have a long walk back to the redoubt."

"Took ignition fuse," Jak said, lifting the tiny item into view from a pocket. "Took spare gas. LAWs and M-60 here with us."

"Besides, the wag is under a sheet of canvas," J.B. added with a grin. "Inside a locked building with a booby trap on the door. That wag won't go nowhere."

"Anybody who reaches it now has my permission." Krysty laughed.

"Sir, it has been quite a while. Should I go spell Dean on the rooftop?" Doc asked, sitting on a stool. He was steadily stropping the blade of his swordstick with a whetstone. The polished steel shone like a mirror in the clear light of the lanterns.

Moving the steaks about so they wouldn't stick to the grill, Ryan glanced at a loudly ticking wall clock. Once they had rewound the mainspring, the machine worked fine. Too bad it was much too big to bring along. And naturally, all of the watches in the display cases were battery powered. Precision timepieces made out of gold and with jewel points, they were useless junk nowadays. He made a mental note to check and see if there was an antique store in the city.

"Not for a while. Two-hour rotations," he stated, sliding another piece of wood into the flames. The grease from the cooking meat dribbled off the grill, making the flames surge upward spitting and crackling. It smelled wonderful. "Don't give him any special treatment just because he's young. He's old enough to carry his share of the load.

"Besides," he added. "Two have an urge to chat, and we're laying low. He'll be fine."

"As you say," Doc replied. He had made the suggestion, and that was as far as he could broach the subject. He knew that the three things nobody should openly discuss were: how to raise a child, how to make up with a lover and how to go to hell.

Finished with the packing, Mildred removed her stiff boots and started to massage her feet when some odd scratching and pops sounded. Across the shop, Krysty stepped away from a weird moving machine. The cranking handle on the side spun steadily, as the platter turned under the huge needle and from the curving horn, a tenor started to faintly sing in another language.

The physician's expression of puzzlement gave way to profound pleasure. "Good God, that's Enrico Caruso," she said. "I can't believe that old Victrola phonograph still works!"

"Built things to last in those days," Doc said proudly, sliding the sword into his cane with a snap. "Nothing electronic or computerized, just springs and honest steel."

"Nothing wrong with science," J.B. said, crossing his feet at the ankles on top of a brass spittoon. "You just can't let it run the world, is all."

Glancing up from a VR helmet he was examining, Jak said, "Purpose of science to explain, not define."

Everybody turned to look askance at the teenager.

"William Blake," Jak muttered in annoyance. They always seemed surprised that he knew anything.

Returning to their respective chores, the companions listened to the singer for a few minutes, then in a crescendo of music, the man stopped and applause thundered. Rising from a stool, Krysty dutifully flipped over the record to the other side. Unfortunately, this was the only disk she could find. There didn't seem to be any jazz or swing in stock which she had heard before and enjoyed, but classical was better than no music, she supposed. After Krysty cranked the handle a few more times, the tenor started another incomprehensible song.

"Rigoletto," Doc said happily. "It has been much too long since I last heard Verdi."

"Beautiful." Mildred sighed, wincing as she slipped on a boot.

At the grill, Ryan arched an eyebrow but kept his opinions to himself, sprinkling some crushed salt over the sizzling steaks.

Vastly amused, Doc beamed a smile. "Incredible, madam, at last we agree on something."

"Had to happen someday." She chuckled, tying off the laces and starting on the other.

Cutting a notch in the thickest steak with his knife, Ryan checked the interior. Pinkish-gray and getting darker. "Almost done," he announced. "Better grab some plates."

"A pleasure, sir," Doc announced, going to a cabinet. Smashing the stained-glass door with the butt of his LeMat, the man gathered a stack of gilded plates from amid the china and crystal.

"Need some help?" J.B. asked, starting to rise.

"No. You stay right there," Krysty said, pushing some steamer trunks together to form a crude table for the repast. The stout brass-and-mahogany luggage would also give good protection to hide behind if they were attacked during dinner and had to fight.

Searching his fatigues for the fork he always carried, Jak pulled into view a frilly red-and-gold tassel. "Son of a bitch," he mumbled in surprise.

"Good Lord," Mildred said, amused, crushing a lump of salt in her hands and sprinkling the crystals over the sizzling steaks. "Is that from the Leviathan?"

"Yeah, from the fifty." Jak snorted, toying with the ornament. "Must have stuffed in pocket after cut off."

"Going to keep it as a memento?" J.B. asked, recrossing his legs to get comfortable.

"No," the Cajun stated, tossing it aside. "I know Shard is dead. Don't need relic."

Just the way the Trader had taught him, Ryan raised a coffee mug full of warm water in salute. "To Shard," he said solemnly.

Everybody lifted their containers to drink to the memory of the hero of Novaville.

ON THE ROOF of the pawnshop, Dean faintly smelled the wolf cooking and smacked his lips. It had been a while since they'd had meat, and he was really looking forward to dinner. Daydreaming about meals long gone, the boy watched as darkness descended quickly over the desert, the dying red light of the departing sun climbing up the one great skyscraper in the ruined ville, going higher and higher until the building vanished completely.

Softly, a sterile wind blew over the dead city, only the fragile barrier of white glass protecting the thousands of piles of dusty bones from being disturbed from their centuries-old slumber, slumped at their office desks or sprawled in their bedrooms. An ordinary day for them, frozen into a hellish tableau from a microsecond blast of supercharged neutrinos when cars and people alike died at the exact same instant.

In the crumbling belfry of a church, an owl softly hooted for its mate. On the streets, lizards darted from one hiding place to another on an endless quest for insects to feast upon. In a city possessing a million lights, blackness reigned supreme.

Leaning dangerously far over the edge of the rooftop, Dean rested his elbows on the cornice as the wind ruffled his hair. There was a park just off to their right, nothing much there except for dead trees and a dried-up lake with a marble statue of a mutie in the center. The woman was half norm, half fish. Creepy, although he did like the way she wasn't wearing anything but a necklace and a smile. Not bad for a mute. Then the boy spotted a sudden movement on the sandy streets below. Black specks moving fast and coming straight this way.

''Must be more wolves,'' he said to himself, and, digging in his pocket, he unearthed some spent shells. Dean carefully counted out three and put the rest back in his pants. There was no need to drop a handful. He was giving a warning to the folks below, but that was no reason to waste perfectly good brass. Reaching over to drop the warning shells, the gray moonlight unexpectedly disappeared and darkness enveloped the boy.

A terrible stench washed over him, smelling worse

than rotting corpses. Dean choked on the fetid reek, almost retching. Backing away, he instinctively pulled out his Browning Hi-Power, and it was slammed from his grip by a powerful blow. He snatched for the flying weapon, but it disappeared into the night.

Pistol gone, the gren in his pocket worse than useless at that range, the young Cawdor decided that this was no place for heroics, turned and sprinted for the tiny kiosk at the rear of the roof, the entrance to the stairwell. But something large landed between him and the exit as another stinking wave of hellish air washed over the boy, stealing the breath from his lungs. A ragged cough seized his throat, and yellow eyes opened wide in the blackness.

Gasping for air, Dean recognized it as the winged mutie from the tunnel. Coughing and hacking, he cradled his aching hand and slowly retreated, trying to circle the beast, get on the other side of the kiosk, then scoot around fast and slam the door. But every move was countered by the winged beast, its great wings spread wide, blocking any chance of escape as if this were a game it played often. Dean knew that some animals played with their prey before killing, and he had a terrible feeling this was one of those breed. He tried to draw in air to call for help and only choked on the awful stench again. It was sort of like skunk mixed with burning sewage, impossible to breathe.

Flapping its huge wings, the mutie hissed loudly, exposing long yellow fangs, and Dean knew the game was over. It was going to attack. When a person had nothing to lose, attack and hope for the best, his father had always told him. Fumbling for the knife on his belt, Dean charged forward, slashing hopefully for the vulnerable throat below the inhuman eyes. The mutie easily dodged

out of the way as silent as a dream. Then white-hot pain
struck the boy's shoulder and he found himself airborne.

Breath exploded from Dean as he landed sprawling
on a hard surface. Looking about, he saw he was on the
roof of the next building over. His chest felt as if it
were on fire, and he wondered if bones were broken,
when clouds overhead parted for a brief instant, admit-
ting a wealth of silvery light. Black wings extended, the
mutie was flying straight toward him, and there on the
rooftop by his boots was the dropped knife. Desperately, he dived for the weapon and collided headlong
with the animal. Something snapped just over his head,
and he kneed it hard as he could in the belly. The mutie
snarled in response and stepped back, its clawed feet
accidentally kicking the knife farther away.

Cursing his luck, Dean snarled back at the thing, hoping to frighten it, then ducked under a slashing wing
that would have taken off his head. Blaster gone, knife
lost, and he was still hacking for air, with no chance of
a good scream for help. Matches, didn't he have some
matches in his pants? That would chase it away. Maybe
rip off his shirt and set it on fire. But he needed a minute
first to get some more room. Had to keep his distance.
He didn't want to go hand-to-hand with the creature
again, not with a broken arm and ribs. The pain was
becoming a warm fuzzy feeling, and the boy knew that
shock was starting to set in. Not good.

The mutie launched itself into the sky, and Dean
dropped and rolled to the left, the rough concrete becoming smooth and sloping sharply upward beneath
him before he realized that he was now lying on the
skylight he had spotted earlier.

Delicately shifting his weight, Dean heard the glass
musically crackle, and he forced himself to go limp to

try to slide off. but one wrong move and he would go through. He had to get off the skylight, find the knife, jab for the eyes and wait for help to come. The others had to be only moments away. All he had to do was stall.

Another warm stench flowed over the boy as the animal landed heavily on his chest, talons racking across his shirt and flesh. Dean cried out in pain, and the weakened glass shattered, sending the boy plummeting into the inky blackness beyond. His last coherent sight was of the broken skylight receding into the distance, the frosty panels of glass framing a black-winged figure, the cold yellow eyes watching him fall.

STANDING AT THE DOOR, J.B. pressed his ear to the glass and tried to hear. "And I tell you," he repeated, "I heard something odd."

"Dropped shells?" Ryan asked intently, pausing in his eating. If Dean had spotted somebody coming their way, the meal was over. The wolf was excellent, but not worth dying for. Hastily, he swallowed the last morsel unchewed.

"Well, no," the Armorer relented.

Ryan relaxed and returned to his rice and steak. Hopefully, they could trade for some cans of vegetables from the ville the next day. He was getting mighty tired of bastard rice.

"But definitely something metallic," J.B. added stubbornly, lifting a corner of the blankets and peeking outside.

"Mebbe lizard on can," Jak mumbled around a mouthful of food.

"Mebbe not," Krysty retorted, wiping her lips on some Irish linen.

"We better do a recce," Ryan said, rising and placing aside the unfinished meal.

The closest, Mildred leaned back in her office chair toward the barricaded door. She heard nothing. "Think the wolves followed us?"

"Possible," J.B. said, placing a gren on the top of a steamer trunk. Laying down the Uzi, he deftly removed the black electrical tape holding the handle in place. A quick yank of the pin and they were in business.

"Great. How many more of these do we have?" Mildred asked, looking at the dull green gren. The color said it was HE, high explosives, with no shrapnel. Not a very good killing device. But enough of them could bring down an army.

"One each," J.B. answered, reaching into his munitions bag and passing them around. "The rest are hidden upstairs in case we had to fall back."

"Sufficient unto the day," Doc declared, both hands busy resetting the hammer on his LeMat to fire the shotgun blast first. "These days, there is no such thing as overkill."

"Agreed."

"Best check wag, too," Jak suggested, tucking his gren into a pocket.

At that moment, something thumped onto the sidewalk in front of the store. Everybody stopped eating as plates and drinks were cast aside and blasters were grabbed.

"That wasn't some empty brass shells," Ryan stated, SIG-Sauer in hand as he went to the door.

"Too heavy and solid," Krysty agreed, peeking outside through the blankets covering the display window. "Gaia, there's a blaster laying on the ground!"

"Browning Hi-Power?"

"Looks like."

"No way Dean dropped his blaster." J.B. frowned, unfolding the wire stock of the Uzi.

"Well, somebody did," Ryan snapped, easing off the chain and darting into the night. With his blaster sweeping for targets, he let his eye adjust to the darkness and glanced around.

Krysty joined him on the sidewalk, with the rest staying inside and covering them from the doorway. Ryan jerked his head to the left. She nodded and he went to the right, but only got a few feet. There on the broken concrete was a familiar metallic shape. Rushing over, he scooped up the weapon. It was a .38-caliber Browning Hi-Power in near mint condition. The odds of somebody else having one of these were astronomical.

"It's Dean's," Ryan said, looking at the roof. Nothing was visible.

"Shit," Krysty swore, craning her neck. "Any blood?"

"No." Placing two fingers in his mouth, he whistled sharply twice and waited. No reply. "We got trouble." They hurried inside and J.B. closed the door, keeping a hand on the busted lock.

"Okay, something is wrong," Ryan stated, grabbing his Steyr and working the bolt. "Dean might have dropped the blaster, but no way he is also asleep on guard duty. Krysty and I'll hit the rooftop. Mildred, J.B., are the anchor here. Doc and Jak recce the ground, then join us topside."

Everybody moved without discussion.

Grabbing a canteen, Mildred poured water over the grill to kill the coals and went behind the steamer trucks. They would give decent protection and offered acceptable vantage of the front window and the door to the stairs.

"We'll fire a round if there's trouble," J.B. said from the doorway, but Ryan was already charging up the stairs.

It took them only seconds to reach the top of the building. Ryan and Krysty burst out of the stairwell, blasters in hand. But the roof was empty, only a warm wind from the desert blowing steadily over the bare concrete.

Frowning, Ryan gave a pigeon coo and listened for an answer, while Krysty moved to a prominent dark spot on the white concrete. She didn't have to touch it to know it was fresh blood. The redhead eased back the hammer on her revolver and whistled sharply three times.

Scowling, Ryan gave an answering coo and they moved out in a crisscross pattern, blasters searching for targets. A minute later, they met at the far corner.

"Anything?" Krysty asked in concern.

"Nothing," Ryan stated grimly. "Think he fell off?"

The woman looked at the three-foot-high wall edging the roof and thought of the five-foot-tall boy. "No."

"Better tell the others."

A nod. "I'll stay here and keep a watch."

"Check." As Krysty sprinted for the door, darkness enveloped them, something large blocking the weak moonlight shining through the dense clouds overhead.

"It's the mutie!" Ryan shouted, the Steyr belching flame and thunder.

A few yards away, Krysty was briefly illuminated by the muzzle-flash of her booming handblaster. Under the double assault, the shadowy figure was hurled backward and over the edge of the roof to disappear.

"Fireblast!" Ryan growled, working the bolt on the rifle and slamming in a fresh clip.

"Creature did the same thing back at the tunnel," Krysty agreed, thumbing fresh shells into her own blaster.

A snarl sounded from the sky above them, and a dimly seen shape flashed by their left side, then the right. But the man and woman held their fire, waiting for a clear shot. Did the animal understand blasters could be emptied? Just how smart was this thing?

"Circling, trying to confuse us into thinking there's more than one," Ryan said, impressed in spite of the situation. "Must be smarter than it looks." Then something juicy smacked onto the metal door of the raised stairwell, and they both heard a steady sizzling sound.

"Blood of the mother!" Krysty shouted, shying away from the dissolving metal. What the hell was that, acid rain? Triggering another round, she kept moving to make herself more difficult to hit when more blaster shots split the night as the rest of the companions poured out of the doorway.

"Watch out!" she cried, bending out of the way of a raking claw. "Damn thing spits poison!"

Standing brazen before the mutie, Doc and Jak now realized why the woman had been bobbing about and quickly followed her example of shoot and dodge.

Bleeding from a score of minor wounds, the frustrated beast spread its wings and took to the air, diving toward Ryan. Leveling his blaster, he stood there until the very last moment, then triggered the Steyr, the muzzle-flame reaching out to touch the beast. There was an audible crack of cartilage, and the creature hit the rooftop, roaring with pain. The left wing drooped impotently while yellow blood poured from the ghastly wound.

Angling about to avoid hitting Jak, Doc waited for a clear shot and placed each slug from the LeMat with extreme care, each impact making the mutie reel crazily. The percussion pistol took minutes to reload and prime. These nine shots were all he had before reduced to his swordstick, and he highly doubted the lethal efficiency of a steel blade against a mutie the size of a gorilla.

As Ryan moved in for the kill, the thing spit loudly. Jak tackled Ryan from the side, and they hit the roof as fluid smacked onto the ventilation fan. The sizzling noise of the acid eating the metal sounded like bacon frying in the darkness.

Ryan grunted his thanks, as they stood and fired both weapons, going for the throat and groin. Krysty and Doc joined them, forming a ragged line, and volley fired at the darting beast. Unable to escape into the air, it spit again and again as the barrage of blasterfire hammered steadily. But its motions were becoming slower as the beast weakened, the useless wing dragging on the roof slowing it considerably. Slashing out with its good wing, its talons narrowly missed Krysty. She stood her ground and fired, blowing out an eye. Now the beast screamed insanely and charged. They broke before the rush, folding away on both sides, then stepping in again. The animal was trapped in a killing box, with every blaster firing from all sides.

A knee buckled, it spit randomly, an arm drooped limply, blood pooled around its clawed feet. It slashed out a clawed wing, and that one drooped as the cartilage was smashed. Pain overwhelming sense, it continued to rush the humans, but the deadly blasters never ceased, one person reloading while the one alongside kept firing, until finally the broken, bloody thing collapsed, pale yellow blood pooling around the riddled corpse. Then Ryan stepped close and cut off its head with his panga.

Jak rubbed a painful spot on his hand where a tiny drop of the poison had splattered on his bare flesh. "Stab again."

Ryan slid his rifle barrel underneath and flipped over the mutie.

"It's a bat," Krysty stated, reloading quickly and watching the sky for any other of the monstrosities. "A night feeder."

"Bastard tough mutie," Jak said, reloading quickly.

"That's no mutie," Ryan stated, shoving a fresh clip into the Steyr. "See that golden blood? Means its from a predark lab."

"Another biological weapon," Doc grumbled, plunging out the charging holes of his LeMat. The chore was normally done sitting at a flat table. He fumbled with the placement of a copper-coated percussion nipple. "Damn them all to hell."

"Good thing Dean gave us a warning," J.B. said. "If that thing had caught us inside with no room to maneuver, we'd be in its belly by now."

"Where Dean?" Jak asked, concerned. Piss-colored blood and spent shells were splashed about, but there was no sign of the boy.

"Don't know. He wasn't here when we arrived," Krysty said, pocketing the spent brass of her revolver.

"Dean!" Ryan yelled. *"Dean!"*

Only the wind whispered in reply. Ryan took in a deep breath and let it out slow. "Well, he's got to be around here somewhere," he said. His hand had trouble holstering the big autoblaster, then an icy calm took the man as if he were in the middle of a firefight, and it slid smoothly into place.

"Mebbe he's hiding, or fell over the edge," Krysty suggested, glancing at the dark streets. Gaia, what a grisly thought.

"Any sign of him on the ground?" Ryan asked, but their replies sounded strange to him as if somebody else had asked if the boy was dead, but not him. He felt oddly distant from the conversation, as if he were speaking to them from over a great length of pipe.

"Not a sign of him," Doc stated, forcing a neutral expression as he holstered his blaster and buttoned down the flap. "Don't worry, it is only three stories onto soft sand. If the lad did tumble, he probably has no worse than a broken leg."

"Jumped another building," Jak suggested, as pragmatic as always.

"Logical," Ryan admitted, unclenching his fist. "I'll check the roof to our west."

A sharp whistle cut the night.

"Here!" J.B. shouted, waving from the east side. "Over here!"

The companions rushed to the edge of the roof. The Armorer pointed across the alleyway to the next building. The rain-pitted expanse of concrete was empty except for a skylight. But one of the milky-white glass panels in the framework was broken, and lying nearby in a splash of red blood was Dean's knife.

Chapter Eight

Tossing Krysty the rifle, Ryan backed away a few steps and charged. At the last moment, he jumped over the low wall and sailed across the gulf of the alleyway to land heavily on the concrete roof of the next building. He went to one knee, but was up again in an instant. Going to the hole in the skylight, Ryan listened for any sounds before cupping his hands and shouting the boy's name. There was no answer.

He turned and barked, "Mildred!"

The physician reached into her med kit and tossed him a small object. Ryan made the catch one-handed and squeezed the charging handle on the tiny flashlight a few times to power the miniature battery inside. It was old and weak, but a hundred times better than a candle. Playing the beam through the hole, he saw an open area directly under the skylight with a balcony on four sides. A staggered staircase of iron lace spiraled down into the building and out of range of the weak beam.

"I'm going in," he said, stuffing the flashlight into his belt. "Meet you on the ground floor."

"On our way," Krysty shouted, already heading for the kiosk.

Carefully testing the skylight for strength, Ryan knew it would never hold his two-hundred-plus pounds. Carefully wiggling the rest of the glass shards from the frame, he tossed them aside. Then, grabbing the part of the framework directly attached to the concrete roof, he carefully lowered himself down. The angle was awkward, but he held on tight. Lowering himself as far as he could, Ryan swung his legs back and forth until he had sufficient momentum and let go.

Pain racked his back as he scraped over the railing, and he landed sprawled on the soft carpeting of the topmost balcony. Scrambling erect, Ryan pulled out his blaster and flashlight. Anything could be inside this place. Just because the roof was untouched didn't mean the front door wasn't wide open. He couldn't chance being caught unprepared.

Playing the beam around, he saw that the central area was squared off by the fancy iron-lace railings. An open framework elevator shaft of the same material stood nearby. Moving along the floor, he noted the array of closed doors with tarnished nameplates lining the balcony. Every one was closed with no signs of busted wood on the jamb showing a forced entry. Lush plastic plants in oak stands adorned the corners, and a squat copier stood reverently in an alcove near a brace of soda machines.

"Dean!" he shouted, his words echoing slightly down the halls. "Son, can you hear me?"

Dead silence. Ryan shook that word from his mind. Negative thoughts would only slow his reflexes. He had to concentrate on finding his son.

Still holding the SIG-Sauer, Ryan placed two fingers in his mouth and whistled once loudly. No response. With a growing sense of unease in the pit of his stomach, the man moved past the elevator and started down the open stairs, shining the flashlight everywhere. At the third story, he encountered an iron grating padlocked shut. Ryan hesitated for a moment, then leveled the 9 mm blaster and shot off the lock. The cough of the silenced weapon was lost in the crash of the exploding metal and seemed to endlessly bounce off the plaster walls, the noise somehow making the building seem even more empty than before.

Two more gates blocked his progress, and by the time he reached the ground floor, the rest of the companions were already waiting in the spacious lobby. The area was well lit by the strong light of the lanterns. Wide couches surrounded low tables piled with magazines, the pale walls decorated with ornate paintings of landscapes and running water. Velvet ropes formed a maze to traverse before reaching the massive reception desk, where a tiny sign sternly announced that no smoking was allowed.

"We heard shots," J.B. said urgently, the Uzi held steady in a combat grip.

"Locked doors," Ryan replied, clicking off the flashlight and returning it to Mildred. "Any sign of Dean outside?"

"Not a trace. You?"

"No."

Shoving aside the soft ropes, Krysty strode behind the reception desk and glanced underneath. Wounded, the boy could be hiding anywhere.

"Lavatories are clear," Doc announced, bursting out of the ladies' room, his frock coat spreading wide in his wake like the wings of some terrible prehistoric bird.

Mildred yanked open an unmarked door and jumped back, almost firing as a collection of brooms and mops piled out, nearly hitting her. "Janitor's closet," the physician reported. "Also empty."

"Dean!" Ryan shouted through cupped hands. The name echoed throughout the old building.

A great rage was building within the man, the fury tempered with the dire possibility the boy was dead and gone. Crossing the lobby past a brace of telephone cubicles, Ryan kicked open the first door. Inside were only chairs, desks dotted with coffee cups and a huge easel covered with a meaningless pie chart showing the excellent performance of something somewhere.

"Okay, we do this systematically. I'll take the left side with Krysty. Jak with Mildred, J.B. stay here and cover us with the Uzi. Doc, sweep outside again."

Scratching her cheek with the barrel of her .38, Krysty spoke. "Remember, that mutie flew. If it wasn't alone, and another grabbed Dean…"

"Then there's nothing to be done," Ryan stated coldly, his features set as if cast in an arctic glacier. "We can't track an animal in flight. So concentrate on what can be done. Search this place room by room."

"Over here!" Jak cried, partially masked by the shadows of the reception desk.

Grabbing a lantern, Ryan shone the light in the direction of the call. The pale teenager was kneeling at the iron-lace railing that cordoned off the middle of the lobby. "Central access not stop here! Down another level!"

In a second, Ryan was already alongside the Cajun, leaning over the railing and shining the lantern around. A chrome-and-steel kinetic sculpture made of sharp panes and angles rose from the dusty center of a dried fountain. Dozens of small tables dotted the floor around it, and lying amid them was a crumpled human body, limbs splayed, a trickle of blood dribbling from his slack mouth.

"Dean," Ryan said softly, almost dropping the light.

"Still bleeding," Mildred stated quickly. "That means he's alive."

"How do we get there?" Krysty demanded, looking around. "The enclosed stairs stop on this level. Where are the ones leading to the basement?"

"This way!" Doc shouted, gesturing with the LeMat.

Staying at the railing, Ryan gauged the distance, then jumped over the banister. He landed next to the boy, missing the granite rim of the fountain's basin by only inches. The others arrived minutes later, charging out of the enclosed stairwell. They maneuvered through the rows of tables and found Ryan kneeling solemnly alongside his son.

"There's no pulse," he announced woodenly, holding the boy's small wrist in his hand.

Pushing the man aside, Mildred expertly placed two fingers on right side of the lad's throat just under the mastoid bone. "There's a pulse," she said, resting a palm on his forehead. "But it's weak and fast, and the skin is clammy."

Already her tone was shifting from concern to impartial. Never think about the person you were treating. Concentrate on fixing the injuries—later on there would be time for celebration, or mourning.

"He's in shock." Ryan frowned, having seen enough in his life to recognize the symptoms. "Got to keep him warm. Krysty!"

"On it," the redhead said. Placing the Steyr on a table, she shucked the bearskin coat and passed it over.

"More," Mildred said, tucking the fur over the boy.

"Done." Krysty holstered her blaster. "Jak, cover me."

The Cajun followed her into the darkness, and soon there came sounds of smashing wood and ripping cloth.

Glancing around, Ryan saw they were in the center of a food court, rows of garish plastic signs proclaiming delicious snacks long decayed into dust. Rows of plastic tables encircled the fountain with the weird metallic sculpture. On the other side of the court was the iron-lace framework of the elevator, adjacent to more public rest rooms, phones and drinking fountains.

Rising, Ryan removed his palm from the floor and flexed his hand. "Bastard tile flooring is ice cold. We've got to get him off this." He started to slide his arms under the boy, but Mildred pushed the man away.

"Don't touch him until I say so," the physician ordered brusquely. Then she ripped open the boy's shirt. His hairless chest was smeared with blood and heavily scarred in spots, but there were no cuts or slashes readily apparent. But his forearm was thick with partially dried blood.

"Clawed," she said, probing the tender flesh. "Some minor discoloration, but no signs of toxic striation."

"The mutie is poisonous?"

"Apparently so, but none got in the wounds." Then she muttered, "However, that isn't what I'm worried about."

Suddenly shuddering, Dean began to have trouble breathing. Ryan started for him and stopped. As careful as if she were handling antique glass, Mildred took his head and tilted it backward an inch, the raspy noise easing somewhat.

"Tissue damage to his throat, just a bruise really, but it can swell and close off his breathing. I better prep for a trach just in case it gets worse." Whipping out a knife, she placed a small piece of soft plastic tubing from a fish aquarium alongside her switchblade knife and a packet of cotton wadding. The med kit held the big instruments, but Mildred always carried small medical items in her pockets just for a case like this.

Then she cursed, bumping her head against the rounded corner of one of the plastic tables. "For God's sake, give me some room to work. And more light!"

With his back to the wall between two fast-food counters, J.B. stood guard while Ryan and Doc started to remove the obstructions. The tables were bolted to the floor, but that didn't hinder the men from clearing a space around the patient and doctor.

As Doc tipped the plastic tables sideways, Ryan set the lanterns close to the shiny plastic tops to reflect the light and amplify the meager illumination. As bright as it was, there was no overhead illumination, and for one fleeting instant, Ryan felt he would have given his remaining eye for a single working lightbulb.

Concentrating on her task, Mildred carefully probed behind the boy's ears for any telltale swelling, then checked his nose for a trace of clear fluid.

"No sign of a skull fracture," she announced, feeling a wave of relief. "That's good news." Furiously pumping the handle of her flashlight, charging the battery to maximum, she gently used a thumb to peel back an eyelid, shining the beam directly into Dean's eyes. The pupils dilated very slowly.

"Goddammit," she cursed. Shifting position, the physician started to unlace the boot on Dean's right leg, her dark fingers lost in the shadows.

Krysty and Jak arrived just then with their arms full of draperies. "No blankets," Krysty announced, depositing her bundle near the boy. "But these are good and thick."

"Need more, we'll get carpet," Jak added, dropping his load of curtains and valances on top of the pile.

"That's enough for now," Mildred said, easing off the boy's Army boot. Drawing a knife, she slid the pommel of the weapon upward along the inner sole of his bare foot. Then she did it again, watching his unresponsive toes.

Doc sat on the edge of the fountain, watching the process with growing unease. He remembered a farming accident from his youth in Vermont and how the local country doctor had done the same thing and what the awful verdict was.

"What's wrong?" Ryan asked, sitting on his haunches.

Sliding the sock back on the limp foot, Mildred looked at him directly. "Your son has a concussion, no way to tell how bad. Thankfully, there doesn't seem to be any loose bone fragments. Might be okay if there's no internal clotting. Couple of ribs, right hand and his left leg are broken, but no compound fractures, thank God. Right arm is dislocated. Painful as hell, but also not serious. Probably landed sideways, breaking his leg, which slowed his momentum enough to stop the impact from smashing his skull open."

Mildred knew she was sounding callous, and her old teachers at medical school would have had a fit about her talking to a patient's parent this way. But those days were long gone. Ryan needed information hard and fast. There was simply no time for courtesy.

Ryan gave no outward sign of concern at the news.

"Partially bit through his tongue. I can fix that with needle and thread good as new, and I have two antibiotic tablets I've been saving for an emergency."

"Use them," Ryan snapped in a voice she had never heard before.

"I had already planned on doing so," Mildred said softly. "However, it's his back that worries me. I'm not getting any autonomic reflexes. It may only be a temporary condition, or there could be significant damage to his spinal cord."

"Oh, hell," J.B. whispered in the background.

"A broken back," Ryan muttered, his knuckles clenched white. "Is...is he in pain?"

"No." Then much as she hated to, Mildred told him the truth. "But he might be crippled, or blind, or completely paralyzed for the rest of his life. Spinal injuries can go a lot of ways, most of them bad."

Ryan's face underwent a series of somber expressions in a heartbeat. Blind. Paralyzed. Unable to fight or run, his son would be as good as dead. Worse, he would endanger the rest of them. His hand brushed against the stock of his 9 mm pistol and jerked away as if struck by an electric spark. Guilt flooded his being.

Tilting her head, Mildred brushed a coil of beaded hair out of her face. "Don't even think about such things yet. There's still a lot we can do first."

He took a deep breath. "Name it. Anything."

"First and foremost, we immobilize the boy completely. He can't be allowed to move an inch in any direction. God, what I'd give for a paramedic airpack." She shook away those thoughts. "We need wood for splints, and rope, or better yet, something flat like a belt to hold him down. And a flat board to get him off this cold floor."

"Blankets no good?" Jak asked, frowning.

"Can't cushion his back. It has to be hard."

Ryan took a lantern from the floor. "Let's move."

In orderly fashion, the rest of the companions separated throughout the food court, the flames of their lanterns bobbing behind counters and disappearing into back rooms.

"What are you not telling him?" J.B. asked softly.

Mildred glanced sideways at the man, the light reflecting off his wire-rimmed spectacles. "A four-story fall onto polished tile," she stated barely above a whisper. "What do you think I haven't told him yet?"

In only a few minutes, Ryan and the others returned with a collection of paneling, a door with hinges still attached, chair arms, shelves and numerous belts.

"Packing strips from the mail room," Doc said proudly, proffering a handful. "A most fortuitous acquisition."

"Damn near perfect," Mildred agreed, examining a woven cloth strip. "Good work. Jak, start cutting the buttons off those coats."

The Cajun nodded as a slim knife appeared in his pale hand and he started to slice.

"Krysty, lay that door right here. Anybody find boards for splints?"

"Bookcase shelving," Ryan said, setting the wood nearby. "From the security office. Way too wide, but we can split them lengthwise."

"Excellent."

"Here," Jak said, handing over the garment.

Laying the coat across the door, Mildred rolled some miscellaneous fabric into a tube and laid it sideways at the low end of the door, then another, smaller roll, near the top.

"Okay, listen up, people," she spoke brusquely. "First thing, follow my lead and move on my command, not one second earlier. We have to do this in unison, or we may kill him right here and now. Understand?''

Ryan started to speak and stopped.

"Okay, everybody gathered around. You too, John." J.B. shouldered his blaster and joined them. "I want everybody except Doc to take ahold of the loose clothing on a limb. I'll hold his head. But not his body," Mildred reminded. "Just the clothing, and try to shift him as little as possible. That's vitally important."

While the others did as directed, Doc positioned himself at the door. Good thing they had removed the knob so it lay flat on the floor.

"Now be careful!" the physician admonished, her hands cupping the boy's head, fingertips resting under his jawline. "We're only lifting Dean an inch. Soon as he's off the floor, slide the door underneath, and keep those supports in position at his knees and neck."

"Understood," Doc rumbled nervously.

"On my call," she said, watching their intent faces. "We go on the word *mark*. Not a second before. Ready? One, two, three—mark!"

The companions lifted in unison, and Dean moaned as he cleared the floor, his clothing tearing a little from the strain.

"Now!" Mildred barked.

Doc eased the door underneath, the loose hinge scraping nosily. "In position."

"Good," she grunted. "We go down on *three*. One, two, three!"

The companions lowered Dean onto the makeshift platform and stepped away. Releasing his head from her grasp, Mildred quickly inspected the boy again. "It's okay for now."

"What next?" Ryan asked, feeling the cold rush of adrenaline as if he were in combat.

"Get my new medical kit," Mildred said. "I don't need the instruments yet, but it's best to have them close just in case."

Then she added, "And when you get the chance, thank God I have something to work with."

"My turn," Jak said, rising and heading for the enclosed stairs.

"Doc, go with him as cover," Ryan ordered. "There might be more of those winged things running around outside."

"Sir, consider me Perseus of Greece," Doc said, and he followed the teenager out of the circle of light.

"Mildred, anything else?" Krysty asked. She knew death was just part of the wheel of life, but this was a friend, the son of her lover, a child she loved very much. Sometimes the wheel of life needed a good solid kick in the ass.

Opening her canteen, the physician sat in one of the plastic chairs built into the tables and took a swallow. "Yes," she decided, screwing the cap back on. "We better start moving our supplies over here. Especially that brazier. And find something to use as a bedpan. We're going to be here for a while."

"That's not a good idea," Ryan countered, sitting on the rim of the fountain, the kinetic sculpture behind glittering like a Christmas tree from the light of the lanterns. "Once you've bandaged his breaks, we can carry him to the redoubt. There's a full medical hospital on level five. Everything you'll need."

"Yeah, sorry, Millie, but we can't stay here. Whatever was out there might come back," J.B. added. "With friends."

Mildred gestured tiredly. "Then shoot him in the head. We take Dean on the road, and it's the same thing. At least chilled by a friend is faster."

A minute of silence passed.

"Absolutely?" Ryan demanded, elbows on knees.

"Hell no. Until he wakes up, there's nothing I know for sure. Except that he's damn lucky to still be alive."

Dean lay on the ground, shivering and trembling, his complexion a deathly white.

"Mebbe we could all lift in unison like before," Ryan suggested, eyeing the impossible stairwell.

"One more jostle and he could die," Mildred stated. "We had to do it the first time, but never again. He's not going anywhere. Not down the hall, not across the hall. Nowhere." She pointed. "That's why a jacket is under his leg to keep it from shifting position."

Sitting upright, Ryan chewed over this unwelcome information. "For how long?"

"Couple of days at least. Maybe a week. I can't tell until he stabilizes and I can chance trying some tests."

J.B. whistled. "Trapped here for a week. Possibly with more of those winged things roaming the streets. Not to mention the wolves and the sec men from the ville."

"They might be able to help, but probably not," Krysty said, her hair coiled protectively against her nape. "Always best to plan for the worst. It comes true more often than not."

"So we dig in for the duration. Should be safe enough once we seal this building," Ryan observed, running stiff fingers through his black hair. "Okay, we definitely have got to do something about the skylight. Mebbe we could replace the glass so it isn't obvious where the accident happened."

"This will never be a hardsite," J.B. stated. "Front door is a joke, and there must be a hundred windows to this place. It's a frigging glass box."

"We can nail boards across the inside of the office windows and jam the hallway doors shut. That'll give any attacker two things to get through," Ryan suggested. He had felt helpless watching the doctor work, but this was a combat matter now, and he was back in control. "However, this bastard central air shaft is begging for attack."

"Mebbe we could lace barbed wire across the railings," Krysty suggested. "That would give us a good three levels of protection. Nothing is going to fly through that. Probably find some in the local hardware store. Nails, too."

"Sounds good. But first we recce the whole building to make sure that we are alone here," Ryan declared, a hand on his blaster. "Then we go get the big conference table from the first floor. Set it over Dean to hide him from sight and protect from any more falling glass."

"That will do for a start," Mildred said. "And then dump furniture into the elevator shaft till it's jammed solid. That's an express route down here."

And to Dean. A chilling thought. "Which leaves the stairs as the only way in or out. What the hell. We can't retreat anyway."

A crash made everybody draw weapons as the door to the stairwell burst open and running figures emerged. Postures relaxed only when the companions recognized Jak and Doc. However, the two men bore serious expressions.

"Gone," Jak said bluntly. "Med kit gone!"

"Along with the Hummer!" Doc added, radiating ill-controlled anger. "The M-60 and a lot of rifles off the wall."

"We've been jacked?" J.B. cried in disbelief.

"Indeed, sir. Curse the Visigoths!"

"Shitfire, we were only here a few minutes!"

Mildred checked her wrist chron. "Well over an hour."

"More than long enough," Krysty said, her red hair a wild, fiery corona.

Then Doc added, "But the rockets are still in the pawnshop. They took the useless predark blasters and left the LAWs. That I do not understand."

"Illiterate," J.B. stated. "Couldn't read boxes."

"Any tracks?"

"Impossible to see in the night," Doc reported, resting on his cane. "Even if the moon were full, the sky is solid with clouds."

"Storm coming," Jak agreed knowingly. "Big one."

Irritably, J.B. pushed back his fedora. "Swell. That'll erase any tire tracks we could trace."

"Then we find the bastard tonight," Ryan stated gruffly. Retrieving the Steyr, he checked the clip. Taking out the half-full clip, the man slammed a new clip into the loading recess and worked the bolt, chambering a round. "Doc, stay here with Mildred and Dean."

The physician stood, clicking back the hammer on her revolver. "If I have to operate, we'll need that kit badly. However, this could be a trap to lure us outside."

"Sure as hell hope so," Ryan stated, starting for the stairs. "That would mean they're still nearby."

Chapter Nine

Outside, the streets were as dark as pitch, the sky a swirling, mottled mixture of greens and reddish-orange. The only faint light came from the twin searchlights steadily sweeping the clouds in an endless pattern.

Spreading out in a standard defensive pattern, the companions moved down the block and into the alleyway. The canvas sheet lay crumpled in a corner near an overturned garbage bin.

Dropping to one knee, Ryan studied the sandy street, brushing the surface lightly with his hand. "Nothing here," he said bitterly. "Can't tell if it was one person or ten."

"One," Jak said. "Used branches to erase his tracks getting here."

"So we can't backtrack him." J.B. cursed. "Frigging pro."

"Yep," Jak agreed.

"Perimeter sweep," Ryan snapped. "Five blocks in every direction, then another five until we find his tracks."

"And there's no need to bring him back alive if you find the med kit," Ryan added in the tones of an executioner.

"That was the plan," J.B. stated, switching the fire selector on the Uzi from single shot to full-auto. "He's going down, my friend."

Any further instructions were interrupted by a shape swooping from overhead, and the companions raised their weapons, staring into the darkness. Ryan whistled twice, and they followed him into the gutted paint store next door to the garage.

"Another one of those damn muties," Krysty said, crouching behind a stack of cans.

Adjusting his glasses, J.B. scrunched his face. "Hate to say it, but mebbe we'll have to wait until morning. In the dark, this thing could ace us one by one."

"Set fire to place," Jak suggested, his arms resting on the front counter, blaster pointed steadily at the smashed window. "Not like light."

The shadow of something flew past the store as Ryan considered the idea. "No, can't risk the flames spreading across the street." As if forcing his hands through mud, Ryan lowered his blaster. Dean couldn't be moved, and the muties ruled the night. They had no choice.

"Let's get back inside," he said, forcibly controlling his anger. At the moment, logic, not fists, would save his son. "We have to wait until morning."

As they returned to the food court of the building, Mildred saw their faces and knew what the situation was.

"Is there another med kit in the redoubt?" Ryan asked hopefully.

"Does it matter?" she asked, confused. "Without the Hummer, it's a two-, three-day walk."

He waved that aside. "The wag was almost out of fuel, and we have the spare can. We might find it only a couple of blocks away dead in the street."

"Well, there isn't another med kit," Mildred mused. "There's an X-ray machine, and I could really use a view of his skull and spine. But it's not portable. And even if there was a portable X-ray machine, the isotopes would have decayed into lead by now. The thulium core only has a five-year half-life.''

Tenderly, Ryan brushed the hair off the boy's forehead. The skin was clammy to his touch. Privately, he cursed himself for a fool. He should have known there had to be a reason why a town full of treasure hadn't been looted. Then he suddenly realized what he was thinking. That could be an answer to their problem.

"These ruins are in excellent shape," Ryan said. "There has to be a hospital somewhere, or a doctor's office. Might find what we need locally."

"Worth a look," J.B. agreed. "You never know, eh?"

"But right now, we recce this dump, and start ferrying over the supplies," Ryan continued, shouldering his longblaster. "We'll eat and sleep in shifts until dawn. Then we do a scout of the neighborhood. After that, we split into teams, J.B. and Doc hunt for supplies. I'll track the thief."

"Plus, we better get to work on the defenses," Krysty added, shivering slightly from the chill in the basement. "We'll need them if those muties come in a flock."

"Can't be many more around," Mildred said, dampening a rag with the canteen and wiping down the boy's forehead. "They're too big. They'd eat all of the wolves and lizards and then start on each other. So unless they're smart enough to open cans, logic dictates there are only a couple at most."

"Sure as hell hope you're right," Ryan growled, glancing at his son, and then upward at the broken skylight four stories away. "Because it took the lot of us to barely chill one of these bastard things, and we have no hope in hell of stopping a swarm.''

THROWING EMBERS high into the sky, a roaring bonfire cast dancing shadows across the bare brick walls and iron gates of the ruins of the predark library. Just outside the circle of light, men patrolled with longblasters cradled in their arms, black scarves wrapped about their faces as protection from the evening chill and to mask their presence from any possible observers.

Laughing and talking, a group of men sat around the crackling fire, throwing in the occasional book to feed the flames. A massive aluminium pot hung suspended over the blaze, the contents bubbling steadily as the fat, bearded man opened another predark can of beef stew and added it to the mixture. He stirred the food carefully with a bayonet, now and then taking a lick.

Most of the men were dressed in bulky plain cloth jackets, more patches than original cloth. But each sported blue denim pants with the price tag still attached, the cuffs tucked into brand-new heavy work boots. Each man was armed with blasters in police holsters, a few with M-16 assault rifles or double-barreled shotguns.

Backpacks and bedrolls were scattered around, along with stacks of canned goods, some with labels, most without. Nearby was an orderly line of U.S. Army MRE packages, and a large stack of ammo boxes next to a huge tarp-covered stack of flat crates. Vehicles stood parked in a ragged line cutting off the street entrance to the library parking lot.

The cook took a sip of the watery contents in the pot, and nodded. "Supper's on," he announced.

"About freaking time," Rev growled, taking a seat

in a beach chair. He was a tall man with pale skin and jet-black hair cut in a military-style flattop. An old leather bandolier of clips encircled his waist like a belt, and a compact MAC-10 machine pistol was slung over a shoulder.

Twelve other men gathered around the fire and took seats on office chairs and park benches while the cook quickly served out steaming helpings of the stew onto tin plates. Slices of canned bread were freely distributed, and nobody talked while the food was being dispersed.

"Not bad," Rev slurped between mouthfuls. "Not bad at all."

The cook, Jimmy, beamed in pleasure. "Thanks."

Spoon poised, Rev eyed the man. "I was talking to the grub. What the hell did you do but open some cans? Moron could have done that."

Others echoed his sentiments as the men used the stale slices of predark bread to mop the plates clean of the thick gravy.

Red fury burned in the man's face, but Jimmy went back to tending the fire, setting aside more cans to open in preparation to feed for the next shift of men when they came off guard duty. When nobody was looking directly his way, Jimmy flavored the stew with a healthy wad of spit. As his father always said, revenge came when you least expected.

"Damn, after nothing but coyote and lizard for the past month, even this shit tasted good," Rev announced as he sucked a juicy morsel from his back teeth. The man loudly belched in satisfaction and tossed the plate in the darkness. A squeal came from the crash followed by tiny scurrying noises.

"Got yourself a lizard there, Rev," said a burly man, wiping his mouth on a sleeve.

"Who gives a shit?" came the brusque reply.

An Oriental man in faded Army fatigues grinned widely as he filled a coffee cup with champagne from a dusty bottle and drank it like water. Best damn hooch he ever tasted. Raided lots of ruins, but never heard of Iron Horse before. Now he'd watch for the stuff. Age didn't seem to affect some booze, occasionally made it taste even better. Damnedest thing.

"Hey, Samson," Wu-Lang asked, refilling the mug. "What did that runaway we captured say the ville was called?"

"Alphaville," the giant squeaked. Nobody laughed at the ridiculous contrast. Samson possessed the voice of a child, but the body of two men and a mind of solid ice. Not even Rev would challenge the big man directly. "Used to be run by some old baron till a new guy took over last winter."

His shaved head gleaming in the firelight, another man laughed. "Don't matter. The ville is ours. They just don't know it yet."

"Yeah," Wu-Lang added, finishing off the champagne. "Can't understand it, though. He hated the place so much he risked traveling through the Deathlands solo. But when we ask for info on the defenses, he clams."

Baldy snorted in contempt. "Dying to protect a ville you hate. Just so your old baron gets a chance to reclaim it from the new boss. Never heard of such a crazy notion."

Reaching into a wheelbarrow placed conveniently near the campfire, Jimmy tossed in some more books and stirred the blaze with the poker. "He lasted long enough under the knife before talking."

"Crazy don't mean weak," Rev stated, reaching into the canvas duffel bag lying at his boots. Finding a carton of cigarettes, he ripped it open, destroying most of the packs, the smokes tumbling to the asphalt. He chose one from the jumble, tucked it between his lips and lit it with a stick from the fire. Rev drew the smoke deep into his lungs with satisfaction. Lighting up a predark cig usually tasted like smoking a turd. These were wonderful.

"And he knew where the old baron had all this shit hidden away," Wu-Lang continued. "I have never seen such weps before!"

"And the foods, the clothes!"

"It's the shits," Rev agreed, smiling as he blew a smoke ring. "The absolute shits."

A soft whistle started to keen from a copper teakettle on the fire, and the cook deftly removed it using arc-welding gloves. They would be wanting coffee soon, and he needed the fire high to get that huge pot boiling before they whipped him for taking too long. Sure would be great when the folks at the ville were hooked on jolt and he had some slaves of his own to beat.

"Where the hell are those guys, anyhow?" Wu-Lang asked, picking his teeth clean with a dirty thumbnail. "Isn't it time for shift change?"

"Yeah, it is," Rev said, frowning.

"Might have found another supply of booze," a fellow with a big mustache suggested. "And they're testing it for quality."

Cig dangling, Rev stood and hooked his thumbs into his gun belt. "Kick their ass if they do. This be a military op. We ain't partying yet. And guards stand rotation.''

''If you say so,'' Jimmy said, tending to his business.

''Mebbe the wolves got them.''

''Lots of them around here.'' He laughed. ''Or those flying muties the sec man told us about before he chilled.''

Holding aloft his rifle, Samson squealed loudly. ''I got the cure for muties right here, boys!''

A slightly drunken chorus agreed with the giant wholeheartedly.

''Hate wolves,'' Wu-Lang muttered, reaching out to take a cig from the loose pile on the ground. ''Hate the way they taste, too.''

Rev offered the man a light from a burning stick. ''Shuddup. They're our key to the ville.'' He turned his head to watch the searchlights sweep the sky. ''Fighting wolves means some of them got to get hurt. Mebbe hurt bad. When we offer to sell predark drugs in exchange for protection from the wolves, the local baron will shit himself inviting us inside the wall.''

''What we gonna call the jolt this time?'' Harlan asked.

''Tell them it's painkillers.''

Samson patted a small wooden crate at his side. ''Or, ah, antibiotics,'' he said stumbling over the long word.

''Either way, one taste and we own them.'' Wu-Lang smirked.

''Aye, it's a good plan,'' Brian agreed, giving a snaggletoothed grin. ''Our best yet. Putting it into the water supply thins down the jolt too much. Some of the stronger folks don't get hooked, and we have a fight on our hands.''

''Takes longer to cook, too.''

"Time wasted working when we could be drinking and fucking."

A skinny fellow with a feverish expression lowered an adult magazine, the pages brittle and yellow with age. "Think of all their women. Clean women! And they got to do whatever we want or no jolt." Harlan rubbed his crotch and resumed looking at the old pictures. "For as long as they live."

"Or least, still warm," Wu-Lang added.

"Yeah..."

Exhaling sharply, Rev cast away his dead cig. "And nothing is gonna stop us. We got it all this time. Food, blasters, wags and fuel." He waved about them. "These ruins are a gold mine. Who knows what we'll find in the next store?"

Just then, the stars overhead blacked out for a moment, and a sudden exhalation of air moved over the parking lot, bringing a hint of the desert heat.

"What the fuck was that?" Harlan demanded, dropping his nudie mag and drawing a huge revolver. The old S&W .357 Magnum was spotlessly clean, the blued barrel glinting dimly in the reflected lights of the bonfire.

"Don't know," Rev said, unlimbering his MAC-10 and snapping the bolt.

Following his lead, the rest of the crew hauled blasters into view. Even Jimmy whipped out a sawed-off double-barreled shotgun from an archery quiver on his back.

Rising to his full height, Samson hoisted his Marlin rifle to his huge chest, working the bolt to chamber a round. Nearby, Wu-Lang lifted an M-16 into view from a packing crate. With clumsy hands, he eased off the safety and fumbled with the bolt. He cursed as it sprang back, almost costing him a finger. Shitfire, the police station SWAT armory had yielded a dozen of the autoblasters, but no frigging instruction manuals.

"Probably just a bird," Jimmy whispered, holding the shotgun as if it were a good-luck talisman. "A vulture mebbe. Or an owl. We heard one before. There are lots of them in these parts."

"Yeah," Harlan whispered, cocking back the hammer on his blaster. "An owl."

"Mebbe it's that flying mutie the runaway was talking about," Brian muttered thoughtfully, holding a revolver in each hand.

"Nonsense," Rev snapped, struggling to keep the terror from his words. Before dying, the sec man had described the terror of the ruins. Covered with his blood, they had laughed at the speech, but now a chill invaded the drug runner's stomach as he scanned the night sky.

A wet crunch sounded from the dark.

"That you, Hal?" Wu-Lang asked. "Step on one of those tarantulas again...? Shitfire!" The man retreated from the night, staring at the ground.

Rolling and bouncing out of the darkness and into the firelight came a bloody human head. The features were slashed, ribbons of flesh hanging off the bloody skull, but what remained of the face was still recognizable as one of their sentries. The neck was severed in the middle, with no ragged marks of biting or chewing. The end of the flesh was smooth as if the man had been beheaded by an ax.

Then a torso plummeted from the sky to land on the bonfire, extinguishing the flames. Darkness enveloped the parking lot.

"Bloody hell!" Rev yelled, spraying a wreath of 9 mm tumblers into the sky above.

Everybody cut loose, rounds ricocheting off the stone walls of the library and shattering glass like crystal thunder.

Calmly waiting for a target to present itself, Samson stepped out of the reddish glow of the dying embers to let his vision adjust when a wind ruffled the hair at the back of his head. Annoyed, he patted it back down and was surprised when he found his hand sticking to his hair. The giant could feel warmth trickling down his neck, into his new shirt, and knew it was his own blood.

Baring his teeth in a wordless scream, Samson triggered the Marlin, explosions of flame illuminating the parking lot for yards. Briefly, something on top of the stack of ammo crates was caught in the flash, and then was gone. A misshapen figure with terrible demon eyes.

"It's them! They're here!" Wu-Lang screamed in panic, firing short bursts from the M-16 wildly in every direction. Spent shells arced out in streams of brass and fell musically to the ground.

Rushing forward, Jimmy slipped on the brass and hit the asphalt hard, losing his blaster. Then with a horrible cry, he was hauled into the darkness and the sound of ripping meat accompanied his piercing screams.

Rev pumped some bursts that way, then the back of his neck tingled and he wildly spun, firing. Something unseen brushed his face, tearing a bloody score along his cheek, and the drug runner knew he had escaped death by a split second.

"Light the torches! We got to see to fight!" Wu-Lang cried, dropping a spent clip and slamming in a fresh one. He pulled the trigger and nothing happened.

Screaming curses, he furiously worked the bolt and started to fire again.

Ever so slowly, as if his bones were melting, Samson slumped to the ground, the Marlin clattering to the asphalt from his dead hands. The entire back of the man's clothes were soaked with blood, and he seemed to have only half a head.

"Regroup at the library!" Rev shouted as he dodged among the piles of supplies to put his back to the stone wall. Footsteps and gunshots headed for the granite building, and as the fight shifted away from him, Rev sprinted for the line of parked wags.

Scrambling into the nearest truck, Rev was startled to find Harlan already behind the wheel, coaxing the big engine into life. With a sputtering roar, the ramshackle engine finally caught and he rolled ruthlessly over fallen bodies of the crew.

"Go for the street!" Rev shouted, "and head for the searchlights!"

"No shit," grunted Harlan, grinding gears and pumping the gas pedal.

A thump shook the truck, and the hood flipped upward, completely blocking their view. Then a line of holes sprouted in the roof, and the windshield shattered, spraying them both with glass. Cursing, Harlan hit the brakes hard, the disks squealing in protest.

The truck was still moving as Rev shoved open the side door and hit the ground running. Firing the MAC-10 over his shoulder, the man scampered into the night. Dark shapes were everywhere, and he clumsily dodged one, only to collide with another.

"Motherfucker!" Rev roared, waving his chattering weapon, hoping for a hit.

Then a charnel-house breath washed over him worse

than anything he had ever smelled, and fiery pain exploded in his groin, moving upward through his belly and deep into his chest. Gutted wide open, Rev tried to scream but only whimpered as red-hot pain filled his world and he fell forever into a bottomless abyss.

Fighting the shuddering truck to a halt, Harlan dived from the vehicle and scrambled underneath for safety. Hiding seemed the smart move. Screams sounded from every direction, and dim headlights came on as another truck lurched from the line. Harlan calculated a jump to the wag, but froze when he saw the truck careen wildly left and right, then accelerate and smash directly into the low stone wall edging the parking lot. A mangled body crashed through the windshield and a winged figure enshrouded the man just as the headlights winked out.

An inhuman figure blocked his view of the wreck, and something grabbed hold of his blaster, crushing hand and weapon into a mangled pulp of flesh and steel. Harlan screamed as he was hauled out from under the chassis. Struggling to escape, the man smacked his face against the frame, knocking himself unconscious. His last conscious thoughts were of a fetid sewer breath and a distant pain in his groin moving ever upward.

The last of the crew now headed for the library, the line of trucks horribly alive with movement. An awful stench tainted the air, and the screams of the dying filled the night. Suddenly, a lone man holding a pistol and brandishing a machete stumbled into view.

"Come get some!" Hal cried, fury contorting his features into a feral mask as he expertly twirled the shiny steel blade about in a glittering whirlwind defense.

"Over here!" Wu-Lang shouted, doing a figure-eight pattern with the M-16 into the sky. The blaster jammed again, and he jerked the bolt to clear the bad round. Frigging predark ammo was for shit!

"Head for the library!" Brian added, shoving shells into the shotgun. When his revolvers became empty, he had simply grabbed the first blaster he found lying on the ground. There were plenty of shells sewn into the strap, enough for a while anyway. However, the man simply refused to notice how sticky the stock was, his mind overwhelmed with the current fight to bother with such trivia.

Hal jumped at the sound of their voices as if startled that anybody else was still alive, then he charged toward them firing his pistol to both sides. But he crossed only a few yards when he dropped to his knees, the machete skittering along the asphalt into the bare shrubbery lining the sidewalk.

Coldly, the others turned their blasters on the latest victim as he was lifted thrashing into the sky. Pistol shots sounded from above, then screams, and then limbs started to fall, closely followed by a bloody torso.

"Get inside!" Wu-Lang screamed, feeling sick to his stomach.

Rifle over his shoulder, Baldy was already tugging on the handle with both hands. "The door's stuck! No, I got it!"

With those words, the door silently swung open and Baldy was dragged inside, the closing door nipping off his fingers as the screaming man desperately clawed at the jamb to stay out of the killing darkness.

Firing their machine guns wildly, the handful of survivors formed a rough circle, keeping their backs tight against one another. It was a plan forged by instincts created by a million years of plains apes learning how to counter a charge by the savage jungle cats.

"They ain't getting us from behind now!" Brian shouted triumphantly over the booming of his shotgun. "Head for the ammo boxes! We'll chill these fuckers yet!"

As they awkwardly scuttled off, a spatter of rain hit the ground exactly where the group had been standing seconds earlier, the asphalt sizzling from contact with the moisture. In stark comprehension, Wu-Lang understood what was happening and cast aside his blaster to frantically run for his life.

"Gutless coward!" Brian spit, training his shotgun on the retreating man.

Soft rain patted down, coating on their hands and faces. Shrill screams of hideous torment sounded as the coldhearts clawed at their dissolving faces while the dark shapes moved among them slashing throats. Moments later, there was nothing alive in the parking lot. The only sounds were the hiss and crackle of the dying embers in the campfire.

Then the echo of running boots sounded from the streets of the ancient city, and the stars winked out as something very large eclipsed the heavens, moving to the sound of snapping canvas.

Chapter Ten

Crackling torches dotted the streets of the ville in reddish light, the illumination reflecting off the honeycombed glass of the many greenhouses. The streets were deserted with every door closed, every window bolted shut, only the murmur of soft voices coming from inside the lower levels of the intact buildings and from underneath the gutted ruins. Beyond the pile of smashed vehicles composing the great wall, sec men watched the sky with blasters in hand as the scintillating beams of the searchlights swept the cloudy sky, endlessly searching for an enemy that would attack without notice. In the far distance, a wolf howled in agony for a lost mate. Cursing under their breaths, grim sec men moved closer to the lights and made sure their weapons were ready for combat.

Cutting through the alleyway between the market place and a partly built greenhouse, Leonard Strichland strode purposefully across the dark plaza heading toward the bright lanterns of the baron's palace. After the revolution, the open area before the converted museum had been painstakingly cleared of structures so that the defenders inside would have a clear field of fire against any attackers. Leonard considered that a practical idea. If the old baron had thought of such things—indeed, if the despot had considered anything other than harshly disciplining his people—then the man might still be in charge of Alphaville instead of a chained prisoner in the dank basement of his former home.

The walls of the predark museum soared twenty yards into the sky, a louvered expanse of granite strips interlocking into a solid homogenous whole of amazing strength. No windows marred the three sides of the predark structure. The entire front had once been a window, but the new baron had bricked up the vulnerable area, both inside and out, giving it a relative stability almost equal to the granite sides. On the roof, sec men steadily patrolled the perimeter of the building, bolt-action longblasters held at quarter-arms.

Secretly, Leonard knew there were also small kegs of black powder with homemade fuses in a locked munitions box up there to drop on invaders. Any attacking force would be met with fierce opposition. Born and bred on the dirty streets of Alphaville, Baron Gunther Strichland didn't make the same mistakes as his dethroned predecessor.

On the ground, sandbags formed a low wall before the double doors, the emblazoned brass marred with dull streaks where soft lead bullets had ricocheted. A half circle of steel I-beams salvaged from the ruins across the Stink River chasm had been welded into tripods to act as a deterrent to attacking wags, or even APCs. Getting past those would take a predark tank. Coils of barbed wire stretched across the ground like dark smoke frozen in time and space. A few strips of stained cloth here and there marked the spots where sec men had thrown the corpses of their fallen comrades onto the wire so they could gain access to the museum and continue the fight to usurp their former leader.

Before being captured alive, Baron ''Mad Jim'' Harvin had unleashed his pet winged muties, but it didn't work. Sergeant Strichland had carefully orchestrated the revolt at first dawn so his troops would be safe from the deadly black bats. Or flying lizards, or whatever the hell the muties were. Leonard had no idea, nor did anybody else, as the creatures only appeared at night and the only folks who got a good view of them died soon afterward, torn to shreds. Not a single one of the creatures had ever been successfully slain.

Leonard walked toward the front doors of the palace so that the guards would see him coming. Five huge men stood behind the sandbags, longblasters over their shoulders, handblasters at their belts. The Elite, the baron called them. The five were sworn to die before allowing invaders inside the home of their baron. To their left and right rested a pair of old muzzle-loading cannons. It had taken two years to unblock the barrels, but the weapons were fully functional now, and the soft cotton bags stacked in the red plastic milk crates were filled with bits of broken glass, bent nails and other tiny scraps of metal. A band of raiders had gotten this far once, and after the cannons roared, nothing remained but bloody clothing and smashed bones. It was the last direct attack.

"Morning, Lieutenant," a sec man said.

"Morning, Sergeant." Leonard smiled, trying not to lose his armload of papers. "Permission to enter, please."

"Granted, sir, as always," the sergeant said, waving him on.

A private pulled open the door and saluted as Leonard walked through. Inside was the mate of the outside cannons, and more sec men standing behind more sandbags. They put aside their card game and snapped to attention.

"Morning, sir. Dropping off a message, or looking for your father?" a grizzled veteran asked, his face mostly composed of scars.

The phrase embarrassed the adopted boy. "The second, Sergeant. Do you know where is the baron?"

"Cellar," said the sec man grimly. "We caught a thief last week. Now he's getting justice."

"One of our own, or a newcomer?"

"Local man. Cobbler. Been here for years."

"Did he lie about the crime?" Leonard asked hopefully. Stealing food was a pardonable crime, and the perpetrator often got no more than a dozen lashes. But lying to the baron was death by the Machine.

The soldier shook his head. "He should have known better."

"Thank you." The boy hurried off, still clutching the portfolio of papers and maps to his chest.

"I hope he toughens up." The private sighed, reclaiming his chair and gathering his cards. "Don't want a momma's boy like Leo there as our baron."

Fanning the cards in his hand, the sergeant shifted them about to hide the straight he had drawn. "Don't be fooled. Boy's still young. But I saw him in the revolt when we charged this place. He took an arrow in the leg and a bullet in the chest and he fought on with his father. Tough as a slut's heart, the both of them."

"Long as he ain't twisted as his old man," the private muttered, laying down a card and drawing a fresh one. "I hate all that screaming in the night."

"Well, got to be worse for them doing the screaming," the other man added wisely.

"Aye, suppose it is." He brushed a hand through his golden crew cut. "Damn, I'm sure glad my girl is a blonde."

SMOKING SLIGHTLY, vegetable-oil lanterns with rope wicks stood in wall niches illuminating the interior. The high vaulted ceiling of the museum was perfect for conducting away the greasy fumes. Hurrying across the terrazzo expanse of the front hall, Leonard turned left and took the main stairs downward, the broad steps some four yards wide. There used to be a brass handrail along the center, but that had been destroyed when the rebels drove an APC down the stairs, chasing the former baron. Caught him, too.

Guards and maids greeted Leonard politely as he hurried along the corridor past the storage room and the armory, past the furnace room and finally the jail. The door was closed, tufts of cloth rimming the jamb of the thick portal, but he could still hear the muted roar of machinery inside and a man pitifully screaming.

Withdrawing a small ring of keys from his pocket, Leonard unlocked the door and entered the deafening charnel house, the air stinking of excrement and exhaust fumes.

"Mercy!" screamed the man hanging from the ceiling by chains. The chains were wrapped about the hanging man's wrists, a trickle of blood flowing down his arms as he struggled to get free.

"Please!" the prisoner wailed, the word barely audible over the muted rumble of the machine directly beneath. A black plume of smoke streamed from its exhaust pipe, and the ceiling was blacker than hell itself from the accumulation of grime from its use.

Squads of somber men in clean uniforms stood about the abattoir watching the suspended victim struggle for life. None of the grim faces were softened by an expression of pity, or even interest.

"Mercy?" Baron Gunther Strichland asked, crossing

his powerful arms across his barrel chest. The red-headed giant towered over the other men, his long fiery red hair moving as if endowed with a will of its own.

"Mercy?" he repeated as if it were a new word never tasted before. "An interesting choice of words for a traitor."

"I am innocent!" the man howled as the chain jerked and once more he was lowered inexorably toward the maw of the churning machine. Between his bare feet, he could see the blur of the interlocking blades whirling at incredible speed. His stomach heaved at the idea of what was happening, but nothing rose into his throat. He hadn't been fed for days in exact preparation for such an eventuality.

"I didn't break the window!"

"No," Gunther said, accepting a silver chalice of cool wine from a busty maid in Army fatigues. "Your son did, and valuable plants were destroyed. Should we punish him instead?"

"Yes! Yes," the man whimpered, rivulets of sweat pouring off his naked body. His toes could feel the vibrations of the Machine in the air. It sent waves of ice through his veins, and the judgement room swirled as he started to faint.

"Not yet, thief," a woman snarled, and threw a bucket of ice water over him.

The shock forced him fully awake, and he squealed like a piglet being dragged to the butcher's block.

"Do you honestly think," Gunther murmured, sipping from the chalice, "that we should kill a child instead?"

"Yes! He did it, not me! Not me!"

With a snarl, the baron dashed the chalice to the concrete floor. "Then you are worse than a thief. You're a coward, as well! Your boy may have done the damage, but you, the adult, hid the fact! By the time we discovered the damage, the sandstorm had killed over half the crops in that greenhouse! How many others may die from lack of food because of your cowardice?''

"Excuse me, High Baron," Leonard said from the doorway.

Furious over the interruption, Gunther turned, his red hair a crimson halo about his distorted features. But when he saw who it was, the man relaxed his posture and his filaments laid down obediently on his wide shoulders.

"Yes, Leonard, what is it?" the baron asked calmly.

The teenager bowed respectfully. "We have a problem."

Gunther turned back to the screaming man. "Then handle it, my son. I'm busy at the moment dispensing justice."

A diplomatic cough. "It is a serious problem, sir."

"Sir, eh?" The baron smiled tolerantly. "Very well, then, let's go." He turned to a sec man. "Lieutenant Kilgore, handle that matter."

A slim, dark, handsome man snapped to attention and briskly saluted. "At once, Baron!"

Gunther reached for the door latch, but Leonard took his arm.

"Father," he whispered softly, glancing at the writhing prisoner, "I know his crime was terrible, unforgivable, the killing of plants, the stealing of food..." He swallowed and his voice faltered.

Baron Strichland rested a hand on the boy's shoulder until he looked up. "Never be afraid of anything. Especially when asking me for a favor. Understood?"

"Yes, my father."

"Is it mercy you wish, for that?" the baron asked, the distaste in his voice painfully clear. "A thief and a liar who places the blame of a crime on his own child?"

"Yes," the boy said forcibly.

Debating the issue, the baron looked directly at the rest of his council. Their opinions were also clear on the matter. The weeping prisoner had drawn his knees to his chest, fighting to keep his flesh away from the churning maw of the wood chipper.

"I can refuse you nothing, my chosen son," the giant said gently. "Mercy it shall be."

Leonard took his father's hand and kissed it. "Thank you, Father."

"Enough," Gunther said, shaking off the embrace. "I'm the baron, not some mucking high priest."

"Sorry."

"Lieutenant Kilgore, show the criminal mercy."

"At once, sir!"

"Come, lad, to my office, where we can talk in private." The baron turned and they left the room.

"Mercy." Kilgore sneered in contempt. "For the likes of you. This is your lucky day."

And so saying, the lieutenant reached inside his camou-colored flak jacket, drew a Colt .45 blaster and fired once. Half of the man's skull was removed by the bullet, blood spraying out in a hideous geyser. Limply, the feet of the warm corpse dropped straight into the blades and disappeared. The crew holding the chains released the tension, and the body dropped without hindrance and a hideous whinnying noise rose as the man was reduced to mincemeat.

"Enough!" Kilgore said after a minute, sliding his blaster away into a predark shoulder holster. "Never waste fuel. Why is that, Private Hanson?"

Caught by surprise, the middle-aged woman snapped to attention. She had been busted four times back to private for not paying attention while on duty, and here it was happening again! "Ah, because the Machine won't run on the alcohol we make, but only on real gasoline."

"That is correct. You there, Corporal, what is the sequence of the mix?"

His mustache merely a wisp of hair across his upper lip, the teenager swallowed and saluted. "Boil the residue twice to remove impurities, then mix him with sand in a one-to-ten ratio. Then add twice-boiled sewage two parts to five. Let it ripen for a week in summer, a month in winter."

"Very good." Kilgore smiled, wiping a tiny droplet of blood off his sleeve. "When he is processed, add the new soil to the contaminated soil of the repaired greenhouse. We may be able to recover some crops from this mess yet."

"Sir, about the child who did the actual damage..."

"He is now a ward of the ville, and upon age will become a sec man trained to kill those who steal food from our bellies." A rue smile. "We do not harm children here, Private. Only thieves and liars."

"Yes, sir," the woman replied, fear a lump of ice in her belly from a carrot she had stolen from the kitchens the previous week.

As THE FATHER and son approached the office on the third floor of the museum, sec men snapped open the door and saluted. The baron waved in passing, and Leonard returned the salute properly.

The office was tremendously huge, covering half of a floor. To the east was a working stone fireplace surrounded by a sunken living room of plush couches. A wooden desk stood in the center of the room, and behind it on the wall was a map of the ville and surrounding lands. The floor was smooth fieldstone dotted with a dozen matching white rugs. To the west was a bookcase made of mirrors and glass shelves, and on display was the first ear of corn grown in the first greenhouse, fancy autofire blasters, all of which worked and were loaded, geodes because they were pretty, hundreds of bottles of liquor and predark wine, a few specially marked bottles expertly poisoned and a small teakwood box nearly full of human ears taken from every man who had ever challenged Strichland to a duel. Assassins simply went into the Machine, and the baron drank a cup of their blood in order to steal their souls and make himself stronger.

As the door closed behind them, the elder Strichland took the chair behind the massive cherry-wood desk and put his boots on the mirror-smooth surface. "Report," he ordered.

"Three people came in yesterday," Leonard said, placing his armload of papers on an empty chair. "But they were chased by only six wolves."

"Bastard birds, or whatever the muties are, have been breeding again," Strichland grumbled, cracking his knuckles, as his hair stirred with impatience. "Every time we find their nest and burn it out, they're back again in a couple of months."

"We may never find the main nest," Leonard stated.

"Obviously." Gunther sneered, his hair coiling in response to his tension. "If it weren't for my searchlights, the things would have destroyed Alphaville months ago. Are the lights in good working order?"

"Yes, Father. Perfect shape. I check them myself every day."

The redhead smiled benignly. "Good lad."

"We could send in more men to search the ruins," Leonard suggested.

Gunther shook his head. "And risk one of them finding the old baron's secret weapons cache and starting a war over the ville? I think not."

"Why did the old baron hide his weapons outside the ville?"

"You've never asked me that question before."

"It never seemed important before," the boy said.

"And now?"

"I...It is my duty to know such things."

The baron placed his boots on the floor with a thump and beamed proudly. "At last, you're taking an interest in ruling our land. Excellent. Baron Harvin did that so in case of a rebellion, he could regroup sec men outside the ville and blast their way back in to seize control."

"But none of the troops stayed loyal."

"A lesson to remember, future baron," the man said sternly. "Always stay on the good side of the troops. That is why a gaudy house was the first thing I built, even before the greenhouses. The sec men go there for free, which makes them happy. None of the farmers' daughters or wives are attacked, which makes them happy, which increases the production of food, which makes everybody happy. These people would willingly march into a rad pit for me!"

And they would someday, too, Gunther added privately. Every last one of the stinking norm bastards, once he had a real son to replace him as baron. That was, if he ever managed to father a true heir and he wasn't saddled with this obedient milksop for the rest of his life.

"Father?" Leonard asked urgently. "Something wrong?"

The middle-aged man smiled gently. "Nothing, my son. Nothing."

Rising from his chair, the baron started to pace the room. "The searchlights, which keep away the muties, also attract more people. Both good things. However, a larger population means more noise, and more activity, which attracts the muties. It's a vicious circle. Our only defense weakens us and makes us more of a juicy target. For ten months, we've been walking the razor's edge. I took the ville from the monster who controlled it before. There are no more random beheadings, no more rape or cannibalism. We have greenhouses and grow enough food for an army. We have trials, and gaudy houses. The population has tripled since I took over. Tripled!"

Gunther stopped at the mirrored wall and toyed with the teakwood box for a moment before replacing it on the shelf. "We have over a thousand people here, son. That's bigger than most predark cities. Clean food, and we burn wood to make charcoal to purify the mountain water. Nobody has gotten ill from the river for months. But we must have those blasters to kill the bats! If the lights should ever fail during an attack, our people would be slaughtered."

"We could use alcohol bombs to set fire to the whole city," Leonard stated, then, seeing his father's darkening face and lashing hair, quickly relented. "Perhaps not."

"Not if we want the weapons. And that has always been the twix, and we must soon decide. The bats or the blasters. It seems we can't have both." Strichland paused, knowing this request wouldn't please his adopted son. But it was time for him to learn that running a ville was often bloody work. "Get the old man."

Leonard stayed in his chair, breathing heavily, then stood and saluted. "I understand. Yes, sir."

Going to the door, Leonard stuck his head outside. Minutes later, two burly sec men dragged a scrawny man into the room. They efficiently tied the near corpse to a stout wooden chair, and upon a signal from Leonard went back outside.

Drawing a revolver, Gunther extracted every bullet but one. Spinning the cylinder, he aimed and pulled the trigger. Harvin jumped involuntarily at the click.

The baron spun it again. "My patience is gone, old man. Tell me where the weapons are."

"Never," the former baron said.

"Then where are the bats hidden, or how can we control them? Colored flags? Special clothes? Some odor, hand signals, whistles?"

For a brief instant, Gunther thought the former baron registered surprise, but then realized it was just a tick brought on by the starvation and torture.

"Tell me!" Strichland shouted, dry firing the revolver again and again.

"Never tell you." Harvin cackled, smiling toothlessly. "Took my ville, but you can't keep it. Keep it. That's a joke. Hee-hee."

Leonard lashed out and slapped the bound man, teeth and spittle spraying across the room. "Obey my father, or die!"

Bleeding freely, the former baron sat there with his head tilted. Then ever so slowly he turned to stare at the hated usurper, the fire of reason burning bright in his face.

"You have trained the little bastard well, thief. He's a most fitting son for a traitor," Harvin said in a clear voice. "And while you managed to steal the ville, you'll never keep it."

Then madness welled within the man. After so many months, he simply couldn't hold the secret in any longer. "Only Harold and I know how to control the guardians!" he shrieked insanely. "And Harold's dead! Which leaves me. Eventually, the muties will get past whatever you're using to stop them, and then it's your day in the barrel.

"You lose," he said, sneering in triumph. "Can't keep it."

Father and son stared in astonishment at each other, then both slowly smiled.

"Excellent." Gunther sighed. "I knew keeping that gimp around would pay off."

"Thank you so much for helping us," Leonard said, feeling a wonderful rush of power from the terror of the old man.

"No, impossible," Harvin whispered, going deathly pale. "You told me months ago that Harold was dead. Showed me his corpse!"

"A corpse," Gunther corrected with a smirk. "An invader who resembled your friend, nothing more."

"No..."

"Harold lives," Gunther stated, coming closer. "And now that I know he has the secret, I have no need of you." Cracking the cylinder of the blaster, the baron loaded every hole.

Sweat began to run off the man. Harvin pleaded,

"No, wait! I can tell you where the weapon caches are! And how to get past the traps!"

"Don't care." Closing the blaster with a snap of the wrist, Gunther spun the cylinder for no reason, placed the muzzle to the old man's chest and shot him dead.

Feeling ill, Leonard stared at the corpse. He had been an enemy of the ville and deserved to die. It was a job to be done, and he did what he had to. Yet there was an odd, almost sexual energy to the act of murder. This contradiction confused him greatly.

"Send out a dozen...no, twenty sec men," the baron ordered. "And tell them not to come back until they have Harold in custody, alive and unharmed. Mind you, he's useless chilled."

"The sarge may be outside the walls," Leonard suggested. "We've had trouble finding him before."

"Then send fifty men, with bolt-action rifles from my private armory and ten live rounds."

"Ten!"

"We can afford it. Besides, if he is out among the muties, our troops will have to defend themselves, and every dead mutie is a point in our favor." Then he added, "But first and most importantly, find Harold!"

HAROLD MOVED through the dank pipeway with the surety of a bullet in a barrel. Feeder pipes lined the main conduit, with rusty water dripping constantly from the corroded openings. His footing was treacherous as the curved walls were slimy beneath his hands, but this was the way back home, and every step made his heart feel lighter. He had something better than blasters. He had a doctor's bag. That saved lives. Lots better than killing. The voices in his head agreed wholeheartedly and complimented him constantly, sometimes painfully loud.

He had really tried to take the big blaster off the top
of the war wag, but he couldn't figure out how to free
the ammo belt. After dragging it behind him for a block,
Harold had tossed it away. Besides, the long dangling
belt was too noisy. Never sneak in here with that.

Scampering noises sounded from the darkness ahead
of him, and Harold quickly reached inside his shirt and
blew on the silent whistle. He felt a stab inside his ears
as always, and the scampering sounds quickly departed.
The man had no idea how the broken whistle could
chase away rats. The voices suggested they had a better
range of hearing than humans, but his chest started to
pound as he struggled to understand the odd words, and
the voices soon ceased, replaced by soothing silence.

After a while, the drain branched into a full six-way
intersection, and Harold carefully jumped across the gap
into the next tunnel. Staying to the left, he counted
aloud on fingers and toes until reaching his right pinkie
toe, and climbed a ladder set into the concrete wall.
Pushing aside the iron grating, he eased out of the storm
drain and glanced around to make sure nobody could
see him.

Over by the big tunnel that went under the dead river,
twin searchlights swept the sky. The air was foggy with
the reflection of the powerful beams. Climbing out, the
hunchback eased the grating quietly back into position,
then, staying close to the wall of cars, he kept low until
finding the faded orange bumper sticker. There were no
others like it anywhere on the wall. One had been similar, and in a fit of brilliance he had removed the bumper
so as not to become confused between the two. But then
Harold spent days trying to figure out if he'd removed
the correct sticker. Life was so confusing sometimes,

and the voices in his head didn't always help, even though they said different.

Grabbing the handle of the Pontiac, he eased the back door open, lifting it slightly so the metal wouldn't squeal. Stepping inside, he carefully locked it behind him and started the labyrinthine return to the ville on the other side. From this point onward, Harold knew he was safe. Nobody could follow him through the wall. Not even the rats.

Chapter Eleven

The cloudy yellow sky was just beginning to lighten in color, slashes of fiery orange streaking across the murky gray atmosphere as dawn struggled into existence. The front door to the government building opened on freshly oiled hinges, and Ryan stepped onto the broken sidewalk.

"Good enough," he declared as the rest of the companions joined him outside. They had spent the night in hurried preparation, blocking the exposed stairwell solid with office furniture, doing the same to the elevator shaft and nailing all of the office doors shut, and driving extra nails through the middle of the wooden panels so that anybody trying to crash through would be badly stabbed. Forming a semicircle across the lobby was a six-foot-tall barricade of metal file cabinets stuffed with books, and backed with the couches. It made a pretty good fire wall, and helped muffle any lights or noises. There was still a lot of work to be done, but it was a good start. Purely precautionary, but experience taught hard lessons over the years. Better safe than dead, as the Trader always used to say.

Unfortunately, Dean was no better by morning, if anything a bit worse, and the necessity of reclaiming the med kit had been escalated to a priority.

Walking over to the garage, Jak knelt on the sandy ground, running his fingers over the faint indentations across the ground. A breeze ruffled his snowy hair as the Cajun stood and walked into the street.

"One man, big," he said. "Walks funny, mebbe wounded. Came from down block."

"He came from the ville," Ryan answered curtly. "Can you track the Hummer?"

Snorting, Jak glanced over a shoulder, his ruby-red eyes deadly serious. "Track through monsoon for Dean."

"Who's to stay?" Krysty asked, shifting her backpack.

"J.B. and Doc," said Ryan, sliding the Steyr off his shoulder and checking the clip.

Ramming the cylinder back into the blaster, he slapped the bolt. "J.B., think you can fix that skylight before we get back with the wag?"

"No problem," the Armorer replied, half of a cigar clenched between his teeth. He discovered the cigar in a humidor in some executive's office, and for the hundredth time since the previous night he started to light the thing, but forced his hand away. "Found some replacement glass for the windows and such in the basement. Won't take me more than an hour."

"Good. Doc, take the roof as lookout. Stay sharp, but don't fire at anything, even another of those damn muties."

"Until young Master Dean is mobile," Doc rumbled, "we shall be the most devout of cowards."

"J.B., when the roof is done, spell Mildred. Make her get some sleep. She's got to be rested and alert."

"Just in case," J.B. said. "I understand. No prob. Get the med kit and chill the bastard who stole it from under our noses."

"That's my plan."

"Wind is increasing," Krysty warned as thunder rumbled softly in the mottled heavens. "And the damn tracks are half-gone already."

"Got go," Jak urged, stepping away.

"J.B., Doc, if we have any live company when we return," Ryan said, his voice implying it was highly unlikely, "we'll use the standard a-b-c codes."

"Gotcha." J.B. clearly remembered when they first invented the alphabet code. If one of their group showed up with strangers, how could the rest know if the new-comers were okay or armed aggressors? The solution was as simple as the problem was basic. If the companions identified themselves, or the stranger, with any name starting with the letter *a*—Alfred, Alexander, anything like that—it meant there was no danger. All clear. If they used a *b* name, it meant bad news. They were being forced to comply with the folks they were with. And if they used a *c* name, it meant the whole thing was crap, kill everybody, including the companion.

"Godspeed, sir," Doc said solemnly. "My prayers go with you."

"I don't think your God would approve of my plans for today," Ryan said, turning to the street.

Down the block, Krysty stood attentively on the corner, while Jak was inspecting the crumpled ruin of a mailbox.

"Freshly sideswiped," he said, then studying the ground and faced north. "Hummer went this way."

Spreading out so they wouldn't present a group target to any snipers, the companions followed the main street until Ryan found a clear set of tracks in some smooth stretch of sand.

"East," he said, the butt of the Steyr resting on his hip.

Cutting through a brick-lined alleyway, they disturbed a nest of green-skinned lizards who turned as pale as sand and scattered at their intrusion. Climbing over a low mound of rubble from a fallen cinder-block wall, they proceed across a bare parking lot, the ancient black macadam partially hidden under the windblown sand and tufts of dead weeds sprouting from the many cracks in the black surface. The lot was edged with a short concrete wall, the kiosk smashed under a fallen telephone pole. No tracking skills were needed to spot the fresh tire tracks in the churned masonry.

"Did he know the Hummer was tough enough to take the wall," Ryan asked, "or was he driving with the lights off?"

"Headlight switch is clearly marked on the dashboard," Krysty said, watching the rooftops for any suspicious movements. "Especially at night, they glow. No wait, shit, I busted one of them yesterday."

"Even so, scared we following," Jak offered, not sounding convinced by the suggestion. Then he pointed. "Ammo box."

Ryan walked over and picked up the green metal container. It was from the redoubt. "Must have lost it when he took the wall."

"Rolled down street. Couldn't do if driving all over place," Jak said thoughtfully. It was an unusually long speech for the normally monosyllabic Cajun. "Damage to box?"

Ryan turned it over in his hands. "Dents and scrapes, but it wasn't hit by the Hummer if that's what you mean. Army ammo boxes are tough, but the five-ton wag would flatten this like a soup can."

Resting a hand on her canteen to stop it from bouncing as she walked, Krysty started toward the intersection. "Then he went this way."

For the next ten blocks, they proceeded quickly, following a set of disappearing tire tracks to a scraped wall, and through the center of a department store, the huge glass window on one side stoved in, and the other side busted out.

"Driving like a lunatic," Ryan observed, treading carefully over the glass shards. "Must have known he was safe by now. We only had the one wag."

"Afraid somebody else might see him?" Krysty suggested. "Mebbe he's a solo who just wandered by, or a rogue living in the ruins, avoiding the sec men of the ville."

"Excited. First time stealing," Jak said, brushing off his knees. "Kid, mebbe."

"Who got past a trap from J.B.?"

The Cajun shrugged in reply.

Too many questions, not enough info. Ryan hated mysteries. Give him a good standup fight any day. Checking a side street, the Deathlands warrior saw that the soft surface was smooth and untouched. "Nothing," he reported to the others.

"Over here," Krysty said, stepping through the ruins of a wooden fence. "Our thief was driving like he was being chased."

"Muties?" Jak suggested, staying close to the woman.

"Or the wolves. Mebbe he was driving like this so the wolves could follow him to the muties," Ryan said slowly, keeping a watch on a dark hole in a broken wall. "Give them something to feed on and leave him alone."

"Like pets?" Jak looked disgusted.

"Not all muties are bad," Krysty said sharply, her animated hair moving about her shoulders and face.

Following the tire tracks through the sand, Ryan took point, and, rounding a corner found himself before a block-long three-story building. It was a school of some kind with a tilted flag pole standing in the front, and an empty parking lot to the east side. The front and side of the structure was marked with bullet holes, the ground churned from explosives, but smoothed again by the wind. The windows were gone, blackened holes with the sky visible where a roof should have been.

Taking refuge around the corner, they used the mirror in turns to study the building. The tire tracks of the Hummer led straight to the side of the building where a gaping doorway stood more than large enough to drive the military wag through.

"Garage?" Jak asked.

Ryan nodded. "Looks like."

"I think we found them," Krysty said confidently. "Looks like a public school. Definitely not private. Those are always surrounded by high walls to keep out the riffraff."

"Must have been a hell of a fight," Ryan added, imagining the battle in his mind. "Blasters, Molotov cocktails and some C-4 bombs. Went hand to hand over there."

"Are those arrows in that fence?"

"Check. Somebody ran out of ammo."

"Five, six months ago," Jak mused. "Depending on rain."

"Think the defenders were fighting the muties?"

Baring his teeth, Ryan exhaled and tried not to think of the passing of time. "Muties? Well, I sure as hell hope there's nothing else in this hellhole that can attack a third-story window.''

"Don't seem to be any sec men on patrol," Krysty commented, angling the mirror. "Area looks empty."

"No snipers or lookouts," Jak agreed, studying the rooftops while unfolding the foil on one of his precious last sticks of Army chewing gum. He folded it in two and started to chew with his mouth closed. Breakfast had been cold wolf, and his tongue tasted as if something had died there.

"Let's take no chances," Ryan told them, the hairs on the back of his neck stirring. He slicked them down with a palm. Something was wrong here; he could feel it. He just didn't know what exactly. "Tracks leading to a burned-out school with nobody around. Smells bad to me. Could be a trap, and we know these folks are tricky. We'll do a tight perimeter sweep, single file, two-yard spread. If there's no activity, we go inside."

"If this is a trap," Krysty stated, taking her weapon in a double hand grip, "then they'll want us alive, which gives us a tremendous edge in chilling them. Because we're only interested in the kit. Don't give a rat's ass about them."

Jak held up a restraining hand. "Wait for wind," he said slowly. "Cover sound of boots. Wait...now."

Moving fast through the ruins outside the parking lot, the trio kept low. A lizard eating a tarantula darted away at their passage, but nothing else responded to their presence. No barking dogs, no gunshots, no cries of alarm.

Reaching a ditch opposite the garage, they slid in and splashed quietly through the brackish runoff water, which reeked of sulfur. Using the mirror first, then chancing a direct look, they could see the Hummer parked amid the cold ashes and burned timbers of the building. The wag was a lot more battered than when they had last seen it; the sides scraped, the radio antenna gone, with the spare tire flat and hanging loose on the rim bolted to the chassis.

Ryan pointed left and right. The others spread out and approached the garage from converging directions. At the doorway, they took positions, listening for sounds, then charged in with blasters at the ready. Jak took the grease pit, Krysty the office, Ryan the tool room. The garage was completely deserted.

Chewing steadily, Jak went under the chassis of the wag, while Krysty stood guard and Ryan circled the wag, looking for trip wires. In the cargo area, he found the longblasters from the pawnshop, but the med kit and the big M-60 were nowhere in sight, which was expected. Those items were the most valuable.

In a few moments, Jak came back out. "Clean. You?"

"Same," Ryan reported gruffly. "The thief just took what he could carry and left. Probably planning on coming back and getting the rest. We can't wait for that. Could be days before he returns."

"How did he start it?" Krysty asked. "Ah, took the radio fuse and inserted it into the ignition. That was stupe."

"Yeah, might have shorted out the engine and blown the whole electrical system," Ryan countered. "It's what you do in an emergency situation."

"Mebbe was for him," Jak suggested pensively.

Sliding in the proper fuse, Ryan hit the ignition and checked the gauges on the dashboard. "At least we know why he abandoned it here. She's out of gas."

Krysty gratefully slid off her backpack, the contents

sloshing as it hit the ground. "We got that covered. Doc was smart to hide the extra fuel in the lav."

She refueled the wag, as the others kept guard, watching the shop and the steel girders above them for suspicious movement. Some yellow papers blew among the wreckage, then lifted away on a breeze into the sky.

"Done," the redhead said, capping the container and placing it in the rear with the rifles.

"Drive?" Jak asked.

"We're too close to the river," Ryan said. "May as well leave the wag here out of sight of the sec men on the wall. Krysty, take all of the fuses and let's do a perimeter sweep for footprints."

Sure enough, only a few yards away they located tracks marked with black soot from the burned-out school. Following the footprints across a football field and through a dry creekbed, they reached the edge of the river. The clouds overhead were a vile green, slashed with fiery orange. If a storm was coming, it was going to be hell on Earth, and that made them move faster.

Reaching the concrete dockyards, they noted that the sluggish river from yesterday was now churning madly, whitecaps crashing on the embankments as the water rushed into the east.

"Scuffle, no, slipped," Jak corrected, scrutinizing the stony concrete. "Check water."

Krysty leaned over the edge. "No sign of a... Wait, there's the M-60! Oh crap, the barrel's bent. Must have hit something on the way down."

"Useless," Jak agreed, scanning the river. "No sign kit. Must kept."

Feeling the pressure on him, Ryan glanced east and west along the river, both directions equally barren of tracks. Every second made the thief farther away, and increased the risk for Dean. Fast decisions and fast action were called for. And if he had to gamble, so be it. This close to the ville, the logical place to look was the tunnel. Maybe he was a refugee, or a guard. The med kit could be only a hundred yards away in the hands of the sec men, pawing through the instruments wondering what they were.

"Let's go," Ryan said, heading toward the east.

Following the embankment, they reached the concrete apron that capped the top of the tunnel they had observed the previous day. Long ago, a fence of some kind had skirted the apron to keep the curious from going over the side. But nowadays there were only a few gutted metal posts to show where the safety barrier had once stood.

Crawling on hands and knees to reduce their exposure, the companions started to creep across the apron when Krysty paused and snapped her fingers for attention. She jerked her head to the left, and they followed her toward a low rise in the concrete.

An iron grille covered a hole in the concrete. On the other side was a pipe with a ladder going down and out of sight. But more importantly, off to the side, a smudged footprint was cut in two by the grating. Ryan touched it with a fingertip, and the ash came off easily.

"Ha," Jak whispered in triumph.

Looking it over closely, Ryan couldn't see an exterior locking mechanism, or even hinges. Sliding the sling of his rifle over a shoulder, Ryan braced himself and tried to lift the grating, but it refused to budge. Krysty and Jak joined him at the task, and the trio put their backs into it. But the grille didn't move an inch. The companions backed off a few yards.

"That's where he went," Ryan said bitterly. "But without explosives we're not getting in. Either it weighs a ton, or else there's some trick to holding it in place. Magnetic seal, mebbe. Or hydraulics."

"Six inches of thick metal, I'm not sure even a gren would do the trick," Krsty countered. "Plas-ex, sure. But J.B. has all of that."

Ryan frowned. "Didn't think we'd need any on a hunt."

"Window no good," Jak said, jerking a thumb. "Use front door."

After a minute, Ryan nodded his agreement. There didn't seem to be any other way into the tunnel without alerting the whole ville to their presence. The thief had effectively blocked any possible pursuit from this direction.

Going to their bellies, the companions crawled forward over the predark concrete, the rough material scratching at their clothes and scraping exposed skin. They stopped at the edge when voices could be heard, men complaining about eating vegetables and some bitch named Patrica. Gently putting down his rifle, Ryan unearthed the plastic mirror and looked around, then withdrew.

"Same as yesterday," he mouthed. "Two guards armed with muzzle-loading longblasters, one with a handblaster on his belt. Searchlights on either side behind a sandbag wall. No sign of the med kit."

Krsty looked at the low buildings nearby, and discounted them. The thief couldn't live that close to the ville and stay hidden for very long. And he headed straight here, so the med kit was in the ville somewhere. Probably in the hands of the baron by now, or whoever ruled the place. They knew nothing of what was on the other side of the wall.

"If they don't have it," Krysty whispered, "then where did the thief go?"

"Let's ask," Jak suggested, drawing a gren from a pocket, a predark pineapple from WWII. The color coding showed it was a concussion grenade, used for distractions and evasions. Useless for battle, as the kill range was less than a yard, it was perfect for taking prisoners.

"Might lose one," the Cajun said callously, wiggling the pin free. "Mebbe two, but only need one."

Considering the matter, Ryan reluctantly vetoed the idea. "Still too damn noisy. If there are more guards inside the tunnel, we'll have a major fight, with reinforcements coming from the ville. We have got to be quiet."

"I say jump them," Krysty said, drawing a sleek stiletto from her boot. "Toss a blaster far down the road, and when they start forward to investigate, we take them from behind. Knife in the lungs and nobody makes a sound."

"Can't breathe, can't scream," Jak agreed, nodding.

"Sounds good." Ryan drew his panga, the curved blade streaked with dried blood from the previous night's interrupted dinner. The sight shocked the man, as he had never gone so long before without cleaning the weapon. He had to take his mind off Dean and concentrate on killing the sec men. Then a familiar rumble sounded from the ruins, and a horn beeped in warning.

"Shit," Ryan whispered. "Convoy!"

The distant rumble of engines became louder, until around the corner lumbered an old WWII jeep jammed full of men. Behind it was a flatbed truck piled with mattresses, and lastly a battered U.S. Mail truck, the driver wearing a gas mask.

"Exhaust-pipe leak?" Krysty guessed.

Scowling, Ryan said nothing, and Jak continued to unwrap the electrical tape from the handle of the gren.

The convoy of predark vehicles pulled to a ragged stop in front of the tunnel, and the drivers got out. The tunnel guards walked over to greet the newcomers, and soon the two groups were smoking pipes and swapping canteens. From the reactions, some of the containers didn't contain water. The desert breezes carried away most of the conversation, with only scraps audible to the companions.

"...bodies slashed to ribbons..."

"...blasters..."

"...muties had a real party last night..."

"...enough for a new greenhouse..."

His ruby eyes going wide, Jak curled a lip in disgust. Krysty turned slightly pale, and Ryan felt sick to his stomach. The local baron was using people as fertilizer in greenhouses? Part of him acknowledged the intelligence of the notion, turning liabilities into assets, but the whole thing was a bit too close to cannibalism for him.

Ryan motioned for a retreat, and the companions crawled back to the river some fifty yards away, where they could converse in private.

"Gaia, eating their own dead," Krysty said.

With a curt hand motion, Ryan interrupted. "Doesn't matter. This is even better than questioning the guards. This is our way in and out of the ville. Everybody agrees the thief must have sold the kit to the baron, right?" Brisk nods answered the question. "Okay, then, so do we. Here's the plan."

"HEY, HARRY," a driver called out, leaning his long-blaster against a truck, the hot engine under the battered hood ticking loudly as it cooled. "You gotta see this!"

Puffing on his corncob pipe, Harry started over as Trevor began to unfold a glossy sheet of paper. "Whatcha got, Trevor?"

"Found this on the wall of a brake shop. Not bad, eh?"

A smile growing wide, Harry gazed at the naked woman, dressed in lace and bound in leather. He whistled in appreciation. "Goddamn, that's hot!"

"'Darla Crane,'" the driver read off the back. "Gotta love them redheads."

"Nyah, blondes do it for me," George said.

"Long as they don't carry knives," Phil added, leaning against the tiled wall and tapping his pipe out in a palm. "Pass her over, boys, give me a gander."

"Just don't drool." Harry laughed, ambling closer.

"And give it back!" Trevor added angrily.

Just then, the sound of a roaring engine broke the silence of the predark ruins.

"Another one of ours coming in?" George asked.

Dropping the poster, Phil grabbed his blaster and cocked the hammer. Only the Wolf Pack got bolt-action blasters, and nobody had autofires anymore. But these muzzle-loaders still killed at a hundred paces, even if they did make enough smoke to blind a man.

"Ours?" Trevor asked, drawing his revolver. As a driver, he got special considerations from the baron. "Hell, no. We're lucky to have these three rolling at the same time. Damn rust buckets are always breaking down."

The noise drastically increased, and a huge vehicle erupted around the corner, sand and dust spraying off the tires as it spun in a circle in the intersection. The driver seemed to be lost, confused or insane.

"This way!" George called out, buttoning his fatigues while waving a hand. "Run for the tunnel. We'll hold off the wolves!"

Obediently, the wag started forward and they caught sight of the driver, an albino with snow-white hair and eyes like rubies.

"Mutie!" Henry screamed fearfully.

Now the driver spun the vehicle in a figure-eight pattern, kicking up a tremendous dust cloud. The sec men covered their faces with neckerchiefs as the desert wind blew the choking cloud over the tunnel opening.

Then the driver slammed on the brakes, the nose of the wag dipping toward the ground and the wheels squealing in protest. As it bounced to a halt, the albino drew his mammoth blaster, the long barrel gleaming in the dim daylight. The driver fired twice, the sounds echoing down the tunnel. Oddly, the slugs hit the tunnel wall, cracking the tiles but nothing more. The pale stranger stomped on the accelerator, the big wag spinning its tires in the sand, raising an even bigger cloud than before as it sped away, zigzagging wildly back and forth down the road.

Leveling the museum-piece rifle, Harry eased back the iron hammer, checked the flint and pulled the trigger all in one smooth motion. Flame and smoke thundered from the pitted muzzle of the two-yard-long blaster. In spite of the moving target, the miniball scored a direct hit on the military wag, but only ricocheted off the armored side. Then the wag took a corner and was gone.

"You muck-eating idiot!" Phil cursed, slapping down the flintlock rifle. "He wasn't going to stop with you shooting at him!"

"He was a mutie!" Harry replied hotly. "Whiter than milk! Probably a stickie from the waist down, or something even worse!"

"Don't care if he was part blood rat. Stop the wag, then kill the driver, fool! How many times have I told you that?"

"Son of a bitch!" George coughed, brushing out his bushy beard. "Let's go get the bastard!"

"No need to chase him," Phil said, holstering his revolver. "He can hide from the wolves during the day, but when night falls and the bats start hunting, he'll come crawling back. Tomorrow, his ass is ours."

"And then we'll make him pay," Harry added grimly.

"Yeah." Wiping the sand off his pockmarked face, George gave a guttural laugh. "They don't all have to be alive. Baron needs corpses, too."

Beating the dust off his caked clothes, Trevor started to agree with the gate guards, when he heard a metallic creak. Turning fast, revolver steady at his hip, the sec man blinked a few moments to clear his sight. Nothing seemed unusual or misplaced. Then he could have sworn that his mail truck moved slightly. He walked over and yanked open the doors.

Human corpses were piled haphazardly on the floorboards of the vehicle, bones and organs exposed, loose limbs and hands lying in the corners so badly had the winged muties clawed the bodies to pieces. Sprawled on top was an intact male corpse without an eye, and a redhead female dressed in military coveralls who didn't appear mauled at all. Trevor studied the curve of her shapely ass for a moment before abruptly slamming the door.

Climbing into the cab, he pumped and throttled the

engine a few shots to get the big-block V-8 firing on the alcohol fuel. The engine finally caught, and he started to roll into the dark tunnel.

"Damn, I got to get to the gaudy house fast," he muttered to himself, pulling the gas mask from a bag on his belt and sliding in over his head. "Been too long without quim when the stiffs start looking good."

AS THE CORPSE-FILLED truck began to move, Krysty rolled off Ryan and both drew their blasters. Crawling over the dead, she looked out the tiny rearview window. The opening of the tunnel shrank in their wake. Dimly seen through the billowing dust clouds, the guards were searching the ground for their dropped cigs.

Ryan tied his eye patch on and pulled a few strands of his black hair loose that got caught in the knot.

"Hope Jak is okay," Krysty said softly.

"We would have heard them boasting if not," Ryan noted in a whisper, retrieving his Steyr from underneath a headless torso. "Okay, we give this convoy a few minutes until we're near the middle of the tunnel. These things are long, sometimes a quarter mile in length. Water damage should rough both ends, but the middle will be smooth. Once the tires start humming, we go."

"At least he's not going very fast," she stated. "Won't hurt much jumping from this crawling can."

"Agreed."

The redhead jiggled the handle on the door. "Locked," she reported. "No surprise. Probably don't want folks robbing the dead of blasters and such."

"Ever hear of a baron who did?"

"Only your family," she whispered, trying to stand but the ceiling was too low. Krysty debated sitting or kneeling, and settled for crouching on her heels. The blood and the guts didn't bother her much. It was the warmth of the fresh corpses, suggesting a terrible mockery of life. Under her breath, she uttered a short prayer to Gaia. During this, the bouncing of the rough road diminished and the tires began to softly hum under the truck.

Patiently, Ryan gave her the moment, then asked, "Ready?"

"Go ahead," she said, covering her ears with her palms.

Placing a hand against the roof as a brace, Ryan aimed the 9 mm SIG-Sauer at the back door of the vehicle, when the truck jounced through a deep pothole. The blaster coughed softly, blowing out the aft window in a loud crash of glass.

"What the fuck was that?" demanded a voice from the other side of the front wall.

The element of surprise gone, Ryan spun fast, estimating three feet off the floor and two feet from the left, then fired again twice more. The corpses and interior of the truck strobed from the flash of the shots. In response, a startled gasp, then wet burbling noises came from the front of the wag. Without a pause, Ryan put another round through the passenger side of the vehicle. The truck started to zigzag wildly, began to slow and abruptly stopped, throwing the companions and the corpses forward into a bloody pile.

Forcibly extracting himself, Ryan kicked open the back door and jumped to the ground. Krysty joined him in a heartbeat.

"Can't chance hiding," he decided. "We're in a tunnel with zero cover and nowhere to run."

The redhead pulled a knife into view. "Then we chill the bastards."

Ryan grunted agreement. Racing around to the driver's-side door, he yanked it open and hauled out the dead man behind the wheel. Climbing into the cab, he fumbled in the darkness for the keys, but they weren't in the ignition anymore. When he got shot, the driver had to have yanked them loose.

Ahead of them down the tunnel, the taillights of the flatbed truck flared brightly red as the brakes were applied.

"He's seen us," Krysty warned, sliding into the passenger seat.

"Working on it," Ryan muttered, scrounging madly about on the floor. Something metallic came under his fingers and pain cut into his thumb. He cursed and brushed it aside. Bastard pulltop from a can! Then a jingling noise sounded as he touched something metallic, loose and on a ring.

"Got them," Ryan said, sitting upright.

Fumbling a bit, he tried a key in the ignition, but it didn't fit. Carefully, sliding that down the ring, he cupped it in his palm to keep it out of the way and tried the next. That key was close, but not quite the correct size. It went in, but not all the way. Probably the key for the back door. The next key was huge and would never fit in the ignition switch.

In the darkness ahead of them, a soft beeping sounded as the brake lights on the truck winked out and the vehicle began backing their way.

"They're coming," Krysty said, patting her pockets for matches or a lighter to help him see. She found a matchbox, but it proved to be empty.

Closing his eye to concentrate, Ryan tried another— too small. The next he passed on, as the stubby key was round and the slot for the switch was long and thin. What the hell did this bastard have so many keys for?

Blaster in hand, the woman opened her door and put one leg out. "Thirty yards," she announced, holding the blaster in both hands and resting the barrel on the window frame, assuming a firing stance.

Lots of keys remained on the ring, but they were out of time. "Last one," he said. "Then we run for it."

Jabbing the worn key toward the slot, he was shocked when it smoothly slid into place. Stomping on the accelerator, Ryan turned the ignition and the warm engine roared into life. Snapping on the headlights, he angled the wag away from the wall and started to creep forward. Krysty closed her door, but kept the S&W .38 out the window in case of trouble.

The truck ahead of them didn't slow, so Ryan beeped the horn. The toot produced was pitifully weak, most likely that way even before the centuries robbed it of power, so Ryan pounded on the horn a few more times. Feeble as it was, the other driver had to have heard the musical squeaks because he stopped the backward progress of the flatbed, and as they came dangerously close, the other truck began to roll forward.

"Thinks we stalled," Ryan guessed, easing the tension in his arms and hands.

"These old engines probably do it constantly," Krysty said, placing the blaster in her lap for fast access.

"Well, we were lucky with this truck," Ryan observed, shifting uncomfortably in the seat. The bullet hole had forced out a spring that was digging into his ribs, annoying as hell. "Can't chance that again with the flatbed. Must have three guys or more riding shotgun. And if they see us, we're in for a fight."

The tunnel gently curved to the left. Ryan had always

wondered why long tunnels did that until Mildred explained it to him. The angle was a break-slope, designed to ease the rush of water charging along the tunnel should there be a midspan break.

"Only three," Krysty said resolutely. "We can take them."

"Can't chance it," Ryan countered. "Getting that med kit is our top priority. If we get caught, Dean could be dead before we could escape."

"He'll be fine. He's tougher than a nail."

"Dean's a survivor," Ryan said, offering his highest compliment.

"We have mebbe ten or fifteen minutes before we reach the end of this tunnel. We have to come up with a plan."

"Yeah, I know," Ryan told her, shifting gears as the curve gently straightened. "I'll have something by then. Mebbe we could— Fireblast!"

Up ahead, faint orange daylight streamed into the tunnel, and tiny figures were walking around on the ground near what resembled a machine-gun nest and a concrete barricade.

Chapter Twelve

Standing guard on the roof of the federal building, Doc checked his windup pocket chron. The timepiece said noon, but the sky above beguiled the fact with streaming yellow clouds streaked with lambent red and blotchy with purple. Even the lizards in the streets seemed to know a bad storm was approaching, as they dug holes in the sand and collapsed the openings upon themselves.

Careful not to pinch his fingers, J.B. lowered the sheet of Plexiglas into the skylight frame. The janitor's closet had been a windfall of material, including replacement glass for the windows and skylight. Unfortunately, the silicon putty had long ago turned into a dried brick, but he had an answer for that problem.

"How's it look?" the Armorer asked, extracting a candle from the bag at his feet. Crushing a pellet of pyrotab so it burst into flame, he lit the wick before the chemical compound burned itself out.

Standing nearby, Doc removed his gaze from the ville around them and studied the repair job. "Good," he finally said, the Heckler & Koch G-12 resting in the crook of his arm.

Rifles weren't his forte, but as a rooftop sentry he needed something a lot quieter and with greater range than his hog-leg .44 LeMat. Dean's caseless rifle fit the bill perfectly, even though this was the last reload. A hundred rounds and the blaster was dead.

"Very good, in fact. That soap you smeared on the inside of the sheet makes it seem sandblasted just like the others."

Tilting the candle, J.B. carefully dribbled the melting wax along the edge of the glass, using a stick to push it into place. He just nodded, concentrating on his work. This window needed to resemble the others in the skylight so that nothing and nobody could tell this was where Dean had fallen through.

"It will last for months if the weather holds."

"More than sufficient," Doc agreed, as he fought back a yawn. "The flask is still half-full. Some more coffee?"

"Hell, yes," J.B. said, starting a second pass over the frame. It had been a long night moving their supplies over to this building, then erasing every trace of the work, using brooms to sweep away their tracks in the sand.

There came the single crack of a blaster.

J.B. dropped the candle and rotated on his heels, his Uzi out and ready. "Muties?" he demanded.

"Skylight," Doc remarked, shouldering the HK G-12.

"Come again?" J.B. demanded, sliding the safety back on his weapon.

"Disguising our location is a logical precaution, agreed? However, I decided to augment the strategy by offering any possible hunters an alternate locale for investigation."

"Ah, you shot out another skylight," J.B. stated, then he glanced about. "Where?"

Doc pointed. "There, a few blocks over. A most prudent expenditure of ammunition, I can assure you."

"I agree," J.B. said with a smile. "But do you honestly think the muties might be smart enough to recall that Dean fell through a skylight, and will check out the other instead?"

"Ryan often remarked that the Trader stated when you underestimate the enemy, what you really do is overestimate yourself."

"Sure sounds like the Trader." J.B. laughed, then paused and stared hard at the streets below. A dust cloud was coming their way. "Incoming."

The two men moved to the corner of the roof and studied the approaching vehicle.

"The Hummer, I see," Doc said, frowning. "And, pray tell, who is that riding with our young Mr. Lauren?"

J.B. scowled. "Beats me. Let's go and find out."

"STOP HERE," Wu-Lang snapped, his blaster pressed hard into Jak's side. The Cajun didn't reply, but brought the Hummer to a stop a few stores down the street from the pawnshop.

"Hello!" a voice called out from the roof.

Trying to hide the blaster, Wu-Lang craned his neck, glancing around. Nobody was visible.

"Hello down there," the voice said again. A man wearing glasses and a hat appeared over the edge of a roof, waving in greeting. "Jak, I see you have company!"

"Answer him," Wu-Lang ordered, putting on a friendly smile.

"So can kill friend?" Jak asked, hands motionless on the steering wheel. "Fuck you twice."

Viciously, Wu-Lang dug the barrel of his S&W .357 deeper into the teenager's ribs. He expected a whimper of pain, but got only a soft grunt.

"Just do as I tell ya, Snowball, and both you and your buddy will live to see another day. All I want is more fuel and some food so I leave this stinking ville," he snapped. "Get me the stuff and I'm gone."

"We live?"

"Of course. You're still breathing, ain't you?"

Jak glared at the man out of the corner of an eye. "Need me get fuel."

"Hey, something wrong?" the man from the roof called out.

"Wave and tell him to come on down," Wu-Lang demanded, twisting the barrel of the gun. Jak grunted again, a reddish stain on his vest slowly spreading out from the spot.

Beaming happily, Wu-Lang clicked back the hammer. "Do it or die. I have nothing to lose."

"No problems!" Jak called out, snapping off a friendly salute. "Come down, Bruce. Want meet old buddy from bayou!"

"The bayou, eh?" J.B. smiled, doffing his hat and waving it twice. "Great! Is this your cousin Charlie?"

"Brian."

The man cupped an ear. "Eh? What was that?"

"Brian. His name is Brian."

The conversation was taking an odd turn, and Wu-Lang was starting to get suspicious. He debated chilling the albino and driving off immediately when a bizarre noise sounded, sort of like a zipper unfastening, only much faster and louder.

Instantly, the windshield of the Hummer shattered into a million pieces and white-hot pain stabbed Wu-

Lang as a flurry of 4.7 mm rounds ripped into his chest. Jak dived from the Hummer just as the coldheart fired his blaster, blowing a hole in the canvas door. Another flurry hit, and Wu-Lang jerked about madly, his chest spouting crimson like a punctured water balloon. The dying man worked his mouth a few times, trying to speak, blood flowing freely over his lips, and he slumped over and hit his head on the dashboard.

Sporting the HK G-12, Doc stepped from the doorway of the federal building. "How are you doing, Jak?" Doc called out, staying in the cover of the partially open doorway.

"Name's Alvin!" the Cajun answered, dusting himself off. Doc relaxed and waved at the roof. J.B. returned the gesture and disappeared from view. By the time he reached the street, Jak and Doc were already hauling the corpse into the back of the Hummer.

"Good idea hiding the body," J.B. said. "The smell of blood will attract animals for miles."

As the hijacker slumped limply into the cargo area, Doc prodded the corpse with his ebony cane. "And pray tell, who was our uninvited visitor?"

"Coldheart who wanted leave ruins," Jak said, holding his side and wincing.

Gathering the dropped blaster from where it fell, Doc inspected the dead man's blaster. "Excellent piece, fine condition." He cracked the cylinder and checked the ammo. The bullets were reloads, but very well done. "Any more in his pockets?"

Expertly, Jak rifled the dead man's clothing. "Nope. Just spoon, can opener, cig lighter."

"I'll take the lighter," J.B. said, and Jak tossed it over.

"Four rounds is it, then," Doc said, and, walking to

the front of the Hummer, slid the blaster into the map compartment. "Never hurts to have a spare."

"How did he get the drop on you?" J.B. asked curiously, tucking the butane lighter into his munitions bag.

"Jumped on hood from overpass," Jak said, making a face. He had been caught unawares like a stupe, and the Cajun felt embarrassed. "Shoved blaster my face. No choice but obey."

J.B. could read the teenager's expression. "I would have done the same myself. What did he want from us anyway, food or blasters?"

"Fuel. Wanted leave bad. Kept looking sky."

"Watching for our winged muties, perhaps?" Doc inquired.

"Yep. Called them demons."

"Good name," J.B. admitted, starting to light his cigar stub, then forcing his hand away. "They're the nastiest bastards I've encountered since Larry Zapp."

"Well, he does not need to fear their arrival anymore," Doc said, raking the street with his hand and tossing some sand on the man. "Ashes to ashes, dust to dust. Where shall we dispose of the body?"

"River," Jak suggested practically. "Water carry to ocean."

"Exemplary, my young friend. Let us be off."

"Wait, I have a better notion," J.B. countered, chewing the stub from one side of his mouth to the other. "Let's drop him off in a vacant lot a few blocks from here with a nice block of C-4 under his ass. Might get a few muties or wolves that way."

"Sounds good," Jak agreed, then he winced as sweat touched the cut in his side.

"Hey, are you hurt?" J.B. asked in concern.

"Just scratch," Jak said dismissively, showing the minor wound. "But how Dean?"

"The same."

"Oh."

"By the way," Doc asked, "where are Ryan and Krysty? Any news on the whereabouts of the medical kit?"

Quickly, Jak told them what happened.

"So they tracked him inside the ville," J.B. said, crossing his arms. "Damn, I don't like the fact that we have no way of contacting them, or even keeping track of their progress."

"Perhaps there is a way," Doc said unexpectedly, studying the cloudy sky. It was difficult to gauge the hour with the heavy blanket of storm clouds blocking the sun. His pocket chron was working fine, but since they didn't know where they were, it could be hours fast or slow in regard to the local time. They didn't even know if this was still America.

"Four, maybe five, hours of light remain," Doc said. "Not nearly enough for my plan. Gentlemen, I suggest Jak stays with Dr. Wyeth to bring her up to date, while John Barrymore and I drop off our guest, and then reconnoiter a few stores to see if we can find some barbed wire for the internal defenses."

Something moved in the cloudy sky and the companions drew their weapons, dropping into combat crouches. The lone sting-wing circled overhead, then moved off.

"Here," Doc said, passing the teenager the G-12. "The Uzi and my LeMat should be sufficient protection for this brief sojourn. But if there is trouble here, you will need the extra firepower."

Accepting the rifle, Jak weighed it judiciously. "Feels light. Ninety rounds?"

"Eighty," Doc said. "I was a bit overzealous eliminating your unwanted passenger."

"Shot him, not me. No complaints." Jak laughed, resting the stock on his hip.

"Thank you. Most kind," Doc said, wiping off the blood on the front seat before climbing into the wag. "Tomorrow morning, we shall go back to the redoubt and load up on all the fuel we can find. Then we go hunting."

"For the muties?" J.B. asked, starting the engine.

"Better," the old man replied, then explained as they drove off.

WIPING THE DIRT off his hand, Gunther breathed in the rich fragrance of the greenhouse and stopped for a moment to admire the beautiful green plants surrounding him in rows upon rows. The shafts of corn were thickly golden, with rich chaff almost bursting to get out. The new tomatoes were small, but growing steadily larger, and the carpeting of soybeans underneath the tall plants was so thick the leaves had a bluish hue.

"Excuse me, Baron," Leonard said from the doorway. "Important news."

"Report," the baron ordered, gently turning a leaf to inspect the underside for any signs of infestation. "Will you look here? That old book we found was correct. Mixing cigarette tobacco and soapy water completely killed those aphids. How clever the ancient gardeners were."

The teenager stepped closer. "We have been invaded."

Retrieving shears from a wicker basket of implements, the baron snipped off a ripe tomato and placed it reverently in a cushion of clean cloth. A special treat for his own dinner this night.

"I do not hear blasterfire in the streets," he said calmly, noticing a meal worm on the stalk. Savagely, he crushed the insect, then wiped his fingers in the rich dark loam beneath the plants. Waste not, want not.

"We found the jolt dealers in the ruins," Leonard said hurriedly. "The muties got them."

The baron tilted his head in thought. The air of the greenhouse was rich, almost pungent with the smell of life itself. "Good. Some of our most recent arrivals had warned us of their coming. Now the problem has been corrected. Did we get much in the way of tools and blasters?"

"No tools, but cases of autofires and a hundredweight of ammo."

"Are you serious? This is excellent news."

"But when the convoy arrived, the last truck, the one carrying the corpses, rammed through the barricade, killing two of our sec men and destroying the big machine gun."

"The driver did this?" Gunther demanded, power flowing into his voice as the last gossamer traces of tranquillity faded from his demeanor.

"No, sir. We found him five hundred yards down the tunnel, shot through the back. All drivers and sec men have been accounted for. Nobody is missing."

"You are my right hand, Leonard," the baron rumbled, his fiery hair flexing and rearranging itself about his shoulders. "There are three possibilities, so we shall start with the most obvious. The fight occurred inside the tunnel, the worst possible location for an attack, so it wasn't a traitor. They would have waited until the trucks were in the ruins, far from our retaliation. So what does that indicate?''

"A corpse," Leonard said.

"We think alike, son. Yes, the guards must have been lax checking the bodies again, one came awake and killed the driver. But it would take a truly exceptional man to accomplish such a task. Our drivers are chosen for their physical strength.''

"And loyalty."

"Fear and hunger make all men loyal."

"So where should we start looking for the corpse? Returning through the tunnel would be impossible without a wag. So he must have taken refuge within our ville.''

Gathering the basket of produce, Gunther stood towering over his adopted son. The boy's hair was red, almost as red as his own, but it was flat and lifeless, the similarity to himself only cosmetic.

"Alert all of our sec men," the baron commanded. "Find the intruder before nightfall."

The words "or else" weren't spoken, nor was it necessary. Leonard understood. Invaders were either spies, assassins or thieves. There were no other possibilities, and all were automatically sentenced to the Machine.

Gunther continued, "Check the market square. That is where he, or she, will most likely try to mingle in with the citizens.''

"Then that is where we shall capture him," Leonard said confidently, snapping his heels.

"Exactly. And capture him alive. If this man is an advance scout, we'll need to know the plans of the enemy.''

"Then he goes to the Machine," Leonard stated, bowing his head.

"Eventually," Gunther stated coldly, then he frowned. "Did he steal the blasters of the sec men?"

"No, Father, which means he has a blaster of his own."

"And a good one. Keep a close watch on the gaudy house. Wild men with good blasters may seek the comfort of a slut where a single bullet buys them hours of pleasure. In fact, arrest all strangers who visit the house tonight. Unless I miss my guess, we'll find our invader among the immigrants."

IN HER OFFICE and bedroom behind the bar of the gaudy house, Madam Patrica took the canvas bag from the hunchback's eager hands. She was suspicious of what could possibly be inside. The gimp had been only gone for a day. If there was a cache of blasters within a day's walk, surely the baron and his army of sec men would have found it by now. They did regular sweeps through the ruins, and every inch of the ville was checked, rechecked, cataloged and indexed. That Leonard had a mind like a rat trap and remembered everything he ever saw or heard. Damn him. No cheating on your taxes with the baron's adopted son doing the tally. Frigging bastard could even add and subtract.

"Okay, let's see what you got for me," Patrica said, loosening the ties. Right off, the bag itself was of some value. There wasn't a hole in the fabric, and the buckles still worked. She shook it and heard a delicious metallic rattle of steel on steel. Perhaps it was a bag full of blasters!

"You like." Harold beamed, bobbing his head as if in church. "Good stuff. Best! I take Laura now."

"Not yet, boy," she stated. "Not until I see in what

condition the blasters are. And how much ammo. We had a deal, remember?''

Harold smiled so wide he drooled. '''Member. Good stuff. You like.''

It took every ounce of control Patrica possessed not to gasp in wonder when she opened the canvas bag and found it full of predark medical supplies in perfect condition. It was a baron's ransom of technology, more than enough to buy half of Alphaville.

''Bah, useless.'' She forced herself to curse, rummaging a hand through the surgical instruments. The flawless steel felt as smooth as silk. ''Where are the blasters? I don't see any blasters in here, just some old junk.''

''Better,'' Harold said, feeling confused. ''Fixes people. Is better!''

''I said blasters, didn't I, boy?'' Patrica stated, crossing her plump arms across her flabby breasts. ''Is this a blaster?''

''Better,'' the hunchback whispered, his fleeting dreams vanishing under her stern gaze.

The madam dropped the pack and kicked it into the corner.

''Useless. I can't do anything with this. Now go get me some blasters.'' Patrica reached out and shook the man. ''You savvy blasters? Revolvers, pistols, boom sticks. Get me blasters, or I put Laura to work tonight!''

Harold shook off the hand and stood to his full height. ''No,'' he said in exacting pronunciation. ''She no work here!'' He grabbed the madam and lifted her off the floor, her shoes wildly kicking to find a purchase. ''She no work here! Wife!''

''Yes,'' the fat woman gasped in terror. ''Of course.

Laura no work here. I was only teasing. Joke. A joke! No work here. Never work here. Okay? Okay?''

"Okay," Harold growled, his face a mask of feral madness. As effortlessly as if he were holding a child, and not a four-hundred-pound woman, he returned her to the floor.

Wheezing for air, Patrica retreated behind her desk and started to open a drawer with a machete hidden under a towel, then thought better of the action and slowly slid the drawer closed. The desire to kill had been plain on his face, and the woman wondered if her game was worth the chance of reward. One wrong move and he would smash her apart. In that instant, her decision was made. Whatever the gimp brought back as payment next time, she would accept as enough and then kill him. He was a golden goose, but one with the fangs of a tiger.

"I go get blasters. Magnum 16s. Remytons. One bag full blasters." Harold started for the door, then stopped and glared at Patrica, his hatred clearly visible. "You obey deal," he growled, rubbing a forearm across his wet jaw. "Or you no friend!"

Shaking more with rage than fear, Patrica watched the door close, the handle ripping out of the wood as the hunchback stomped away in barely controlled fury. A wave of outrage swept over the madam, and her gaze shifted to the spot where he had dared to lay a hand on her as if she were one of the sluts working upstairs, just another common whore! That was where the gimp would die, his guts spilling out onto the floor, screaming and weeping for his life as Patrica hacked away at his limbs until the misshapen body was reduced to flesh and bones.

Striding to the wall, she opened a battered cabinet

and withdrew a knotted leather whip, a speciality item reserved for the baron himself when he visited on tax day. Her back twitched in memory of those awful hours. Expertly coiling the banded leather, Patrica cracked the whip and cut a chunk of wood the size of a plum out of her desk.

Leaving the office, the madam closed and locked the door carefully, then lifted a fat leg and started to climb the stairs for the next level, the long length of the bull-whip trailing behind.

"Party time, retard," she wheezed, the knotted tip bouncing off every step as she waddled higher and higher.

Chapter Thirteen

Soaring from their honeycombed nest, the winged muties swirled in the cloudy sky to hide the location of the home as the First One had taught them so long ago. The moon was full, but the clouds heavy and the light was perfect for a hunt tonight.

Then a scout cried out and swooped to the ground, sailing over the still body of a dead male. The passage of his wings ruffled the corpse, scaring away the lizards feeding on the lifeless form.

Furious, the whole flock took up the cry of his demise, the ruins reverberating from the high-pitched squeals of rage. Swarms of creatures swooped down to snatch scurrying lizards and grind them alive in powerful jaws. The tiny squeals of pain were music for the tasty meal.

Staying above the fighters, lost amid the breeders and the young, the First One was silent in her thoughts as she winged over the ruins, studying a broken skylight. A hunter was dead, and there was a new hole. A connection was made in her mind, and she called for fighters to investigate. Abandoning the lizards, dozens of the muties poured into the insurance building, smashing the skylight apart in their mad rush to gain entrance. The creatures spread across every floor like locusts, and down the staircase to the lower levels.

The largest of the beasts went straight to the bottom

and sailed around the basement, searching for any sign of the prey. But the air was stale, with no blood smell or sweat to spark the killing urge. This was another empty place like the rest of the hunting ground. No food here.

Soaring above the ruins, the great First One studied the sand and stone of her domain. The soil between the stone hives was still radiating away the heat of the day, and prey could easily mask its presence on the ground. But that would only last for a short while, and then the screaming flesh would be easily visible with nowhere to hide.

Peeping a command to the rest of her flock, the leader winged off between the towers of stone, black eyes scanning the night for the telltale glow of living flesh. She didn't understand how the two-legs could kill a fighter or evade the flock, but so much the better. Food always tasted better after a hunt.

Screaming a challenge, the First One banked to the left, folding both wings to dive for the ground, soaring beyond the stinking waters where hundreds of prey walked. Enough meat to feed the folk and the young hatchlings for a week! Unfortunately, the blinding columns of sunlight were moving through the sky, and it hurt the old mother to even glance in that direction. But the slaughter from the previous dark time had taught the fighters a new trick. Perhaps this night the hated two-legs would fall before the flock and the feasting could truly begin.

SITTING IN A CHAIR on the second floor, Mildred sipped a cup of stale coffee, the Heckler & Koch caseless rifle balanced across her lap and a primed LAW at her feet ready for instant use.

Below was an irregular plan of mismatched drapes and curtains. That was J.B.'s idea. They had found enough barbed wire at a local hardware store to criss-cross the central area of the building twice. So they put one layer at the topmost level directly under the skylight to help fend off falling glass, and the other on the ground level. The lower spiderweb of steel they carefully blanketed with the drapes to block any possible light from below, and hopefully to hide from the muties the fact there was a basement. Mildred didn't care how bizarre their biochemistry or physiology was. They had heads the size of a toaster and thus couldn't be very smart no matter how many folds their brains might have. Small was stupid, end of discussion.

Suddenly, the skylight brightened and the woman realized the storm clouds had to have parted, finally allowing moonlight to seep through. The physician debated awakening J.B. so he could shoot their position with his sextant, but she declined. It didn't matter where this zero city was. Location wouldn't help their predicament.

Basked in the reflected moonlight, the government building was eerie in the silence, without even the drip of water or creaking wooden floorboards to disturb the thick silence.

Time passed slowly and steadily, the physician relaxing in the comfortable office chair, conserving her energy and thinking about her odd life and where it has taken her, daydreaming about what might have been, wishing and hoping....

With a start, Mildred jerked awake, the blaster tight in her hands. Damn, she'd fallen asleep in spite of the military coffee. The woman glanced at her wrist chron and saw hours had passed. Listening intently, Mildred tried to hear what had awakened her from such a deep sleep. There was no commotion from below, which was a good sign. J.B. was asleep next to Dean just in case the boy had any more trouble breathing.

A tiny noise came, sounding like a mouse running across the floor, fast and fleeting. Only it wasn't coming from below or behind. In horror, Mildred glanced up and saw a dark shape outlined in the frosty glass of the skylight, the maze of barbed wire between them blurring any possible details.

Reaching out, she tugged on a piece of string tied to the railing, the other end securely wrapped around Jak's forefinger.

Soon there came an answering tug in a two-three-two pattern, meaning the teenager was awake. She tugged one-two-one, and he replied in kind, showing he understood the situation. The men would be awake in seconds to guard Dean, but the physician was the first line of defense should the animals breech the glass.

Releasing the string, Mildred stood slowly and raised the blaster toward the distant skylight, flicking off the safety. The blood was pounding in her veins, and Mildred seemed to have preternatural senses. She knew it was only a fear-induced adrenaline rush, but it still seemed as if she could almost see the winged muties on the rooftop, prowling around, searching for an opening, a hole, any way to reach the human food inside.

Controlling her breathing, Mildred aimed the blaster, slid the fire control to full-auto and waited for the sound of shattering glass.

LONG PINK TONGUES lolling from the desert heat, a pack of wolves padded through the stone forest of man. The flat-faced mountains rose into the distant sky, and when the soft sand gave way to hard slabs of black rock, their claws clicked on the odd material. The evening wind was blowing steadily from the east, the smell of old blood fueling their fury and forcing them onward. A pack of man had somehow slain all the males of their pack, and the stink of the skinned flesh wafting through the night ignited a savagery in the wolves that bordered on madness.

The two-legs in the iron forest had taught them to herd man to them in exchange for food. The wolves liked the game and feared the two-legs with their boom sticks. But this was a matter of blood. The killers had to be killed. It was the way of their world, the law of the new jungle.

And over the years, the wolves had learned to attack man from behind, or strike from the shadows, and the deadly boom sticks would only make noise, but nothing more. And without the stick, man was easy food.

Furry ears pricked upward as a faint trace of smoke in the air made the wolves snarl in response to the possibility of fire. Then the lead female growled and the rest kept moving, warily stalking around a corner. Smoke was the scent of man. The prey was near.

Suddenly, a breeze washed over the animals, carrying the reek of rotting meat, and they froze motionless, recognizing a familiar danger. Nostrils flared, eyes darting, they sought the source of the stench when there was a blur of movement and a young bitch fell over with her head gone, warm blood pumping from the gaping neck wound.

Snarling wildly, the wolves formed a hasty circle, baring their fangs as they faced in every direction. The wind washed over them again with an odd snapping sound, and another tumbled over dead. The pack went wild, darting around in a circle trying to find the unseen attackers. However, nothing was visible and the numbing stench completely blocked their ability to sniff out even a general direction.

Then a struggling wolf was lifted bodily into the dark, warm blood sprinkling down like gentle rain. Self-preservation overwhelmed loyalty, and the pack ran for the safety of the distant dunes. But as they raced down the sandy street a third was beheaded, a fourth disappeared, a fifth howled in unimaginable agony as most of its back was violently removed. Whimpering in terror, a few of the wolves rolled on their backs to expose their bellies in total surrender. Others desperately crawled underneath broken stonework, while the rest fled in blind panic, moving like gray ghosts in the darkness.

Nothing worked. Soon only scraps of warm fur and slowly spreading pools of blood marred the sandy stretch of roadway as deathly silence returned to the ancient ruins.

The bodies of the wolves were nowhere to be seen.

ALMOST DROPPING his smoking lantern, a sec man on the wall of the ville yelled a warning as another started beating a hammer on a metal bell taken from the fallen tower of a church. The bell rang loudly under the blows of the hammer, the noise awakening the citizens, spreading lights and cries across Alphaville.

"Incoming!" a private screamed, fumbling with his musket.

"Hit the lights!" a sergeant ordered, rushing out of a guardhouse, pulling up his pants. Behind him, a woman guard was doing the same, her face a combination of annoyance and terror.

Blasters clenched in sweaty hands, sec men rushed to their posts. From the darkness near the tunnel came the sputtering cough of the lawnmower struggling to catch, then a roar as the engine came to life. Now came the rumble of the big diesel generators turning over. The exhaust pipes spit out black smoke, the whole assembly shaking until the machinery revved to a sustained roar of power.

Switches were thrown, and the searchlights crashed alive, the twin beams stabbing high into the sky and catching dozens of the approaching muties. The beasts keened in agony, two of them clawing at their faces and dropping like stones while the rest wheeled crazily to avoid the horrible illumination.

The men working the searchlights zigzagged the beams across the sky, searching for the airborne enemy. Suddenly, a dark shape plummeted to the ground and bounced off the protective bars covering the Plexiglas lens of the searchlight.

"Dead wolf!" shouted a man on the wall, just as another slammed onto a woman carrying a lit torch. She went down and the torch was extinguished, creating a small zone of blackness.

Raggedly, a rain of wolves plummeted from the night, smashing lanterns and pounding the searchlights with triphammer blows. The protective bars bent, but held for the moment.

A truck in front of the tunnel turned on its headlights and the interior was brightly lit. The five muties crawling on the ceiling froze in position as the sec men opened fire with crossbows and muskets. Off to the side, the deadly .50-caliber machine gun lay disassembled where the frantic repair crew had stopped for the night, unable to continue the work in pitch-dark. The muties retreated from the light, except for a fanged male who madly charged the men, flying straight toward them only feet off the ground. The sec men stood their ground, steadily firing, until the mutie was among them. It careened off one man, knocking him aside as it angled toward another. The first man dropped to his knees, screaming hideously while trying to hold together the bloody ruin of his face. The rest scattered, diving underneath vehicles and into water troughs placed just for that purpose. But the mutie got two more before returning to the flock, its talons dripping red as it soared away.

Then brilliant blue-white globes dotted the night as reserve troops arrived, carrying lanterns. The wicks in the glass flumes burned fast, but threw off an intense nimbus. Oddly, the sec men placed them on the ground, and then retreated. The reasoning was made clear when greenish rain fell from the sky, impacting on the hot lanterns. The flumes cracked, and the contents whooshed into fireballs as the mutie poison reached the wicks and ignited.

The alarm continued to sound as an APC arrived, the back treads throwing off a cloud of sparks as the wag charged down the paved streets. A .50-caliber machine gun on top of the military wag sprayed short bursts into the sky as the side door slammed to the ground, forming a ramp, and out stepped a large muscular man. He was wearing what resembled a policeman's uniform with the insignia removed, and elaborate needlework on the cuffs and collar.

Drawing a fat blaster from a shoulder holster, Baron Strichland pointed it skyward and fired. The weapon thumped, sending a sizzling rocket high into the night, then a small explosion occurred and sizzling light filled the sky as the magnesium flare started to gently drift to the ground on a parachute.

Caught between the flare and the searchlights, the muties swirled blindly, screaming their rage as the APC burped green tracers skyward, and the sec men steadily banged away with revolvers and longblasters.

Then a winged shape fell to the ground, impacting with a sickening crunch. The guards ignored the fallen creature, but swarms of old women and children charged out to savagely beat the mutie with baseball bats and lead pipes until it was utterly deceased.

A second mutie dropped to its death as another flare arced for the heavens. Then the searchlights traversed the air over the battleground, showing the winged monsters flapping back toward the ruins. A flurry of crossbow bolts arched after them, and one more tumbled from the sky, its body a pincushion of feathered shafts.

IN A GREENHOUSE, Ryan and Krysty watched the fierce battle while sipping some water and trying to ignore the ache in their bellies. This was the fourth greenhouse they had visited. The crude handmade benches lining the structure were filled with thick growths of bushy carrot tops on one side and plump cucumbers dangling from support sticks on the other bench. The smell of the fresh food was heady, intoxicating, but they knew what the dark loam in the stands was partially made of, and in spite of being hungry, the two could find no appetite for this food.

Moving closer to the wall, they watched the firefight near the tunnel, the stuttering flashes of the blasters and the searchlights.

Lying on the floor behind them was a bound sec man,

tied hand and foot with strips of his shirt, a sock jammed into his mouth.

"They got it down to a science," Ryan observed, "with ground crews mopping up the wounded."

"I wonder if the sec men are really good," she mused, "or if they've just fought the same battle so often they have it down to a science."

"You think this was staged?"

"What better way to stay in power then endlessly save your citizens from a terrible enemy?"

Ryan considered the notion. "The local baron can't keep control with the food supplies. If the people ever found out where the soil came from, they'd revolt."

"Remember Mildred and Doc telling us about compost heaps? Wonder why they don't boil their garbage until it's sterile and mix that with the sand."

"Mebbe they don't know that trick."

"But they can make alcohol."

"Everybody has a still. That's booze for partying and fuel for wags. A yard-long piece of seamless copper tubing is more useful than a thousand airplanes."

Krysty's reply was cut short by the sound of talking outside the greenhouse. The two quickly moved beneath the table in the center aisle seconds before the door opened and sec men entered, one holding an alcohol lantern, the other a tiny revolver. It was only a dinky .22, hardly fit to be a starter's pistol for a race. But Ryan knew in the right hand and at the right range, it could kill as fast as a .50-caliber Desert Eagle. Shoot a man in the shoulder, and the little rounds would rattle around inside, bouncing off bones and piercing every vital organ before tumbling out his stomach. Nasty stuff.

"What crap," one man said, walking along the aisles of plants, the lantern sizzling and popping. "Nobody is going to steal a carrot during an attack and risk going to the Machine.''

''Better than wall duty,'' his companion replied. ''You see how many we lost tonight?''

''Three or four. Pretty bad.''

''Aye.''

Reaching the end of the greenhouse, they turned and started down the other aisle. ''Damn lucky the fat slut found a predark med kit....''

Instantly, Ryan was behind the man, the long curved blade of his panga tight against the sec man's throat. ''Don't move,'' he whispered hoarsely.

The other sec man stepped backward, drawing his revolver, and Krysty rose to slam a wooden stool over his head. With a sigh, the man crumpled to the ground.

''You're the invaders,'' the prisoner said until Ryan tightened the blade, a trickle of blood flowing from the wound.

''Here's the deal,'' he growled as Krysty took away the man's weapons, a knife and a muzzle-loading pistol. ''You get to live if you tell us about that med kit.''

''What med—?'' He gagged as Krysty placed the muzzle of her .38 against the man's crotch and clicked back the hammer.

''One lie, one ball,'' she said coldly. ''Two lies, no balls, Three and you lose anything remaining.''

The man broke into a sweat, his hands flexing helplessly in the air.

''Gaudy house,'' he finally whispered. ''Northeast corner of the market. Big fat bitch, Patrica, said she found a med kit. Baron doesn't believe her, but she turned it in as you're supposed to so we can't touch her.''

"Where is it now?" Ryan demanded, tightening his hold slightly.

"Vault in the palace. Don't have the combination. Nobody does but the baron and Leonard."

"That his lover, captain of the guards?" Krysty asked.

"Son!" Panic took his eyes. "Don't kill me!"

In spite of his promise, Ryan was torn on the matter. He knew it was the smart move to kill the man. But a deal had been made, and he gave his word. That didn't mean shit in the Deathlands, except to the man whose honor backed the pledge.

"Get some rope," Ryan said.

Holstering her piece, Krysty nodded and turned away, then cried out and dived to the floor. A woman was at the door holding a scattergun. Ryan shoved his prisoner forward as the weapon boomed. The discharge lifted the sec man off the ground, and he crashed amid the green plants, blood and organs splattering everywhere.

The armed guard thumbed back the second hammer of her blaster as Ryan shot her in the knee from under the table. The shotgun fired again, blowing away a dozen panes of glass as the sec woman fell to the ground screaming in pain. Something white-hot scored Krysty's cheek as she shot the sec woman in the throat, then again in the head. The screaming stopped.

Quickly searching the corpses, the companions found a rough map of the ville, spare cartridges for their blasters, a piece of honeycomb, half an apple and some jerky. Krysty carefully smelled the meat, then risked nibbling a corner.

"Wolf," she declared thankfully.

The pair divided the food, devouring the scraps as a

group of people bearing alcohol lanterns started to come their way.

"Hey, Sue," called out a voice. "You okay?"

Moving to the far door, Krysty cut loose with a full throated scream of terror as Ryan shot the lantern lying on the floor with his silenced pistol. Instantly, a pool of burning alcohol spread across the greenhouse, igniting the clothing of the dead.

"Intruders in the greenhouse!" a sec man shouted, firing his longblaster wildly into the sky.

Others took up the fight as the companions quietly retreated from the commotion into the blackness of the night.

"Patrica first?" Krysty asked after they had reached a safe distance from the growing conflagration.

Thumbing some fresh rounds into his ammo clip to replace the spent cartridges, Ryan nodded. "She's our ticket to the baron."

"And he's our way out. Let's go."

Chapter Fourteen

Dragging a brace of window curtains behind it, the Hummer rolled to a halt in front of the nameless skyscraper. J.B. killed the engine and set the brake.

"Any tracks?" he asked, looking backward out the window.

"Not a thing, John Barrymore," Doc replied.

"Good," the man said, sliding out from behind the wheel. "Last night was too close of a call. If those muties had gotten inside, we would have been chilled for sure. Sure as hell don't want any of the frigging sec men finding our bolt-hole."

"I wholeheartedly concur, my friend," Doc agreed, stepping to the ground and closing the door. "And here is the solution to our security dilemma. Voilà! The Tower of Babel!"

"Not quite. But, yes, it is tall."

Somber and impressive, the truncated facade of the skyscraper fronted the apex of the corner, its ten stories of windows frosty white from erosion and age. And if the building had once possessed a name, it had been removed by the rain and the winds long ago.

"Got that list from Millie?" J.B. asked, slinging a LAW over his shoulder. He had given the S&W M-4000 shotgun to Mildred, as Doc had done with Jak and the Heckler & Koch, including a few of the LAWs and their only Hafla napalm rocket launcher, leaving the pair as well armed as possible. J.B. sported only his 9 mm Uzi, one LAW and a lot of grens. Doc carried his LeMat, and a backpack of Molotov cocktails, a special treat for the muties should they be caught outside when night came.

Doc patted his shirt pocket, the gesture making his backpack tinkle and clatter. "Right here, sir. Our dear madam physician is most clever indeed. I myself never would have thought of looking for helicopters to find a hospital."

"Yep. The sign may be gone, and the building too dirty to tell if it's white or what," the Armorer agreed, removing the ignition fuse from under the dashboard, "but from above, if you see a short building with a heliport, it's either the local PD or a hospital. Apparently, every hospital had them in her day."

"Are you not going to booby-trap the seat?" Doc asked, curious.

"Too dicy. We might come back running," J.B. countered, walking away while checking his blaster. "Best to leave us a fast escape route, just in case."

"Most wise, John Barrymore. If we wish to use the structure as a lookout point to survey the ruins and ville, who is to say the baron and his sec men have not thought of the same idea, and are already there waiting for us?"

J.B. paused to clean his glasses with a pocket rag. "That's why we're going in slow and silent," he said, tucking them back into position on his bony nose.

The Armorer jerked his head to the left. Doc nodded and took a position at the side of the building as J.B. checked the revolving door. Made of unbreakable Plexiglas set in a steel frame, it had survived the ages in excellent shape. But the lock was standard office issue and easily fell open to J.B.'s nimble fingers.

Once inside the building, Doc reached into his backpack and withdrew a lantern. J.B. ignited the wick with a butane lighter. One hundred years old and the lighter still worked. Without it, he'd be banging rocks together for sparks. They found pyrotabs sometimes in the redoubts, but not often enough.

Under the assault of the bright light, they could see that the foyer was littered with bottles and leathery scraps of what appeared to be the remains of briefcases and shoes. A pair of glasses frames lay near a pile of pinstriped rags in front of the double doors to the elevator bank, and a baby carriage covered with cobwebs stood alone by the telephones. A receptionist kiosk was situated along one wall, near a newsstand and snack shop, and a huge digital clock was a dull blank circle on the wall.

Hopping over a purely ornamental gate, they ignored the powerless elevator and headed for the emergency stairs. The door creaked loudly as they forced it open, disturbing a horde of lizards. The tiny reptiles changed color as they scurried away in every direction.

"Boo," J.B. said, as they started up the long flight of stairs.

An hour later, the friends finally reached the observation floor of the tower. The desert wind moaned softly across them as they walked across the bare floor. According to the sign in the stairwell, this had once been a posh restaurant reserved for the rich and powerful. The entire floor was empty except for a scattering of marble pillars supporting the ceiling. Probably just concrete faced with marble. The walls had obviously been an array of gigantic windows to afford the diners a spectacular view of the city. But storms had shattered the fragile glass this high up with no other buildings to buffet the tempest of the desert winds. Jagged snowy daggers lined the four sides of the window frames, and twinkling transparent shards lay scattered across the floor like a smashed sheet of ice.

Crunching the glass underfoot as they walked, neither man spoke as they separated and went to opposite corners. Below them stretched a desolate vista, the sprawling metropolis reaching outward for miles to the distant desert, where soft rolling dunes marked the end of the ruins. The once mighty city had been reduced to crumbling mounds from the bombs of its builders, and the greatest destroyer of all, implacable time.

"No sign of any hospital to the south," Doc reported, the wind ruffling his longish hair.

"Same for the east," J.B. said, holding on to his glasses to keep them from flying away. The wind was brisk at this height, and he was having difficulty staying on his feet.

"There's a library," Doc said, pointing, his other hand holding tightly on to the window frame. "Always a good repository of…" The oldster squinted hard. "I say, are those trucks in the parking lot?"

"Vehicles?" J.B. asked, coming over to extend his telescope. "I would have thought the sec men had gathered everything with wheels for that bloody huge wall. Hey, those are U.S. Army trucks, and they're filled with crates of military supplies. Hot damn!"

"Hmm, I do recall Jak saying that the sec men retrieved bodies from an attack by the muties," Doc rumbled, his coat spreading out like wings from the stiff breeze. "That must be the location where they struck."

"And the sec men took the bodies but left everything

else?'' J.B. admonished, lowering the telescope. ''But that doesn't make any sense... Oh, they took half of the supplies. A little something for the baron, a little for them.''

''And more for us.'' Doc smiled, marking the location in his mind. ''I wonder where they located the military supplies, still intact?''

''Can't be the redoubt. If they got in, they would never leave. So it must have been a bomb shelter,'' J.B. said thoughtfully as he lowered the telescope. ''Just look at all the government buildings this city has! It must have been the capital of...well, wherever the hell we are. And the predark government always built plenty of bomb shelters to save the pencil pushers and ass kissers.''

Stepping away from the opening, Doc straightened his collar and smoothed his hair. ''A most logical assumption, my good sir. What say we swing by there on our way back and see what the gods of chance have laid at our altar of need?''

''Sounds good,'' J.B. said, checking his compass. ''North is that way. Let's see if we can spot the ville.''

''Certainly.''

As they walked around the burnished-metal rectangle of the elevator banks, neither man seemed to notice as the doors slid silently apart behind them, exposing the blackness within.

To the west was endless desert, only the hint of mountains lost in a purple haze of the horizon. But directly north of the skyscraper was the yellow river, and beyond that the nameless ville.

''By the Three Kennedys, look at those greenhouses,'' Doc said, shielding his vision from the weak daylight with a raised hand.

Tilting back his hat, J.B. whistled. "Must have a hundred of them. Where the hell did they find any clean dirt? From under the ruins, mebbe?"

"Or they made it themselves," Doc said, rubbing his chin. "Simply mince and boil your own night soil until it was sterilized, then mix with sand."

"And that will grow crops?"

"Without question."

Whew, the things the old man knew. "Searchlights to attract people and protect the ville from the muties, trained wolves and now greenhouses," J.B. muttered, lifting the telescope for a view. "Their baron must be a genius!"

"Or a farmer."

"Farmer with an army," J.B. stated, spotting a commotion in the ringed compound. Adjusting the focus, he swept the milling crowd gathering before a raised platform. "Looks like they're having a meeting of some kind."

"Any sight of our comrades?" Doc asked worriedly, pressing his boot against the frame of the window. The gusts of wind tugged at their clothes, whipping about the loose cloth and keeping them slightly off balance. It was necessary to hold on to the window frame to keep from going over.

"Not yet," J.B. replied. "Here, take a gander." But turning to offer the telescope, he saw a furtive movement near the elevators. Then the man went cold as he spotted the tip of a gray wing sticking out from behind one of the support pillars.

"Ah, Doc," he whispered, pocketing the telescope.

"Mm-hmm?"

J.B. casually withdrew a grenade. "Muties."

Slowly, the oldster brushed back his billowing coat and drew the LeMat. "How many?"

Just then, they heard a skittering noise, like dozens of claws on a hard surface, followed by the faint crack of a piece of glass.

"Too many," J.B. answered, prepping a gren. The awesome power of the LAW slung across his back was useless for this kind of combat. The antitank weapon took thirty seconds to prep, even if the creatures should offer a nice grouped target. Hardly likely. "Hate to say this, but I think we found their bastard nest."

"Congratulations."

"Thank you."

Easing back the hammer on his blaster, Doc glanced over the side of the building, looking at the distant streets and the tiny Hummer, no more than a dark jot in the tan sand. There was no convenient fire escape or any other way down. Even if they were over water and jumped, a fall from that height would kill them.

"Could we reach the stairs?" the old man asked out of the side of his mouth.

"Not a chance. Ready?"

"So it would seem I must be. On your mark, my friend."

"Go." J.B. turned and threw the gren, while Doc spun and fired the LeMat in a single smooth motion.

The blast of the HE blocked their view of the floor and threatened to throw them off the building, but as the smoke cleared, both men started to fire at the crowd of muties crawling around the elevator bank and coming straight for them.

SWADDLED IN DIRTY CLOAKS, two people walked through the bustling market square of Alphaville. The tall one carried a rolled-up blanket on his back; the other was shorter and most definitely a woman despite attempts to hide the fact.

On this side of the river, the ruins of the predark city had been extensively rebuilt, and while the new mortar between the recovered bricks didn't precisely match the colored bands of the ancient concrete still supporting pieces of walls, the homemade concrete did seem to be holding the patchwork of bricks and cinder blocks together, which was all that really mattered.

A former gas station was serving as a stable for a few skinny horses, and a tavern was open for business on the corner across from a pottery shop, a dozen people inside spinning clay by hand on rotating tables. A tailor was cutting garments for an impatient child, while the mother was giving unneeded directions. A bookstore was a burned-out shell, with workmen digging through the wreckage to haul away the trash. A cooper was frowning in frustration, a water barrel before him leaking water from every seam. A cobbler, a baker, a barber, a school for small children, a gallows, a defense nest of sandbags and sec men. And everywhere were the greenhouses, the glass glistening clean, folks inside doing things with the rows upon rows of lush green plants while grim-faced sec men stood guard at the doors, muzzle-loading rifles at the ready.

Shuffling along, talking to nobody, the pair reached the main market square and stopped. Here hundreds of people were exchanging items, buying vegetables or haggling over the cost of rat poison. Set between a greenhouse and a barracks, across from a dentist, was a gaudy house. Topless women leaned out the second-floor balcony, dangling the goods for sale.

The ville was thriving with activity. Tables galore in

the market square were piled with salvaged tools, scrap wire, mismatched shoes and even a few books. A plump woman with a babe in tow haggled prices with a merchant and came away with a mason jar to be used for canning food. She paid for it with a small loaf of fresh bread from the basket on her arm.

"But no weapons," Ryan said, adjusting his scarf to hide his eye patch. "Not even knives." More than a few folks had similar wrappings, and once again Ryan wondered where they were.

"No butchers, either. Baron keeps a taut ship," Krysty said quietly. A hood covered her head to hide her unusual hair. There was a faint reddish streak across her cheek where the bullet had grazed her face the previous night, but it was already fading. She always healed fast.

The crowd surged from an influx of people coming out of a steaming laundry, and Ryan got bumped hard from behind. Instantly, his hands flew to check his weapons, and stopped.

"Sorry," he muttered, hurrying away. He couldn't afford to draw attention to himself. They were here to find that med kit and leave. Nothing more. Besides, this seemed to be the nicest ville he'd ever seen since his own barony back in Virginia.

"Hey!"

Ryan turned, his hand resting on the handle of the panga inside his shirt. Hopefully, it appeared as if he were merely scratching an itch. But the stranger's throat was one fast step away from eternal silence.

"Yeah?" Ryan asked bluntly.

"Nice boots," the big man said, displaying a mouthful of broken teeth. His hands were covered with the fine scars of brawling, his ears lumpy from badly thrown punches. But he stood on the balls of his feet, not the flat soles. This was a professional fighter, not some alleyway thug. Krysty eased herself away from the two and started to edge behind the newcomer.

"Yeah?" Ryan said noncommittally.

The thug stepped closer. "I could use a pair like those, and they're in my size."

Ryan knew where this was going. No chance of him backing out, and he couldn't just chill the man. He'd have to do this the hard way. Bending his fingers at the knuckles, Ryan kept his hand flat and started forward when he froze motionless.

Over the man's shoulder, Ryan could dimly see minuscule flashes of light from inside the shadows of the skyscraper. A firefight was raging on the top floor, and the strobing muzzle-flashes could only be autofire blasters. The ville sec men he'd seen had only bolt-action rifles and revolvers. And they certainly would have used autofire blasters the previous night. Which meant it was J.B. and his Uzi, or whoever was using the HK G-12.

"Hey, I'm talking wid you!" the man stated gruffly, grabbing Ryan by the shoulder and spinning him. "Now gimme the boots, punk!"

Ryan bent over as if to comply, then stood fast and rammed his fingertips straight into the man's throat. Gasping for air, the thug backed away. Swinging a boot, Ryan caught the man between the legs. Breath exploded from the thug, and as he bent over in pain, the one-eyed man raised his knee to catch him on the way down. The impact straightened out the thug, almost flipping him over. Arms flailing, he hit the ground like wet newspaper and lay there, bleeding from the ruin of his face.

Some gasps rose from the crowd nearby, but most kept moving, unwilling to become embroiled in a fight that wasn't their concern. Some shopkeepers closed their doors, and a few folk turned into alleys to avoid the clear space that had magically appeared around the combatants.

"What's going on here?" a man demanded, pushing a path through the milling throng. The man was big and muscular, wearing good clothes, with a revolver holstered on his hip, a stout club in his grip and a red band of cloth on his arm marked with a white circle and a big blue letter *A*.

But all of the identifying items of a sec man were unnecessary. As soon as he had spoken, Ryan knew it was a guard from his attitude toward the crowd. They weren't people to serve or assist, but a problem the man had to handle quietly before he could get back to his interrupted drinking.

"All right, gleeb," he barked, fixing Ryan with a menacing stare. "Did you attack this man? We got laws about fighting near the greenhouses. You bust a pane of clear glass, and it's fifty strokes of the whip."

Aside from an acknowledging grunt, Ryan didn't reply, calculating his chances of making a break into the open doorway of the blacksmith shop. Once out of sight and over the bellows, he could ace the sec man and find someplace to hide. He noticed that Krysty had already gone, blending into the crowd. They had agreed upon that. If one got caught, the other stayed free to finish the job. The clock was ticking on Dean, and minutes counted.

Then four more sec men converged on the sleeping giant, and Ryan knew there was no escape. He'd have to talk his way out of this mess. A difficult matter when he didn't even know the name of the ville or the baron who ruled there.

"Trouble?" asked the leader of the new group, a hand resting on the butt of his blaster. The others fanned out behind him to establish a greater presence of authority.

"Yeah, I think so," the first guard murmured.

Ryan noted that several shops had closed their doors, and folks were avoiding this section of the street. He had a gren, and wondered how best to use it—blow up a greenhouse or try to kill as many sec men as he could. Both had their downside.

"Hey, Roberto!" called out a thin man eating an apple as he walked over from the market square.

The first guard scowled for a moment, then relaxed slightly. "Hey, Dawson. See what happened?"

"Sure. Crusher tried to roust the new guy," Dawson said, munching contentedly. "Bad mistake."

"Didn't think anybody could take Crusher but the hunchback," said one of the other guards.

Already the tension was starting to diminish, and Ryan felt the muscles in his arms unkink. Somebody had vouched for him, and as far as the sec men were concerned, the matter was already over.

"Did he, now? Fair enough, then. You want to kick him some more while he's down?" Roberto asked, still brandishing his club. "Somebody attacks you for no reason, you get to pound them. It's a law we got to discourage brawling."

"Nah, he ain't going to bother me none again," Ryan said.

The second group of sec men seemed satisfied, and moved on, but one of the men stared hard at Ryan before leaving, as if trying to memorize his features, or worse, recall them.

Dawson finished the apple, then tucked it into a

pocket. "Pretty good with your fists," he acknowledged. "Got an assignment yet from Leonard?"

"Tomorrow. He was busy," Ryan risked saying. Then on impulse, he threw back his cowl as if having nothing to hide.

Roberto laughed. "Yeah, the kid tries to run the whole ville. But then, he'll be baron when Strichland dies."

"Seems like an okay guy."

Tapping the wooden club against his leg, Roberto frowned. "Don't let that smiling face fool you, newbie. The baron would toss his own mother into the Machine."

"Ain't that the truth," Dawson added, his face as somber as the tone of his voice.

There was that word again. Ryan filed that phrase away, along with the sound of real fear in the guard's voice. "Meant Leonard."

"Oh, yeah, he's okay. Pretty good in a fight, too. And smart. He's the one who thought of the greenhouses. We call him the Brain in the barracks." The club was brandished. "But you didn't hear that from me."

"Hear what?" Ryan asked blandly.

A slow smile. "Quick. You're very quick. What's your name?"

"Finnegan," Ryan replied, recalling an old friend who no longer walked the Deathlands. "Friends call me Finn."

Dawson licked his sticky fingers clean. "Any good with a blaster?"

"Some."

"Yeah?" Roberto scratched his head with the club. "Know how to turn a regular lead bullet into a dumdum?"

"Fucking carefully," Ryan stated honestly.

Both men laughed. "You'll do, Finn," Dawson said, smiling. "After your stint in the muck, try for security. We always need tough guys." He glanced at the supine form in the sand. "And I think you'll fit right in."

"Thanks."

"Better than weeding," Roberto added, as he turned and strolled away. "Or wall duty."

"Yar, anything is better than that. Well, see ya later, Finn."

"Later," Ryan agreed.

Having said their piece and ascertained there were no problems, the sec men went back to their business, and the crowds flowed around Ryan again. The fight was over, and the disturbance in their ville had been settled. Life went on again.

Some kids darted out from the legs of the crowd and started going through Crusher's pocket, and Roberto halfheartedly chased them away.

Retreating to the safety of the market square, Ryan looked for Krysty, but she was nowhere to be seen. Finding a gap between some of the buildings, he next studied the distant skyscraper. But without binocs, he couldn't see any details and nothing seemed to be happening anymore. The fight either was over, or it had gone hand to hand. The muties! The building had to be their nest. Ryan flexed his hands, then stuffed them into his pockets and strolled away. There was absolutely nothing he could do to help from where he was. He had to concentrate on the task at hand, get the med kit and get back. Until he got across the river, his friends were on their own.

From out of the cloudy sky, a sting-wing darted toward the mob of people. A blaster boomed, and the dead mutie tumbled to the ground out of sight. Rooftop guards, Ryan realized. This ville was very well protected, and by damn good shots, too. Suddenly, he was glad he decided to talk his way out of the problem.

Moving toward an eatery, Ryan saw folks pay for bowls of vegetable stew with local jack, big predark silver coins stamped with a crude letter A, just like the armband of the guards. Someone had to have shaved off the original embossing and hand-pounded on the new face. He'd seen it done many times. Made sense. The stuff couldn't be duplicated anymore, and wouldn't wear out like the old paper stuff.

Taking a seat at an empty table made from an industrial cable spool tipped over on its side, Ryan started to think about how to find the baron's private vault. But the smell coming from the wood-burning stove was shifting his attention. It had been too long since he'd had a good night's sleep, so food was important. Ideas would come with a full belly.

"What'll it be?" a barmaid asked, wiping the table with a damp rag. She wore a very loose dress with a mechanic's apron tied around her trim waist.

The top didn't button closed very well, and a lot of her was viewable. Ryan guessed that not only food was sold here. "What do you have?"

"Veggie stew, cold roasted potatoes and some green beer that won't make you puke much."

"Any bread?"

She looked at him for the first time. "Sure. All you want. That's free from the baron. You new here?"

Damn, he walked into that one. "Stew," he said. Then took out a single round from his shirt. "This should cover it."

The woman gasped and swept the bullet off the table

and into a pocket of the apron. "Are you insane?" she hissed, leaning closer. "No, that's right. You're new here, right? Thought so. Guards didn't search you very well. We ain't allowed to have blasters or ammo. Only the baron and his troops."

That was standard for most villes. But if the baron had all the blasters, why was he so nice to the civvies? Mebbe he had blasters, but little ammo. Might be a bargaining chip there.

Resting the tray on a round hip, the barmaid, leered suggestively. "This'll get you meat in the stew, or a romp with me. I'm Dolly."

"Finn. Thanks, but I just got laid," he lied. "Only want some food."

"Suit yourself." The barmaid eyed him up and down. "But if you change your mind, we can use the back room here. No charge, stud."

"What about some info?" Ryan said, laying his hand on the table and pushing forward another 9 mm round.

Dolly licked her lips while eyeing his hand. "What do you want to know? If it's jolt you're looking for, we don't got none. Baron forbids all drugs. Says it slows us down building greenhouses."

"Fifty strokes?" he asked.

She blanched. "You get caught with jolt, you go to the Machine."

There was that phrase again. It had to be some sort of torture device. Probably the rack. "What does he care if we have fun?"

"He's got the blasters," the woman said. "Besides, he's the best baron we've ever had. And I've lived through four of them." She grabbed her breasts and jiggled them. "Tits like these keep you alive, as long as they plump. The last one tried to make rules about

everything, including fucking. His own sec men turned
on him and made their leader baron.''

Dolly jerked a thumb. ''Put up the gaudy house right
off. No more rape in the back streets at night. Guards
go for free, but everybody else pays. Fair, I guess.
Them's the ones fighting those winged devils. Baron
Strichland is tough, ten lashes for lying to a sec man.
Twenty for stealing, fifty for rape or stealing food. And
it's the Machine if you damage a greenhouse.''

Ryan merely grunted and waited for her to continue.
Most folks talked to a serving girl, not with them. Shut
up and listen, and they were always a mine of data. She
bent over the table, her breasts almost spilling out, so
he patted her ass and stroked her partially exposed leg.

''You sure about the back room?'' Dolly asked,
sounding wistful. She liked this one; he was cleaner
than most, and darkly handsome in a frightening way.
The eye patch didn't bother her; she bet the other guy
had come out a lot worse in that fight.

''Would if I could.'' He smiled politely. ''Tomorrow,
for sure.''

A pro, Dolly accepted the rebuff. ''So what do you
want to know?''

''I'm looking for somebody,'' Ryan said, tucking the
live bullet into her apron. ''A woman called Patrica.''

''Fat Pat? Sure. What you want with her?''

Ryan stared at the woman.

Her smile faded like ice in the sun. ''Right. Not my
business. She's the madam of the gaudy house down
the street. Anything else?''

''Stew,'' he said, adjusting his hood to hide his features once more.

She shrugged, checked her pocket and walked away,
hips expertly swinging to avoid bumping the tables.

Watching the crowds stream by in an endless procession, Ryan started to feel better about the task at hand. They were in the ville, and he knew who had the med kit. Now all he had to do was get hold of this Patrica, get an audience with the baron and find the vault. The rest would be simple stealing. What could he offer to sell? Mebbe where the muties nested? That might work.

The food arrived in a not overly clean bowl with a big chip in the side and a plastic spoon that had seen better days. But the stew was hot, and Ryan wolfed it down as if it were his last meal. He was nearly done when a gong began to sound, slow and steady. The man lowered his spoon. Another mutie attack? Couldn't be; this was daytime. But everybody in sight stopped whatever they were doing and started to walk down the main street of the ville, heading in the same direction. Dolly and the sec men included.

Leaving his food, Ryan mingled with the crowds, keeping an eye out for Krysty. Usually, her fiery red hair would be an easy find amid the collection of brunettes and blondes, but this day she was wearing a hood.

A fortified building of some sort stood at the head of a large courtyard, and the crowd was forming a half circle in front of the structure. On a wooden platform stood a redheaded man in embroidered military fatigues, and a few more folks less ornately dressed. Could be the baron and his flunkies, Ryan realized. Better and better. There were sec men on the ground behind a sandbag wall, holding very clean blasters, but they had a relaxed appearance, as if this were nothing unusual.

Then the man on stage lifted the med kit into view, and Ryan had to stop himself from rushing the guards.

There it was, only a hundred yards way. Ryan grimly swore it wasn't going to leave his sight again.

"Will you look at that, a predark medical bag. Bastard thing must be worth a ville itself," muttered a dirty-faced bald man dressed in tattered clothing.

"More," a tiny woman agreed, her cascade of golden hair reaching to her knees. The luxurious tresses were braided into a thick ponytail. "Wonder what's going on?"

"Good morning, citizens of Alphaville," the baron boomed, the med kit dangling by a strap in his hand. "First off, I want to tell you that the traitor who broke the windows of greenhouse fourteen has been caught and dealt with."

A murmur swept through the crowd.

"I prayed the poor bastard would escape," said a giant in a leather apron. He was holding a massive hammer and reeked of sweat and hot iron.

"Nobody escapes Alphaville," said a tiny rat-faced man wearily.

When the noises died, Baron Strichland continued, "The plants have been saved, the soil replenished and there will still be enough food to last us through the long dark winter."

Applause broke out from the attendees.

"That's something," a dour old woman snorted, her hands as gnarled as tree roots. She stank of lye and soap, and a hand-carved clothespin jutted from a skirt pocket.

"And on a more positive note, we have a new addition to our ville, Brian and Tasha." The baron gestured to the couple and they dutifully stepped forward. Ryan recognized them as the folks chased by the wolves the previous day. The man seemed thinner, more haggard, his face a stone mask. The woman was red eyed and sniffling, the baby cradled in her arms. Their daughter wasn't in sight.

"Unfortunately, their daughter Lucia was killed by the muties last night," the baron said sadly. "So this is a time of joy and sadness. Joy, that we have two more citizens, and sadness at their terrible loss."

"Must have been a redhead," the rat-faced man muttered, and many others growled agreement.

"It's awful," Ryan said, hoping to prompt more information.

The blacksmith nodded glumly. "If my wife gave birth to a redhead, I'd do the babe a favor and drown her on the spot."

The words were said so casually, but with such vehemence, Ryan didn't doubt the man for a moment. What the hell was the redheaded baron doing with the girls? It wasn't really Ryan's problem, until he realized Krysty's situation. If her hood slipped, the woman might be taken captive and find out what was happening to the females of the ville.

Quickly easing his way deeper into the attentive throng, Ryan reached the edge and frantically searched for the woman.

"We are also here to punish a traitor!" the baron boomed, raising the med kit high. "This woman is Patrica, the madam of our gaudy house. Favored with easy work, she has grown fat, but her work is important and we did nothing. So some of this is our fault for allowing her to think she was above the law."

"None are above the law!" shouted a teenager near the huge baron.

"None," the redheaded man agreed, and the crowd roared its agreement.

Elbowing his way through the throng, Ryan heard the words, but was concentrating on every hooded person in the crowd. He found Krysty amid some bare-chested men holding shovels, and grabbed her shoulder.

"Don't show yourself," he whispered.

"Why?" the old woman demanded, sliding back the hood to expose a wealth of gray hair. "What do you want? Who are you?"

"Sorry, wrong person," Ryan apologized and moved on quickly.

On the platform, a gang of sec men pushed a fat woman into view, coils of rope binding her. A cloth gag filled her mouth, and even from this distance, Ryan could see the blind panic in her face.

"This is our enemy, and all that is to transpire will take place here in the justice square," the baron said formally. "I hide nothing in the darkness of basements or hidden rooms."

The guards lashed the fat woman to a wooden stake, binding her at the neck and waist. The prisoner struggled frantically and achieved nothing. A sec man removed her gag, and she spit out another wad of cloth.

"It was a mistake!" the woman screamed in desperation. "I hadn't gotten to the baron yet when they caught me. I have done nothing wrong!"

"Lies!" the redheaded teenager spit. "When we went to pay her the reward for finding the doctor bag, the sec men found a cache of blasters in her room. Not one, or two, but many!"

The crowd voiced its shock and disapproval.

"Even one blaster is punishable by the Machine," the baron intoned, spreading his arms. "But why so many? Who needs more than one?"

He advanced upon the bound woman, shouting at

every step, "Why were you building an armory? Are you working with outsiders to overthrow the ville? Confess, traitor, and die a clean death!"

"Liar," a man whispered to the person next to him. "Big words, and a knife in the back is all you get here."

"Just like they did my cousin who found the searchlights," the other man agreed, hands stuffed deep into his pockets.

"No, it serves her right," a young blonde in a colorful dress said with a sneer, hands on her hips. "That bitch Patrica was the meanest madam a slut ever worked for."

Ryan stopped at those words and stared at the struggling prisoner on the platform. She was his key to the baron? Oh hell. Good thing he already knew where the med kit was.

"Mercy!" the madam shrieked. Blood trickled down her forearms as she tried to escape from the ropes.

Clearly, the baron wasn't moved by the outburst, almost as if he had heard it all far too many times before. "Strip her."

Leonard approached with a knife and cut away her clothing, until the woman was nude to the waist, her giant breasts squeezing out either side of the wooden post.

"Start with the whips," the baron said calmly, crossing his arms.

In the anxious throng, a young woman started to guide her children off the square.

"You, there!" Leonard shouted. "Stay, mother, and let them watch. This traitor to our ville dies so they may live in safety. That is the gift—knowing is the price!"

Going pale, the teenager curtsied and hugged the trembling children close, their eyes wide with fear.

A sec man on the platform removed his shirt, displaying a Herculean torso of rippling muscles. Expertly, he uncoiled a long whip, the knotted leather moving across the cracked concrete like a writhing snake.

"Wait!" Leonard ordered, holding up a hand.

Everybody watched in silence as the youth stepped forward. Even the baron seemed caught by surprise with this unexpected move. Hope blossomed in the madam's face, and the executioner turned toward the teenager. "Yes, Lieutenant Strichland?"

"Do not kill her quickly," the boy said fiercely, shaking with barely controlled rage. "Make this filthy traitor feel the terrible guilt of her crimes!"

Bursting into tears, Patrica soiled herself and started to choke.

"I shall obey, my liege," the executioner said with a bow, and the whip cracked forward, blood spraying into the air.

The fat woman screamed with a wild animal sound, every inch of her soft body jiggling.

Nauseated by the obvious pleasure Strichland was getting from the torture, Ryan forced himself to watch for a while to appear normal. Hopefully, Krysty was doing the same, blending in and staying low. Then he noticed a commotion among the crowd on the other side of the courtyard.

"Wait!" the baron shouted, staring into the crowd. "What's going on there?"

A cloak went flying, a man bent over double clutching his gut, a woman screamed and Krysty burst from the bystanders running across the open courtyard. Her hood and cape were gone, her long fiery hair billowing behind her. Instantly, sec men charged from behind the sandbags.

"An outsider!" Leonard shouted, pointing with the knife. "Guards, capture her!"

As if poleaxed, Baron Strichland openly stared at the woman as if unable to believe what was happening. His hair fanned out around him in a wild corona of astonishment.

Deciding to risk a shot, Ryan drew the silenced SIG-Sauer but balked at the sight. The man's hair was the same as Krysty's. Exactly the same! Suddenly, Ryan knew what the baron was doing with all the redheaded girls who came to the ville. He was searching for another of his kind, searching for a mate. And now he had found one.

As the crowd linked arms to form a wall blocking her escape, the troops converged from every side. As Krysty raised her blaster, the men in the sandbag machine-gun nest fired a short burst. The rounds struck the ground at her feet, rising a line of dust clouds.

"Halt or die!" the baron commanded, the wanton lust and need on his face brutally on display.

Forgotten at the post, Patrica savored the scant few seconds without pain, knowing this was no release from her death sentence, but merely a brief delay.

Surrounded on every side, Krysty turned wildly, as if searching the crowd. Then she found Ryan. They exchanged glances. He nodded, and she stopped running, dropping her blaster and raising both hands.

"Alive!" the baron roared, climbing down from the platform. "Take her alive at all costs!" The sec men swarmed over Krysty.

Returning the blaster to its holster, Ryan merged with the excited crowd and disappeared from sight.

Chapter Fifteen

The ramshackle old pickup truck rattled noisily down the sandy street, resembling the loser in a car crash. Its tires were bald, the muffler was held on by wire hangers, and the doors were composed almost entirely of duct tape.

But deadly serious armed sec men were in the cab and sitting in the open back. They had been boastful and confident in the ville, but now amid the ghostly ruins of the city, their conversations were brief and to the point. Death lurked everywhere among the crumbling structures: falling masonry, poisonous spiders and lethal plants. Hell-flowers, they were called. Beautiful plants, with gorgeous flowers. But take a sniff and you stopped moving until a buddy dragged your sleeping body away. Something to do with spoors, or such. But if you were alone, the victim would stand there locked in a perfumed dream until he toppled over dead from starvation. Then the plants would feed on the rotting carcass. Before the fuel started running low, the sec men used to firebomb the plants on sight. They hated the filthy things. It was no way for a man to die, stupefied like a drunk in a gaudy.

Worse, outsiders come to loot the ruins—once cannibals, another time a predark war machine. And then there were the human muties who wandered in from the glowing red pits beyond the mountains, plus the local winged muties. Sometimes, even their own wolves turned against them for unknown reasons.

"Hold it!" Sergeant Benson cried, leaning out the passenger-side door. "Right here."

The driver applied the brakes, and the truck slowed, squealing every foot of the way.

"Henders, check out that body!" the sergeant directed, pointing to a vacant lot. A sprawled form lay amid the wolfweed and wreckage. Lizards were chewing on his flesh, and what seemed like a perfectly good longblaster was in the bones of his hands. The triple-damn reptiles always seemed to eat the hands of the dead first.

"Sure, Sarge," the private replied, puffing away on his pipe.

Strolling over, Henders used his bolt-action rifle to chase away the lizards, then pinched his nose shut against the stink of the decomposing flesh as he inspected the corpse.

"Nobody I know," he reported, choking a bit. "Dead for a day, mebbe more."

"Get the blaster!"

"Sure." Bending over, the private picked up the rifle and felt the slightest tug from a string attached to the stock. His face registered curiosity, then horror for a full second before the lot was filled with an expanding fireball that vaporized the man, corpse and a hundred lizards, before reaching the sidewalk and dissipating.

Shrapnel peppered the truck, sounding like hard rain, and a man in the back toppled over with a cry, falling out of the vehicle.

"Skydark!" Benson roared, holding on to the sagging door of the battered truck and painfully lifting himself off the ground.

There was no need to recce the blast zone. Smoking shoes and a burning skull told the story. Henders was gone. The ground was a charred pit with flaming wreckage scattered for dozens of yards. Shaking his head to ease the ringing in his ears, the sergeant watched as the mushroom cloud of the blast rose into the cloudy sky. Damn explosion resembled a plas-ex blast, but nobody had any of that anymore. Not even the baron. Stuff crumbled over the passage of time, became unstable, then dried into a hard, useless brick.

"Hey, Sarge!" a private called, stepping into view from behind the truck. His empty hands were dripping blood. "Pete is dead. Got a chunk of rifle barrel right through the belly."

In wordless fury, Benson glanced around the intersection at the movie theater, garage, pawnshop and office buildings. Nothing stirred—not a soul was in sight. But he knew the hunchback was somewhere near.

"Okay, Harold!" he yelled. "You got two of us with the trap! Well, enjoy the victory, 'cause you ain't getting any more!"

Silence answered the comments, and drawing a knife from his belt, Benson stabbed it into the street. "You see that?" he asked, pointing at the knife. "There's where I'm going to stake you out like a dog! Baron says we got to bring you in alive."

The sergeant took in a deep breath, then bellowed, "But alive doesn't mean with eyes! Or fingers!

"Get moving!" Benson barked at the squad. "I want a five-block perimeter sweep of the whole damn area. Smash open every ground-level door that looks suspicious."

Clutching their longblasters, the sec men rushed to comply, fueled by their own anger and hatred.

"No prisoners," Benson growled, cracking open the top of his .44 Webley revolver and loading every chamber. The hell with rationing. "Shoot first, and we'll loot the bodies afterward."

"And find me that son of a slut Harold!"

THE BASEMENT of the government building was brightly lit, mirrors from the bathrooms on every floor now ringing the sleeping Dean on each side. Mildred remembered reading how Thomas Edison assisted the doctor operating on his mother by boosting the candlelight with mirrors, and the trick worked. If necessary, the physician had no doubt that she could do an operation on the boy's spine. That is, if Ryan returned with the field kit.

Sitting on a plastic milk carton, Mildred was rubbing gun oil into the stiff leather of her new boots. They fit better every day, but still needed a bit more softening or else she'd have blisters on her heels for a month.

Finishing the first boot, Mildred took a drink from her tin cup of coffee. It was room temperature, but she needed the caffeine to help stay awake. Sipping the brew, the physician listened to the stillness. The old building was as silent as a grave, and even her breathing seemed to echo slightly amid the empty stalls and bare walls. Jak was on the ground floor standing watch, and the others were out on recce, so she was alone again with Dean. Even if the group had working radios, they wouldn't be so stupid as to waste precious batteries on idle conversation.

Placing aside the empty cup, Mildred dutifully started on the other boot, removing the laces first so they wouldn't become oil soaked and impossible to tie anymore. But then the physician jerked her head toward the sleeping boy lying under the conference table. Had his breathing just changed a little?

Putting aside the boot, the doctor padded over. Suddenly, Dean started to hack and cough. His left arm ripped lose from the binding, and he clawed at the restraining straps.

Grabbing the limb and pulling it away, she knelt on the arm to keep it still, and the boy stopped breathing. Immediately, Mildred started to apply CPR, but then realized pressing on his chest to force air into the lung would only aggravate the possibility of a puncture from the broken rib. Pinching his nose shut, she inhaled deeply and exhaled into his mouth, their lips pressed tight together. His chest rose and fell at her ministrations, but the boy didn't stir and his pallor took on a faint grayish tinge.

"Come on, Dean," she panted between breaths, feeling light-headed from hyperventilating herself. "Live!"

EXPLOSIONS SOUNDED from the ground floor of the skyscraper, then the front door exploded in a spray of glass. Firing steadily, Doc and J.B. stumbled into the tinged sunlight, their blasters booming and chattering.

Backing into the middle of the street, the two men paused for a moment as they quickly reloaded.

"Looks—" J.B. paused to swallow and moisten his throat "—looks like we made it."

"By Gadfrey, what foul magician conjured these dark visitors!"

"Here they come again!" J.B. cried, snapping the bolt on his Uzi and triggering the blaster.

Doc was only half finished reloading the LeMat, but he leveled the blaster and discharged the scattergun barrel. Smoke and thunder blasted from the muzzle, and something inside the building screamed in pain. His heart pounding, Doc pulled a paper cartridge from his pocket, bit off the top and poured the black powder into an empty recess of the nine-shot cylinder, then placed the lead ball from the package into the recess and lastly tamped down the paper to hold the charge and lead in place. He shifted the selector pin from the shotgun back to the revolver. God's blood, how many of the damn muties were there?

Doc reached over his shoulder and hauled out a Molotov.

"Light me," he ordered, proffering the rag fuse.

But J.B. started for the Hummer. "Let's get out of here while we got the chance," he retorted. "Then we'll blast them with a LAW from down the street."

"Brilliant," Doc said, as a window on the second floor exploded and a black shape sailed across the street to land heavily on the hood of the military wag. The bat clawed and bit at the sheet metal covering the engine, its large eyes shut tight against the blinding sunlight.

J.B.'s Uzi barked a dull staccato of death. The 9 mm rounds knocked the mutie off the wag, yellow blood spraying out from the impacts. The men rushed forward just as a dozen more of the muties leaped from the ruined front door of the building and landed in the middle of the street.

The companions froze, trying to be as quiet as possible while the creatures raised piglike snouts and loudly sniffed the air, turning their misshapen heads this way and that. In the tainted light of the cloudy sky, the beasts were mostly wings, their bodies no bigger than a dog's. Their ears were almost a full foot tall, their mouths filled with rows of needle-sharp teeth. The wings gave a semblance of size, spreading well over eight feet wide, the elongated elbows sticking high over their bodies and waggling ridiculously as the killers crawled about in a gross pantomime of walking.

In slow motion, J.B. took a careful step toward the Hummer, the sand softly crunching beneath his boot as he shifted his weight. Instantly, the muties turned toward him and a few started scuttling forward. The Armorer raised his leg, and one darted directly underneath the boot.

An odd noise caught Doc's attention, and he glanced over a shoulder to see two more bats directly behind him sniffing the air. Sweat broke out on his brow. He knew that primates sweated ammonia, and once any animal realized that, it could track a human forever. He didn't know if bats naturally had a good sense of smell, but these certainly seemed to. Thankfully, they were stone blind in daylight, and it was only the soft breezes from the coming storm in the desert that was keeping the muties from finding them immediately. However, if the wind shifted, or one got too close, it was all over. This close, sight wouldn't be necessary for the monsters to claw the men apart.

High above them, thick smoke poured from the broken windows of the skyscraper where the Molotov cocktails had set the building on fire. The fuel bombs had done a good job blocking the stairs and slowing the advance of the winged muties. But the elevator shaft was more than their nest apparently. It was a highway reaching from the cool dark basement to the observation tower. No wonder nobody had ever found them before. Who would search for aerial creatures underground? Smart, too damn smart for his liking.

Aiming his LeMat at the largest of the bats, Doc dangled the rag of the last Molotov before the barrel. When he fired, the muzzle-flash would ignite the rag, then he'd drop the bottle and dive out of the way. Hopefully, the noise of the gun would attract several of the muties into the flames before they knew what was happening.

Spreading out from the building, the bats crawled across the street and sidewalks in an instinctive search pattern, just like a flock of birds in flight. The similarity was unnerving.

Wiping the sweat off his brow, J.B. reached into a pocket and tossed a few spent cartridges down the road as a diversion. The empty brass landed quietly on the soft sand, and the bats started to go that way, then returned to their unified pattern. The Armorer mouthed a curse and started to unwrap a thermite gren.

Tucking the Molotov under his arm, Doc tried the same trick with his whetstone, but this time throwing the stone underhand.

It hit the side of the skyscraper, and two of the bats leaped upon the spot, sniffing and clawing air for the prey. The large bat squealed questioningly at them, and they chittered angrily in reply.

Oh yes, way too damn smart, Doc decided.

Surrounded on every side, the old man reached out and touched J.B. on the arm. The man turned with the gren ready. Doc tapped his wrist where a chron would be, and J.B. lifted three fingers, then made a zero with thumb and forefinger. Doc understood and chose a direction to run. If they shot one, all of the others would converge in a swarm. But an explosion would get several and hopefully stun the rest. Ears that big had to be sensitive.

Doc had already tossed his only gren into the elevator shaft, hoping to seal the passageway. The detonation only roused more of the monsters, including the big male they now faced. Its head was twice as large as the others, so if he wasn't the bull of the nest, he had to be the leader of the hunters. Nature abhorred a vacuum.

Accidentally, two of the bats bumped wingtips, and they leaped on each other, clawing and slavering, until realizing the mistake. From behind them, a clanging sound announced that the wounded bat was crawling back on top of the Hummer. Probably thought the heat of the engine meant there was a living thing inside the shell. Judiciously, Doc aimed the LeMat at that particular mutie. Let them reach the Hummer and... No, the ignition fuse still had to be reinserted into the fuse box under the dashboard. That would take precious seconds they couldn't afford. Where the hell were they supposed to run? Back into the dark recesses of the skyscraper was certain death. What else was around them? The park with the dried fountain, some burned-out buildings without doors or windows. An apartment complex, which meant too many doors and windows. A tennis court, a bank, a parking lot and a library.

The library had thick stone walls and slit windows much too small for the bats to crawl through. Unfortunately, the door was out of sight around the corner. It might be locked, or missing entirely. Either of those would cost the men their lives.

J.B. waved to get Doc's attention and vehemently shook his head. The old man nodded in understanding, then pointed northward up the street to the Hummer, and next to the library. J.B. placed the ignition fuse between his teeth and pointed at the vehicle. After a few moments, Doc hesitantly nodded his agreement and braced himself for the concussion, holding on to the LeMat as if it were a good-luck charm.

Sliding the Uzi over a shoulder, J.B. removed the sticky electrical tape from the gren and placed the tape on his shirt to get it out of the way. Holding the bomb tight in his left hand, he started to rotate and wiggle the pin.

Shifting his weapon away from the Hummer, Doc leveled the LeMat at a sniffing bat dangerously close to the Armorer, then realized another was moving toward himself from upwind. Once it passed Doc and got downwind, they would be discovered, and that meant a fight whose lethal outcome was anybody's wild guess.

With a dry mouth, J.B. released the spoon of the grenade. The curved handle sprang away with a snap, and the bats swarmed toward him until he lightly tossed it at the main group of the muties. It landed with a thump, and they reversed course to converge on the military explosive.

Tucking away his glasses, J.B. opened his mouth and covered both ears to cushion the effects of the blast. Doc copied the position just as the Army charge cut loose. The street erupted, sending out a stinging sandstorm and flaming chunks of flesh everywhere. The men went sprawling, but so did the bats. Screaming so loud their wails keened into the ultrasonic, the surviving muties took flight and wheeled madly around in the sky, constantly colliding with one another, seemingly impervious to any injury incurred.

Standing, Doc fired the LeMat, blowing the head off a bat and igniting the rag. He dropped the Molotov and took off at a run, with J.B. right beside him, the Uzi firing into the sky.

Then a bat careened off another and plowed straight into the driver's seat of the Hummer, squealing in protest. The mutie on the hood took up the cry and the rest flapped toward the Hummer, covering it with their wings, clawing at the metal, ripping the seats and canvas doors apart. The five-ton wag rocked under the assault, and one of the tires hissed loudly as it went flat. The bats screamed in triumph as if making a kill.

In midstride, the companions changed direction and headed for their only remaining hope.

"Head for a truck!" Doc shouted, turning to fire, then taking off once more. At his words, the bats went terribly still and started sniffing the air again, cawing their hunting cry, searching for an echo. Both men knew moments were all they had remaining.

"They might not run," J.B. countered, bounding over a low stone wall. He stopped, spun, fired the Uzi twice, then dropped the exhausted clip and reloaded.

As the men angled around the corner of the granite building, the muties were out of sight, but their cries were coming strong and fast. The effects of the blast were wearing off the survivors.

Stopping near a stack of crates, the men saw the line of trucks and knew why the villes sec men hadn't taken them away. The vehicles were wrecks, riddled with bullet holes and discolored in numerous spots as if splashed with acid.

The men checked their weapons and surveyed the neighboring buildings. They were ramshackle structures without doors or windows. Worse than useless. The double doors to the library were to their left, the brass bound portals wide open and inviting. The interior of the building was pitch-black, and numerous dried bloodstains marked the front step. This was where the others had been slain.

"Got another grenade?" Doc asked, frantically reloading.

"Nope. Molotovs?"

"Negative."

The hunting cries of the muties started to get louder.

"We aren't going to outrun them, and the Hummer is out of commission," J.B. stated grimly, lighting the tiny stub of his last cigar. He drew in the dark, then exhaled in satisfaction. "Library is our best bet."

"Once inside, we are trapped," Doc told him. "The sky is already starting to darken."

Drawing a knife from his boot and tucking it into his belt for easier access, J.B. growled, "Same can be said for them."

"A mousetrap?"

"Yep."

The sky rumbled ominously, as Doc studied the broken line of trucks. "Might work. If there is still fuel in the tanks."

"Only one way to find out," J.B. said, lowering his voice to a whisper as the first of the bats crawled over the stone wall.

The muties looked ridiculous waddling on their chicken feet and tiny clawed hands, those impossibly long elbows sticking high into the air. But their feral faces removed the clownish appearance. These were man-eaters on the prowl. Only six left, but that was more than enough.

Dropping the sheath of his sword, Doc tossed the ebony cane away. It clattered on the sidewalk, but the muties made no move toward the noise. They were learning.

"Left door?" J.B. asked, firing short, controlled bursts at the creatures. The bull mutie charged him, raising a cloud of dust in its wake.

"Right. I mean correct!"

Doc assumed a firing stance, the old LeMat boomed and the bat flipped over sideways, its muscular body blown in two. The ones behind climbed over the dead, unstoppable in their rage to reach the men.

Constantly firing, they stepped back closer to the library and parted, one to either side of the outside doorway. Now angling his aim above the oncoming muties, J.B. stitched the first Mack truck across the lot, punching holes in the steel canister set under the step of the cab. Nothing happened.

Resetting the hammer on his weapon, Doc triggered the shotgun and blew off a bat's wing. The victim yowled, and the others recoiled from the buffeting of the discharge, but didn't flee.

J.B. directed their remaining LAW missile at the second cab. A fireball engulfed the vehicle. The gasoline blast lifted the wag into the air, tires coming off and windshields shattering.

Their tall ears flattened, the muties screamed at the explosion, fleeing from the painful concussion straight toward the two friends.

Waiting until the very last moment, Doc and J.B. grabbed the ornate handles of the big library doors and swung them farther apart, pinning themselves between the brass doors and the marble building. Trapped in a triangle of shadow, the battered men couldn't see what was happening. They heard crackling fire, another explosion, the bats screaming and several thumps against the doors they clutched tightly.

Doc waited for as long as he could, then whistled sharply and frantically shoved. His heavy door moved in smooth timing with J.B.'s, but just before closing, an inhuman arm thrust out of the narrowing gap and shoved back, clawing for their faces. J.B. slashed at the limb, cutting off a finger, and something coughed in reply.

Thrusting the pitted maw of his blaster into the slim crack, Doc fired the LeMat. A piercing scream answered the ploy, the bleeding arm was withdrawn and they closed the doors in perfect harmony. But they noticed a minor flaw.

"Dark night, we have no way to lock them in!" J.B. said, his cigar drooping as he brushed the smooth brass plate around the sturdy handles.

"Then find something!" Doc shouted, shoving his arm through the looped door handles. Almost instantly, the brass shuddered from a violent blow, and high-pitched keens came from inside the building. The door shook again.

"And find one fast!" Doc grunted, digging his heels into the loose sand, "because our captives are most displeased with their new home and desire to leave post-haste!"

Across the parking lot, another fiery blast ripped apart the overturned truck, sending pieces sky high.

J.B. sprinted around the corner and returned with a length of chain from the winch of the Hummer. Shoving the stout links through the handles, he and Doc carefully exchanged positions and tightened the chain before wrapping the length through the handles as many times as it could. The screaming and spitting was increasing inside the library, and the sounds of assorted destruction could be dimly heard over the continuing explosions of the trucks.

"Success," Doc panted, stepping away. The doors shook and rattled, the loose ends of the chains dancing madly, but the library was sealed. No number of muties would force their way through that much military steel.

Losing his hat, J.B. tried to speak and staggered to his knees. Doc grabbed the man to keep him from toppling over and saw that he was badly flushed, his eyes dilated, his breathing labored. This was a chemical reaction!

Straightening J.B.'s clothes, Doc found a bleached spot on his friend's shirt, the fabric rotting away even as he watched. Ripping off the garment and casting it away exposed a spreading purple splotch on the Armorer's arm, the flesh inextricably turning a deadly necrotic black. Frantically rummaging through his coat, Doc found a butane lighter and, playing the tiny flame over the blade of his pocketknife, he then slashed the area open. A few drops of red blood rose to the surface, along with a greenish icher.

Squeezing the wound produced little more, so Doc began to suck the incision as hard as he could, turning to spit when a horrible sizzling filled his mouth and his tongue went numb. Great God in heaven, did these things spit poison or acid?

Again and again, Doc repeated the procedure until only clean blood was coming from the cut, the discoloration already significantly diminished. Laying the comatose man on the ground, Doc dropped wearily next to him, feeling totally exhausted. Plus, there was a terrible aftertaste that didn't seem to be lessening. Oh, no.

He hawked and spit repeatedly, but the world was starting to get blurry for him, as if a dense ocean fog were creeping over the landscape. The fire in the trucks seemed distant, surreal, like a movie on a badly tuned television, and the man sluggishly realized he had accidentally swallowed some of the poison. Summoning his last vestige of strength, Doc stuffed fumbling fingers down his throat, trying to make himself vomit. But the universe started to spin faster and faster until he slumped over unconscious.

Meanwhile, tiny hands squeezed out of the library windows, clawing at the granite walls, trying to enlarge the narrow slits to get free.

Chapter Sixteen

The dirty daylight streaming through the barred window of the cell was beginning to fade, and Krysty was still struggling against the chains. The links were solid steel, welded to a massive ring set in the tiled floor. The guards had been painfully thorough in searching her for weapons and lock picks, but oddly none of them tried to assault her. Aside from the occasional quick grope, she hadn't been harmed in any way. Yet.

The woman bitterly cursed the frightened child in the crowd. Krysty had felt sorry for the babe and removed her hood to cover his eyes from the torture. But the instant her face was exposed, the crowd started gasping and pointing. One man dashed off shouting for the guards, and an elderly couple tossed their own clothing over Krysty to mask her head, but it was too late by then. Knowing she was trapped, Krysty pushed into public view to try to draw attention away from Ryan. If he was free, there was hope of his rescuing her and their finding the med kit for Dean. Hopefully, the boy was still alive.

As the tainted light from the cloudy sky faded, she was thankful for the odd bluish illumination that came from the lanterns on the table. It smelled like moonshine, almost pure alcohol. The cell was a bare room of cinder-block walls. The paint was peeling off in strips from moisture, and there was a definite stink of mildew.

A former storage room, it was oddly on the third floor. Dungeons were usually in the basement. The only furniture was a table with leather straps, the wood darkly stained, a padded bench with straps for the obvious function of forced sex and a small wooden stool with a hole in the center and a bucket underneath. The furnishings were crude and simple, but the door was of rusty metal hung in a metal frame with four hinges. A formidable barrier.

As if waiting for her to make this appraisal, the door swung open and in strode a tall, muscular man flanked by two sec men holding bolt-action blasters. The tall man was painfully handsome, his features finely chiseled. His ornate uniform was spotlessly clean, and twin blasters rode at his hips, the handles turned inward for a cross draw.

"Leave us," the man ordered with a gesture.

The sec men snapped their rifles to their chests in a salute and departed, closing the door behind them.

Krysty saw all this peripherally, as she could only stare at the tall man's hair. She had noticed it seemed to be moving a lot more than anybody else's on the outside platform, but now she could see the truth. His hair was the same fiery color as her own, exactly the same color. Slightly more than shoulder length, it constantly moved and flowed as if stirred by secret winds, even now in a locked room with no ventilation. Her own hair coiled tightly to her head in response, and cold flooded her stomach as Krysty realized he could be kin. A distant cousin perhaps. Or even her unknown father. Krysty could actually feel him standing close, the same way she used to be able to sense her mother in another room.

"Yes," the man said, as if reading her thoughts.

"And do you know how long I have been searching for you?"

"For me?" she asked incredulously.

"You specifically? No, although if I had known you existed, I would have traveled the Deathlands to find kin. I was referring to how long I have been searching every redhead I could find to locate another one of us."

His sharp emphasis of the last word wasn't lost on Krysty. And deep inside, the woman was forced to admit she would have done the same. In a world of norms, where all muties were looked upon as a filthy evil, to find blood kin was her deepest wish.

"But I'm being rude, my dear," he said with a slight bow. "Please allow me to introduce myself. I am Baron Gunther Strichland, master of Alphaville."

Krysty said nothing in return.

"And you are...?" he prompted with a beguiling smile.

"Nobody of importance," she muttered, testing the chains.

In blinding speed, Strichland drew a blaster and fired. Krysty flinched as the round burned past her face and embedded in the cinder-block wall.

"What was that again, please?" the baron said with a smile, twirling the blaster by the trigger guard.

He was insane. Good, that gave her an edge. "Krysty Wroth."

"Of?"

She shrugged. "The Deathlands. Nowhere. Everywhere."

"Ah, a wanderer." Gunther lifted a leg and rested it on the corner of the table. He appeared to have something wrong with his left leg. "And now you have come home to me. I was starting to think I was the only one of my kind, doomed, to breed with the norms, casting my superior genes into the stagnant pool of their monkey blood.''

''We're all the same,'' Krysty said, trying to keep a calm expression.

The baron laughed. ''Are we? Do they heal like us? Have the same control of their muscles as we? Can they sense things in other places? Oncoming danger? Have you ever seen one of them getting a haircut?'' Rising, he spit the words like a curse, his hatred contorting his handsome features.

In spite of herself, Krysty flinched at the memory of the companions giving each other a trim. It had been horrible. The slightest tug on her hair was painful, combing was agony and cutting was worse than getting shot. Her hair was as alive as her fingers and toes, not just dead protein filaments.

''Yes,'' Gunther said softly, standing very close. ''I can see you have, and the sight affected you the same as it did me.''

Krysty didn't reply, estimating the range of her chains and the distance to the stool. Any weapons were preferable to none.

''Can you lift things with your hair?'' the baron asked unexpectedly. ''My mother could, and I could as a child, but that has left me with age.''

Her hair went still as Krysty stared at the man. He seemed in the prime of health, certainly no more than thirty years.

''I'm sixty-three,'' he said. ''Our kind age very gracefully. Or, at least, I do.''

The mystery of her own parentage suddenly welled within her as an unstoppable force. ''Who was your father?'' she asked desperately.

Snarling furiously, Gunther slapped her across the face. Krysty swung her head to avoid the blow but not fast enough, his jeweled rings raking her cheek like knives.

"That question won't be asked again. Do you understand me!" he screamed, drawing a golden dagger from his belt and waving the blade about. "Your sight isn't needed to give birth to a son. Nor your hair!"

With his free hand, Gunther slapped her again, then slammed his fist into her stomach. Caught by surprise, Krysty doubled over, gasping for breath. "Do you understand?" he asked, his voice silky soft as he stroked her crimson hair with the flat of the blade.

Shivering from the touch, Krysty did understand and tried her best to cower, to appear helpless and whipped. This was a threat that nobody else had ever made.

Encouraged by the silence, the man fondled her for a while with his free hand. Her skin crawled from the touch, but she gave a little gasp of pleasure, her sight riveted to the handles of his blasters only inches away from her chained hands. Just a little closer, fool…

"Yes, oh yes," she murmured. But as Krysty raised her smiling face to the madman, her true feelings were betrayed by her hair, which fanned out in a wild corona of unbridled hatred.

With a snarl, Gunther stepped back quickly. "So, I see you are indeed kin and will never submit willingly. No matter. A baroness would be desirable, but not necessary. I was even willing to use the new med kit to ease the pain of childbirth. But so be it, bitch. Guards!" the man shouted abruptly.

The door slammed open and sec men rushed into the room, weapons at the ready.

"Yes, Baron?" A bearded private saluted.

Strichland rested a leg on the table again. "Kill all of the other prisoners. I have no need for them anymore."

"At once, your liege."

Then he rapped the wood with his knuckles. "And replace this table with a birthing bed. I'll mount this bitch until she becomes pregnant, and then she'll give birth still strapped to the bed, and die some day when she can no longer give birth."

He turned to face the woman. "Your cooperation isn't necessary or desired. Fight me, scream and rage. It will fuel my son, make him strong! A true heir to rule my ville after me!"

The first guard seemed puzzled. 'But, Baron, I thought that Leonard—"

"Will be regent until my son is of age, then he'll step down willingly." The lies came so easily to him, they almost seemed the truth. Leonard's death had been sealed the moment Gunther found this woman. "I have already taken steps to ensure that no one ever rules this ville without my blood in their veins."

The baron gestured. "Get the bed. I wish to start immediately on my dynasty."

Krysty strained against the chains, and for a moment debated calling on Gaia for strength and breaking free to kill these men before exhaustion claimed her. But for all she knew, he could be a match for her.

Conflicting emotions raged within the woman, and she hesitantly eased her stance. The proper chance would come some other time.

Misreading the acceptance as surrender, Gunther smiled lustfully. "Obey my whims and life can be very good. How good, you have no idea."

"Mercy!" she cried, throwing herself against the

chains and rubbing against the man, her manacled hands clawing at his clothing. "Mercy, please!"

With a snarl, he punched the prisoner in the chest and backed away, grabbing for his blasters. The ivory-handled pistols were still in their oiled holsters, but one was angled halfway out.

Krysty blinked innocently and smiled sweetly like a virgin on her wedding day.

"You are dangerous," the baron snarled through clenched teeth. "Iron, pure iron. A most worthy mate.

"Guards! Bring in the bed for her to see. But come no closer than this stool."

"Yes, Baron."

"And no food," the redheaded man added thoughtfully. "After a few days, she will be too weak to try such tricks again, and there will be no trouble binding her to the birthing frame. Will there, my sweet bride?"

Pivoting on a heel, Krysty kicked at the man's throat, the chains stopping the silvered toe of her Western boot a fraction of an inch from the vulnerable flesh.

Strichland laughed as she slumped to the cinder-block wall, gathering the chains around her for protection.

"I'll return in a week, my dear bride," he said, sneering, and turned to leave, the sec men smartly holding the door open for him.

Craning her neck to see, Krysty got only a brief glimpse of the corridor outside. More cinder-block walls and lots more guards. Hopefully, they were only an escort for the baron and not a permanent detail to guard the prisoners.

Strichland turned to speak, when the window shattered and the man's shoulder exploded blood as he spun wildly, dropping to the floor.

The sec men had only a split second to register the

fact, when a black dot appeared on the forehead of the private with a beard and he toppled over, exhaling deeply. The second man dived for the door, but spewed a geyser of red as his throat was removed. He landed sprawling, twitched once and went still.

Stretching out her boot, Krysty snagged the baron's cloak and carefully dragged the body closer. Kicking him over, she grabbed a blaster, then searched his clothing. A ring of keys was found in his pants, and in seconds she was free.

First checking the corridor, she then closed the door and went to the window. A tiny figure waved on top of the building across the market square, then pointed to the north. Knowing Ryan could see her clearly through the scope of his Steyr rifle, she mouthed, "Med kit here."

The figure nodded and moved into the shadows once more.

Grabbing the baron by his frilly collar, Krysty hauled him to his feet and slapped him twice before he responded with a moan.

"Where is the med kit?" she demanded, pressing the barrel of the blaster into the ghastly wound.

The baron writhed in pain, and she eased the pressure.

"Don't die yet, cousin. Where's the med kit?" she repeated, clicking back the hammer.

"My...office," he gasped. "Down...hall..."

"Let's go," she said, throwing him toward the door.

In the hallway, some sec men were walking their way, so Krysty ducked behind the baron and shot them both dead. A third stepped into view from around the corner, blaster in hand, when the hallway window shattered and the man crashed against the wall, then sagged to the floor in a bloody heap.

"Any more around?" Krysty demanded harshly.

"That's all…" he gasped, reaching for his wound. "I wanted…privacy with you.…"

"Now you got it," she stated, slapping his hand away with the blaster while tightening her grip on the collar. Get him in submission and confused. He was a danger like none ever faced, and her only hope was intimidation through pain.

Jerking the baron about, she slammed him against the wall, then forced the bleeding man down the hallway until reaching an ordinary-looking door.

"Here…" he wheezed, his face deathly pale.

Twisting the blaster into his side, Krysty made the man open the door himself, then shoved him through in case there was a reception committee of sec men.

The office was empty.

Kicking the door shut, Krysty slammed the pistol against his temple, and the baron crumpled to the floor. Quickly searching the office, she found the med kit on a glass shelf of a mirrored wall. The rest of the shelves were filled with assorted weapons, including her own .38 revolver. She checked the load and tucked the dead sec man's blaster into her belt as a spare. The weight on her hip was reassuring. A teakwood box was filled with grisly trophies, and she tossed it aside. But from the rest of the armory, Krysty took a boxy MAC-11 submachine gun with an acoustical sound suppressor, and a sleek 9 mm Skorpion rapid-fire blaster. She had no preference among the weapons. These were simply the blasters with the most ammo clips stacked alongside. Krysty checked the clip on the Ingram MAC-11 and worked the bolt, when a dark shape rose into view reflected in the mirror.

Spinning, she fired the MAC-11 as the baron charged past her, crashing into the glass shelves. Incredibly, the man rose again, brandishing a sliver of glass as a dagger. He lunged again, and Krysty stitched him from crotch to crown, emptying the entire clip. The force of the bullets drove him back, but the baron thrust for her one last time before slumping to the floor pumping out his life onto the white carpets. Taking no chances, Krysty reloaded and fired again until there wasn't enough left of his head to identify the corpse as human.

Cries and bootsteps sounded from the corridor. Krysty waited behind the desk, and as the door swung aside, she riddled the sec men coming through, driving them back against the wall, their bodies jerking like mad puppets under the stuttering fusillade of rounds.

They dropped, and she chanced a peek outside. Clear. Heading for the stairs, Krysty shot another man coming out of the torture room, but he was already bleeding freely from the ruin of his face. More evidence of Ryan's sharpshooting.

Stopping at the window, she mouthed the news the baron was dead. A match flared for a second, showing Ryan's face. He pointed down and closed his hand into a fist, then raised one, two, three fingers. As the match died, Krysty nodded in understanding and headed for the ground floor.

On the second floor, she found a few more bodies sprawled before an open window, the curtains full of holes. Then a door opened wide, and out came a busty maid with an armload of clean bedsheets. The woman inhaled sharply, preparing for a scream, and Krysty buried a boot in the woman's gut. The maid dropped her load of linen, gasping for breath.

The redhead moved in close and administered a swift blow to the back of the head with the butt of the Ingram. With a soft moan, the maid dropped. Quickly checking her pulse to make sure the servant was alive, Krysty moved on. The maid would have a headache when she awakened, but unlike the baron, she would survive.

Tiptoeing down the staircase, Krysty paused as the brick wall of the first floor came into view. And so did a cadre of sec men, playing cards and smoking pipes behind a sandbag wall, a muzzle-loading cannon pointed at the front door. She had spotted them as the guards who had dragged her into the building only a few hours earlier. They were big and hard looking, but relaxed, obviously depending upon the security of the external guards way too much.

Staying hidden in the shadows just beyond the bluish light of their alcohol lanterns, Krysty checked over her borrowed weapons. The clip for the MAC-11 was down to two rounds, but the Skorpion was full. Exchanging 9 mm Parabellum rounds from one weapon's clip to the other, Krysty finished just in time to hear a series of muffled grunts and clatters from the other side of the front door.

"Hey, Lieutenant, what the heck was that?" said a guard, placing aside his cards and going to the door.

The officer stood and reached for his rifle. "Let's go see. Hannon, you're on—"

Stepping into the harsh light, Krysty mowed the men down where they stood with the silenced MAC-11, the hissing stream of 9 mm rounds sounding no louder than a tire gently going flat.

Stepping over the tumbled corpses, Krysty opened

the door and there was Ryan, SIG-Sauer in hand. The market square was well illuminated with a ring of torches, and she could see the exterior guards sprawled on the ground, weapons and bodies jumbled on top of one another, in the terrible throes of unexpected death.

"Clear?" Ryan whispered.

"Clear," she said, stepping through and closing the door quietly. "I have the med kit."

He touched the bloody cheek. "You okay?"

"Nothing a bath won't cure."

"Good. Let's go."

Chapter Seventeen

Carrying a plastic tray of covered dishes, Leonard walked up the stairs to the third floor. The baron hadn't asked for his dinner yet, so the youth was bringing it to him. And secreted in his pocket was a piece of stale bread for the female prisoner. It wasn't much, since the kitchen kept a close tally on the stocks, even for the nobility. Every scrap meant another day. But nobody should be allowed to starve.

When Leonard reached the third floor, the tray dropped from his hands, crashing onto the floor when he saw the bodies scattered along the hallway. The coppery stink of fresh blood filled the air, and red fluid was splashed everywhere, brightly dotted with the shiny spent brass of an autofire blaster.

Feeling stunned, he moved toward the baron's private office. At the detention room, the door was ajar and he glanced inside. The chains were empty, the prisoner gone, two additional dead sec men sprawled on the floor.

Leonard could only hear the pounding of his heart as he headed into the office. More blood and shells. The mirrored display shelves were smashed to pieces, and there amid the shining wreckage was the crumpled body of the baron. Kneeling on the glass shards, uncaring of the cuts received, Leonard tenderly turned over the body, hoping for a miracle.

The entire universe shrank to just the ruined face of the man who had saved him from the stickies in the desert as a small child, raised him, taught him to write, to sing, to read, bandaged his leg when he broke it in a fall, indoctrinated him as a warrior, the sovereign leader of their ville.

"Father," Leonard cried, hugging the bloody corpse to his chest. "I'll get her, Father. I swear. If it takes my whole life, I'll kill that bitch for you...."

THE GURGLING of the nearby river was a low background noise to the sec men walking along the top of the Alphaville wall.

"Damn flies," one of the men grumbled, waving a hand about. Something had buzzed past him, and he could only assume it was one of the fat black bugs that bred in the river. Horrid things, the bites stung worse than the rain and took weeks to heal.

There was another buzz, and a man several yards away made a juicy noise, falling to the ground and dropping his blaster.

"Billy? You okay?" he asked, coming closer, working the bolt on his rifle. Something strange was going on here. Then the buzzing sound came again and he stopped caring.

A FEW MINUTES LATER, the still of the night was violently shattered as a bright flash washed over the ville, followed by a roll of thunder.

"What the hell was that?" a grizzled sergeant demanded, walking out of a guard shack holding a cup of steaming soup. The man started to take a sip, but the cup dropped from nerveless fingers as he watched a column of flame stretch into the sky, along with assorted bits of machinery, the blast echoed by the crackling crash of a thousand windows shattering.

"Holy shit, the brewery blew," a private gasped, coming out of the barracks and sliding on suspenders.

"Damn fools got drunk again," another man drawled, chewing on a pipe. "Quality control, my ass."

"That blast must have taken out every greenhouse for blocks."

"What?" a young private said, suddenly wide awake. "But without them, we starve!"

Sergeant Zanders turned. "No shit, genius. Corporal Linderholm!"

"Sir!" the sec man barked, coming to attention in his underwear.

"Beg, borrow, steal blankets, then get your squad over there to cover those bastard plants before the night chill aces the whole fucking crop!"

"On it!" The man dashed off.

"MacPhillips, gather civvies and start lighting torches around the greenhouses to keep the area warm."

"Will that help?" the man asked, sliding on a boot while standing on one foot.

"Am I a farmer? Get!"

Not bothering to salute, the sec men rushed to the task, knowing their lives depended upon moving fast.

Window shutters were opening in every building, throwing shafts of light onto the streets. People stumbled out asking one another endless questions and gawking at the running sec men.

An officer sauntered from the tavern on the corner. "What's the commotion, Zanders?" Removing a small box from his vest, he took a dainty sniff of the pink powder inside, closed the box and returned it to his pocket, instantly more alert. "Muties? A jail break?"

"Stuff it, ya junkie!" the sergeant snapped hatefully. "Go wake the glazers and get their furnace going. We start repairs, right fucking now!"

The officer stared at the noncom coldly. "I'm in charge here, Sergeant," he said sourly.

"Great. What are your orders, sir?"

A minute passed as the lieutenant buttoned his jacket closed. "Carry on. I'll alert the glazers."

"Fucking officers," Zanders muttered, tapping the revolver at his belt. Then his expression melted as a rain of flaming debris plummeted from the sky across the ville, crashing onto stores, tents and rooftops.

"Sound the fire alarm!" the sergeant shouted to a group of gawking sec men. "Now, ya fools!"

Soon a metallic clanging sounded and people charged into the streets, carrying buckets of sand and brooms. Some beat at the small scattered fires on the street, while others started forming a bucket brigade to smother a large chunk of blazing debris dangerously close to the gaudy house. Inside, the naked women were screaming and throwing things out the windows.

"Sentries, any sign of rooftop fires!" Zanders yelled at the wall. There was no reply to the summons. "Captain of the guard, report!"

The searchlights moved back and forth along the palisade, and the guards should have been easy to spot in the glare, but he didn't see a soul. As he marched closer, his suspicions grew until he spotted a bloody arm dangling over the side of the wall, dripping red onto the streets below. Shit, poor bastards had to have been hit with shrapnel from the blast. Then the sec man drew his blaster. Or maybe Alphaville was under attack. This whole thing would make one hell of a great diversion.

"You three," the sergeant barked, pointing with his

blaster. "Get the fuck up there and see what's the trouble."

Hesitantly, the men obeyed, climbing the ladders welded to the side of the cars and leading to the wooden walkway on top of the wall.

"Well?" Zanders shouted. "Any signs of muties?"

"No, sir," a private called down. "Just dead men without faces."

"All of them?"

"Yes, sir!"

How odd, muties usually attacked from behind.

"Hey, Sarge! Here's Leonard!" a sec man cried out.

The sergeant knew that Leonard had recently reconditioned a big batch of predark fire extinguishers and had to be hauling them over for the troops to use. Good man. The kid was worth ten of the father.

But the squat APC rolled straight down the street past the burning wooden skeleton of the brewery, then turned right and charged directly toward the tunnel, traveling much too fast to ever stop in time.

The sergeant couldn't believe his eyes. That idiot lieutenant had been correct. "Jail break!" Zanders bellowed, leveling his blaster and cutting loose, the rounds ricocheting off the armor plating of the military half track as if he were throwing stones. Several of the other sec men followed his example, but the .75-caliber lead miniballs of their muzzle-loaders did even less damage.

With everybody else out fighting fires, the lone sec man in the machine-gun nest swiveled the repaired blaster on its stanchion and started firing in controlled bursts as he expertly tracked the approaching war wag. The half-inch-wide bullets punched a line of holes through the chassis of the armored personnel carrier.

Then the machine gun mounted on top of the APC

chattered nonstop as it raked the nest, sandbags spitting dust, sparks flying off the ground and car bodies of the wall. A lantern burst, and the lone sec man cried out and dropped. Unencumbered, the vehicle vanished into the tunnel, spewing oil from a punctured housing.

"WE MADE IT," Krysty said, shifting the med kit on her back, struggling with the bolt of the machine gun to free a jammed round. The baron didn't take good care of his weapons.

"Any damage?" Ryan asked, shifting the steering levers.

"We got a line of holes along the aft end of the half track. Nothing much."

The road ahead was poorly lit by the predark headlights, and Ryan cursed as he worked the gears. He was unfamiliar with this machine. "Get ready to jump. We should be in the middle of the tunnel soon."

Krysty glanced at their cargo. The wag was stacked with all of the ammo and fuel they were able to load from the garage in the few minutes they had after killing the driver. "Think it's enough to collapse the tunnel?"

The APC took a pothole with only the smallest jounce. "Damn well hope so. With this closed, they have no way to chase us."

"No sign of anybody yet," she announced, checking through the aft ob slit. "Must be too busy fighting the fires. Nope. Here they come."

"Buy us some time," Ryan snapped, killing the headlights. He had already smashed the taillights of the wag before leaving so it would be difficult for snipers to triangulate on the wag. Unfortunately, feeble as they were, the headlights outshone the aft bulbs and silhouetted the APC in stark relief, making it a near perfect target. Driving by the yellow parking lights was tough, but the vehicle took the potholes with ease.

A small wag of some kind roared into the tunnel, and its driver foolishly clicked on its headlights. Bracing herself against the moving vehicle, Krysty pointed directly between them and fired, moving the stream of bullets slightly upward, the phosphorescent tracers creating a dotted line along the tunnel. The wag veered wildly and slammed into the wall, whooshing into flames.

"Got one," she stated, savagely clearing another jam. "But more coming."

Ryan didn't reply, concentrating on his driving.

Krysty swept the tunnel with the machine gun until down to her last linked belt. However, the next vehicle didn't repeat the mistakes of the previous one, but drove through the blackness, visible only by the fiery flowers of the muzzle-flashes from the blasters of the sec men. The steady ricochets off the back armor of the APC spoke highly of their accuracy, and the lack of a blaster powerful enough to punch through the 12 mm alloy plating.

Climbing from the top gunner's seat, Krysty joined Ryan in the front of the wag.

"Ammo?" he asked, pumping the brakes for a test. Good thing they were going EVA soon. The engine temperature was climbing like a rocket. The wag had been damaged back in the ville. Cooling system, oil system, something like that. And at the rate the engine was warming, it would never reach the other end of the tunnel. But that wasn't the plan.

"One belt left," she answered. "Can't use that if we want to get out of this alive."

By the dim glow of the dashboard, Krysty disassembled a grenade. Hers had been taken by the guards, but Ryan still had his from the armory in the redoubt. Now it was the key to their escape. Extracting the plastic explosive from inside, she cradled it in both hands and climbed back to the gunner's seat atop the war wag.

"Hold on!" Ryan cried, yanking the steering levers hard in opposite directions. Tires squealing, the aft treads dug into the macadam and the APC was brought to a shuddering halt across the middle two lanes of the roadway.

Reaching under the dashboard, he pulled out handfuls of wires. "Engine is dead," he stated.

"Blaster is set," Krysty added, climbing down and swinging past the chairs to reach the door.

They hit the ground running and took off into the darkness. Pausing for a moment, Ryan fired his silenced pistol at the vehicles as they braked at the APC.

Some scattered rounds came their way, and Krysty fired the MAC-11 back at them a few times. "Wonder how long it's going to take them to think of using the APC's machine gun on us—"

A fireball erupted atop the wag, closely followed by an even louder detonation, the concussion knocking the companions off their feet. Burning men dashed about shrieking as an inferno grew in the tunnel, the black lump of the shattered APC a hulking shambles amid the crackling flames.

"J.B. was right," she said grimly. "A little plas-ex in the blaster barrel and they blow themselves to hell."

Another explosion shook the tunnel, and the entire passageway shuddered, a low creaking moan sounding from the walls. Tiles rained off the ceiling, and chunks of concrete were starting to come loose.

"Seems to have worked too well," Ryan commented,

taking her arm and starting to back away. "Fireblast! If the containment sleeve cracks, the river will flood in and we're dead, too."

The pair sprinted down the tunnel, trying not to imagine the millions of tons of polluted water pressing against the weakened tunnel walls and struggling to get in.

IN THE PREDARK RUINS, a pickup truck rattled to a noisy halt in the parking lot of the library, and five sec men disembarked. The alcohol lanterns hanging from the grille of the wag showed the ground was churned with explosions, spent brass everywhere. A line of smoldering trucks edged the parking lot, and two corpses lay sprawled on the sandy asphalt, an old white-haired man, and a short guy without a shirt. Neither man was armed.

"Well, well," Benson said, stepping from the pickup. "Look what we have here. Charles, Hawk, recce the area, see if there are any more folks about. Fred, check the trucks."

It took only a few minutes to check the perimeter of the parking lot before the men returned, giving the all-clear signal.

"Great! Let's check for loot, boys." Benson beamed happily.

"But what about the muties?" a nervous private asked. "Shouldn't we be inside?"

"Not going back to the ville before we find Harold," the sergeant admonished. "Besides, between the searchlights and our lanterns, no mutie is coming anywhere near this spot."

That sounded acceptable, and the men spread out, hunting for anything usable.

"Hey, Sarge!" the private called out from near the

smoking chassis of a destroyed Mack truck. "Some of this stuff isn't burned much."

"Anything good?" the sergeant asked, walking closer, his boots crunching on the packed sand. With the lanterns behind him, his legs cast long shadows across the parking lot.

"Don't know. What's an MRE?" The sec man tried to open the foil pack and started to turn red from the effort. There were directions clearly printed on the package, but the squiggles were meaningless to the man.

Keeping a careful watch on the sky, the two sec men proceeded to the library while the driver kicked over the white-haired corpse in a weird coat. The man's shirt was covered with so much blood it was impossible to tell if it was his or came from the other fellow. "These must be the last of those jolt dealers the muties aced," the driver theorized. "They came out of hiding to reclaim their stuff and kilt each other."

"Good." A toothless sec man laughed happily, rattling the library doors. There was no sound from inside. "More for us."

The foil finally ripped apart, spilling out an assortment of smaller packs and pouches. "Hey!" the man cried in delight. "These are food packs!"

"Hell, no wonder they fought," the driver commented. "Let's see what else they got on them."

Fred rubbed his chin. "Mebbe a little jolt?"

"Could be." The driver grinned, bending over the old man when there was a sharp metallic click. The driver recoiled just before his chest exploded, and he flew backward to slam into the pickup with a hole the size of a dinner plate in his torso.

"Sumbitch!" Benson cursed, clawing for his blaster.

But the other corpse rolled over, firing a squat machine gun from a prone position. The sec men near the library died on the spot. The sergeant drew his pistol and got off a wild shot before the LeMat removed his head in a grisly spray of bones, brains and blood.

The last sec man jumped over the low stone wall and took off for his life. Stumbling after him, J.B. and Doc both fired their blasters, but the nimble man disappeared into the ruins.

"Bedamned, we are shaky," Doc rumbled, clumsily reloading his blaster.

"Just be glad we're still alive," J.B. panted, leaning against the library wall. He was exhausted from the minor exertion. "When I saw those stupes going for the library, I almost shot them right there."

"They were not a good pattern yet."

"I know. That's why I waited."

Finished reloading, Doc holstered his piece and took a lantern from the pickup. Hurrying over to the library, he lifted it to a window. Instantly, there was a rustling of bodies and the snapping of wings. He ducked quickly and a juicy gob flew across the lot.

"Our guests seem most perturbed by imprisonment," Doc stated, closing his eyes until a wave of dizziness passed. "Perhaps we should amend the terms of their captivity."

"Too dangerous to shoot them through the windows," J.B. said claiming his rumpled hat from where it had dropped. He winced from the pain in his pulsating arm as he beat the dust off the fedora, then reset the crown and brim. "That bat venom is bad news, and they spit way too accurately for my taste."

"And mine, sir." Moving about, Doc found his sword and ebony cane. "Think there is enough fuel in the—well, let's be polite and call it a vehicle—to burn them to death?''

Forcing himself to keep standing, J.B. donned the hat, then tilted it an inch to the proper angle. Dressed again, the man felt more like his old self. "No way, even if the tank was full."

"How inconvenient," Doc commented, glancing at the skyscraper rising about the ruins. The upper levels were lost in the distance of the nighttime sky. "And I can only postulate that we did indeed capture them all, or else we would be long dead and eaten while we were unconscious."

"Screw them. Let's blow," J.B. said, shivering slightly. "It's colder than a baron's witch out here, and I'm starving."

Doc slid off his frock coat and it was gratefully accepted. "I shall fix the flat tire on the Hummer while you shop among the trucks for undamaged MRE packs. It will be warmer than the exposed street."

"Okay, by me," J.B. chattered, buttoning the garment shut. Lying on the sand, he had been warmed by the stored heat from the day. Standing, the desert winds took it away, chilling him to the bone. Hadn't been this cold since the Zarks. "Just hurry, okay?"

"I shall endeavor to do so, sir," Doc replied. As he rounded the corner, he leaned heavily on his cane, the lantern held high to light the way.

Watching where he stepped, J.B. poked though the glowing rubble, gathering items and stuffing them into the voluminous pockets of the coat. Actually, Doc had been correct; it was a lot warmer here amid the twisted metal, and the Armorer felt better with each passing minute. Whatever the toxin was the bats made, it clearly wasn't lethal. Maybe just knocked a victim out so the muties could feed at their leisure. Grisly thought.

Several minutes later, Doc drove the Hummer alongside the ruined trucks, and J.B. stumbled inside, the frock coat bulging.

"Ah, thanks." He sighed, rubbing his hands before the vent. The military heater was turned on full force, sending out waves of hellishly hot air. "Feels wonderful."

"My own pleasure," Doc said, starting to drive, both hands streaked with grease, a knuckle bleeding slightly. "If I owned a brass monkey, it would now be singing soprano."

J.B. laughed. "Good one."

"Find anything?"

Feeling the numbness leave his cheeks, J.B. patted the bulging coat. "A few souvenirs, and enough food to keep us going for a week."

"Excellent. Now our top priority is to get inside and get you outside something hot."

"Sounds good." With fumbling fingers, the Armorer snapped the window shut just as there came the faint sound of blasterfire.

Immediately, Doc killed the lights and slowed the Hummer. "That was close by. Could it be our escaped sec man?"

"Wrong caliber. He had a .38, those were smoothbore muzzle-loaders."

"Perhaps additional people being herded into the tunnel by wolves," Doc suggested, as if not believing the notion himself. He sucked on the cracked knuckle and flexed his hand.

"Or Krysty and Ryan leaving in a hurry," J.B. countered. "We better go check, just in case."

The noises came again. A machine gun chattered, the dull thud of a gren, and one of the searchlight beams disappeared.

"That's them," J.B. said, hauling the Uzi into view. "Go!"

Shifting gears, Doc stomped on the gas, and the Hummer peeled away from the curb, leaving billowing dust clouds in its wake.

Chapter Eighteen

A hand reached around the sagging door frame of the wooden barrier closing off the front of the tunnel and blindly fired a blaster three times. The shots zinged off the tiled ceiling and into the distance.

"Now," Ryan snapped, kneeling behind some garbage and carefully aiming the Steyr SSG-70.

Krysty cried out in pain and fell to the tunnel floor. After a few moments, a sec man peeked around the door and Ryan blew away a chunk of his temple. The body collapsed onto the sandy ground, his rusty blaster rolling out of sight. Unseen hands dragged the corpse out of the doorway. Once again, all that could be seen through the sagging door in the barrier was a waist-high sandbag wall and the ruins beyond.

"That's two down," the woman said, getting back up. "How many were there to start, four or six?"

"Don't recall," Ryan growled, firing at the left side of the barrier. The 7.62 mm round slammed into the wood, but didn't penetrate.

"Fireblast," he cursed. "Damn thing is made out of different kinds of planks. Sometimes I get through—most often I don't."

Glancing over a shoulder, Krysty noted the tiny specks of lantern light were a lot closer. She sprayed a few bursts at them, but got no answering cry of pain. Damn sec men had to have the lanterns hanging from the ends of sticks or something. No way she could target the guards.

"Range?" Ryan asked, the Steyr held loosely in his grip, his single eye wide for any indication of the guards.

"Too damn close," she replied, trying the MAC-11. The hissing autofire hosed a full clip down the tunnel with no results.

High up on the frame, a shiny square edged past the door, and Ryan shattered the mirror, a finger dropping to the ground. A stream of curses sounded and again several revolvers popped into view, firing wildly.

Ryan shot a blaster out of its owner's grip, the weapon spinning away over the sandbags. Then Krysty gave a spray from the noisy Skorpion. Lacking a suppressor, its bullets hit harder, blowing chunks of wood from the frame, leaving clusters of splinters sticking out.

Shifting the med kit on her back, Krysty mentally wished she hadn't thrown away the dead gren. It would have bought them seconds of shock when they were forced to rush the doorway. Caught between an unknown number of armed sec men behind, and only a few ahead of them, a frontal charge was the logical way out. At least the ville guards were on foot. None of their wags had gotten past the burning APC. Yet.

Easing a fresh clip into the Steyr, Ryan fired randomly at the barrier, but only two holes showed daylight and nobody shouted in pain.

Just then, shots boomed from down the tunnel, and a miniball impacted on the ground between them.

"Shit, they can see our silhouettes," Krysty spit, crouching lower and firing back. This time, she got a hit, but it was only a single voice.

"And they have our range. This is it. We got to

chance a charge," Ryan said, rising and drawing his SIG-Sauer. "You ready?"

Standing, Krysty worked the bolts on both of her weapons. "See you in hell, lover."

For a precious second, the man and woman exchanged private glances, then started to creep forward, but froze motionless when a long sharp whistle sounded from outside, closely followed by two more.

Separating to the opposite sides of the tunnel, Krysty crossed her arms at the wrists and aimed her blasters in both directions as Ryan chanced an answering whistle. A guttural voice on the other side of the barrier asked a question to somebody in the negative just as the wooden slats furiously shook from a barrage of machine-gun fire and the telltale discharge of the predark LeMat. Men screamed, handblasters discharging from their death convulsions. Bodies fell into view. The Uzi chattered once more, followed by another thundering round from the LeMat, then silence.

Whistling again, Ryan got an answer. Exiting the tunnel, the companions relaxed a notch as J.B. and Doc walked from the idling Hummer parked near a curb. But the smiles on the two men quickly faded when they saw the serious expressions on the man and woman.

"You folks okay?" J.B. asked in concern, cradling the Uzi.

"Gaia, no," Krysty replied, scrambling over the sandbag wall. "We have an army on our tail."

"Then we must leave, posthaste!" Doc said, waving away the tendrils of smoke from the muzzle of his black-powder hog-leg.

Shouldering his rifle, Ryan snarled, "Fuck that. Got any grens, or plas-ex?"

"Not a thing. Used it all killing the muties," J.B. said. "Even our one LAW is gone."

"How about spare fuel?"

Seeing where the man was going, J.B. got the idea. "No, but we have two alcohol lanterns we took from some sec men. That should do the job."

"Get them. You two, block the doorway," Ryan ordered, going for the Hummer.

Moving fast, Krysty and Doc holstered their weapons and started tossing sandbags from the wall in front of the open doorway until the stack was chest high. J.B. and Ryan returned at a run, lit the wicks on the lanterns and threw them onto the barrier. The lanterns crashed high on the wooden half circle of the tunnel's mouth, the flaming alcohol flowing down the planks and spreading until the entire front was crackling and smoking.

"That won't hold the baron's men for very long," J.B. stated.

"Not supposed to," Ryan said, blinking in the pale daylight. Rumbling with thunder, the dirty clouds were low in the sky and a lot darker in color. Lightning flashed, and the winds increased slightly. The storm that had been threatening to break ever since they first arrived was now only hours away. Acid rain or a sandstorm, either could be an advantage if handled correctly.

"Please elucidate, sir," Doc asked, confused.

"I only wanted the fire to get rid of the wood," Ryan said, heading for the Hummer and climbing behind the wheel. The engine caught the first time. "Now let's get the hell out of here, so we can come back and finish this."

"To fight an army?" Krysty asked, dropping the med kit on the floorboards as she took the passenger seat.

Making room for Doc in the back, J.B. was smiling, as if he already knew the answer and highly approved.

"Hell no," Ryan stated, driving away. "We're going to *stop* the baron's army. With one shot."

THE BURNING BARRIER smashed apart, the smoking timbers tumbling to the ground as a bulldozer effortlessly plowed through. Right behind the rattling predark machine were a hundred sec men with blasters, then a dozen carts full of supplies. The dozer plowed the front of the tunnel clear of planks, sandbags and corpses as the sec force spread out, immediately setting up defensive posts and starting a perimeter sweep for enemies. A few carried muzzle-loaders, but the rest sported autofires, loot from the baron's private armory mixed with the fancy blasters recovered from the dead jolt dealers.

Cradling M-16 submachine guns, the Wolf Pack marched into view followed by a sky-blue Cadillac convertible with the top down. Leonard was standing in the passenger's seat holding on to the windshield. His longish hair was now a crew cut, and the teenager was dressed in a black jumpsuit, with leather bandoliers full of ammo crisscrossing his chest. A silver Desert Eagle rode at his right hip, and a Navy flare gun rested in a shoulder holster.

The driver was a grizzled man with an unhealed gash across his face from the destruction of the greenhouses. A sawed-off shotgun lay on top of the dashboard before him, his shirt pocket jammed with homemade shells.

The crowd of sec men moved out of the way for the Caddy, and it stopped in the middle of the access ramp for the tunnel.

"Sergeant," Leonard yelled, indicating a soldier, "have the men establish a perimeter, then recce the local buildings for snipers. I want a safety zone of two full blocks. A storm is coming, and I want that bitch and her friend found before it hits."

"Sir!"

Leonard watched the activity bustling around him as more wags rolled out of the tunnel. The trap with the APC had been extremely clever, but failed. The tunnel was severely weakened there, and the river was steadily trickling in, but the predark storm drains easily handled the flow and diverted the water…well, someplace else. He didn't know or care where as long as the underground passageway stayed clear for his sec men. Timbers hoisted by car jacks reinforced the ceiling, making a maze for the wags to carefully maneuver through. But it worked. They were here and ready for a fight.

"Establish camp here, Captain," Leonard commanded. "We can retire at night inside the tunnel in case of muties."

"Or a storm," the driver added, listening to the angry sky.

"Is that a good idea, Lieuten—? Baron?" Captain Zanders asked, running an uncomfortable finger along the interior of the collar of his new uniform. Anton Zanders an officer—his mother would have died with pride. "Shouldn't we make camp inside the sports arena or the high school? They're both in good shape. Gives us lots of room to maneuver."

The young baron stared hard at the grizzled veteran until he felt flush with unease.

"Safety first, Captain. But thank you for the opinion," Leonard said with surprising gentleness. "My father had favorites among the troops whom he would promote out of friendship. I do not. That idiot officer in charge of tunnel defense was the first man I sent to the farmers.''

"Sent to till the farms, you mean, sir,'' the captain offered as a correction.

Looking over the men, the youth said nothing in reply.

Zanders tried to hide his pleasure and failed.

"The man was a total jackass,'' he spit. "Should have told me, sir. I would have turned on the Machine myself and tossed him in.''

"Which is why you are in charge now, Captain.'' Baron Leonard Strichland stepped down from the Cadillac and walked about.

"However, I do agree with you about mobility. This area will merely be our base camp. From here, we spread out through the ruins, systematically checking every street, every building.''

The former sergeant scratched his ear. "I don't know, Baron. That might drive her into the desert.''

"I'm prepared for that,'' Leonard replied, watching a team of specially chosen hunters head out into the dunes. They were his insurance. If this should fail, their job was to track the woman until they brought back her head. The families of the hunters would stay safe and warm in Alphaville as security to guarantee their allegiance to the task. Fear and hunger made all men obedient. In a well of emotions, his chest ached with the thought of his slain father, then the youth forced himself hard again. Only the strong survived, and the weak didn't rule.

"Baron, the area is secure,'' a sec man reported, crisply saluting. "The buildings on both sides of us are clear, cellar to roof.''

"Good. Thank you,'' Leonard replied, wiggling uncomfortably in his new stiff boots. Sneakers were more comfortable, but didn't look impressive. Power knew no pain. His father had also told him that many times over dinner, or at an execution.

"Any footprints or tire tracks?" Zanders asked brusquely.

"None, sir."

"Well, they didn't fly away, moron. Have the trackers search again."

Another salute. "Yes, sir."

Zanders slapped the hand down. "And stop doing that, ya gleeb. The boss looks bad enough in his new uniform. You want to tell a sniper exactly who to shoot at?"

Walking slowly forward, the Cadillac right behind him, the baron arched an eyebrow at the statement, but didn't speak. Was he overdressed? Damn. Mebbe.

"Oh." The sec man had obviously never considered that. "Sorry, sir." His hand twitched but stayed at his side.

"Better," the captain grumped. "Now, have we checked the skyscraper yet?"

Watching a squad of men dig foxholes, Leonard turned and interrupted. "Is that necessary, Captain? The top is so far away, what weapon could possibly..."

His words faded as a contrail of white smoke moved across the sky from the top of the tall building, traveling straight for them.

"Incoming!" the captain bellowed, diving for the ground, pulling the baron with him.

The contrail arced down to impact directly inside the mouth of the tunnel. The world shuddered from the explosion, bricks and tiles shotgunning out to fell scores of screaming men. Another contrail streaked in to punch through the bulldozer, the ground underneath the machine rising to tear it to pieces. Then a third and fourth contrail hit the tunnel again, cracking apart the concrete apron in strident fury. With the groan of a dying giant, the tunnel crumbled apart, the steel support beams screaming as they twisted out of shape. In slow grandeur, the opening crashed shut, spewing thick billowing clouds of acidic concrete dust.

"Rockets!" a man yelled in panic. "They'll wipe us out! We surrender! We surrender!"

Rising, Leonard drew his blaster and shot the man where he stood, the .50-caliber round from the Desert Eagle spinning the man like a top before he fell over.

"There are no more rockets," the young baron shouted, holstering the piece, his wrist aching from the recoil. "If they had more, they would have used more. Do you hear any more explosions? No. The attack is over."

Sullenly, the troops got to their feet and retrieved dropped weapons. For most of them, this was a lot different than bullying civvies or shooting escaped prisoners.

"Captain, I apologize," Leonard said, offering the man assistance. "Get a squad up there immediately. Or should we set fire to the building?"

There was no response from the still form, and the young baron noticed an unbroken tile sticking out of the back of Zanders's head, his exposed brains a pulpy mass of soggy red tissue dribbling onto the dry soil. Leonard turned away from the corpse, his eyes stinging, his heart pounding. So fast, it had happened so fast.

"Lieutenant Kelly, you are now in charge of the men," he barked. "Get a team to the skyscraper and kill anybody you find. Then set fire to the bastard thing!''

''Sir!'' the officer barked, saluting.

The young baron ignored that for the moment. ''Sergeant Jarmal, divide the men into thirds. One group starts clearing the tunnel, the second finds that high school Zanders mentioned and begins fortifying it, the third salvages anything useful from the wreckage.'' Leonard paused for longer than he meant to. ''And the dead.''

''Yes, my lord!''

''It appears,'' Leonard said grimly to nobody in particular, ''that despite my wishes, we're trapped here until further notice.''

Chapter Nineteen

Sweaty and bloody, Mildred stumbled out of the tent in the basement of the building. The exhausted physician was holding a lantern. Every other lantern the companions owned was inside the bedsheet tent, backed by a mirror, the glow infusing the food court with almost noontime clarity. The air of the entire level reeked with alcohol, and the floors shone from a fresh scrubbing.

Five anxious faces watched her approach. Nobody spoke. Ryan sat in a chair holding a full cup of cold coffee. Earlier in the day, it had been steaming hot. Krysty sat nearby, her hand on his. Doc crossed his fingers. Trying hard to appear calm, J.B. and Jak both looked as if they were about to defuse a bomb.

"He'll live," Mildred reported, removing her homemade surgical mask and mopping her damp brow. Just a few layers of white cloth cut from a shirt and boiled clean, but it served the job. Her gown was a kitchen apron, bleached white and boiled in antiseptic mouthwash.

Ryan started to rise, then sat down again. Krysty squeezed his hand, while J.B. slapped him on the back.

"Told you so," the Armorer said, grinning. "Dean's tough as shoe leather."

"He's young and strong, and everything went textbook perfect. Oh, he'll have some scars, but the rib will be fine and there's no danger of paralysis or blindness."

Walking to a punch bowl filled with bottled water and contact-lens cleaner, a mild solution of boric acid, Mildred washed her bare hands clean, using a spare toothbrush to scrub extrahard under her fingernails. Apparently, in predark days, business executives traveled unexpectedly a lot. Most of the offices here had travel packs in the desks. The old materials were a perfect mix for surgery—mouthwash, soap, floss. And the first-aid box in the receptionist's desk had given her enough iodine solution for postop, once she revitalized the dried crystals with sterile water.

"So he'll be okay," Ryan said without emotion.

Patting her hands dry, Mildred snorted. "You should be so healthy."

On a nearby table, a glass pot of MRE coffee was simmering over a candle. J.B. poured Mildred a cup, added two sugars and brought it over. She accepted the brew gratefully and slumped into an empty office chair. Mildred took a sip and for the first time in a long while didn't grimace in distaste. By God, even this military boot cleaner was good after six hours of meatball surgery. Homemade masks, flour, water and newspaper to make papier-mâché for the cast, fishing line for sutures, vodka to wash the floor…Hawkeye Pierce, eat your heart out.

Seeing her actions, Ryan drained his own cup untasted and stiffly stood. "Can I see him?"

"Sure. You couldn't wake Dean with a bomb. I shot enough sodium pentathol into him to keep him asleep for hours. Had to guess at the dosage, it was so old and weak. But he'll be out for quite a while."

"You sure?" Ryan asked, taking a spare mask off the small pile on a restaurant countertop.

Typical concerned parent. Mildred kept her voice

soothing. "Yes, Mr. Cawdor, everything went fine. Dean will be his old self in a few months."

"Months?" Krysty repeated. "Mildred, we can't stay here that long."

J.B. offered the physician a refill, but Mildred waved it off. Sleep was what she needed most now. "Don't have to. We can leave as soon as Dean wakes. Maybe tomorrow."

"Hallelujah." Doc sighed.

"We just have to take it real easy going over those dunes," Mildred continued, fighting a yawn. "I don't want my fine stitching to pop and have to go in again. I'm out of 4-0 silk, and you folks can't afford the blood."

It was true. The companions were exhausted from the transfusions. Just prior to the operation, Mildred had taken a pint and a half from each of them, the maximum that could be safely drained without endangering the giver. Only Ryan's blood type matched his son's, so the rest went into mason jars and they were swung overhead at the end of a rope for hours until the clear plasma and the blood cells separated. Mismatch blood types, and a patient suffered horribly. But anybody could accept anybody's plasma. Some mighty fine engineering there by the Lord, as her father used to remark during his Sunday services.

Not bothering to try to stifle her next yawn, Mildred noticed a lack of enthusiasm from the others.

"I said he's going to be fine," she stated irritably. "Why all the long faces?"

"Skyscraper on fire," Jak said, resting his elbows on his knees, his snowy hair tumbling down to hide his scared features.

The physician frowned. "Still? I thought J.B. said the

fires died from the cocktails he and Doc used on the muties.''

"This is the new baron's work," Ryan said, stepping from the bedsheet tent, carrying the other lantern. Mildred was right; the boy seemed fine. He put down the lantern he had brought out and turned off the wick. No sense wasting fuel. Dean would sleep regardless, and they were low on juice.

"Set fire to a whole building, just to get rid of us?"

"More likely to flush us out of hiding," J.B. stated, polishing his glasses on the sleeve of his new shirt. Smelled a bit musty, but it was nice and thick.

"Me, specifically," Krysty said, tearing open an MRE pack. Suddenly her appetite was back with a vengeance. Using her teeth to open a foil envelope of corned-beef hash, she dug in with the attached plastic spoon. One hundred years old at room temperature, and it tasted like ambrosia.

"Damn." The physician nervously glanced at the covering of barbed wire and curtains above them as if able to see the tall building fifty blocks away. "Is the blaze spreading?"

"Thankfully no, madam," Doc replied, resting his chin on top of his cane. "We kept careful track of its progress until the danger passed."

And they didn't inform her so she could concentrate on Dean. Smart move. "Think he'll set fire to the rest of the ruins?"

"I doubt it. Too much here yet to be salvaged. Probably just removing a potential source of danger," Ryan said, reclaiming a chair and laying the Steyr across his lap. Nimble hands began stripping the blaster for a cleaning. "After all, that's where I launched the rockets from.''

Mildred chose her next words carefully. "Yeah, about that, why didn't you use the Hafla to kill the sec men? It carried four rounds. Should have been more than enough. Or do you have a plan cooking?"

"No plan. Just common sense." Disassembling the rifle without looking, Ryan patiently explained to Mildred that armor-piercing weapons were almost useless against troops. The damn rockets went through a heavy steel bulldozer before exploding. Shoot a man, and they would bury themselves underground. Only kill one or two at the most that way. But seal the tunnel and there were no more reinforcements coming. What troops and supplies Leonard had with him was it until they dug free.

"At least we are safe for a while," Doc said, getting himself a cup of coffee.

"But while he's digging in, the others will be digging out," Krysty said, tossing the trash into a receptacle. "We may have only bought a few days."

"More than we had before," Ryan stated, laying aside springs and levers.

"The guy should be delighted we made him baron," Mildred said, rubbing a tired hand over her face. "Unless Strichland was his father or something."

"Blood feud." Jak frowned. "Nasty."

"Can't be." Krysty chewed a brick of gray U.S. Army cheese. "The baron was different, like me, and he wanted to breed a son. So it can't be a member of his family. He didn't have any.

"No, wait," she added, blinking. "A guard did mention something about a boy named Leonard."

"So it's his adopted son who's after us."

A low moan sounded from above, the windows softly rattling.

"I have a theory," Doc rumbled, adding powdered milk and thoughtfully stirring the brew, "that the personnel of our redoubt established this ville. The military hierarchy, the greenhouses, the tunnel in just like our tunnel out."

Jak looked up from scratching at the bandage on his side. "Shit! New redoubt."

"Would explain a lot," Ryan mused, adding a few drops of homogenized oil to the trigger assembly. "And thankfully, they don't know about the real base in the mountains anymore."

Muted thunder rumbled somewhere.

"What's that noise?" Mildred asked, changing the subject. "Storm finally hit?"

"Sandstorm," Ryan said, sliding the assembly back into the bottom of the stock and tightening the screws. "And a real bastard. That'll buy more time. It's why nobody is on guard duty. We can't even open the door against the pressure of the wind."

"Once Dean wakes up, I'll do a few tests and we can leave."

"Useless to go hunting in a sandstorm," the Deathland warrior continued. He inserted the bolt into the receiver slot and worked it back and forth a few times to make sure the action was smooth. A drop more oil was added. "Wind blows right down the barrel, and the grit clogs a blaster solid. Can't get off more than a single shot before they jam."

"Autofires," Jak said grimly. "They got muzzle-loaders. Be okay."

"No, my friend," Doc stated. "Those will jam also. Much more grease in an iron works of a muzzle-loader than a modern rifle." He affectionately patted the LeMat on his hip. "Trust me."

Jak accepted the rebuff. Doc would know.

"Got knives."

"Sure, but the wind is still too strong. Even if they had diving weights tied to their shoes, the storm would smash them against the buildings like bugs on a windshield."

"Wonder how the greenhouses survive intact?" Mildred asked pensively.

"Not care," Jak said. "Their prob."

"However, when the storm stops, we can expect company."

Finished with her repast, Krysty wiped her mouth on a tiny moist towelette from the MRE pack. "Think Dean will be ready to travel by then?"

Mildred shrugged. "Hopefully."

"We aren't waiting that long," Ryan said, dropping in a clip of fresh round and ramming the bolt home. "Once the wind dies down a bit, Krysty and I will move out to hit them hard. Cut down the numbers of the opposition as much as possible."

Unwrapping a stick of sugarless gum, the redhead nodded. The matter had already been discussed between them.

"During a sandstorm," Doc said, slowly arching an eyebrow.

"How?" Jak asked pointedly.

Mildred added, "Can't wrap blasters in cloth as protection from the grit. Bolt action and autos would jam immediately on any loose fold, and the revolvers would set the material over the cylinder on fire."

"Nothing like that." Ryan laid the assembled weapon across his lap. "True, we'll need some speciality equipment, but I spotted the place to get it when driving back here."

"Don't remember any scuba shops or anything like that," J.B. said, scratching under his hat. "Mebbe a pharmacy. Going to put condoms over the barrels? No, the guts would still be exposed. What's the place?"

"Shoe store."

As the desert winds fiercely rattled the windows again, the companions stared blankly at the one-eyed man. Already knowing the answer, Krysty allowed herself a half smile waiting for the man to explain.

Only J.B. burst into laughter. "You crafty bastard. They'll never know what hit them."

"Agreed. As soon as the storm breaks, we attack."

IN THE NORTHERN section of the ruins, sec men were using the butts of their blasters to nail boards across the inside of thick Plexiglas windows. Boards were already on the outside, but the white expanse of the drive-through window shook from the fury of the storm, so it seemed a wise precaution. The front door of the bank wasn't even visible through the stack of sandbags offering them protection from the storm.

At a teller's cage, the quartermaster was frying onions in a skillet held over a small fire of paper money to add to the soup for dinner. A lone corporal was playing harmonica in the lobby, while the night crew was sleeping in their bedrolls down in the cellar. Some officers were upstairs throwing dice for cigs. One enterprising private was skinning a lizard he'd caught, and the rest of the sec men were sitting on their duffs, ritually field-stripping their blasters merely for something to do. Out of the seventy-four men, only six stood guard duty with loaded weapons.

"Hey, Marv, play something snappy," a corporal asked, dry shaving with a straight razor.

Tapping the moisture out of his harmonica, the musician seemed offended. "I was."

"Oh, yeah. Sorry."

Playing poker at a table with other sec men of various ranks, a lieutenant muttered, "Son of a bitch only knows four songs, and we've heard them all twice by now."

"Better than quiet," the private said, drawing a new card.

A snort. "That's your opinion. I bet two cigs."

"Fold."

"I'll cover that. Whatcha got?"

"Read them and weep."

"Shit."

Using a paperclip to scrape the warm ashes out of his corncob pipe, a private asked, "Anybody got some corn silk? I can trade."

"Whatcha got?" a corporal asked, stitching a hole in a sock.

"Token from the gaudy house for an hour with the new girl."

The quartermaster looked up from the sizzling onions. "You mean Laura? The one who's so wild they gotta tie the bitch down to keep her from breaking your back? I'd trade a whole cig for that."

"How about a nice lizard?" the hunter offered hopefully, proffering his filleted catch at the end of a bloody knife.

"Dream on, gleeb. I'll take the cig." The exchange was made.

"One day," grumbled a private off by himself, stabbing at the carpet with a knife. There was concrete under the flooring so the blade couldn't gain purchase and kept falling over. "We leave the ville, the tunnel explodes, ten guys croak and now we're stuck in a freaking sandstorm. In a single day. Shitfire!''

"Could be worse," another sec man suggested.

"Yeah?"

The man winked and nudged his friends. "Sure. Might also have to listen to some loud-mouthed blowhard whine like a mutie with a broken bottle up its ass."

The knife took on a more aggressive posture. "Oh yeah, lard bucket?"

"Cork it, the lot of you," Sergeant Jarmal said low and menacingly. He was sitting against the wall, his thick arms crossed, with his battered cap covering his scarred face. But that didn't always mean the coldheart was asleep. "Any more chatter and you'll both walk the perimeter. Outside. Get me?"

That dire announcement stopped conversation for a while, but over the long hours the voices slowly returned to the usual mix of lewd jokes, dreams, suggestions, bitching, yawning and lies, the ageless talk of bored soldiers.

Reading a paperback war novel found in a desk, Leonard was sitting on a cot in the vault of the bank, the open door letting him listen to the troops. They were restless, but had good reasons to be. Luckily, he had the foresight to bring along extra provisions and supplies. Leonard thought they might be needed if the chase went into the desert. Now the rations were keeping them alive while trapped by the storm, although they were low on water and he was getting mighty sick of fried-onion soup and baked potatoes.

Outside, lightning flashed and the winds howled.

"How bloody long will this last?" the young baron growled, placing aside his book. Too many of the words in it were unfamiliar to him, and he detested feeling like a stupe. In a fit of pique, he tore the volume into pieces, the pages fluttering to the floor like dead leaves in autumn. There, who was the stupe one now?

Thunder rumbled again.

"Seen worse," Jarmal drawled from under his hat.

"I doubt it," Leonard snarled. "Captain Kelly, any word on the tunnel? Have the civvies broken through yet?"

The officer turned from the poker game. "Unknown, my lord. I twice sent men to check." He hesitated. "But none ever returned."

"Then send more," the baron ordered impatiently. "Lash them together with ropes, tie bricks to their feet, but get me some information!"

"As you command, my lord," the officer said coldly.

Then Leonard saw the faces of the sec men, the fear, the unwillingness to do the job, that first fledgling trace of resentment, the brother to hate.

"Cancel that, Captain," the youth stated, fear a knot in his belly. Then, in forced gaiety he added, "Quartermaster, break out some wine. That'll cut this dust from our throats. There were a couple of bottles in the trunk of my wag. Use them all! Give every man a half cup, starting with privates, then the officers. I'll be last."

A score of heads turned his way, tired faces showing interest, with a dash of disbelief.

"B-but, my lord," the man stammered, rubbing his hands as if in absolution. "There won't be enough to go around."

"Do what you can, but the men come first," Leonard said with a straight face.

"Three cheers for the new baron!" a private called out, and the rest took up the cry.

Eagerly, the sec men formed a line for their liquor ration, and Leonard retired to his bulletproof room. He was a fool, an idiot! One of the very first lessons he learned was to always stay on the good side of the men. Whoever had the blasters was in charge. That was a fact of life he could not afford to forget again.

And when the winds eased in force, the men could then prove their loyalty by bringing in that cursed redhead alive. How well he remembered the fierce beauty of her face and those ample, womanly curves. Starting a dynasty with the redhead had been a splendid idea of his father's. Yeah, a very good idea. And after they were safely back in the ville across the river, his troops would burn these ruins to the ground, removing the problems of the wolves, the winged muties and the hidden weapons cache permanently. But first, he had to find the bitch.

To hell with waiting for the storm to stop. Just as soon as the winds eased in force, Leonard would unleash all of his troops and let the final hunt begin.

REEKING YELLOW WATER swirling around his patched boots, Harold slogged through the sewer of the ville, a tiny candle in his cupped hands lighting the way. A voice inside his head said a major storm had to be raging for the river water to be this high, and the hunchback was forced to cover his face in an effort not to choke on the chemical stink. Even if the acid rains didn't reach the ville, the runoff from the mountains raised the level of the river until it flowed back into the normally dry sewers. Splashing in the wastewater, a rat scurried by, already dying from the diluted acid. There was no sewage down here. Alphaville saved its solid waste for the greenhouses.

Counting the feeder pipes carefully, the hunchback reached the last familiar intersection. Here was where he usually turned left to reach the ruins, but not today. Patrica was dead, the deal was off and he was going to claim his bride. A strange kind of cold anger was building within him, and he was eagerly looking forward to meeting anybody who tried to stop him.

The previous day, Harold had reached the secret place where the old baron used to hide blasters. Oddly, the basement of the skyscraper was completely deserted, not a mutie there. But the sergeant left the bundle of food for their young anyway, took what he went for and departed again. The hunchback hoped his pets were okay. They were so innocent and shy.

The two huge blasters rode heavy at his hips, and the rifle slung across his back was the biggest in the plastic trunk. Did he remember to release more argon gas into the trunk after he sealed the lid shut? He shook off the thoughts. It didn't matter now. Harold knew he probably wasn't going to survive this journey. But that was okay. He and Laura could be together in death.

Reaching another intersection, the hunchback paused, waiting for the voices to tell where to go. He had never been in this section of the sewers before. It was forbidden for any to go down there, twenty strokes, and owning a map of the sewers was death by the Machine. The faint light of his candle displayed several side tunnels, extending out from a central pit. At the bottom was a main feeder pipe, and in a rush he knew that was his destination. A ladder was bolted to the side of the pit, and, starting to climb down, he stopped halfway as there came the telltale squeaking of rats. Lots of them.

Holding on to the rungs, Harold lit a match and dropped it. Before the sulfur tip burned out, he caught a glimpse of what was below. Lining the bottom of the pit were river rats, hundreds of sleeping rats, their naked pink tails lashing about as the piles constantly shifted and moved. Real fear seized the man, and he had trouble breathing. This was bad. The hunchback knew the appetite of a rat. A pack like that could take the meat from his bones before he covered the few feet to the main pipe. Instinctively, he knew the silent whistle wouldn't work here. Scaring the horde would only make matters worse.

Several voices shouted conflicting suggestions to him, but only one rose above the others in clarity, ordering the hunchback to give the rats exactly what they wanted. All the food they could eat.

Drooling slightly, Harold eagerly nodded. Yes, that should work fine! Pulling out his eating knife, the man carefully cut off the sleeve of his shirt, then realized he had no rocks. Taking one of the blasters, the hunchback tied it tightly inside the sleeve, leaving a nice long tail hanging loose. Then, stabbing his thumb with the knife, he squeezed out blood and rubbed it over the bundle until it was good and soaked.

There was a flurry of movement among the rats, and Harold waited with a pounding heart until the rodents succumbed to sleep once more. One particularly large rat lying prominently on the very top of a pile yawned until its jaws threatened to crack, then blinked sleepily and settled back into position.

Taking hold of the end of the cloth strip, Harold began whipping the bundle around and around, building speed until it started to hum, then released the makeshift bolo. Off it flew over the rats and landed with a clunk in a side tunnel, bouncing and rolling for another yard or so.

Suspended above the furry killers, he clung to the ladder and watched. His vision was becoming adjusted to the darkness, faint streamers of light coming in from a street grating far overhead.

In the side tunnel, a pink nose twitched as a rat at the far end of the pack lifted its head and glanced around, sniffing curiously. Waddling from its cozy position on the bottom of the gently breathing pile, the yawning rodent ambled over to the pistol and took a sniff, then a lick, then began happily gnawing on the bloody rag. Its squeal of delight roused another rat, which joined the first. Their quiet nibbling awoke a third, then a fourth. Soon a group was working on the warm morsel, and as more arrived, rats began crawling over one another to get to the food. Wiggling for position became shoving, then teeth were bared and hissing turned to snarling. One savagely bit another, and blood spurted. Its squeal of pain aroused hundreds more, and the wounded rodent was torn apart and eaten by its comrades.

Soon dozens, then hundreds from the pile joined in the cannibal feast, the hot smell of fresh blood driving them insane. Screams filled the sewer as the hungry rats turned on one another, slashing and clawing in a wild feeding frenzy.

Quickly reaching the bottom of the ladder, Harold tried not to step on any of the scampering rats underfoot as he crossed the pit into the tunnel. A few scurried after him, and the hunchback waited until he was a good distance away from the feeding frenzy before stomping them to death. One seemed less mangy than the rest, and he stuffed it into a pocket for dinner later.

Moving fast along the pipe, he found more ladders leading into access shafts. The voices counted merrily until reaching number fourteen, then screamed at him to climb exactly here. Shivering under the chorus of commands, the hunchback obeyed meekly. A heavy iron grating blocked the top of the shaft. Harold quietly lifted the covering and gently set it aside as he climbed from the sewer.

Standing, the hunchback saw he was in a storage room, boxes and barrels stacked haphazardly about in careless abandon. Moving quietly to the door, he peeked through the keyhole and saw Jimmy in the next room brushing his teeth at a dirty sink, humming a tune. The voices had done it. This was the gaudy house. The next part was his alone to complete.

Lifting the door by the handle so the rusty hinges wouldn't squeak, Harold crept forward, and, releasing the door, he drew the knife. A creak from the settling hinges caught the bouncer's attention and as he turned, the hunchback charged and smashed the skinny man against the wall, knocking the breath from his lungs.

Gasping for air, Jimmy desperately slashed at the brute with his straight razor, but Harold knocked that aside with a meaty arm and grabbed the bouncer by the throat. Jimmy left the floor kicking, his eyes bulging as if about to burst from his head. Jamming a hand into his pocket, the bouncer partially drew the homemade zip gun when something loudly snapped in his neck. He trembled, then went completely limp, the razor dropping from twitching fingers.

Squeezing some more until he was sure the man was dead and not trying a trick, Harold laid the corpse on a filthy bunk in the corner and covered him with a thin blanket. Now drawing the .44 AutoMag from his holster, Harold started up the dank wooden stairs to the first floor of the brothel, his face an inhuman mask carved from ice.

Let the storm rage and thunder outside—this was his wedding day.

Chapter Twenty

Digging in their heels and shouldering the door to the shoe store open, Ryan and Krysty burst onto the street. Instantly, the wind slammed the door shut, shattering the glass. The sandstorm invaded the shop ruthlessly, overturning displays and sending shoes flying madly about in a whirlwind. Sacrosanct for a century, it was now just another dead store amid the crumbling predark city.

Hunching over to walk against the fierce gusts, the companions started toward the destroyed skyscraper. The once mighty edifice had been reduced to a mere ironwork skeleton from the fires, but it still served as a landmark to direct them through the madness to the tunnel.

Thunder rumbled in the murky sky as the quieting sandstorm still raged over the ruins, the winds howling along the barren streets, driving the sand before it with pounding fury. The windows of the buildings shook, and loose debris flashed by to disappear into the maelstrom. More than once, they found a dried splotch on a wall, marking where a lizard had braved the storm and had abruptly become part of the landscape.

The pair was completely wrapped in strips of cloth bleached to mottled colors to help blend into the storm. Desert camouflage. Their right hands were swaddled in lumpy balls of oily cloth. Even their faces were hidden behind overlapping layers, only their eyes showing through the narrowest of slits.

The wind noticeably lessened as they moved to the lee of a bowling alley, and Ryan and Krysty paused to examine a dead man embedded in the ground, his mouth packed solid with sand. The body was flayed to bones in spots from abrasion, and a smashed muzzle-loader that lay nearby showed he was from Alphaville. Tightening their own masks, the pair moved on.

Suddenly, there was a tremendous crack and a billboard flew by overhead, tumbling end over end as the winds tore it apart. As if renewed by the destruction, the storm rose in power until the whole world seemed on the verge of shattering. The pair was forced flat against the wall, helpless to take a step in any direction. Then the winds diminished, dropping to a soft breeze. The lightning and thunder also eased, then died away completely. For a few moments, the companions stood listening to the blood pound in their ears as they adjusted to the unexpected silence. Then the tempest returned, but not as strong as before.

"Almost over," Ryan shouted, using a knuckle to rub the windblown grit from his eye.

"Too fast!" Krysty replied. "We need another hour!"

"We aren't getting it! Better hurry."

A single strand of her fiery hair flying free, Krysty gestured onward with her cloth-wrapped hand when a figure walked around the corner of the building. The man was dressed in military fatigues, with a handkerchief covering his mouth and an M-16 assault rifle in his grip.

Instantly, Ryan raised his swaddled hand and fired, the silenced SIG-Sauer coughing once inside the big shoe box, the rags outside muffling the noise to almost inaudible. But the wind shifted his aim and the sec man staggered, only wounded in the shoulder.

Snarling in pain, he pointed the M-16 and savagely pulled the trigger to no results. The dirty autofire was hopelessly jammed. Lunging forward, Krysty stabbed the sec man with the stiletto knife in her free hand. Dropping the blaster, the sec man fell backward clutching his gushing throat.

Kneeling, Ryan finished him with a slash of the panga. Reloading their blasters was impossible until out of the storm, so every bullet counted. Which meant no mercy shots for the merely dying. Checking the body for any explosives, Krysty found none and the companions moved away from the site.

"Fireblast, we better watch that wind shear," Ryan cursed, lowering his arm so the hot shell rolling about in the shoe box didn't rest on his bare skin. "I almost chilled the both of us with that."

"Got you covered, lover," Krysty said, nudging him with an elbow.

He grunted in reply. No matter how good you were, mistakes happened to everybody. But mistakes got you chilled in the Deathlands.

A few blocks later, the pair froze and retreated into a recessed doorway. Standing in the middle of an intersection and making no attempt to hide was a sec man holding a bolt-action rifle, a towel tied across his mouth. His hair a wild frenzy, the red-faced guard bowed under the gusts of wind, but stayed right there, squinting against the dust and sand.

"Perimeter guard," Ryan said, his hand double-checking that the safety was off his blaster.

"We're close," she agreed grimly, making sure her

own MAC-11 was set on single shot. "Double-team him?"

"On the next upsurge. Check."

Lightning flashed, and the storm increased for a few moments, blinding the sentry completely. Covering his face with an arm, he rode out the buffeting until the wind eased. Dropping the arm, he recoiled as a mummy charged out of the dust clouds. He raised his blaster and white-hot pain took him in the kidneys, then the throat. A terrible cold washed over the sec man and he dropped to the ground, pumping out blood. The dry soil absorbed the fluid on contact, the storm covering the crimson fluid and the dying man with ruthless efficiency.

Systematically, the companions moved sideways along the picket of guards, traveling from man to man, until finally reaching where they started.

"None of these men were large enough," Krysty said, wiping the gore off her stiletto.

"So let's find more," Ryan replied.

Two more guards were encountered and dispatched, along with a lieutenant found asleep in a telephone booth, before they reached the sloped ramp that led to the tunnel.

Moving toward the embankment, the companions reached the tumbled entrance to the underground tunnel, the jagged pieces of concrete and twisted steel beams already partially buried under a softening blanket of sand. Four men struggled to haul away some of the smaller pieces of rubble, while a burly sergeant with an M-16 wrapped in a sweater stood guard. That was the right idea, but it was nowhere near enough protection for the weapon against the billowing sandstorm. However, the scuba mask on the sergeant's face gave him an unobstructed view through the stinging dust clouds, and that was trouble.

Quickly, tactics were discussed, then the companions moved. Approaching from the direction of the wind, Krysty took out the sergeant first with the stiletto between the ribs, twisting the blade to enlarge the hole and deflate his lungs. No pressure meant no sound.

Ryan grabbed the blaster to stop it from hitting the ground, as the sec man sighed out a warning and died. Laying the useless blaster aside, the man and woman simply walked behind each of the armed workers and shot them at point-blank range.

Removing the jackets of the two largest men, Ryan and Krysty bundled the garments into an empty bag and took refuge behind one of the searchlights. A few handfuls of sand rubbed out most of the blood spots. Trying the jackets on over the camou wrappings, Krysty's fit perfectly in spite of her top-heavy figure. But Ryan's was too small in the shoulders, and he had to leave the jacket unbuttoned. Hopefully, nobody would notice.

Now resembling sec men, they crawled out from behind the searchlight and studied the buildings on either side of the access ramp. Several windows were gone, probably from the concussion of the rockets. It also removed those places from the list of possible campsites for the baron and his men. A liquor store with an iron grating over its front window seemed a good location until they noticed a sandbag wall that closed off an alleyway, alongside a massive granite building on the corner. Boards covered the windows on both stories.

"That's their base," Krysty said, tucking a loose strand of hair away, only to have it immediately fly free again.

Ryan agreed. "Wags must be in the alley to cut the wind."

Just then, light flared inside the liquor store directly across the street from the bank, then it was gone.

"And there's the guard station," Ryan said, sounding disgusted. "Some fool is smoking on duty."

Without a comment, Krysty started to crawl that way, but he stopped her. "Wags first."

Rising, they darted across the street, hitting the wall, and waited for a response. None came. But now they could faintly hear the strains of a badly played harmonica. Moving to the sandbags, they climbed over to find a dozen vehicles draped with window curtains and carpeting. Krysty stood guard while Ryan opened the gas cap of each vehicle and slid a thin block of C-4 into the gas tank, the tiny timing pencil sticking out of the top like the wick on a candle.

Crossing to the bank, Ryan stood guard while Krysty dug a small hole in the sand in front of the front door, placed a wrapped package gingerly inside, then smoothed the sand again. This process was repeated four times as they crossed the street.

Reaching the sidewalk, the companions straightened their jackets, boldly walked over and knocked on the door to the liquor store. Nothing happened, so Ryan knocked harder to be heard over the gusting winds. There hadn't been any lightning for a while, and that was making the man anxious. If the storm died now, their attack would completely unravel. Without the masking effect of the dust clouds to hide them, this was a suicide mission.

"Yeah, yeah, I'm coming," a male voice said, and the door swung aside, showing a sec man with a napkin around his throat and holding a can of spaghetti with a spoon sticking out. "What the fuck is it now, Sarge? Rotation ain't for another hour."

"Thanks for the info," Ryan said coldly.

The SIG-Sauer coughed, and a hole appeared in the man's forehead. The corpse tumbled off to the side, and they pushed their way into the store.

The wall shelves and refrigerated cases were empty, along with the racks and displays. Not a speck of food remained anywhere. Even the cash register was broken, apparently from a sledgehammer blow judging from the damage.

A fast recce revealed a back room with a couple of folding chairs, a table piled with supplies and a snoring man in an old Army cot against the far wall.

"Wake up," Ryan said loudly, kicking the cot.

The sec man awakened and froze at the sight of the strangers. His hand darted for his belt and found the empty holster at his hip. His gaze flicked to the table, then back to the masked people standing with a wad of rags swaddling their right hands.

"Who the hell are you gleebs?" he asked, the ragged edge of sleep blurring his words slightly. "What's with the bandages—you hurt? Burned?"

"Not important," Krysty snapped.

"Talk to us about the baron, and you can live," Ryan added.

"Whatcha gonna do, hit me with your bad hands? Fuck this," he snarled rising off the bunk. "Hey, Sal! Sal!"

Ryan moved closer. "Sal is dead. Shot through the head."

"With invisible blasters?" The sec man laughed.

"Our blasters are protected from the storm."

"Yeah? Show me."

A head shake. "Takes too long to wrap them."

He smiled tolerantly. "Of course." And with that, the man darted across the room toward a table covered with clothing and equipment.

"Stop or die," Ryan warned, raising his shoe box.

The man shoved an arm into the pile, and as he started to withdraw something, both companions fired. The sec man buckled under the double assault and fell, sprawling to the floor.

"Never considered the possibility he wouldn't believe us," Ryan said, sounding annoyed. "Stupe."

Spotting an Uzi on the table, Krysty checked it over to make sure it was a 9 mm, then slid the spare ammo clips in her bag for J.B. Ryan slid his panga into its sheath and took the Uzi itself.

"Well, we can't uncover," the woman said. "It would take forever to get the strips right again. Want to try and capture another one alive? Mebbe we'll have better luck with the next guy."

"Don't believe in luck," he said, awkwardly setting the Uzi for full-auto with one hand. "Besides, we can't risk it. The baron or a sec boss has got to notice that something is odd soon, and then it's show time."

Moving to the front of the store, they took positions near the front door and watched the street and corner. Dust devils danced along the gutters, a steady stream of sand blowing past them. It was like looking at a river.

"Gaia!" Krysty said, spinning on the man and staring at his face in frustration. "We are idiots!"

"What's wrong?" he asked. "Everything is going according to plan."

"Your eye."

Ryan touched his good eye, then scowled under his

mask. "None of them have patches. They'll spot me for a phony immediately."

"Just a minute." The redhead went into the back room, then came out and checked behind the counter. "Ah, knew there had to be some in stock. Here."

He took the item and unfolded them. Sunglasses. They would cut down his vision, but it was their best bet. Sliding them on, he tucked the ends under the wrappings and shook his head violently.

"They're not coming off," Krysty said, brushing back her loose strand of hair again.

"Good." Peeling back the rags on his wrist, Ryan glanced at his chron. "Too long. They're taking too long."

"Prime the pump?" she asked, raising her shoe box.

"Use this," he said, giving her the Uzi. "You shoot, I'll do the rest. Haven't seen any women guards yet."

"Agreed." Stepping outside, Krysty fired a burst into the air, and Ryan yelled as if gut shot. Then the woman peppered the front of the bank with the rest of the clip, and they ducked back inside the store.

Seconds later, armed men poured into the street by the dozens. Some hit the ground while others spread out in a defensive pattern.

"A lot more than we bargained for," Krysty whispered, dropping the exhausted blaster.

"The more the better for this job," Ryan countered grimly.

"What the hell is going on?" demanded a sec man in bare feet.

"Where are the sentries?" a sergeant asked gruffly, cradling a longblaster. "Phil, Kaja, check the tunnel!"

The couple jogged over and returned just as fast.

"They're all dead, Sarge!" Phil reported.

"Shot and stabbed," Kaja added.

Suddenly, the door to the liquor store swung open, and out came two sec men with cloth covering their faces as protection from the storm.

"Hey, guys, see anything?" a sergeant shouted over the noise of the storm.

"No, sir," replied the big guy in sunglasses. Then a tremendous blast filled the alleyway and sandbags cannonballed out, slamming into the stores across the street, smashing windows.

"Rockets!" a sec man shouted, and he started to fire wildly at the rooftops. A dozen more joined in shooting at anything and everything. But the weapons jammed constantly, and frantic hands struggled to clear the clogged mechanisms. But opening the breeches only made matters worse.

Deadly calm, Krysty and Ryan moved through the shouting crowd, their shoe boxes softly chugging. Sec men fell over, clutching their chest and bellies, blasters dropping.

"Snipers!" the corporal cried as a dead man collapsed at his feet. "Brewer, get on the roof and kill anybody you find!"

"Sir!" But the sec man took a single step before he also fell.

With the wind howling, another blast ripped apart the alleyway, spewing out chunks of vehicles, a flaming wheel rolling through the crowd of sec men. Stepping out of its way, Krysty shot the corporal in the throat to stop his commands.

Killing four more, Ryan reached the bank and kicked open the door. There were only a few people inside, and behind a teller's cage was the youth from the platform in the ville. Only now he was dressed in a clean black uniform dripping with weapons, but it was his carriage and bearing that showed he was in charge, the new Baron Strichland. Their gazes locked for a moment. Registering shock, the teenager frowned and reached for his fancy blasters.

"Goodbye, Leonard," Ryan said, firing three times.

But the bullets slammed to a stop in midair directly before the startled teenager, a spiderweb of cracks radiating from each impact point. Ryan cursed and retreated outside fast. Fireblast, this was a bank and the kid had been standing behind a sheet of bulletproof glass. His one chance to end this matter permanently had gone to hell.

Only a heartbeat behind, sec men burst out the door, and Ryan shot the ground at their feet. The buried charge went off, blowing them to pieces and showering burning gasoline across the front of the building. The desert winds fanned the flames, but instead of extinguishing the blaze, actually seemed to feed the fire with every gust.

Retreating amid the enemy, Ryan knew that was a speciality of J.B.'s, mixing thermite with a Molotov to create an unstoppable chem fire that lasted for minutes even underwater. Nothing but time could kill those flames.

Just then a section of the road exploded, harming nobody, merely throwing sand at the sky. Everybody moved away from that location and the street under them now erupted in a series of blasts, pieces of bodies flying everywhere.

"Rockets!" one man cried, dragging a broken leg. "Run!"

"Land mines!" yelled another, clutching a bleeding arm. "Nobody move!"

Right on schedule, the alley thundered again as lightning flashed, and Ryan and Krysty moved through the shouting men, their weapons chugging steadily, bodies dropping in their wake like harvested wheat.

A corporal standing too near realized what was happening and turned his blaster on the pair. He got off a hasty shot, missing Ryan completely and hitting one of his own men. The one-eyed man chilled the corporal and met with Krysty on the far corner away from the burning bank.

"I've got six rounds," the woman said.

"Four," he replied. "Time to go."

"Check."

Placing their last few shots on just officers, Ryan and Krysty backed away from the baron's army, and paused to stand directly on a smooth patch of sand between a bare metal mailbox and hydrant.

"Hey! The sniper ran this way!" Ryan shouted, waving to the sec men. Several caught the call and passed along the news to the others. Soon a crowd of the men was coming their way.

"This way! Hurry!" Krysty added, waving.

As the sec men got near, the companions took off fast at a run. Thinking they were chasing the sniper, a dozen sec men charged and reached the smooth section of sand almost exactly as the big ticking bomb buried there detonated.

The men on top of the explosive charge simply vanished, the thunderclap and fireball knocking the rest to the ground covered with flames. Shrieking, the human torches dashed about amid their brethren, setting others on fire, spreading terror until the troops started firing on one another in confusion.

Dropping their stolen jackets, Ryan and Krysty disappeared unobserved into the dying storm.

SMASHING HIS FIST onto the Plexiglas shield of the teller's cage didn't dislodge the jammed rounds, and Leonard savagely turned upon his troops.

"Boxes! They used boxes!" the young baron shouted. "I saw it! Blasters inside boxes with strips of cloth to hold them in place!"

"Smart," Sergeant Jarmal grumbled, bandaging a wound in his arm. He had a good suspicion it was from his own men, but that was a matter for later. The sec men had just gotten their butts kicked and were burning for revenge on the faceless enemy.

"DeLellis, what is the death toll?" Leonard snapped, pointing at the man with a clipboard.

"Sixty-four, my lord," the corporal reported, brushing sand from his face to read the hastily scribbled list of names. "Mostly officers. Which leaves us thirty."

"Wounded?"

"Nothing serious. Only minor flesh wounds. The snipers killed damn near everybody they hit."

The troops murmured uneasily at that news.

"Stack the dead. We'll bury them later. No sec men go into the Machine."

"Yes, sir."

"What about the wags?" the baron asked, crossing his arms and trying to radiate a positive attitude he didn't really feel.

"Gone. Along with our extra water and all of the fuel."

"Well, we don't really need any fucking fuel without vehicles, do we, Lieutenant," the youth snapped.

"Corporal, sir."

"Not anymore." The baron walked among the men. "You're a corporal now. You are a sergeant, you're a corporal and you are a lieutenant."

Beaming faces spread through the motley crowd, and the weary bodies sat upright, holding their bolt-action pieces with renewed determination.

"Let's kick ass, sir!" a private cried.

Tolerantly, Leonard allowed the familiarity from the lower class drone. Odd, how quickly he was learning to think like his father and consider them as merely workers, tools to be used and discarded, nothing more.

"Jarmal, you're in command now," the teenager finished.

The grizzled veteran had seen this coming and wasn't thrilled by the battlefield promotion. The commanders of the sec men had a bad habit of dying in the Strichland reign. "Thank you, Baron. May I suggest we stay here until the storm dies, and then we go home?"

"What did you say?" the youth whispered, staring at the older man with a near deranged expression.

Jarmal sighed. With his wife and children still in Alphaville, he had to follow the little lunatic straight to hell if need be. Afterward would be another matter. Alphaville needed a strong baron, but not another madman in charge.

Then again, people died in battle. Even barons sometimes.

"I said we should attack immediately," the CO corrected.

"Absolutely!" Leonard cried, then he pointed to the nearest men. "You, you and you! Rip this place apart and find some boxes and rags. Private, you're the quartermaster. Gather the weapons from outside and field-strip the autofires until you have enough clean blasters for everybody.''

''We each get an autofire, sir?''

Leonard took the Desert Eagle from his left holster and tossed it to Jarmal. ''Everybody,'' Leonard stated. ''Then we go after this bitch and her one-eyed lover and blow them to hell.''

The sec men cheered and got to work with a fever.

''One eye?'' Jarmal asked, checking the load on the huge blaster. ''Isn't she with Harold?''

''Apparently not. When that man tried to shoot me, his sunglasses slipped and I saw he wore a patch on the left side.

''Oh yes, and one more thing, Captain,'' Leonard added, brushing his hands across the Plexiglas.

''Sir?''

''Send some men to the supermarket and see if we have any wolves still alive. We'll use the beasts to track this pair to their bolt-hole and take the battle to them this time.''

''Still want the redhead alive, sir?'' Jarmal asked slowly.

''No,'' the young baron said without hesitation. ''No prisoners. Kill them both on sight.''

Chapter Twenty-One

Resembling freshly unearthed mummies, Ryan and Krysty slipped into the government building and Doc closed the heavy glass door tightly, sliding the wedge of wood under the jamb to help it stay firmly in position. Overhead, the storm was noticeably weaker. Thunder rumbled again, but the lag between noise and lightning was increasing. The Deathlands tempest was almost finished.

"How's Dean?" Ryan asked, uncovering his mouth. "Can we leave yet?"

"I do not know, sir," Doc said, offering a canteen. "Dr. Wyeth is spoon-feeding him broth, and most of it stays down."

"Most? That doesn't sound good." Ryan took a healthy swig of the tepid water. "Damn."

Yanking down her mask, Krysty accepted the canteen and took a long pull. "Whew. Thanks," she said gratefully, stripping off the cloth holding the shoe box on her arm.

"You seem undamaged," Doc said, pleased. "May I assume the mission was a success?"

"Shit, yeah." Ryan coughed, also removing his box. Holstering the blaster, he flexed stiff fingers.

"Excellent."

Doc returned to watching the street outside as the man and woman raised quite a dust cloud while unwinding the intertwined rags covering them before reaching clothes. Feeling pounds lighter, they climbed over the barricade of file cabinets and started downstairs.

"Any problems?" J.B. asked, rising from a chair, a napkin tied around his throat and an open MRE envelope in his hand.

"Went like clockwork," Krysty announced, dropping the stack of ammo clips on a table. "Found these for you."

"Thanks."

"Is that spaghetti?" Ryan asked, amused for some reason.

The Armorer blinked at the odd question and checked the foil package in his hand. "No, corned-beef hash. Want some?"

"Mebbe later." Maneuvering through the sea of tables, Ryan reached the bedsheet tent and scratched on the cloth.

Mildred came out, stooping to clear the fold. "You're back. Thought I heard voices. Any damage that needs mending?"

"Just bruised and tired," the big man replied. "How's Dean?"

The physician glanced backward. "Stable, nothing more. I've done everything possible. It's a waiting game now."

Cawdor took her shoulder and squeezed gently in understanding. She shrugged, apologizing for not being able to do more.

"How many dead?" Jak called out. The albino teen was lying on a crude bed of sofa cushions with his boots off, an arm draped over his face to keep out the lantern light. The first rule of surviving combat, after not getting shot, was to always grab as much sleep as possible.

"Thirty or so," Ryan replied, going to a punch bowl full of water and washing his hands and face. Krysty joined him, and the water was almost black when they finished.

"Any chance you were followed?" J.B. asked, finishing his meal. He tilted his head to listen for any noises outside, but only heard the soft moan of the desert wind and Doc humming that damn Caruso opera song again.

"They were too busy dying to worry about us much," Ryan stated confidently, using his wet hands to brush back his unruly crop of black curls. "We hid and waited at a couple of locations, never saw a soul."

"Besides, we did a loop into the desert twice," Krysty said, drying off with a piece of a yellow towel. "Went over a few walls, and through that burned-out high school. Nobody could follow that trail."

"Unless they got dogs," Mildred agreed.

Lowering his arm, Jak sat up and frowned. "Or wolves."

"Those were trained wolves," Mildred said slowly. "And we never met the females of the pack."

"Think any are still around?" Krysty asked, instinctively going for her blaster.

"Sure as bastard hope not," Ryan grumbled, taking a pencil stub from a pocket and drawing a map of the ruins on the smooth stone floor. "But just in case, we better concoct a battle plan. We got them scared, but when the sky clears, the baron and his men will come boiling out of that bank hot for revenge."

"We can set up an ambush," Krysty said. "Certainly

enough locations in these ruins for us to stage one hell of a firefight.''

"Thirty to five? Bad odds.'' Jak frowned, lacing his shoes.

"Agreed,'' J.B. said, disposing of the remains of his meal. "So how do we change them?'' With explosives, J.B. knew no master, but strategy was Ryan's field of expertise.

He stabbed a finger at the crude map. "We're here, the baron there. So we send out Jak in the Hummer to swing past them real slow, dribbling oil out of a puncture can.''

"Breadcrumbs,'' the Cajun said, rubbing his unshaved chin.

"Exactly. You leak a trail away from us and into the desert dunes.''

Mildred paused for a moment, listening to the sleeping boy, then said, "These guys are pretty smart. Do you really think they'll fall for that old trick?'' Then her expression changed. "Oh, I see, they're not supposed to believe.''

"Right. But the baron will still have to check it out anyway, just in case,'' Ryan said. "I estimate he'll send ten, mebbe half his men after Jak to double-check.''

"I'm bait,'' the teen said, slowly grinning. "But not trap. Lure away driving slow, hurry back.''

"Could buy us another day,'' Mildred said, massaging the back of her neck. "And hours count at this point.''

"Still leaves the rest for us,'' Krysty stated.

"I've done the best I can with this building,'' J.B. said, coming over closer and sitting on the edge of the fountain basin. "It's tight, but I sure don't want to have a major fight here.''

"Not here," Ryan countered. "We'll make it a fall-back."

"We can't move the boy," Mildred reminded them.

Adjusting his eye patch, Ryan frowned. "Not that kind of a fallback. There's a ton of weapons in the pawnshop. We choose a good location and arm it with the useless blasters. Then mine the place with boobys. Jam the barrels of the blasters so they explode."

"Yeah, might work just fine," J.B. added, glancing at the kitchen he had converted into a weapons lab. Bottles were stacked everywhere, several of them bubbling away softly, steadily building pressure that would soon demand to be released.

"Yeah," he repeated with a smile. "I got some stuff brewing that will ace the bunch of them if we can gather them in one tight area."

"Poison gas?"

"Not quite, but close."

"Fuses?"

"Nope. Just break the glass and the chems mix."

"Good. Bastard fuses give away too much."

"Check."

"Sounds okay," Mildred admitted. "It's us or them, so you know my vote."

Krysty pursed her lips, then nodded. "Let's do it."

"Anybody got a better idea, speak now," Ryan said gruffly, glancing at the barbed wire and curtains of the makeshift roof. "From the sound of the wind and thunder, the storm is almost gone, so we have to move fast."

There was no dissent.

"Okay," he said, "We hit them hard and fast. Don't give the baron a chance to plan or regroup. Keep him off balance. The sec men outnumber us, but we have automatic weapons and the Hummer. Firepower and mobility.''

A knife appeared from out of nowhere in Jak's hand, spun on its pommel in his palm, then was slid smoothly back into his sleeve. "Dead meat," the teenager stated confidently.

Off in a corner by itself, the string from upstairs jerked, making a spoon in a glass tinkle like a tiny bell. The sound startled everybody.

Slowly at first, then faster, Ryan started across the basement to tug back to see if it was a warning, or just Doc asking for a piss break, when there came the stitching zip of the HK G-12 caseless from overhead, followed by screams and the raging snarl of wolves.

"Dark night, they found us!" J.B. cursed, drawing his blaster.

"Already?" Mildred gasped, doing the same.

Weapons out, Ryan and Jak were heading for the door to the stairwell with Jak close behind.

Grabbing his bag of munitions, J.B. stopped at the stairs and turned. "Hey, Millie!" he shouted, and tossed over the M-4000 shotgun.

"Just in case," the Armorer said softly.

The physician nodded, then reached into a pocket and tossed him a gren. "The last one. Don't miss, John."

J.B. tucked it away, threw her a smile and took off at a run.

Bursting out of the stairwell, the companions found Doc behind the reception desk firing the Heckler & Koch at a swarm of sec men climbing over the barricade of file cabinets. Ryan and the others opened fire, and the invaders fell back screaming and cursing. Two bleeding bodies stayed where they were, draped motionless on the metal banks.

Advancing to the barricade, Ryan rested his blaster on top of a cabinet between the dead men. They would give good cover. "Volley fire at the windows," he ordered softly. "On my mark...now!"

A hellstorm of lead shattered the remaining panes of snowy glass, exposing thirty sec men armed with autofires standing in the sandy street.

"Chill them!" Ryan shouted, riding the bucking Steyr SSG-70 as he worked the bolt and fired steadily.

Their bodies dancing under the impacts, six sec men fell to the ground before the rest could scurry away. A snarling wolf leaped on top of the files, and Jak shot it in the face with his .357 Colt Python, the muzzle-flash igniting the fur as the head exploded and the body tumbled off. In seconds, the street before their building was clear of live targets.

As Ryan shoved in a fresh clip, he scowled at the garage directly across from them where the Hummer was hidden. So bloody close, but it might as well be on the moon for all the good it could do them now.

"Doc, cover fire from the roof and watch for jumpers," he snapped. "Krysty, take the first floor in case somebody gets past us or tries a window."

"On it," the redhead answered.

"Godspeed all," the oldster rumbled.

As the pair disappeared into the shadowy interior of the predark building, there came the sound of running boots, and a mob of yelling sec men charged into view carrying sheets of glass before them as shields. The companions coolly opened fire, but the rounds simply knocked the men back, becoming embedded in the soft clear material.

"What the... Shitfire! It's that Plexiglas from the bank!"

Heartened by their apparent invulnerability, the troops rallied and charged again, firing their automatics around the sides of the resilient plastic.

"Shoes!" Ryan shouted, lowering the barrel.

The companions concentrated on the shuffling boots of the sec men. Leather toes erupted, spraying blood. A man fell and was trampled by the others. Another dropped, losing the shield, and his exposed comrades died. Then the rest were inside the building, shouting and whooping like madmen.

Maintaining steady fire, the companions fell back to the receptionist desk as the sec force tried to shove aside the cabinets. But filled with books and with every handle lashed together with spare barbed wire, the barrier was immovable.

"Gren," Ryan ordered, dropping the rifle and drawing his handblaster, working the slide to chamber a round.

Holding the Uzi with both hands, J.B. carefully aimed at the ceiling on the other side of the barrier.

"No need for that yet," he spit, and fired.

The ceiling tiles broke apart, displaying a dozen plastic bottles tied to the rafters. Riddled with bullets, the containers poured out their pale blue contents onto the sec men. Shrieking with pain, the horrified men dropped their weapons and shields, beating insanely at their melting flesh, white bones and pulsating organs already in plain view.

Advancing, the companions slaughtered the dissolving victims, and caught a couple of unhurt men trying to leave the hellish lobby. Two shots and the cowards fell face first into the sizzling puddles.

"What was that?" Ryan asked, backing away from the cabinets. The pungent smell was horrific, beyond description; his nose was running and eye watering. "Acid rain water?"

Moving to a safe distance, J.B. grinned without humor. "Liquid drain cleaner, spiced with a little of my brew. I found a whole carton in the janitor's closet. Great stuff. They won't hit here again for a while."

"Got more?" Jak asked, snapping off a shot at a dashing wolf and missing. He cracked the cylinder, dropped the brass and reloaded.

"No," J.B. said solemnly. "Got a bunch of stuff cooking downstairs, but it's not ready, and this is it for traps. We're on our own."

DOWN IN THE BASEMENT, a scratching noise drew Mildred's attention from the commotion upstairs. Grabbing a lantern, the physician moved through the fast-food restaurants, tracking the disturbance until finding a manhole cover in the floor of a back utility room. The round disk was rotating, as if unscrewing, and faint voices murmured on the other side.

Turning off the lantern, she took a position behind a cold furnace and patiently waited. Finally, the cover was gently lifted and a face peeked out of the hole, eyes glancing quickly about.

"See anything?" asked somebody deeper inside the access shaft.

"Looks clear," the first sec man replied, glancing about.

Mildred stretched out her arm and neatly shot the man in the temple. His head jerked, and he dropped out of sight down the shaft, the heavy iron lid slamming back into position. Dim cries came from below as the falling corpse apparently knocked several sec men off the access ladder.

Holstering her ZKR .38, Mildred ignored the water heater and furnace as too heavy for her to move, and passed by a stack of spare doors as too light to be of any use. Ramming her shoulder into the side of an upright freezer, the woman managed to shove the piece of equipment forward one foot at a time. The manhole cover was starting to move again, when Mildred strained against the awful weight, but managed to topple over the freezer to resoundingly crash on top the sewer hatch. If there was any reaction from the other side, it was muffled by the four hundred pounds of steel and ceramic lying across the lid.

Searching the shelves, the woman placed a few cash registers on top of the sideways freezer, along with a fifty-pound bucket of floor wax. The container didn't feel that heavy. The ages had to have stolen every drop of moisture from the compound, lightening it considerably, but even twenty extra pounds of weight was useful.

Leaving the door to the utility room jammed open, Mildred went back to her post at the fountain basin where she could keep a watch on the back room and the stairwell. Suddenly, the mammoth freezer shifted a bit with a muffled thump, and she knew there would be no more trouble from below. The physician could only imagine the awful mess in the sewer when the explosion failed to penetrate and the back-blast hit the unsuspecting sec men. They had to have been instantly pulped. The basement was secure again.

Just then, a violent explosion rocked the building to its very foundation. Reclaiming the shotgun and laying it on her lap, Mildred glanced skyward and wondered just how badly the battle upstairs was going.

Chapter Twenty-Two

On the rooftop, Doc emptied the HK, raining death from above on the sec men as they scampered about for safety. Drawing the LeMat, he heard a thump and, leaning way over the roof, saw a group of men ramming a park bench against the metal door on the side of the government building. He ignored them and watched for others in the streets. That weak point in their defenses was blocked by an entire room jammed full of office furniture. Even if they got inside, it would take them an hour to dig through the mess. Then again…

Leaning way over, Doc pumped a few rounds from the LeMat their way, blowing a slat out of the bench and sending a bald sec man down for the count. The group broke ranks and fled, firing wildly in return. A chance ricochet chipped the stone lintel of the roof and bit his upper arm.

Staggering back, Doc dropped the LeMat and tried to staunch the wound with his handkerchief. There was little blood, the wound didn't hurt much and his fingers could still move, which meant a small-caliber bullet that hadn't hit bone or artery. Thank God, just a flesh wound. The sick feeling in his stomach was just a natural reaction to being hurt. Perfectly ordinary. However, he knew that the numbness would soon wear off and his arm would ache like the dickens. He had to move fast.

"Come on, Theophilus," he grunted, trying not to pay attention to the red stain spreading down his shirt. "No pain, no gain."

Biting a corner of the cloth, Doc managed to tie off the wound, then slid his cold right hand into his belt to help keep it still. Clumsily lifting the powerful .44 LeMat revolver in his bloody left hand, Doc experimented with the weight, trying to get a feel and balance for the weapon again. The stickiness was making things awkward, but he felt confident if the target was close enough he could handle the handcannon. Well, hopefully.

Unfortunately, there was no way he could reload now, or even change the selector pin to discharge the shotgun. Five more rounds and he was out. Feeling a bit dizzy, Doc sat on the concrete roof and tried to catch his breath.

He just could not faint, he thought. He could not die yet. He had to stay awake.

WHILE THE BARON'S troops peppered the defenders with steady blasterfire, a sec man sneaking along the wall of the pawnshop lurched forward and hurled himself at a ground-floor window of the government building. The glass shattered and he fell back, bleeding from a dozen spots. The nails sticking through the wooden boards covering the inside of the window now dripped with his blood. Then from the opposite side of the building, another man stumbled into view, an eye dangling on his cheek, blood pumping from his wounds with every heartbeat.

In an alleyway between a paint store and a ramshackle garage, Leonard stood on a box behind a metal trash bin and watched the battle. His personal guards, the last members of the Wolf Pack, stood close to the youth to protect him from ricochets or any other dangers.

The young baron smiled as his men charged the building again, then frowned as they retreated, clothes smoking, faces bleeding and with more bodies lying on the ground. He had no idea if they were killing any of the people inside the building, but his men were being slaughtered. He was already down to twenty men in a matter of minutes. Who were these people?

"Enough!" the teenager stated, and turned to the men beside him. "Okay, Jarmal, we gave it a try. But this is going nowhere. Burn them out."

"My lord, this is the dry season," the captain said patiently for the tenth time in an hour. "We could lose the whole city, and the flames could even spread to the ville. The river has caught fire before."

"Damn the river, damn the ville and damn you!" Leonard shouted. "I want those people dead. Do you understand? Dead at any cost!"

Touching the blaster on his belt, Jarmal debated killing the teenager right here and claiming it was a chance shot from the defenders. But the Wolf Pack watched him with knowing faces, their autofire blasters already drawn. It would be best to get the young baron mixed into the fighting, then Jarmal could safely frag the lunatic. Most of the sec men stayed loyal because of the food, and the threat of the Machine being used on their families. They wouldn't give a shit about who was in charge. But the Wolf Pack and others followed the baron because he gave them the authority to kill in safety, allowed them to wallow like drunkards in human blood. Cowards hiding behind a madman. But cowards with blasters who were damn good shots. Perhaps an assassination wasn't going to work.

Jarmal snapped a salute. "Yes, my lord. Of course. At once, Baron."

The boy seemed to notice a difference in the sec man, then dismissed it, attributing the change to combat. Killing made some men uneasy. Personally, he enjoyed it immensely. "How many Molotov cocktails do we have?"

"Only the six, my lord. Lots more bottles but no more fuel. This is every drop that survived the alley fire."

"More than enough. Take your strongest men and firebomb the front door and roof simultaneously. Let's see them stop that!" Leonard scoffed in triumph. "Ha!"

"If this fails, sir, will we leave?" Jarmal asked.

"Wh-what was that?" the youth asked in a hoarse whisper.

"Leave. Depart. Go. We're getting slaughtered and for no reason!"

The teenager stared. "Are you mad? They killed my father!"

"After he kidnapped and almost raped the woman." Then, unable to stop the words, Jarmal said, "The crazy old bastard had it coming for years! Served him right!"

Leonard grabbed his blaster, then released the weapon. "Captain, you're relieved of rank," the new baron said in an icy tone. "You will lead the troops in the next rush on the building. Take his blasters."

The Wolf Pack closed on the man, and under the muzzles of their blasters he was stripped of weapons.

"Haven't got the guts to just shoot me here, eh?"

Jarmal snarled, with nothing more to lose. "That's a death sentence and you know it."

Calmly, the youth returned to watching the losing battle. "Do as you are told, or your children will beg for the mercy of the Machine."

Sporadic blasterfire continued from the building, and the sec men shot back from behind mailboxes, vending machines and inside the paint store.

"How did we ever let you get in charge?" Jarmal asked woodenly. "What the fuck were we thinking? You're worse than Gunther."

Leonard smiled. "I'll take that as a compliment. Now go die."

"You heard the boss—git," one of the Wolf Pack said, sneering, jabbing the former captain with a rifle. "And make us proud, or else I'll take care of your wife myself."

"Mebbe we will anyway," another stated, and the rest agreed, making vulgar suggestions.

Outraged, Jarmal tensed to charge them, then forced himself to calm down. Ignoring their catcalls and taunts, he turned on his heel and marched into the ranks of the sec men. Too furious to think clearly, Jarmal almost registered surprise when somebody pressed a knife into his hand. Keeping his expression neutral, he slid the weapon away quickly. Then a revolver was slapped into his palm, and the troops closed around their old sergeant, hiding him from sight as he checked the load on the blaster and tucked it into his shirt.

"You there, Private," Leonard snapped, crossing his arms and posing as if on the display in the ville and not in the middle of a firefight.

The sec man turned slowly. "Sir?" he managed to croak.

"You're in charge now. Firebomb that rad-blasted pit into rubble!"

"Yes, sir," the sec man replied with a salute. If the baron noticed it was with his forbidden left hand, he didn't comment on the fact.

Shouting orders over the blasterfire, the new captain directed men to take positions and six Molotov cocktails soared into the air. Two of the bottles streaked right into the open front of the building, spreading fire across the metal cabinets. The other four arched high, going for the rooftop.

STRUGGLING TO STAY conscious, Doc jerked awake as he saw the Molotovs soaring through the cloudy sky. As he grabbed the blaster with both hands, fresh blood gushed from his wound, but the old man took careful aim and fired the LeMat again and again. The first shot missed completely. So did the second. But the third and fourth hit. Two of the bottles burst in midair, forming burning blossoms that rained harmlessly to the ground.

The third Molotov impacted dangerously near Doc, and he dragged himself away, the gasoline spreading across the concrete but finding no pursuit to feed the hungry flames. The fourth hit the skylight and shattered, raining fire and glass into the building. The burning debris landed on the curtains and barbed wire of the third floor. But dry as dust, the predark cloth instantly ignited and the interior of the structure was harshly illuminated with hellish light. Soon red-hot embers floated downward, drifting harmlessly onto the terrazzo floors, and elevator cage. But several reached the first floor. Now only yards away from the basement, tendrils of smoke rose from the hot flakes on the carpeting, tiny glowing specks that pulsed with every breeze as if living things.

GRABBING THE FIRE extinguisher from the wall niche, Krysty sprayed carbon dioxide foam over the whole expanse of the material. The canister died quickly, but all of the hot spots were quenched. However, more and more embers were drifting downward. Already the woman could see huge sections of bare wire above, the strands snapping from the accumulated heat. The next Molotov would drop through, falling straight to the basement, and she had nothing but blasters to stop the advance of the deadly fire.

"THEY'RE NOT TRYING for a capture anymore," Ryan snarled, coughing from the thick clouds of smoke blowing in over the barricade. It reeked of the drain cleaner, and he tried his best not to breathe any of the bluish smoke directly. Who knew what it would do to his lungs.

Fanning himself with the fedora, J.B. said, "How about we make a run for it? Try and lure them to the library and set the muties free?"

"Too far," Jak said, slapping shut the cylinder of his reloaded blaster.

The temperature was rising fast from the two fires. Ryan wiped the sweat off his brow with a sleeve and glanced around the building, counting their options. They were low on ammo, with no more bombs, missiles or grenades. The building was on fire, and surrounded by the enemy who wouldn't consider a surrender. The stairs were clear. They could reach the roof easily and jump to the pawnshop, but then what? There was no way across that street without the sec men seeing them, and night was hours away.

"Can't sit here," Jak drawled, brushing an ember off his sleeve. The crackling of the fire was getting louder, as the flames found new fuel in the floor tiles and wall paneling.

"What do you want to do, charge them?"

Jak hawked and spit to clear his throat. "Element surprise."

"Sure as shit would surprise me," J.B. agreed angrily.

"J.B., what did you mean nothing was ready?" Ryan asked brusquely.

The Armorer took a moment to mentally shift gears. "You mean the stuff downstairs? Well, I have some poison-gas bombs cooking, but they're still green. Wouldn't make a kitten ill. Tomorrow, they will be lethal as a nuke."

"Tomorrow isn't today. Would they smoke much?"

"You mean now? Sure. But it's just smoke."

Jak barked a laugh. "Once burned, twice shy."

Sidestepping some embers, J.B. grinned. "They'll think it's another sandstorm gag, us attacking under cover of the smoke."

"Work?" Jak asked pointedly.

"Better," Ryan said, starting for the stairs.

MINUTES PASSED as Leonard watched the fire spread throughout the building, a thick plume of smoke rising into the sky. Then he gasped as a barrage of glass bottles came hurtling from the roof to loudly crash on the street. He flinched, expecting gouts of flame from Molotovs to erupt at each impact. But instead, volumes of grayish-green smoke flowed from the puddles. Billowing clouds of smoke filled the street, flooding into the alleyway and stores. Suddenly, a volley of blasterfire erupted from the defenders. In horror, the young baron realized it was a deadly repeat of the fight at the bank. Visibility dropped to zero, and the sec men started to pull back, unwilling to chance contact with the dense smoke.

"Attack!" Leonard shouted, pounding on the garbage bin. "Attack now, you stinking cowards!"

The desert breeze was already starting to thin the chem fog, and so the sec men slowly began to advance into the dark clouds, disappearing from view. Drawing his own blaster, the baron waited impatiently for the sounds of combat to renew when somebody coughed a few more times in the alleyway behind him.

"Shut up, fools," he snapped irritably. "It's only smoke." But then something hot and hard pressed painfully against the back of his head.

"Freeze," Ryan ordered, grabbing a fistful of hair to hold the youth motionless. "Tell your men to stop attacking and start shoveling sand."

"What?"

"Put out the fire!"

Breathing hard, Leonard glanced down and through the thinning clouds of smoke. He could see the still forms of his bodyguards lying on the ground, most of their heads missing.

"Who the hell are you?" he asked through clenched teeth.

Ryan shook the teenager hard. "Doesn't matter. Give the order to your men, or I'll blow your fucking brains out."

"I don't think so," Leonard said smoothly, sensing a weakness to exploit. "You need my men, so I stay alive. What with the fire, your bitch is trapped in there?"

Ryan wasted a live round jacking the slide so the noise would startle the man. "Last chance."

"And then I die anyway," the teenager retorted, shaking with restrained fury. "Fuck you. Go ahead, chill me!"

A thunderous report shook the alleyway, and Leonard jerked free of Ryan's startled grip. Stumbling off his box, the teenager staggered against the garbage bin, and from out of the smoke strode Jarmal, the blaster in his hand bucking and jumping as he emptied it.

"That's for my daughter," Jarmal said, reloading as he strode forward. "Your father took her when she was twelve. Twelve years old!"

"My sympathies," Ryan snapped. "Order the men to put out the fire."

The big man swung about, the pitted maws of their deadly weapons now aimed at each other. Time passed in tense silence. The thinning smoke exposed the group of sec men on the sidewalk, and the burning building across the street. Grips on weapons were shifted as the men waited for a sign of what was happening.

"Ryan," Jarmal said on impulse.

The one-eyed man narrowed his gaze. "You know me?"

"No. Heard of you in a tale around a campfire."

"And who are you?"

"Uther Jarmal."

"The new baron," Ryan said.

He almost smiled. "Looks like."

"Give the order. Fast."

"Why? Let it burn, you're safe out here."

"My business."

The former sergeant locked gazes with the Deathlands warrior. "You have a man trapped." It wasn't a
question.

Ryan debated on responses and chose the truth.
"Yeah."

"Everything is for sale," the man prompted.

"Blasters," Ryan spit.

"Got lots. And more food than you'll ever see."

"The Hummer."

"Your wag? No thanks."

Watching the growing conflagration, Ryan racked his
brain for a bargaining tool. "I know the secret location
of the last six live muties," he said in desperation.

Jarmal narrowed his eyes. "Bull."

Knowing it was time to go for broke, Ryan lowered
his pistol. The sec men seemed stunned.

"This is how much I want the fire out and my son
saved," Ryan stated, holstering the piece. "How bad
you want those things dead?"

"Your son?"

"One of my girls had red hair," a sec man said,
hatefully gazing at Leonard. "I joined the guards to try
to get close enough to his father to ace the freak."

"Me, too," said another.

Ten long seconds ticked by before the new baron
slowly lowered his blaster and tucked it in his belt.
"Bucket brigade!" he shouted. "You, you and you! Get
some metal pails from the paint store. The rest of you
gleebs form a line from the street and start throwing
like you mean it!"

"Hey!"

Everybody turned. The rest of the companions stumbled out of the pawnshop, Dean wrapped in a blanket and tenderly cradled in Mildred's arms.

"Hot pipe, what's going on?" Dean asked weakly, blinking at the dim daylight.

Epilogue

A week later, dust devils danced along the sandy street in front of the pawnshop as the companions loaded Dean into the rear cargo area of the Hummer. The desert winds were starting to increase once more, and they wanted to leave before the next storm arrived. Next door, the government building was gone, just another blackened hole in the ground like the skyscraper.

"You okay?" Mildred asked, tucking the blankets tighter around the boy.

"Headache," he whispered. "Did I really fall through the skylight? Don't remember."

Sliding behind the steering wheel, Ryan glanced at the physician in concern.

"A common reaction to head traumas," Mildred said soothingly. "Nothing to worry about."

"Damn straight you did," the elder Cawdor replied. "Fell four stories. Good thing you landed on your head."

Dean chuckled, then abruptly stopped. "What's that smell?"

"Food," Jak said, munching on an apple. "Bushels of food. Corn, tomatoes, beans, lots of taters."

"The word is *potato*," Doc corrected, wiggling into the back seat, a canvas sack on his lap.

"You peel, you name."

A smile. "I see your point, Young Jak. Taters it is."

The albino teen grunted in victory.

Curiously, Dean reached out to touch one of the baskets stacked nearby. It was made of reed and seemed to be filled with live lizards. "Meat, too," he said, astonished. "But where did it come from?"

"We caught the lizards," J.B. said, snuggling next to Mildred. "It's easy once you know how."

"And we traded with the local baron for the vegetables," Krysty said, climbing into the passenger seat.

"Oh, yeah. The blasters."

"Actually, no," Ryan stated, starting the engine. "He had lots of those. We traded with something he didn't have, and wanted very much. J.B.'s formula for smoke bombs."

"Knowledge is power," the wiry man beamed, adjusting his glasses.

"So we staying here for a while?" Dean asked.

Ryan eased off the brake and slipped the wag into gear. "Can't. There was some trouble. We're not on a chill list, but we aren't welcome any longer, either."

"Oh." The boy thought about that. "So what about the mutie? Is it dead? Who runs that ville? Did we...could—"

"Enough. Sleep," Mildred ordered, pressing a finger to his lips. "We're going to the redoubt for a while, let you rest and get your strength back. Tell you all about it there."

"Still have no idea where we are," Krysty complained, staring at the cloudy sky.

"Locals call the ruins Zero City," J.B. said.

"A bastardization of the military term 'ground zero,' I would assume," Doc rumbled, wincing as his shoulder wound throbbed.

"Mebbe after a couple of years, when things calm down," Ryan stated, putting the Hummer in gear and pulling away from the curb, "we'll come back and ask them."

LYING ATOP an old horse blanket spread on the white sand beach before the azure ocean, Harold felt himself rising again from the electric touch of Laura's naked breast on his chest. But his wife was asleep, and the man forced his passion to cool. There had been a lot of sec men in the gaudy house that night, but oddly nobody attacked when he appeared with his blasters. They simply watched as he took the young woman from her bed and departed. So much preparation for nothing. Carrying her in his arms, he had raced through the sewers and taken a boat he had built himself down the dirty river to the sea. There he rowed for hours until finally reaching a small island where nobody else lived. Deep in the lush greenery was a hut built by the old baron, the cellar full of food, ammo and tools. His secret escape place was now their honeymoon oasis. That night under the stars, they kissed like adults and did many other wonderful things.

As he gazed at the sleeping woman, Harold's heart swelled with love for his tiny bride. The naked goliath gently stroked her long flowing hair, so soft to the touch of his massive scarred hands. He didn't care about her many scars. She was his angel, and nobody would ever harm her again.

Shifting position in her sleep, Laura pressed warmly against the man and reached out to stroke his misshapen face with fingers as gentle as a prayer in church. A single heartfelt tear flowed down his ravaged cheek, and the deformed man closed his eyes in complete contentment.

"Good doggie," the woman murmured softly. "Good boy."

Lost in reverie, Harold never heard the words and he fell asleep with a smile, happily dreaming about how fine and strong their many children would be.

**A journey to the dangerous frontier
known as the future...
Don't miss these titles!**

JAMES AXLER

DEATH
LANDS.